RICHARD D ROSS

Eye of the Hybrid Storm

A James Macrae Thriller – Book 2

To Margrit

'We must just KBO.'

Winston Churchill – 11th December 1941

****

'Hybrid methods of warfare, such as propaganda, deception, sabotage and other non-military tactics have long been used to destabilise adversaries. What is new about attacks seen in recent years is their speed, scale and intensity, facilitated by rapid technological change and global interconnectivity.'

Jens Stoltenberg, NATO Secretary General

Contents

Preface

Jeremy Hirons – MI6 Special Agent

<u>**Other Characters**</u>

Ben Armstrong – Owner Pair-Tree Capital

General Shen – Chinese general

Li Ming – Private secretary to Jiang Zemin, President People's Republic of China.

Meili Shabani – PR representative Shanghai Port Authority

Greg Driver – Journalist *Mercantile News*

Phil West – Editor, *Mercantile News*

Charlie Thornton – Former partner of Jack Carter

Harry – Employee and driver for Charlie Thornton

Otto Van den Berg – Director-General Transport Division EU Commission

Andre Laffite – Chairman Marseille Port Authority

Pierre Bourellier – Supervisor, Jules Bordet Institute

Geoffrey Ravenhurst – Lawyer

Scott Farmer – Private detective

DCI Thomas - Metropolitan Police Task Force

DI Stella Hudson - Metropolitan Task Force

All characters, companies and events in this book are fictitious. Any similarity to real persons, living or dead and companies is coincidental and not intended by the author.

Real world characters are only used in the fictional context.

1

Chapter 1

S**pring 1995**

Am I going to survive long term?

In the dark early hours of the morning, the deserted city streets stretched out in front of him. A sudden breeze whipped up dust and garbage, toyed with it momentarily, and then redistributed it across the empty pavements. A black cat ventured out to cross the street, caught sight of the headlights and quickly reversed direction, scurrying in between two dimly lit buildings. James Macrae felt invisible in his quiet Range Rover cabin, completely separated from the outside world. He was a silent observer scrutinising everyone and everything from a distance. It was a good time to reflect on his inner self as he tried to unpack his memory. The events of the last year had had a profound effect on him. He had been pushed to the brink of disaster. He had nearly lost his wife and the family business. His own actions had later shocked him, once the adrenaline and anxiety of what had occurred, finally fell into the rear-view mirror. Now that the true reality had sunk in, a dark side to his character had emerged. His use of his own physical force, as well as the killing of two people, had been a revelation. *'Have I really done that? Did I dream it?'* He had questioned himself repeatedly and the answer always came back the same. *'Yes, you did.'*

The traffic lights in front of him turned red. From a side street a garbage truck emerged, crossed the junction, and entered a flat yard. The truck lowered a set of hydraulic forks over the front of the cab and hoisted a large metal garbage bin into the rear of the truck body. The sound of the garbage falling into the body and the subsequent crash of the bin returning to the ground jolted James out of his dark, reflective mood. He shook his head. Feeling more in the moment, he further reflected that his past actions had been fully justified. If he looked back at his earlier life, he hadn't been pushed around by anybody. He had always stood his ground. He wasn't so shocked anymore at what he had done. *'I guess this is who I really am,'* he murmured to himself, *'and what's more I would do it again if I had to.'*

His introspective mood started to lift as he felt his confidence growing. He turned on the radio tuning into BRMB, the local Birmingham station. They started to play Glenn Frey's song, 'You Belong To The City'. The lonely drawling notes of the saxophone introduction added to his sense of isolation and then each word of the song hit him head-on. Listening intently to every single lyric, it was as though Glenn Frey had written the song exclusively about him.

As the traffic light changed to green, James slowly accelerated his vehicle. The road widened and straightened out in front of him. A series of junctions, each with their own set of traffic lights came into his vision. The intelligent traffic control signals on this section of the city were synchronised and sequenced for approaching vehicles in this early hour of the morning. The lights ahead turned green every time he approached a junction. By the time James arrived at work at 1:00am, ready to liaise with his overseas terminals, he was singing along with the song. He smiled to himself. He was going to be alright after all. At least that was what his present mood told him. If he was honest, deep down inside, he still had a sense of foreboding.

2

Chapter 2

S **pring 1995**

Hugh Stanfield groaned as he lay back on the battered metal bed in his cramped Brixton prison cell. Around him, the scarred brickwork was layered thick in a dull grey paint plastered on multiple times over the prison's two-hundred-year history. Initials of former inmates were carved into the brickwork for anyone who cared to look. His new home was becoming more claustrophobic by the day. Sparsely furnished with only a bed, washstand and stainless-steel toilet, there was a small barred window which just allowed him to see into the small yard below. Not much light could penetrate from the outside through the dull and grimy window. The lights remained on all day every day.

As he closed his eyes, his mind was grinding away. It had been over six months since his conviction with multiple life sentences being handed down to him in the London Central Criminal Court for mass murder. To think that after all his hard work building Euro-Asian Freight Services, a successful international maritime business, he had ended up here with all his assets sequestered by the authorities. They had even found his secret Swiss bank accounts, his financial gain for arms dealing and seized those as well. He knew he would never be considered for parole. His attempt, on behalf of the Chinese Communist Party, to take over the Macrae Shipping Company with their four European port terminals had failed miserably. James Macrae had outsmarted him, good and proper. Hot blood started to rise up through his neck. Firstly, the bastard had stolen some of his major customers and then he'd killed his friend Jack Carter while rescuing his wife. If only his taxi from Heathrow hadn't been delayed reaching the Bulldog and Beaver pub then his life would have been completely different. Somehow, he needed to get even with Macrae.

It was hard to bear. He felt isolated, trapped, lonely and, worst of all, devoid of hope. Desperately needing a way out, time was not on his side. He would soon be transferred to the recently opened HMP Belmarsh top-security prison in south-east London; his stay here only temporary. As a category-A high-risk prisoner, his new home would be the most secure prison in Europe.

Escape. How to do it? Overcrowded and understaffed at the best of times, Brixton was guarded by a skeleton screw on Sundays.

Charlie Thornton from Bethnal Green would help me on the outside.

The small metal observation hatch slid open on his cell door, revealing a pair of eyes. The heavy cell door opened and a burly older prison guard with thinning grey hair entered his cell. His movements were slow and repetitive, reflecting the countless hours he had worked in the same prison.

'Hello, Mr Clarke. How are you today?' Stanfield enquired.

'Oh, you know, another day in paradise. Bin doing this too bloody long. I need to check your cell,' Clarke replied in his thick cockney accent.

'Go ahead,' Stanfield said in his warmest tone as he stood up and waved an inviting arm for his guard to proceed. 'I know you've told me before, but remind me again how long you've been working here?'

'Pretty well forty years now. Nothing's changed much in all the time I've bin here,' Clarke replied, lifting the thin mattress. 'I'll be retiring in six weeks. Even though I'm counting the days, it's a scary thought, eh? Won't know what to do with meself.'

'Oh, you'll have a good pension after forty years, I would imagine. That should allow you to do all the things you've dreamt of with your wife over the years, eh?' Stanfield replied.

'Stanfield, if you can Adam and Eve that, you'll believe anything. We was hoping to buy a little bungalow on the coast, but we just can't afford what we want. Wanted to 'elp our daughter buy her first house an' all. Bloody house prices down there are ridiculous. Every time you think you've got enough money, the soddin' price goes up again!'

'Well maybe there's a fairy godmother out there some-where?' Stanfield said, laughing.

''Ere, don't go saying things like that or you'll get me locked up in ere!' Clarke replied.

'Well, a little friendly advice from you might, let's say, help with your moving expenses?'

'You're very kind, Stanfield, but I could be locked up here and lose what little pension I have. Now that's not a good idea, is it?'

Stanfield laughed again. 'No, I suppose it isn't.' He paused. 'You know, it's been a long time since I went to church but being in here has made me reflect on my crimes. Would I be permitted to attend Mass?'

As Clarke looked inside the toilet cistern, he replied, 'I would think it's okay. The guv likes inmates to show remorse. First step to repentance. Let me find out for you. Right, that's me done for today. See you tomorrow, Stanfield.'

'I'm not going anywhere.'

Stanfield lay back down, hands behind his head expecting the same daily instruction at this time of the day.

A shout from outside his cell came right on cue. 'On your feet, Stanfield.' As the cell door opened, the sound of shouting and clanging steel doors brought him back into the real world.

The new guard on the late afternoon shift constantly punched his open palm. He escorted him down two flights of metal stairs for his hour in the prison exercise yard. Taller than most men, Dan Nash was already out there striding alone across the other side of the quadrangle. Nash had been Stanfield's accomplice in – including but not limited to – murder, blackmail and extortion. As the government broadsheets occasionally lamented the parlous state of the British prison system with overcrowding and building stock not being fit for purpose, Nash was also awaiting transfer to Belmarsh.

As Stanfield emerged into the exercise yard, other inmates gave furtive glances and immediately stepped away from him. Stanfield and Nash's reputation had preceded them, allowing them a clear passage of rights.

The prison smell of sweat and black water began to subside in the open space as Stanfield fell into stride next to Nash.

'Howya doing?'

'Oh you know. Wears thin, doesn't it?' Stanfield replied, quietly. 'How about you?'

'I miss horizons. We have to get out before it's too late.'

Stanfield nodded. He checked no one was in earshot and lowered his voice. 'Damn right we do. Once we're in Belmarsh, there'll be no chance. I would say helicopter, but look.'

Nash didn't look. 'Yup, wires over the yard knocks that one on the head. Plan B?'

'I've found God.'

'Whatever it takes, I suppose.'

'Beyond his help, mate. No, the chapel is on the ground floor next to that yard at the side of the prison. Closer to the outer wall. I'm going to attend Mass.'

'I suppose I could repent and redeem myself.'

'It would take a show of force, but I'm almost there with one of the screws. He's standing strong, but he needs money.'

Nash stopped walking and looked at Stanfield directly. 'Sounds complicated. It's not Mexico or Columbia, for god's sake!'

'What have we got to lose. Really?'

'There is that.'

'If we do escape, would the Chinese come after us? We could still be a threat because we know too much. They might try to silence us.'

'Bloody hell. Are we better off in here or out there?'

'We have to do it before they transfer us to Belmarsh. Otherwise, there's no hope.'

3

Chapter 3

'**I**s everything alright, James?' Sarah asked her husband. James Macrae nodded, smiling warmly into Sarah's hazel eyes. Wearing a smart navy-blue skirt suit with a white silk tie blouse, she looked stunning. 'Sorry. I was just thinking how far we have come in the last nine months. Here we are today, for the launch of the new company, when only last year we were fighting for our lives as well as the survival of the company.'

'I know. Thank goodness we were able to pull through. With the marriage of the two companies, I think everyone deserves this celebration for helping the merger go so smoothly.'

As the early afternoon sun reflected brightly off the newly constructed steel and glass Macrae-Claybourne Logistics head office, dozens of visitors' cars were being parked neatly outside in the transport yard. Two to three hundred guests were starting to gather in the large imposing glass-fronted reception area of the headquarters, located in Birmingham. It was the official launch of the new private company, merging the Macrae Shipping Company together with Claybourne

Cartage. James Macrae and Chris Claybourne had been close friends and business associates for many years and were now solely responsible for the companies they had recently inherited from their fathers. Originally James had approached Chris to start the rumour of a merger between the two companies that would help divert the previous takeover attack from Euro-Asian Freight. The more he kicked the idea around with Chris, the more they realised that a real merger could work.

They had agreed to create a mega logistics company; partly to increase efficiency and partly to ward off any future takeovers, especially from the Chinese.

The new enlarged headquarters were located in the existing Claybourne Cartage transport yard and warehousing complex. James had moved his staff into the new office block, amalgamating the staff. The old Macrae offices in Gas Street Basin were now the headquarters of Macrae Holdings LLC, owning and operating all the former properties of Macrae Shipping.

Catering staff in white and black circulated, carrying trays of canapes and pouring champagne. James, Sarah, Chris Claybourne and his wife Jenny stood on the mezzanine. They were joined by the parents of both James and Chris.

Ken Claybourne, Chris's dad, put his arm around Richard Macrae's shoulders. They were old friends.

'Look at these two boys of ours! They are going to take this company forward to another level neither you nor I could ever have imagined.'

'You are so right, Ken. With their collective vision and the new technology available to them, I believe it will be a great success! You and I can retire care-free.'

'Amen to that,' said Ken, raising his glass in a toast.

'You have taken what we started and become a world leader

in ocean, land freight and warehousing with all the logistics efficiencies our customers have come to expect. Thank you, ladies. Without your support and love through thick and thin, we wouldn't be here today.'

Outside the main office and reception were neatly parked trucks and trailers proudly displaying the new company logo: MCLO. The adjoining service workshop doors were open, with staff ready to show the guests around the premises once the ribbon-cutting was over. Across the extensive vehicle marshalling yard stood the huge cold storage warehouse with its loading and unloading docks all fully utilised.

James looked over at Chris. 'Chris, I think we should start the ceremony.'

Chris smiled brightly back at his new partner. 'Okay, let's do it!'

Both in suits and over six feet tall in their forties, they stood proudly together behind the microphone ready to address the guests. James's close-cropped light-brown hair and Chris's slightly longer black hair reflected a sheen from the sun shining through the reception windows.

James spoke first. 'Welcome everyone. Welcome.' The buzz of the reception quickly died away with all eyes focussed on the speaker.

'Ladies and gentlemen, thank you for honouring us with your presence here today marking the official opening of our newly merged company – Macrae-Claybourne Logistics.' He paused, looked around at all the guests and continued.

'Logistics are the lifeblood of every successful company and every economy. Indeed, winning is all about having superior logistics. Our vision was to create a mega logistics company worldwide that could offer all our customers, whether at home or abroad, worry-free door-to-door service with delivery tracking 24/7. Accurate and swift delivery times are essential today to minimise interruptions in the supply chain and save our customers money. With our synchronised overland and maritime services, we can now guarantee shorter and more efficient delivery cycles. Later, on the tour of our facilities, you will be able to see how we accomplish this. Our new and innovative mission control centre, where every vessel, truck and trailer in our fleet is tracked by GPS, brings you tomorrow's technology today.'

Chris came forward to the microphone.

'We have a long list of people to thank today, including all of our valued employees who have worked tirelessly to help us put this altogether. I also want to introduce to you, our local Member of Parliament, the right Honourable Clare Short and Sir Richard Knowles, Lord Mayor of Birmingham, who will jointly cut the ribbon and officially launch our new company.' There was a loud round of applause.

After the official opening, the guests broke up into smaller groups to each tour the company's separate operations. Janet Rushton, Vice-President IT, welcomed her group into the mission control centre. The expansive, quiet and dimly lit control room was full of computer terminals, world time zone clocks and large wall screens. Janet stepped forward to the microphone.

'Good afternoon, everyone! Yes, it's 1995, but today you see the future. The future of distribution in action today! What people have dreamt of for years, we have achieved. This is CSM: Complete Supply Chain Management. You will witness a revolution in the handling of goods being distributed globally. Utilising our own proprietary software systems, we can offer our customers the status and delivery times of their goods in real-time 24/7.'

She paused and moved over to a large screen covering one complete wall and clicked a hand control. Instantly the screen lit up with a plethora of information, rather like a flight information board. She paused momentarily to allow the audience to take in the detail that had suddenly sprung to life in front of them.

'Imagine you are a supplier or a customer of time-sensitive goods, such as fresh fruit or meat, or you are a supplier or a customer of automotive components that have critical time deliveries to your point of destination on the other side of the world. What if you could access the exact location of your goods and expected time of delivery to synchronise with the exact demands of your own customers or factories, without even leaving your office desk or your home computer? Your pipeline of goods, weight tickets, way point, delivery receipts and invoicing is now completely seamless.'

She paused again and then radiated a huge smile, knowing exactly what she was going to say.

'And we sure all love to collect our receivables quickly, don't we!'

There was a lot of laughing and nodding in agreement.

She put up her right hand in the air.

'But that's not all! Just when you thought it couldn't get any better, it does!'

She turned to another huge blank screen behind her. The screen immediately lit up. The visitors gasped when they saw the progress of goods from all points of the world to their destinations with real-time arrivals at their intended docks, the transfers into the fully integrated truck and rail transportation system, completing the last section of the delivery cycle to customers' premises.

'The bar-coded goods, containers, ships, trucks and trailers are all linked by GPS to the system that can be accessed by both the suppliers and customers anywhere in the world.'

There was an enthusiastic round of applause and chatter.

James Macrae stepped forward to the microphone.

'Thanks, Janet. So, you are all probably wondering what happens if goods are too early or too late for a customer. Well, we've got that covered too. We can provide a safeguard in your supply chain by using our temperature-controlled and bonded warehouses to act as a buffer stock for you. Our system can help you set the minimum stock level, that is, if you think you need them. Bottom line; a seamless and even flow of goods – worldwide.'

James and Janet smiled at each other as they watched the group of business and transport journalists scramble to get every detail down, ready to publish in their next editions. There were also several influential leaders from major manufacturers and retailers that nodded in satisfaction at what they had seen. It was impressive.

'So, are there any questions?' James asked the group. At the far side of the room a hand shot up.

'Yes, sir.'

'Thank you, Mr Macrae. Greg Driver, *Mercantile News*. Janet, has the logistics system been developed entirely by yourselves or is this an application that could be purchased on the open market?'

Janet stepped forward to the mic again.

'Excellent question, Mr Driver. Yes, the software system you see here today is exclusively proprietary and our very own creation. We searched extensively for a software solution to suit our particular needs, but there was nothing like this anywhere in the world. Bottom line, it was created out of our collective vision of what transportation systems should look like. As both James and Chris said earlier, it brings our customers tomorrow's technology today.'

Greg Driver remained standing.

'Janet, do you see a time when this technology would be made available to the open market?'

Janet smiled.

'Right now, we do not. Let's face it, this is our main competitive advantage over our competitors. We have invested a lot of money and resources into developing these unique systems and will continue to upgrade them as we go forward. By the way, for those customers and potential customers here today, Chad Greening, our Director of Sales and Marketing will be happy to provide further details and quotations on our logistics services.'

There was another round of enthusiastic applause from the guests.

At the back of the audience stood a lone figure. A Macrae-Claybourne employee.

4

Chapter 4

General Shen stepped outside his plain government office. Protruding air-conditioning units perched each side of the small windows buzzed away, constantly dripping spots of water down the brick and plaster exterior walls. His office was in the west building of the vast and sprawling Zhongnanhai Compound in Beijing. The bright sunshine caused him to squint and shield his eyes. He took out his sunglasses from his crisply pressed olive-green uniform and strode north, the half kilometre or so, alongside the elongated lake surrounded by carefully manicured lawns and gardens. The air was heavy with the scent from the bright-red, white and purple tulips that swayed gently from side to side in the warm early summer breeze.

North Zhongnanhai was the headquarters of the State Council of the People's Republic of China, including the offices of the premier and the vice premiers. He was responding to a request from Li Ming for a meeting to discuss China's economic expansion. Li Ming was now the private secretary of Jiang Zemin, the President of China, who had taken over from Deng Xiaoping.

Many thoughts were running through his mind as he threaded his way through the gardens along the winding path. He wasn't sure he could trust Ming. Ming was an opportunist and brown-noser who took any chance he could get for power. It was interesting. Ming wasn't a politician, nor was he a military man. Yet he would often make requests of people who were never quite sure if these were the actual wishes of the premier or Ming himself. To question Ming's instructions was dangerous; if the request had indeed come from the premier, that would be treason. No one wanted to risk that. The downside would be fatal.

General Shen entered Li Ming's cool air-conditioned and well-appointed office. It had the air of a sanctuary with its high ceiling and red-panelled walls. He felt his highly polished boots sink into the deep-pile carpet as he stood in front of the ornate mahogany desk.

'Please sit down, General Shen.'

'Thank you, Mr Ming.'

'General, the president has asked me to seek your opinion on certain matters.'

'I'm honoured and ready to oblige, Mr Ming. How may I help?'

'Well, it goes back to last year when you and I were working together, following orders from Deng Xiaoping to help extend and expand China's economic and political influence worldwide. President Zemin wants to continue in the same direction and build on Deng's economic and political policy. Like Deng, he does not seek to achieve his aims militarily, but by a means that is viewed by the world, shall we say, as being *friendly and cooperative* with other nations. Now, how should

I put it? We need rapid results that can be achieved using all methods that avoid open confrontation. Perhaps we could use such delicate terms as "soft power" or "public diplomacy?"'

'With respect, Mr Ming, those terms mean nothing to me. I don't know what you mean. I am a military man. I follow specific instructions and commands.'

'I see.' Ming stood up from behind his desk. A mid-height man, he stood straight, dressed in his smart light-grey suit. He ran his fingers through his short black hair and turned his back to Shen. He remained quiet for a few moments, then, seemingly to make up his mind, turned to face Shen again.

'Look, the only way we can do this is by coercion, using all means possible. You and I can never admit this, but we must develop a concise and cohesive plan that utilises all non-military means possible to achieve China's long-term economic plan of dominating the world. If we look back in history, the British ruled two-thirds of the world from their tiny little island in the northern hemisphere. Not only did they plunder the world economically, they also established British bases on a global scale that could be used for military purposes. In fact, they had the biggest naval force in the world at that time. It is our goal to rule the world. We need a solid economy, and we need worldwide naval bases. Our navy will become the biggest in the world, superior to the United States and Russia. China has been pushed around for too long. It's our turn now.'

Shen nodded. 'Mr Ming. We tried that method when we were the silent partner of Euro-Asian Freight Services and look where that got us.'

'Yes, of course. You are right. That was a complete failure due to the irresponsible actions of Hugh Stanfield and his team. Clearly, we can't use that approach again. Let's see if we can come up with a list of ideas that can help achieve the chairman and president's ambition of expansion using alternative, more palatable, subversive actions.'

Shen leaned back in his chair and inwardly smiled. Ming was a weasel of the first order. To come up with a list of actions would be easy, but, and it was a big but, if it all went wrong, who would own it? It certainly wouldn't be President Zemin since he had not issued these orders. Shen doubted Ming would own it, claiming he was a mere private secretary. There was no doubt Shen would be the fall guy. He decided, there and then, that he needed an escape plan.

'Okay, Mr Ming. Let's stop pussyfooting around with all the flowery language and cut the bullshit. We need to say it like it is. Here's what I think, but you have to tell me whether I should proceed.'

'I see. Well, go ahead and then we can decide whether to move forward with them or not.'

General Shen stood up, moving around the office as though he was addressing the men under his command.

'Right! To start with, we should start with a simple plan and execute it surgically. We can always add more variants later, but we need some early successes. We should launch a four-pronged assault on our enemies to achieve the expansion of our economic and political objectives.' He held up one finger of his left hand.

'One: Set up a mergers and acquisitions company, based offshore of course, to buy up all the seaports that we consider to be desirable. This includes the ports Macrae Shipping own. They are strategically positioned for us to use Turkey as the gateway into Europe and create footholds along the

Mediterranean Sea and southern Europe.' He put up a second finger on his left hand.

'Two: Step up our cyber warfare to discredit, cause chaos and confusion to weaken our enemies. Again, we still need to include Macrae Shipping, amongst others.' He put up a third finger.

'Three: Influence world public opinion by coercing international journalists to write favourable reports on Chinese developments.

'Four: Continue to invest heavily in our revised "Silk Road" policy but then push the investment-receiving countries into debt, so we can be repaid by taking over their strategic assets that we will need in the future to achieve our objectives.'

Shen stood still, nodding and digesting what he had just said.

Mr Ming's eyes were alight. He was also carefully filtering what he had just heard.

'General Shen, you never fail to amaze me. That is brilliant! If we can carry these four actions out under a cloak of what I would call "respectable secrecy", we can certainly enhance the president and chairman's agenda. Leave these ideas with me. I will get back in touch.'

General Shen shook hands with Ming.

'Thank you, Mr Ming.'

He turned and left the office. Walking back to his own office through the compound, he wondered where his plan would end up. Who would approve the resources needed to execute it? Where would they come from? Who would he report to? Interesting, very interesting. This Chinese expansionist plan of his, if approved, would need a huge amount of money to finance it. Maybe he could take some of the funds for himself so he could arrange an escape from China if it ever became necessary. He was more convinced than ever that he would be the first to be fired and to take whatever other punishment followed. Who was really running China? Was it truly Jiang Zemin or did Deng Xiaoping still have considerable influence on China's economic and foreign policy behind the scenes as a power broker? Maybe it was even Ming, hiding behind the president's title? Whoever it was, Shen found himself boxed in.

5

Chapter 5

James Macrae opened the BBQ lid and turned over the chicken breasts and rotated the spicy chicken and mango sausages. The blue smoke swirled all around him. It was hard to beat the aroma of grilled meat, especially if you had a cold beer in your hand and the sun was shining. He looked over to the back lawn where his family were kicking a soccer ball around. Sarah had owned the small Welsh stone cottage when James had first met her fifteen years ago. They now used the cottage for their weekend escapes to spend time walking in the rugged mountains and valleys surrounding the home. Since that first meeting, they had got married and had three children. Olivia was now five, Mia seven and Mason nine. There was plenty of giggling, fighting and running about going on. James smiled. How he loved his family. Trouble was that life seemed to be flying by at warp speed these days.

Olivia came over to join her dad.

'Dad, I don't like soccer because the others all try to take the ball away from me. It's not fair!'

James laughed in response.

'Can't help you with that one, Olly. That's what soccer is all about. You try to keep the ball from the other team and then score a goal against them. How about if you and I challenge the others later and see if we can beat them?'

'Yes!' She ran off, shouting, 'Daddy's coming to play and help me later!'

Sarah left the children playing and came over to James. She put her arm around his waist and gave him a kiss on the cheek.

'This is bliss. It doesn't get any better than this. A Saturday evening BBQ on a warm summer evening here in Wales with our family.'

James smiled back. 'You're right. I was just thinking the same thing. We are very fortunate.'

'Yes, we sure are fortunate!' She paused thoughtfully for a second. 'You know, James, we could start to think about finding a bigger cottage now the children are growing up and we're financially stable again. Somewhere with enough room for your mom and dad to stay from time to time. Let's face it they are getting older now.'

What do you think?'

'I agree with you, though I wouldn't want to be too far away from here. There's not much available in Llanberis but Caernarfon, where your parents live, might be an option.'

'That's not a bad idea. We would still be on the doorstep of the mountains, and we could keep an eye on my parents as they grow older.'

James sipped his beer contemplatively.

'We would need to find a place that we can keep very secure, though. I'm scarred by the events of last year. I don't want anything like that to ever happen to us again. I think you've dealt with the situation better than me.'

'You know, James, I've had to for the children's sake. We must live a normal life rather than one dominated by fear. Fortunately, the children were not old enough to quite realise what was happening. You are the one that took the brunt.'

'I guess that's true. It certainly gave me an inner strength I never knew I had, or maybe it was always there, but I never knew it. I know I am harder than before. At least I'm always on my guard and better prepared, should there be a next time.'

He checked the BBQ again. 'Listen, can you grab the children and I'll dish up. Everything is done here. The garlic bread and salad are in the kitchen.'

****

The following morning, they were on the meandering path around Llanberis lake. The air was fresh and still with a cloudless sky. There wasn't even a ripple on the water. The mountains reflected their perfect silhouettes on the still surface of the lake. As the children chased butterflies, Sarah and James walked behind them, arm in arm.

'You know, James, I was thinking in the night about our idea of finding a bigger place. If I remember correctly, I think my mom mentioned a while back that one of her friends was considering moving house. As kids growing up, we would visit there with my parents. It was a big place. That might be an option for us to explore.'

James bent down and threw a stone into the lake. 'Why don't you follow it up?'

'Have I lost you again, James?' Sarah asked with a smile on her face.

'Oh, sorry. I'm at it again. It's always about this time on

a Sunday when I start thinking about work, especially with what's coming up next week. I've got a meeting tomorrow morning with Dad to discuss the Macrae Terminal property leases and then a meeting with Chris in the afternoon. He's very concerned about our company security; to the point where it's keeping him awake at night.'

****

'Good morning, Dad.' James gave his father a big hug in the car park of the Hereford and Worcester Shooting Club. 'How are you feeling?'

'Good morning, Son. I'm good. Since the operation last year, I've got a lot of my energy back. Come on, let's grab some breakfast in the clubhouse, get the business over with, then we can get on the range.'

They sat down in the bar that also served as the restaurant. The heavy oak-beamed room, with its imposing stone fire-place and log fire, created an atmosphere that was more like a large farmhouse rather than shooting club.

'Good morning, Richard and James. Good to see you both. What can I get you?'

Richard smiled back. 'Hi, Henry. I'll have fruit and yoghurt, please. I'm afraid my bacon and egg days are over!'

James chuckled and put down the menu. 'I'll get the same with coffee and toast, please, Henry.'

'Okay, Dad. Let's look at the leases.' Richard bent down and pulled a file of papers from his briefcase.

'It was a good idea of yours to split the property with the operations side of the business. With two companies now, it certainly makes it harder for anyone to take over the business like they tried last year.'

'It's true. Not only that, but it also gives you and Mom a substantial income for your retirement. Chris has done the same with his dad and their property as well.

James went over the leases. 'This is all good and exactly as we agreed. I'll sign them off.' He signed and dated each form as well as the copies.

After breakfast, they locked up the papers in the cars and retrieved their guns. They went out to the range.

'So what guns do you keep at home now, James.'

'I followed your lead, Dad. I've got two shotguns, two pistols and a rifle with telescopic lens. Plenty of ammo, too.'

'Let's see what you can do with that telescopic lens of yours.'

James put on his ear defenders and lined up his rifle and sight with the target. He fired several shots off in quick succession.

Richard looked at the target through his scope. 'Bloody hell, James, I wouldn't want to be your enemy!'

6

Chapter 6

General Shen sat at the round conference table in the meeting room adjoining Li Ming and the president's office. He presumed he had been summoned to follow up on his previous meeting with Ming. No further details had been given to him and there was no one else present.

Ming entered the room and smiled as he took the chair opposite Shen.

'So, General Shen, you have the go-ahead to coordinate and proceed with your four-pronged strategy to enhance China's economic and political policies. I will oversee all the finances you will require. You will only use the necessary staff that you have under your command that have access to the highest level of security.'

Shen smiled back at Li Ming.

'That is excellent news! I shall proceed immediately. Are these directives to be confirmed in writing?'

'No, General Shen. I repeat, you have the go-ahead verbally to proceed immediately. Since our last meeting we have been busy at the executive level in preparing for the launch of your initiative.'

Shen felt a rising tension in his neck muscles. He now knew he was *owning* his suggested initiative even though it had appeared to have been endorsed by the Party. Ming had used the term 'your' and there would be no documentary proof of the orders he was receiving. If this failed, he would definitely be the fall guy.

Ming continued. 'As well as giving you the green light today, I have been authorised to give you an update on some of our foreign activities that you can utilise for your plan to succeed. Firstly, we have taken over a Merger and Acquisitions company based in Boston, Massachusetts. The head of this M & A company is an American venture capitalist by the name of Ben Armstrong. The company is called *Pair-Tree Capital*. Armstrong is hungry, greedy and an asset stripper. It will be ideal for us to use him to front our operation. His knowledge of the marine industry is good, so he will be a valuable asset for us. Of course, you will need to keep him between the guard rails. We cannot afford another Hugh Stanfield debacle.'

'Mr Ming. You have worked fast, but why do we need this man? We have vast financial resources at our disposal, so why not just approach the harbour terminals that we wish to take over directly, using a Chinese private company? We can then go in with extremely lucrative offers that no one can refuse. Let's face it, everyone has a price.'

'Yes, you are right of course, but foreign governments can often block attempts by outsiders to take over their key assets, irrespective of the size of the offer on the table. They feel they will lose their sovereignty to another country. Our M & A company will propose in each case a merger of the selling organisation to our legitimate American venture capitalist. It will be perceived as a private commercial deal rather than a political sell-out. In turn he will then "sell" his shares to us at a later date. Of course, he will make a profit. Bottom line, we will have majority shareholdings in all the ports we need!'

Shen leaned forward over the table and clasped his hands together in front of him, 'Can we trust this man?'

'Well, that is where you come into your own, General Shen. You will need to keep this man under surveillance and use whatever tactics are necessary to keep him in line. At the first sign of anything untoward, get rid of him.'

'Does this man understand what we are doing?'

'Yes, he does. Our embassy staff in Washington have briefed him accordingly. Remember, he is greedy. This is an excellent opportunity for him to make guaranteed money, irrespective of any market forces that he is used to. He would be stupid to ignore the gains he will achieve. Needless to say, our agents have uncovered certain deals this man has made in the past using insider trading to his advantage. We are keeping this knowledge to ourselves for the time being, but will not hesitate to use it to alert the American authorities if it becomes necessary. We should always have levers ready to pull at any time. Our ready cupboard is well stocked,' said Ming, grinning widely.

'Good, please arrange for this man to meet me in Singapore. I do not want to be seen to be visiting America, nor do I want him to come here.'

'Consider it done, General Shen. Now, let me continue with more of our foreign activities that we have been pursuing since our last meeting. We agreed that we still need to take over all of Macrae's Shipping terminals. We now have an asset inside their new company in their IT department.' Ming let the statement hang in mid-air.

'What!' Shen sat up straight. He was stunned. An asset inside Macrae-Claybourne Logistics would give them a huge insight into the direction the new company might follow, but it could also provide an opportunity for sabotaging the company's internal systems. Not only was this a major breakthrough, it also proved that Ming was not just the private secretary of the president. He was clearly the head of the MSS, the Ministry of State Security which handled state security and intelligence. As a military man himself, Shen had joined the army at the age of eighteen after studying Economics. He had been fast-tracked by his superiors once they recognised his high intellect and decision-making capabilities. Now in his forties and still single, he was a career officer. This would be the first time, at least to his knowledge, that the MSS and the army would be cooperating together.

Ming continued. 'Yes, we have. You look surprised, General.'

'I am surprised. That is the last thing I expected to hear.' Shen quickly gathered his thoughts together.

'So, who is this asset and how do I communicate with this person?'

'Code name is Zichan. Zichan will send you periodic updates via your secure communications link with our embassy in London. Since our last dealings with Macrae Shipping when we lost our CFO contact, Hal Spencer, they have been busy. They have amalgamated with another company to form a mega logistics company. Their terminals are now owned by a separate new company called Macrae Holdings Ltd. We have to find a way to take this company over.'

'Leave that to me, Mr Ming. I'm sure I can devise a plan to combine the expertise of Pair-Tree Capital with knowledge gained from Zichan. I will also compromise some of the key journalists to influence their audience on how progressive and cooperative China is with the rest of the world. Of course our adversaries will find themselves embroiled in all kinds of scandals and negative news.'

'Excellent, General. Now, one more thing. You and I need to stay in touch whatever time of day or night. We must demonstrate some early wins after the set-back of Euro-Asian Freight last year. Understood?'

'Perfectly, Mr Ming. You have provided me with more than I could have asked for at this stage. Thank you.'

Shen walked back to his office, taking the longer winding path through the compound. His head was exploding with all kinds of ideas to not only take over Macrae Shipping and their new partner but also add to the list of foreign terminals for China to succeed in its expansion plans.

If James Macrae and his new partner thought that their troubles had ended with the imprisonment of Stanfield and Nash, they had no idea about the barrage of hybrid non-conventional weapons that were about to hit them.

7

Chapter 7

James Macrae and Chris Claybourne each took a glug of bitter. James leaned forward and placed his glass down on the restaurant table between them. 'Aaaah! I needed that. I've been talking non-stop this morning!'

They had nipped across the road from the office to the Bartons Arms for lunch. The Victorian pub was over one hundred years old and a well-known landmark in Birmingham with its rich mahogany woodwork, stained-glass windows and decorative tiles. They sat at their usual quiet corner table in the restaurant.

'What are you having for lunch, Chris?' asked James.

'Well, another pint of bitter after this one and then maybe a sirloin steak. We have a lot of talking to do so I'm going to have a proper lunch for once.'

'Yes, you're right. I'm sick of a sandwich at my desk or in a meeting room every day. I'm going to have the ribs.'

After giving their order, James checked to see that there was no one in earshot.

'So, Chris, what's concerning you with regard to security?'

Chris sat forward in is chair and looked directly at James. 'Did you see that article in the *Sunday Times* on the trend in computer malware and ransom demands on companies?'

'No, I didn't.'

'It was a special report on commercial computer systems and the increasing dependency of companies on them. It covered security and how many companies had already been victims of hacking. It's on the increase. One example in the article was one of our national competitors, Trelease Transport. The business was in a downturn. They couldn't figure it out at first, but when they asked their customers why they had lost their business, in every case their rates and terms had been beaten by one competitor or another. Long story short, their systems had been accessed and their rates and contract terms were on the open market.'

'Yes, there's no doubt, we're all becoming more dependent on computer systems. In many cases, especially our revolutionary proprietary software system, it has become so important it is now our competitive advantage.'

'James, you and I have always placed security at the top of our priorities. God knows we have millions of dollars of expensive machinery and equipment to protect. Trouble is, these are tangibles. We can see them, so we can protect them. It's the intangibles that worry me. The information that we handle every day is worth billions of dollars and the software systems we use to process this information is our lifeline.'

James nodded in agreement.

Chris continued. 'So, what bothers me the most is we have computer terminal operators that we think we know and trust, but we don't know who the other people are on the receiving end. Now we have reached the point of being so far ahead of our competitors, we are likely to be more of a target ourselves. With new technology developing at an exponential speed, are we sure our safeguards are enough to ward off an attack?

Chris didn't wait for an answer, but carried on. 'It's not only that, but what if someone breaches our systems midstream? They can insert viruses, steal information, hold us to ransom and so on. The new system we have is wonderful. Don't get me wrong! There's nothing like it anywhere in the world, but I worry that we are now more vulnerable to our competitors or to saboteurs than ever. Let's face it, what you encountered with Euro-Asian Freight was horrendous. Stanfield, Spencer and others might be behind bars, but what if someone else wants to take a swing at us?'

James nodded in acknowledgement.

'You're right. This could be our Achilles' heel. What you say is correct. Let's look at what we've got so far. We've got Janet Rushton as our VP of Information and Technology. As you know, she's highly qualified and always trying to stay on top of the rapidly evolving technology. In fact, she was instrumental in helping us fend off Euro-Asian Freight. She knows how to defend us from such threats. Then we have Lisa Taylor, who reports directly to Janet. She was already working for you when we merged the companies. Janet tells me she is highly experienced and qualified as director of IT. I know they work very closely and regularly report in to each other when it comes to software development.'

'James, that's all well and good. We both respect them, but I repeat it's our security of these systems that worry me. We have a number of database programmers and software developers in the company, but do we really know everything about these people? They operate 24/7 on a contract basis.

We can have all the firewalls we like, but it's a leak from the inside that concerns me.'

The waiter brought their meals and they tucked into them, suspending the conversation for several minutes. James leaned back, using his napkin to wipe some rib sauce from his lips. He looked at Chris.

'Chris, you and I are partners and the best of friends, but, to be honest with you, I've never told you the truth about how Janet helped us fight off our enemy.'

Chris put down his cutlery and sat forward.

James continued. 'I instructed her to hack into certain competitors' websites and a couple of our employees. We have a highly skilled contact who is at arms' length from us that we use. We have a code name and call him 'Shad'. Yes, it was illegal, but my back was against the wall and my enemy certainly wasn't playing by the rules, so I decided to do the same. I never told anyone. Janet is the only person who knows, but now we are partners, so it's important you know.'

'Can we trust Janet? She obviously knows an awful lot,' Chris asked.

'Yes, we can. She gave up a huge job in London and moved her whole family to Birmingham. Her children are now happily settled in school and her husband was able to transfer with his own company. Not only that, if she blew the whistle on us, she would be implicating herself. No, rest easy. She's with us all the way.'

Chris took another sip.

'Okay. I appreciate you telling me this, James. Rest assured, no one will ever hear anything from me in this regard. Knowing this then, how does this affect "my", or should I now say "our", concerns for IT security?'

James looked up at the decorative tiled wall on the other side of the restaurant and then back at Chris.

'Full disclosure, Chris. I owe it to you. We started off as good friends, then we trusted each other in business and now, having taken the reins of our father's businesses, we are equal partners together. I'll take it one step further, we are now brothers.'

'We sure are. Neither you nor I would have done what we did if we didn't trust and respect each other. I have no regrets. On the contrary, I'm excited about our future together, but I do worry about what we now must protect. We both know it's a big bad world out there. I've had my share of corporate battles, but nothing like what you were subjected to.'

James nodded in agreement.

'I feel like I'm in confession mode, but you need to know that I'm not the same person I was a year or so ago. Before, Dad took care of all the business decisions, and I was never really exposed first hand to some of the harsh realities of business. Then, when I took over the company and several of our employees were murdered and others injured, I became harder and more ruthless than I ever thought possible.'

'I know what you mean, James. We were shielded by our fathers. Now, no one can ever say that if we ask someone to do something, we haven't done it ourselves. We both know what makes our company successful. It's the solid workforce. My dad always used to say, "look after the little guys and they will look after you".'

'Yes, our fathers did the right thing with us. It was a good initiation, but here I am today, and I know I'm a different person. As a company, we were heavily under attack from an invisible enemy. When Sarah was kidnapped, I went on the attack. I've now done things that I could never have dreamt of doing in a million years. I've fought and I've taken out two men in order to save my family and business.'

Chris's eyes widened.

James continued. 'MI6 call it justifiable homicide and are perfectly aware of all the details. It was the only way I could help my family survive. I had no choice. So, bottom line, I'm a lot harder than I ever was and somewhat cynical in my belief of the goodness of mankind. Greed, money and power get people to do the most horrible acts. The sad part is they think it is justifiable.'

He closed his eyes momentarily, with an air of sadness.

'I'm so sorry, James. I knew you were heavily involved in turning everything around, but I had no idea to the lengths you had to go to. It can't be easy to share this, so I appreciate you trusting me with this information. I will always be at your side, no matter what.'

'Thank you, Chris. That means everything to me. I'm here for you and yours.'

'So, let's get back to the subject in hand. You are worried about our new logistics software and our personnel. Right?'

'Right.'

'Okay, Janet and I are the only two people who know about this. Perhaps I should have spoken up earlier, or maybe I'm just learning about what it's like to have a partner. Fact is, we are monitoring every IT employee behind the scenes. We are only interested in anything that can harm the business. In addition, the contact that I mentioned, Shad, we keep at arms' length. He is constantly being challenged to break through our security and firewall protocols. Yes, we pay him to do this; in fact, I pay him from my own pocket to keep it off the books. If he spots a weakness, it is immediately plugged. In addition, Shad has created a number of tripwires, so if anyone tries to copy the system code and export it over the internet, we can trace it immediately. All passwords and security codes are safely locked away. Remember, our software developers only work on their individual databases. Of course, all these separate databases are linked, but access to them is all permission-based. Only Janet has full access to all the linked databases, and I keep a copy of all usernames and passwords in a safety deposit box off-site. This means no one can actually see the full version of computer script except Janet. This would make it very difficult for someone to steal or copy the entire software program.'

James sat back, finished his beer, and stared at Chris.

'I don't know what to say, James. On the one hand, I'm shocked you didn't tell me before, but on the other hand I'm beginning to understand why you acted in the way you did. No one should ever have to endure what you went through.'

Chris let the words hang in the air while the waiter collected their empty plates and glasses.

The waiter smiled at them both. 'Coffee, gentlemen?'

'Yes, please,' Chris replied.

When he had gone, Chris continued.

'When I asked the question about security, I didn't realise I would be questioning Newton's third law of motion.'

'I'm not sure I follow you, Chris?'

'Well, the way I see it, you have re-written Newton's third law. Instead of "for every action there is an equal and opposite reaction", it is now "for every action there is now a greater than equal and opposite reaction". I'm thinking I like your version better. Waiting for our enemies to attack us and then reacting, doesn't cut it anymore. We need to be ready to strike back with a vengeance.'

'Good,' said James. 'So do we let Lisa Taylor, our IT director in on what we are doing, or just keep it between the three of us; you, me and Janet?'

Chris tapped his finger on the table for a few moments.

'No, let's keep it between ourselves for now. Lisa is a great person, but I'm not sure how long she will be with us.'

'Oh, why do you say that?'

'It's just a feeling I've got. After her divorce, she moved back here from a high-profile job in London to live with her parents. I always felt that Birmingham was just a short-term safe harbour for her. Once she's on her feet again, maybe, she'll be off.'

James nodded.

Chris continued. 'Okay, let us three meet every week to monitor the situation unless Janet uncovers anything in between. If that happens, we can swing into action immediately. One thing's for sure, our enemies will not have given up. They will come for us again.'

'Sad but true. Our enemy plays by their own rules. As Churchill described Russia once, "a riddle, wrapped in a mystery, inside an enigma"'.

'A bunch of slippery fuckers.'

8

Chapter 8

What the hell am I going to write about?

Greg Driver sat in his cubicle in the *Mercantile News* office, staring blankly through a window at a facing brick wall. Chewing the end of his pen, his head was completely empty.

He'd already typed up his article for the monthly magazine covering the launch of Macrae-Claybourne Logistics. It was a glowing report headlined, 'Tomorrow's Technology Today'. His editor, Phil West, had been pleased and had placed it as the lead article that month. Greg scratched his head as to what to write about for next month's issue. It was the same every month. You started with an empty locker of information and then scrambled to compile relevant news by the end of the month. He got up to grab a coffee and ran into his editor at the machine.

'Greg, how's it going?'

'Same old, same old. Trying to dredge up news for next month's issue.'

'How about this? I've just received an invitation from the Chinese to visit the Shanghai port terminal. Apparently, they have some breaking news and want to share it with us. I can't go as it's too close to my wife's due date. Since you are turning out some excellent work, I want you to go.'

'I don't know what to say.'

'How about, thank you? I know you just got married, but it should be easier for you to get away.'

Greg took the invitation back to his desk. He read the details, hardly believing his luck. It was an all-expenses paid trip. British Airways business class and accommodation at the Mandarin Asian hotel in Pudong, Shanghai. His stay would be three days. Two days would be spent touring the extensive port facilities and one day would be left for sightseeing. There would be journalists there from other countries. This was to be a major event and he would be leaving in five days. Never having been to China before, Greg vowed to pick up as much knowledge as he could of the port's history before he got there.

Shanghai had both a deep-sea port and a river port. In the last four years, since 1991, it had grown exponentially when the central government of China allowed the port to implement economic reforms. Clearly, this was going to be a major story.

****

'Welcome to the Mandarin, Mr Driver. I hope you enjoy your stay with us. If there is anything that you need, please let us know. I have an envelope to give you and here is your room key. Your suite overlooks the Huangpu River and is on the twentieth floor.'

'Thank you. I'm excited to be here.'

'Thank you. You are very kind.'

Greg stared out of the floor-to-ceiling windows of his suite. The river view with its towering skyline on the other side was stunning. He showered and changed into clothes more suitable for the climate. He opened the envelope that he had been given in Reception and sat on the bed, studying it. A representative from the Port Authority would meet him for dinner that evening. The next two days would be spent attending formal presentations in the port with tours of the facilities to follow. He picked up his cell phone to call his wife to catch her before she left for work. He was eight hours ahead.

'Hi, my love. How are you?'

'Hi to you too! Are you in Shanghai now? How was the flight?'

'Yes, I'm in the hotel. Got here safely about an hour ago. Gosh, I wish you were with me. I miss you already. I have a great room overlooking the city.'

'Sounds wonderful. I wish I was there too. Nothing much happening here except it's been raining ever since you left. Other than that, no news.'

'Seems it's going to be a busy couple of days so I'm not sure when I can phone again, given the time difference.'

'That's okay. As long as I know you got there safely, that's good.'

'Alright. Got to go now. I love you!'

'I love you too.'

Greg descended to the hotel reception just before six pm. The lobby, decked out in polished marble and brightly coloured mosaic walls was busy with people coming and going.

Greg stood holding a light suit jacket over his arm with a clean open-neck white shirt on. In his mid-twenties, he took care of his appearance with neatly cut hair and classic good looks. He stood with his back to a large potted shrub, scanning the entrance and reception area with its decorative, circular lights suspended high in the ceiling. He watched several Chinese men enter the hotel, all of whom went straight to Reception. None of them looked around for someone to meet. A lady entered the hotel and walked straight to the house phone. As she held the receiver, she turned to face the lobby. Well dressed in a straight skirt suit, she was very attractive with short black hair and a slender figure. She waited for a while, not speaking, and then put down the phone. She looked around the lobby and spotted Greg. Greg saw her approach him and was even more surprised when she spoke in perfect English.

'Excuse me. Are you Mr Driver?'

Greg looked at her, completely stunned. For some reason he had thought it would be a male representing the Port Authority. Instead, he was taken aback at how strikingly beautiful she was close up; probably in her late twenties with flawless olive skin. He shook himself out of his thoughts.

'Oh, I'm so sorry. Yes, I am. To be honest, I was looking out for a man. I didn't expect a lady. No offence.'

She smiled back at him and held out her hand.

'No problem. I get that a lot. I'm Meili Shabani, customer liaison officer for the Shanghai Port Authority.'

'Meili. It's a pleasure to meet you. Please call me Greg.'

'Welcome to Shanghai, Greg. We are pleased to have you as our guest for this important occasion. I hope you had a good flight?'

'Yes, thank you. I did. I arrived earlier this afternoon. Fortunately, I'm one of those people that can sleep well on planes so jet lag is not much of an issue.'

'Oh, that's good. We want you to have the best experience possible over these next few days.'

'Thank you. I'm very pleased to be here and looking forward to the next few days. Are there other journalists here too?'

'Yes, there are. They are mostly from Europe, but we do have some American guests as well. As everyone arrives at different times, we have assigned each journalist a liaison officer for their stay. As for tonight, it is such a pleasant evening, I thought we could take a walk along The Bund before we have dinner.'

'The Bund?'

'Yes, it's a beautiful riverside walk. It's particularly nice at this time of day.'

'Sounds wonderful.'

They walked along the promenade running along the west bank of the Huangpu River.

Meili stopped and pointed at the buildings alongside The Bund.

'Over the last century this area has a rich history of culture. The area is known as "the museum of grandiose buildings", with an abundance of European architecture, including gothic, baroque, and neoclassical styles. Many of the old English and French buildings now serve as restaurants, boutique stores, galleries and offices.'

Greg stared in awe. 'This is not what I expected.'

'No, it probably isn't. You have to remember that China was invaded by the British in 1839, starting the first of the Anglo-China Opium wars and what we call the "unequal treaties" that followed them.'

'Unequal treaties?'

Meili stopped and placed her hands on the metal railing overlooking the river. Greg moved and stood beside her.

'Yes, unequal treaties were foisted upon China by many foreign powers between the mid-1800s and 1900s. As a nation we were taken advantage of for too long. All the architecture that you see here reflects the European influence.'

'I didn't know that. I obviously need to study your history more!'

Meili pointed again towards the buildings.

'You can see the previous headquarters of the Hong Kong and Shanghai Banking Corporation with its magnificent cupola and now look at the harbour customs office with its imposing bell tower. There's the old Peace Hotel and the Bank of China.'

'I'm really impressed!' said Greg. 'Shanghai is a complete surprise!'

They returned to the hotel and the exclusive Yong Yi Ting fine dining restaurant. They sat in one of the booths separated by splendid floor-to-ceiling engraved glass partitions depicting Chinese culture. As they ate an array of fish delicacies, Greg looked questioningly at Meili.

'Meili, can I ask you something?'

'Of course, go ahead,'

'Where are you from originally?'

'Well, my father is Iranian and my mother Chinese, so I have lived in both countries. As well as Mandarin, I speak obviously English, Farsi and Cantonese. This is why I have this job. Because China is fast becoming the world's industrial powerhouse, I was selected to look after key international customers as well as VIP guests. The port of Shanghai is now the busiest port in the world and tomorrow you will see its latest developments.'

After dinner, they shook hands 'Thank you for a wonderful evening, Meili. I have enjoyed it very much. See you in the morning.'

Greg went back to his room completely blown away by Meili. It was all he could do to behave himself. She was just downright gorgeous. *'Stop it, you idiot! For god's sake, you just got married!'*

The following day, Greg attended the formal presentations with Meili. They were joined by eleven other journalists from the maritime press spread across the world.

Sitting in a purpose-built auditorium, they witnessed the history of the port with its ambition to become the biggest container port in the world. It could now receive the largest container ships ever built. With 100+ ton lifts, as well as fixed, mobile, and floating cranes, the port had over 136 berths, including 67 deep-water berths. Later, they toured the south waterway of the mouth of the Yangzi River and the Huangpu River by boat to fully grasp the scale of the biggest port in China. Greg mingled with the other journalists, scrambling to take notes and photos as the guide pointed out all the points of interest. None of the guests had ever seen anything on this scale before. The guide came back on his microphone.

'So, ladies and gentlemen, yet another surprise awaits you. Even the scale of this port is not enough for us.' He paused. 'Yes, you heard me correctly. Today these port facilities have a berth utilisation ratio of between 80 and 90 percent. This is much higher than the average utilisation of other main ports in the world. This could be viewed as being very positive, but because Shanghai Port is extremely forward-thinking, we are constructing new ports at Waigaoqiao and Luojing which you will see tomorrow.'

Greg talked to another journalist from Germany.

'Bloody hell. Impressive, isn't it?'

The German replied, 'Us Germans pride ourselves on our efficiency, but this is off the scale!'

Later that evening, back at the hotel, Greg took a shower and lay down in his bathrobe. He was exhausted and dozed off on the bed. A knock on his door awoke him. He got up, checked who was there through the peep hole, and opened the door to Meili. She was dressed in a low-cut silk blouse and tight skirt. A shawl was draped over her left arm.

'Hi, Greg. I'm here to pick you up for dinner.'

'Oh, I'm so sorry! I must have fallen asleep after the shower. Please, come in. Can you give me five minutes? You can wait here. I'll get dressed in the bathroom.'

'Yes, I can do that,' Meili said. Their eyes met and chemistry sparked between them.

Greg got flustered, grabbing fresh clothes. 'I'll just be a minute.' He went to the bathroom and closed the door. He got dressed, then looked at himself in the mirror again. *'You bloody fool.'*

As he came out of the bathroom, Meili was standing with her back to him, looking out of the window. The silhouette of her shapely body, in her high heels, against the glittering lights of the evening skyline took his breath away. The faint scent of her perfume invaded his senses even more to the point he was past the point of no-return.

'Meili.'

She turned slowly to face him, deep eyes and moist lips

enticing him even further. She remained silent.

Greg walked slowly across the room and stood close to her. She took his hand and squeezed it gently.

"Isn't the view marvellous at this time of day?"

Greg did not reply but remained still. She leaned forward and kissed him. Greg's eyes widened but remained motionless. She placed her arms around his neck and pulled him closer to her. Greg responded clasping his arms around her slim waist and kissed her in return. She broke away from him.

'I'm not supposed to be doing this! I'm only to have a professional relationship with you but I find you completely irresistible."

Greg smiled, 'Are you sure you want to go out to dinner?'

He looked into her large brown and green flecked eyes waiting for an answer. She looked back at him, shook her head, and said, more to herself, 'I shouldn't be doing this.' She placed her handbag on the dresser facing the bed.

'Maybe just once, but tomorrow we have another full day and then the gala dinner with everyone else.'

9

Chapter 9

Lee Yuen took a long swig of his cold beer. 'Ahh, life is good!' He sank back into his couch, tilted his head back, closed his eyes and let out a long, satisfied sigh.

He looked around, admiring his new luxury apartment overlooking the exotic Winterbourne gardens in Edgbaston, Birmingham. The peace and tranquillity of the lush gardens, shrubs and trees contrasted starkly with the concrete maze he had grown up in.

In his mid-twenties, he was reminiscing on the last few years of his life and what he had been able to accomplish. He had been brought up in Hong Kong by his single mother who had fled from an abusive relationship with his father. Living in the district of Sham Shui Po, they had eked out a bare living of subsistence. With no air conditioning, frequent power outages and a leaking roof, he knew what it was to be poor. His mother, Jinni, was proud and honest; working seven days a week at a local grocery stall. The pay was low, but she was allowed to take home some of the older and left-over fruit and vegetables, which helped them get by. From an early age Jinny had pushed education as a way to get them out of poverty. She spent every waking minute, when he wasn't in school, teaching him English and maths. Eventually, they were able to move to England, having been able to secure British citizenship. Lee was twelve years old when they settled in the Deritend district of Birmingham. His mother's insistence on education paid off and he flourished at secondary school. His efforts landed him at the University of Birmingham where he gained first-class honours with a degree in Computer Science.

Lee had tried to bring Jinni with him to his new apartment, but she preferred to stay in the small terrace house in Deritend. It was near her job at the Chung Ying Cantonese restaurant and all her friends lived close by. She also wanted Lee to start his own life, but they always spent Sundays together.

Lee finished off his beer, thinking about money. It always came back to money. Hong Kong culture had moulded him that way. It didn't matter where you were in Hong Kong or who you were with, the main topic of conversation was always money. People judged you on how much wealth you had. Having a big heart or an engaging personality meant nothing. The more money you had, the more people looked up to you. For Lee, this culture had permeated his whole upbringing and it was irreversible. Money was also an insurance policy against poverty. Money was god.

Just before he graduated, the University of Birmingham sent out invitations to organisations and businesses to introduce their soon-to-be qualified students. Their CVs were circulated amongst hiring companies and open days were arranged where each student could meet with potential employers. Lee had been sought after by both the Chinese Trade Commission as well as several blue chip international corporations. One of those corporations was Claybourne Cartage. Lisa Taylor was their Information and Technology director. She pitched the company to Lee by telling him about their upcoming merger with Macrae Shipping. The merger sounded like a huge opportunity for growth and would likely provide him with the challenges of computer systems development that he revelled in. The salary, benefits and pension were extremely attractive. To make matters more interesting, the Chinese Trade Commission also offered him a consultancy contract that would allow him to advise their staff and members on new hardware and software that were available in the market. He could even draw this fee when he was working full time for another employer. A monthly retainer was agreed.

Lee had worked for Claybourne Cartage for a year. It had been challenging. With the merger of two IT departments from both Claybourne Cartage and Macrae Shipping, they had formed one team creating the software that would run the entire logistics operations of road, rail, sea, and air worldwide. There were no redundancies. Instead, embarking on this futuristic vision meant that the IT department grew even more.

Lisa Taylor was now the IT Director of Macrae-Claybourne logistics, reporting to Janet Rushton, Vice-President IT. Now the merger was complete, and the logistics software had been beta tested, it was ready to go live. Lee had played a significant role in the development phase of the software. His contribution had been added to the other developers work and then uploaded to a steering and quality control group that operated behind secure password protected firewalls.

Lee placed his beer back on the coffee table and leaned over to pick up the remote for the TV, when his cell phone buzzed.

It was his contact from the Chinese Trade Commission.

'Hello, sir. This is Lee.'

'Good afternoon, Lee. It's been a year now since we worked together. Your reports have been thorough and useful, however it is now time for you to start earning your retainer. If you can forward us the information we require, this monthly retainer could be increased substantially.'

'What is it that you require, sir?'

'You will provide us with a complete copy of the coding for the entire software system of Macrae-Claybourne Logistics.'

10

Chapter 10

Greg heard a faint sound. What was it? He tried hard to decipher what it was before the persistent sound finally revealed itself. The alarm clock buzz finally pierced his consciousness. It was 7:00am. He tried hard to remember where he was and fumbled around to turn it off. Lying on his back, he rubbed his eyes to drag himself out of the deep sleep he had been in. The sheets on the left-hand side of him were ruffled and empty. Meili had left a note to say she would pick him up at 8:30am.

With his eyes fully open, Greg remembered in vivid detail the night he had spent with Meili. It had been more than a spectacular and erotic dream. He sniffed her pillow, arousing himself yet again with her scent. At the same time, he felt a deep sense of guilt start to creep in. He had never cheated on his wife before, even when they were courting. If he called his wife now, he knew it would be a difficult conversation, so he convinced himself it was too late at night back home to call her.

Greg and Meili joined the rest of the journalists at the

Waigaoqiao Port. There was a lot of laughing and revelry as the guests exchanged some of their stories from the night before. Greg smiled and listened. He was smitten. The same guide from the day before greeted them on the tour bus.

'Good morning, everyone! I hope you all enjoyed your night in Shanghai and sampled some of the sights and exciting activities the city has to offer.' He smiled and added, 'From some of the looks I'm getting back, I can see you did!' He laughed. Greg smiled again to himself. His guilt had worn off and he was hungry for more of Meili. He also noticed a few other guests smile.

'This is our newest port facility and was opened late last year in October 1994. It handles general cargo and is integrated with our other ports serving the economic activities of the Pudong area and Yangtze River Delta.'

Like a line of giant dinosaurs, rows and rows of red and white striped gigantic gantry cranes towered over all the dry bulk vessels tied up below them. The tour guide became silent as the classical waltz, 'The Blue Danube', by Johann Strauss was played over the tour bus sound system. The whole scene in front of the journalists transformed itself into one giant delicate mechanical ballet. Cranes, rail cars, truck and trailers and conveyor belts all moved and meshed themselves together as the cranes moved back and forth in circular motions above their heads. The bus became silent. It was a mesmerising moment, never to be forgotten.

The bus moved on further down the quayside. 'Now, look as far as you can see. It's a three-kilometre stretch of land that is being developed for another deep-water port and an additional international container terminal. You can see the rail lines going in ready to receive the straddle cranes to feed the quayside cranes.'

There were further gasps from some of the other journalists. A flurry of clicks and scribbling went on.

'Okay, so now we will go to the Luojing terminal.' The bus continued the tour to yet another harbour terminal, still part of the Shanghai Port.

'So, here we are! Here you see the break-bulk port facilities serving the Shanghai steelworks and all the area's iron-ore merchants. This extensive loading quay can accommodate ships on either side. Again, you can see where we are developing the adjoining land for further handling of bulk cargo, general cargo and roll-on/roll-off for wheeled cargo.'

Even though he was impressed by the presentation, Greg struggled to pay attention; the night with Meili invading his mind. Trying hard to concentrate, he took more photographs and more notes on the proceedings. On some of the photos outside the bus, he made sure Meili was included in the shot. Another journalist from the US approached him.

'Are you taking any photos of the terminal or are they all about your companion? If she's anything like the one I have, you will fill an art gallery! It's all I can do to keep my hands off my girl. What a night!' He nudged Greg, winked and walked off again.

Greg looked around and noticed that many of the other journalists seemed to be preoccupied with their liaison officers.

After lunch, the group found themselves back in the auditorium. The president of the Port Authority addressed the group.

'Welcome, everyone. By now I'm sure you are probably exhausted and surprised by the tremendous scale of our recent developments revolutionising port facilities worldwide. Not only have we passed Singapore port in size, but we have the best automated systems to handle the vast scale of our business. It's now my pleasure to show you the final highlight of your visit. This is the behind-the-scenes systems software that powers the handling of all the goods that pass through this terminal and around the world.'

Greg sat up in his chair, listening and looking intently at the screen shots of the software being shown. It was identical to what he had seen several weeks ago at the Macrae-Claybourne logistics launch. His jaw dropped open. *Holy shit!* He nearly said it out loud. *I can't fucking believe it. How could this happen?*

When the president wrapped up and asked if there were any questions, Greg was the first to stand up.

'Mr President. Greg Driver – *Mercantile News*, UK. Firstly, I have to say that I am immensely impressed with your rapid development and progress, managing the import and export of all the commodities that you handle. Can you tell me, though, about your new software system? How did it come about?'

'I'm sorry, Greg. I didn't understand the question; how did it come about?'

'Oh sorry, sir. I wanted to know if this software is your own creation or is it a system that can be purchased on the open market?'

'No. This system is entirely our own creation. We have a whole team of software engineers that purpose design all our systems. Obviously with the gigantic size of the operation we need the latest technology to cope with the volume of business and the number of exporting companies we have.'

Greg wrote down, word for word, what he said.

*****

Later, Greg and Meili attended the gala dinner with the rest of the journalists at The Bund waterfront restaurant, facing the ultra-modern Pudong district. The night view through the panoramic windows was spectacular; the skyline full of high-rise buildings with their lights gleaming and dazzling across the Huangpu River.

Greg took an aperitif of baijiu from one of the circling waiters and mingled with the other journalists.

'Wow! This stuff is powerful!'

One of the others replied, 'You bet! The Chinese didn't just invent gunpowder, you know!'

'So, what did you think of these past few days?' Greg asked.

The Italian journalist looked up. 'To me, it's been five star! Let's face it, Shanghai port has clearly set the bar very high for customer expectations.'

Several of the others nodded in agreement.

Greg posed another question. 'So, what did you think of the software that was presented this afternoon?'

The Spanish journalist replied. 'Honestly, I've never seen anything like the scope of the software they showed us. It's visionary!'

Another journalist in the group stepped up. 'Greg, I saw your article last month in *Mercantile News*. Isn't this software the same as what you described in your article?'

Greg looked back at him and nodded. He knew he would have to investigate this further.

Nothing was spared in terms of food choice and the wine selection. After dinner, Greg chatted further with the other journalists. They exchanged business cards.

Meili mixed with her co-workers. She looked stunning in a long black strappy silk evening dress. Greg was in awe. After the farewells with the port staff, hosts and other journalists, Meili came back to the hotel with Greg. Again, she placed her handbag on the dresser facing the bed. She undressed in front of Greg. Standing there in her black lace panties and bra, Greg reached for her and pulled her towards him. He went to turn the bedside lights off, but Meili stopped him.

'No,' she said. 'I want to make love in the light with you. I want to see and taste every inch of you.'

They lay there afterwards, spent and happy.

'Meili, what would you say if I said that the software program that we saw today wasn't original?'

Meili laughed. 'Of course it's original. There's nothing like it anywhere else in the world! I should know. I work with these people every day.' She paused and drew back from him. 'I don't understand?'

'I saw the same presentation last month at the launch of the new Macrae-Claybourne Logistics company. It was also a working "on-the-fly" demo using actual real-time dynamic data, whereas your presentation appeared to be a series of static screen shots.'

Meili sat up immediately and turned to face him directly. 'This is nonsense! The software system we showed you was our original work and was live. Don't tell me otherwise! In any case, Macrae Shipping has a very poor reputation. As a customer liaison officer, I should know! I hear many complaints about their poor service and exorbitant prices from many shipping companies. They are price gouging the customers who pick up and drop off at their Mediterranean ports. I wouldn't trust a word they said. They are a completely unethical company.' She got up from the bed and started to get dressed. Greg reacted immediately.

'No wait, Meili. I didn't mean to upset you. I was just telling you what I thought I saw.'

'Well, you're wrong and I'm upset you said it! We've worked hard at being the world's number one port. I was wrong to go to bed with you; I've made a huge mistake. I'm even more sorry because I thought I was falling in love with you, even to the extent of wanting to come back to the UK with you.'

'What? I didn't realise! Oh shit!' Greg swallowed hard. His eyes widened. 'I thought this would be just a couple of nights thing.'

Meili became even more angry and started to shout. 'You did, did you? Well, I don't jump into bed very easily with anybody. I thought we had something real going on between us.'

'Oh, Meili! I'm so sorry.' He paused and then blurted out. 'That's not all though. I can't continue this relationship because...' He paused, looked down and said quietly, 'I have to confess, I'm married.'

Meili burst into tears and finished dressing in silence. As she left the room, grabbing her handbag, she said, 'I'll see you tomorrow morning. I will pick you up at 10:00am and take you straight to the airport.'

Meili got back to her own apartment and immediately made a phone call using a special line. A voice answered.

'This is General Shen. How did it go, Meili?'

'Everything went according to plan, General. I have two nights' worth of video. I will pick him up tomorrow and deliver to him the exact press articles that he will need to publish word for word, otherwise his marriage and career will be over.'

'Excellent! You have done well. I will let Mr Ming know.'

11

Chapter 11

'Tomorrow,' Stanfield whispered as they exercised together. 'With the bank holiday, they will have a reduced number of guards. It's now or never.'

'Did you get everything we need?' Nash asked quietly.

'Yes, my contact managed to get hold of a mouse gun and concealed it in the new trainers I managed to get brought in. I'll try to do the handover at Mass tomorrow.' They parted, continuing to exercise separately.

It was already a very hot Sunday. Hugh Stanfield sat on his cell bed with his back to the wall. After an unsettled night, he felt uncomfortable. The odds of escape were extremely poor, but he had to chance it.

'Come on, Stanfield! Get a move on! We haven't got all bleedin' day!' the surly guard shouted. 'While I have to look after all you arseholes, every family in the country is spending time together and having fun.'

'I'm coming! I'm coming!' He stood up in his new trainer shoes.

'Come on, hurry up. God's not gonna wait for you!'

As another guard waited outside the cell, the surly guard gave Stanfield a rub-down search before moving him to the stairway. Another guard had Nash ready outside his cell. The three guards then escorted both of them to the prison chapel on the ground floor for the first mass of the day at 9:15 am.

There were already a large number of prisoners in the chapel and noticeably fewer guards present than on a normal Sunday. The air inside the small room was already oppressive.

Inside the chapel, they sat in the back pews with the stained-glass windows behind them facing the altar. The three guards stood behind them. As Stanfield turned to sit down, he noticed the guards mopping their brows.

Surly shouted again, 'Sit down and shut up! No talking!'

The priest crossed himself in front of the altar and turned towards his congregation.

'We will now sing the hymn, "The King of Love my Shepherd is".

> *And so through all the length of days*
> *Thy goodness faileth never;*
> *Good Shepherd, may I sing thy praise*
> *Within thy house for ever.*

As the notes of the last verse died away, the priest announced,

'We will now pray.'

The congregation started to kneel in their pews with bowed heads when one prisoner towards the front of the church fainted on cue and fell to the floor in the aisle at the side of his pew. Immediately a couple of guards went to his aid and take him out for fresh air. There was a buzz of chatter before peace was restored.

Stanfield covertly slid his left hand down into his new

trainers. He eased a small gun from inside the heel of his left shoe and clasped it in the palm of his right hand. The gun was an American-made Raven MP-25 automatic, also known as a mouse gun. The Raven was no bigger than the size of the average adult hand and contained a magazine of six bullets. Stanfield slid the gun carefully to Nash, who concealed it in his big left hand. Sweat poured off Stanfield. Still, he did not look out of place, given the oppressive heat inside the small chapel.

After the service had finished, Stanfield and Nash were escorted by the three prison officers to return to their unit. Once inside the main building they started to walk in single file down a narrow, windowless brick corridor poorly lit with overhead lights. Stanfield was between the first and middle guard. Nash was between the middle guard and the last one.

Nash stopped. He turned and, back to the side wall, produced the gun, firing a shot up into the roof of the passage. The bang resonated back and forth from the cold bare walls and roof. Jagged fragments of brickwork showered them all from the crumbling ceiling of the passageway.

'Get down! Get down now!' Nash screamed.

The three officers stood frozen, trying to comprehend what had just happened.

'Get down or you'll be a gonner!' Nash roared.

All three officers dived down and lay flat on the bare concrete floor. Stanfield and Nash dashed forward with grim, determined faces. As Nash passed the first officer, he reached down and grabbed him tightly around his neck. Yanking him forward, he held the gun to his head with his right arm and used him as a hostage.

'If you struggle, you're a dead man!'

He turned and looked back at the other two guards, still lying flat on the concrete floor.

'Stay where you are, or he gets it in the head!'

'Don't do this, Nash! You'll make it worse for yourself!'

Nash screamed back at the two men. 'Shut up. I've already got life for murder. A few more won't make any difference!'

Doubled-up and staggering, Nash dragged the horrified officer forward, away from the other officers.

'Get his keys, quick!' Nash yelled at Stanfield.

Stanfield got hold of the long key chain hanging from the officer's waist. They pushed their way forward to a solid steel door on the right.

Nash's face was ashen. 'Hurry up!'

Stanfield fumbled with the keys for what seemed like an eternity but managed to eventually unlock the heavy steel door.

'Follow me!'

Nash followed quickly through the door, still holding his stumbling hostage.

They ran down another narrow corridor, the two guards still chasing them from a short distance. The alarm went off and, within seconds, more prison officers approached them down an adjacent narrow passage.

'Stop, you two! You'll never get out of here!'

On seeing them, Nash stopped at the head of the passage and pointed the gun at them. 'I warned you!'

He fired the gun at the officers. One of them fell immediately. The rest ducked for cover.

'Come on, Dan, I've got this door open.'

Nash dragged his hostage through the door while Stanfield opened another reinforced outer steel door. Gasping for air, they piled out into a small yard, still within the prison.

'Hold him tight while I lock the door again.'

'Leave the key in the door. That should buy us some time!'

Stanfield quickly looked around. 'This is it, Dan! There's the shed. Follow me!'

Three more guards ran out from another door and tried to approach Nash holding out their hands in front of them.

'Keep back!'

The officers kept coming forward, so Nash levelled his arm at them and fired another shot, injuring one of the officers in the stomach. The guard screamed in pain and fell to the floor. The other officers immediately froze and then leaned down to try to help the injured guard.

Letting their hostage go, stumbling to the floor, Stanfield and Nash scrambled onto the roof of the shed, their arms and legs working frantically to gain a purchase to help them climb higher up.

Nash yelled at Stanfield, 'Go up! Go up now. I've got you covered!'

Stanfield dug his fingers into the exposed bricks as hard as he could. His soft fingers began to immediately bleed from their rough edges. Pain shot back down his arms. He tried to ignore it and managed to scale the outer wall to the top.

He lay on top of the wall, dangling his arm down towards Nash.

'Give me the gun. I'll cover you!'

Nash jumped up, arm outstretched towards Stanfield's bleeding hand – trying to pass over the gun. As he did so, one of the guards clambered onto the roof of the shed and made a dive for Nash's leg.

Stanfield shouted down to Nash. 'I've got it!'

Nash tried to free his leg from the tight grip of his pursuer, but the guard wouldn't let go. Nash kicked him in the head with his other leg, but he still wouldn't let go. More guards tried to climb onto the roof of the shed.

Stanfield steadied his aim and, without any warning, shot downwards at the lead guard and hit him in the head. The guard's head fell back and he collapsed in a heap below Nash. With his leg now free, Nash quickly scaled the wall. They both threaded their way through the razor wire as carefully as they could and then dropped down the outer wall, landing heavily on the service road below them. Running on adrenaline, their clothes ripped and bloody, they stumbled across the road to a grassy area and through a small iron gate onto Brixton Hill.

Stanfield gasped, 'I hope to god Charlie's in position otherwise we're done for. Nobody's gonna pick us up looking like this!'

Nash didn't have the breath to answer; he was doubled over.

A black London cab drew up beside them. The driver, wearing a Scottish plaid cap, poked his head out of the window and shouted, 'Stanny! Get in quick!'

Stanfield and Nash piled into the back seat, gasping for breath. Nash managed to slam the door behind them. The driver closed his dark-tinted widow and accelerated the cab as fast as he could down Brixton Hill.

'Bloody hell, guys, you've made it! I've been driving around here for last half hour. Fucking A! You can't be spotted now. The blacked-out windows will see to that. Let's just hope we don't get stopped in any road-blocks now the alarm's gone off!'

Nash and Stanfield lay back in the rear seat, scarcely believing they had pulled it off. With their mouths wide open, panting for air, they both closed their eyes and tried to slow their heart rates down.

Stanfield's inside information of the layout of the prison from Mr Clarke, the prison guard, had paid off. He had paid Clarke seventy-five thousand in cash through his outside contact, Charlie Thornton. Hopefully Clarke and his wife could enjoy their imminent retirement in Brighton after all.

Clarke had also made sure that the trainers Stanfield had had sent in were inspected by another officer when he was off duty. The particular guard was known to be lax.

Stanfield opened his eyes.

'Charlie! Thanks, mate! It would not have been possible without that gun. Just like old times, eh! I see you are still using the hackney carriage technique?'

'Sure am, Stanny boy! Perfect camouflage. This one's a bit different, though. It's beefed up in a few places and with bullet-proof windows. Has to be, the bloody narks are getting tooled up too much these days. 'S not like it used to be.'

'Are we going back to the transport yard?'

'Yep, although I will need to stay off the main roads.'

'Dan, meet my old friend Charlie. We go back a way.'

'Hi, Charlie,' Nash said. 'Thanks for your help. We were just about running on empty when you picked us up!' Turning to Stanfield, he put out his hand across the back seat. 'Here's your gun back. Might as well take it now. We just about used up all the bullets. It was a close thing!'

'We're not out of the woods yet. Let's hope Charlie can thread his way out of the area. If we're caught now, I can't imagine what they would do to us behind closed doors. We've probably killed three guards.'

'Fucked if I care. At least we can suck in some outside air, even if it is short lived.'

They passed through rows of terraced houses and then more open space emerged with people strolling and picnicking freely in various parks. Stanfield wondered if he would be able to do that or would he be back in Brixton by nightfall?

Charlie drove north-east towards the city of London, avoiding the A3. They snaked through the back streets of Camberwell and Bermondsey and approached the river Thames to use the Rotherhithe tunnel to get to the other side. The traffic slowed and crawled slowly along.

Eventually, they crossed the Thames. Charlie weaved his way back east and drove down a succession of back streets towards Canning Town. They eventually entered the Blackwell Trading Estate and arrived in front of a gated fenced yard. Jack pipped the horn, and the solid gates were opened by an older man bent over with age in a shabby short coat. Once inside the yard, they drove into a large warehouse fronted by a set of metal roller-shutter doors. The warehouse was well over one hundred thousand square feet and contained several trucks and semi-trailers. The old man immediately closed the outer gates and the warehouse door.

'Bloody hell, is Billy Blowtorch still working for you?' Stanfield exclaimed.

Charlie laughed. 'He sure is. This is his retirement, but he can still handle a sawn-off shotgun and a blowtorch to persuade people to talk! Okay, guys, time to follow me.'

As they got out of the cab, Charlie stood back from them. 'Bloody hell! You two need to get cleaned up and put some new clothes on. Look at the state you're in!'

Both Stanfield and Nash were cut and bleeding from scrambling through the razor wire.

'Let me show you to the apartment and you can wash and change. I've got some clothes and food in to get you started.'

They moved to the side of the warehouse and went up a flight of wooden stairs and through a solid metal door. Inside was a kitchen, bathroom, shower and one bedroom with two single beds. There were no windows except two sun tubes from the flat roof that provided the only natural light in the ceiling.

Stanfield looked at Nash. 'This is going to be our home for a while, at least until the initial search for us starts to die down.'

Nash gave a nervous laugh. 'You know, I was kinda getting used to my prison cell. I guess we can make do with this!'

Stanfield grabbed Thornton by the arm. 'Thanks, Charlie! You don't know what this means to me.'

Thornton smiled wryly. 'You're not going soft on me, are you, Stanny boy?'

'Certainly not, but it needed to be said. On the contrary, we need to generate some quick cash, plan to move on from here and get even with the Macraes. If I don't do that, everyone *will* think I've gone soft!'

12

Chapter 12

'What's wrong with you?' Greg Driver's wife questioned him, in tears. 'You've hardly looked me in the eye or touched me since you've been back! You don't communicate with me and when you do, you're rude.' She waited for a response from her husband, but he just gave her a blank stare.

'Please! Tell me what's wrong or is it me? Have I done something to upset you?' When he remained silent, she just stamped her foot. 'I'm off to work!' She grabbed her coat and slammed the door behind her.

Greg cast his mind back to the shocking cab ride he'd endured from Shanghai to the airport for his return trip. He could hardly stop thinking about it.

He had been picked up from the hotel by a heavy-set Chinese man in a chauffeur-driven limousine. He looked more of a thug than a representative from the Shanghai Port Authority.

'Get in, Mr Driver!'

'Who are you?'

'I have taken Meili's place and will be taking you to the

airport. I suggest you listen very carefully to every word I say.'

Greg remained silent as the car set off from the hotel.

'Firstly, Mr Driver, understand that nothing will happen to you if you carry out our explicit instructions. Do you understand?'

Greg nodded.

'Here are a set of press articles prepared for you that you will publish on the dates we tell you to. You will be the exclusive author of each of them. You are not allowed to change one word of any of them. Failure to publish these articles or even change them in any way will cost you your marriage, your job and your career. We will wreck your whole life. Are we clear on this?'

Greg started to shake. He nodded as best he could.

'If you don't carry out our instructions or even communicate or hint at this conversation, we will instantly release a complete unedited video of your sexual encounter with one of our employees. Copies will be sent to your wife, her family and yours, your employer and all the other media involved in the industry. In short, your life, marriage and career will be ruined!'

Nothing more was said on the ride to the airport.

Greg shakily pulled out the first prepared article from his briefcase that he had been ordered to print by the Chinese. He read it through and started to sweat. Mopping his brow with his handkerchief, he felt like a cheap tabloid reporter, a complete bottom feeder with absolutely no morals or scruples. The article would cause a sensation, especially after such a glowing article the month before on Macrae-Claybourne Logistics.

Greg made his way to work and read the article once more at his desk. He felt guilty, confused, angry and depressed, all at the same time. What a bloody fool he had been! He had been making good headway in his career and now he sat teetering on the edge of a giant precipice. All for the sake of a quick bonk with someone he really didn't know. And to think it was Meili who initiated it as well. Stupid fucker! Yes, it was a set-up, but he had fallen into it willingly.

'Hi, Greg. Welcome back! How was the trip?' Phil West asked.

'Oh hi, Phil. It was great, though very tiring,' said Greg, desperately trying to sound positive. 'The Port Authority was very generous with their hospitality, but they worked us hard.'

'Yes, you look tired. It's a long way to go in such a short time but hopefully you've got some good stuff ready for print. I'm giving you the front page for this piece so it had better be good.'

'Thanks, boss. I'm right on it!'

His whole body began to shake. He knew credibility was a valued commodity and needed to be safeguarded in life, because you could only lose it once. Once it was lost, you could never fully regain it. His credibility as a person, a husband and a journalist would be gone forever.

'Shit! The front page is the last thing I need with this story. It's a bomb waiting to go off.'

****

Detective Chief Inspector Thomas stood up to his full height of above six feet in the special operations room at the London Metropolitan Police headquarters in front of his team. As a career detective with a broken marriage, his profession had become his religion. Unlike many of his colleagues who had simply allowed middle age to catch up with them, he had fought hard to remain fit and slim. In short, he was dedicated to track down criminals no matter how long it took. This was not a nine to five job in his mind. He wanted officers on his team that would willingly go the extra mile.

'Good afternoon, everyone. We all know why we are here. Stanfield and Nash, having escaped from Brixton this morning, will be our focus until we catch them. They are considered armed and dangerous. In view of the seriousness of the situation, we need a speedy result. From the PM down, we will be under close scrutiny. You all know by now each line of inquiry you will be following up. We must move fast. Assisting us will be MI6, Interpol and I want to introduce to you now, my assistant on this case. This is Detective Inspector Stella Hudson from the West Midlands Police.'

DI Hudson stood up and acknowledged everyone as she put her hand up. She was tall, in her thirties, and also looked extremely fit.

DCI Thomas continued. 'I asked for DI Hudson as there are strong links between Stanfield and the West Midlands that she will follow up on. She has an excellent track record and will be invaluable in consolidating all the police forces that will be assisting us in recapturing Stanfield and Nash.'

There were a few murmurs in the room.

'Okay, the trail is still hot right now. Let's get on it before these villains get a chance to skip the country.'

Chapter 13

Politicians make me sick!

Shen's eyes were closed. He was mulling in his mind the ridiculous language that all politicians seemed to follow like Pavlov's dogs. Trying to be 'nice' and accommodate everyone's opinion all the time was downright stupid. Leaders needed to be decisive and act. In his mind the new President Zemin fell into the 'nice' category. At least Deng Xiaoping had a vision and executed it. In fact, if it wasn't for him, his country would still be wallowing in self-destructive idealism. *'No, it's my time now. I've climbed up the ladder, I need to make a push for the top. The question is "when"?'*

General Shen opened his eyes and placed his table back into the armrest at the side of his seat and raised his chair to the upright position as the Singapore Airlines Airbus A340 banked slowly for its final approach into Changi airport. The flight had taken just five and half hours from Shanghai to Singapore. As the flight descended over the Singapore Strait, he could see scores of cargo and container vessels all patiently waiting at anchor to offload or load in the port. Wearing a smart business suit and tie, his papers identified him as Lei Wen, Managing Director, Shanghai HVAC Controls.

He took a limousine to the Shangri-La hotel, a deluxe oasis nestled in the middle of the city. He would meet Ben Armstrong, the American venture capitalist who owned Pair-Tree Capital. The company had taken the place of Euro-Asian Freight and would covertly represent the Chinese in acquiring strategic port terminals worldwide. They would meet that evening in the Waterfall restaurant located in the hotel's garden wing. The restaurant was renowned for its Italian cuisine.

General Shen sat quietly savouring a Bombay Sapphire gin and tonic. Even though he was a communist, he enjoyed living well whenever he travelled abroad on his country's business. After all, he needed to play the part of an international businessman. He already knew what Ben Armstrong looked like and his background from the files in Beijing, but he needed to meet the man face to face. This way, Armstrong would know first-hand who was in charge. It wasn't difficult to spot the American when he entered the restaurant. He was a medium-build man, slightly overweight with a rather elongated head, swept back greying hair and metal-framed glasses. He paused as he entered the restaurant, looking around to find his new boss. Shen raised his arm and then stood up to meet him. Shen was taller than Armstrong and was surprised at the American's limp handshake for such an apparently wealthy and influential man.

'Good evening, Ben. It's a pleasure to meet you.'

Armstrong looked a little stiff and uncomfortable. 'Thank you, Mr Wen. I have been looking forward to meeting you too and begin our business together.'

'Will you join me in an aperitif before dinner?'

'Thank you, I will.' The waiter appeared, and Armstrong ordered a bourbon on the rocks.

'So, Ben, tell me about yourself. I understand you are a venture capitalist. How did you get started?'

'Well, it wasn't that difficult really. I am the grandson of Damian Craven, the inventor of modern-day printers. Once the Craven corporation commercialised his invention, there was plenty of money to go around. I simply took my inheritance and looked for undervalued businesses, bought them, straightened them out and then sold them. Many businesses I broke up and sold the individual pieces. That way the sum of the parts was greater than the whole.'

Shen nodded in appreciation. 'Excellent, but how did you gain your knowledge of the shipping industry?'

Armstrong took a sip of his bourbon as the ice tinkled in his glass.

'Simple, really. I think they call it learning on the job.' He laughed and started to relax.

'For me to be successful I must have eyes and ears everywhere. For some time, I kept hearing that several shipping companies were getting tired of using the port of Boston. Their docking fees and turnaround times were not as competitive as they could have been. My ears pricked up, so I looked north to the port of Portland, Maine. It's only one hundred miles from Boston. Portland harbour was run down, so I quietly looked at their facilities. The harbour was sound but needed new cranes, handling equipment and an upgrade in road and rail links. Their real estate was undervalued, so I swooped in and bought the port authority. Using a clever leasing arrangement, I invested in new machinery and facilities. I then attracted new oil tanker, container and cruise ship business. Once I had expanded the business substantially, I sold it again for a handsome profit. I learned a lot about the marine industry doing that, so I went and purchased the port at Wilmington, North Carolina and did the same.'

Shen smiled. 'Impressive. Let's eat. Do you like fish?'

'I have to say I do. Anyone who lives close to the sea appreciates fresh fish. What do you have in mind?'

'They have a signature seafood stew that has fresh lobster, prawns, clams, mussels and other fresh fish. It is for two people. I can recommend it.'

'Let's do it.'

The dinner arrived and they got stuck into it, making small-talk in between. Afterwards, Shen leaned forward after ordering a cappuccino.

'So, let's get down to business. I, and only I, will be issuing instructions to you which you will scrupulously follow to the letter. Is that understood?'

'Yes. It is, Mr Wen.' Armstrong stiffened as he looked into Shen's suddenly cold and distant eyes.

Shen's eyes penetrated Armstrong even further. 'I want to make sure these ground rules are fully understood. There must be no deviations from my instructions, or you will be finished. How should I say this? He paused for effect. 'In more ways than one.' He paused again. 'Remember, our reach is extensive.'

'You can rely on me, Mr Wen. I'm only interested in making money and this can be a lucrative partnership. I'm certainly not going to jeopardise that.'

'Good. So, we have our understanding?'

'Yes, we do!'

Shen nodded and smiled. He knew he had frightened the hell out of Armstrong.

'Our cover is my HVAC business in Shanghai. I am looking for a rundown HVAC manufacturing plant in the US to purchase, so we will have the perfect cover for meeting when necessary. You will be acting as my agent and would be a partner in this venture. Any funds you require will be funnelled through the Caymans. Communication will be by secure link phones, which our embassy in Washington will provide. Any questions so far?'

'No. I understand perfectly.'

'Good! So here is your first assignment. The port of Zeebrugge in Belgium was previously purchased by Euro-Asian Freight Services but had their assets frozen by the European Union. Once it was discovered that Euro-Asian was owned by the Chinese government, in the interests of European security, we were unable to capitalise on the ownership. You are to buy the terminal and set it up with all the necessary investment in infrastructure. Next, I want you to buy into the port of Marseille. The port is somewhat rundown and needs investment. It should not be too difficult for you to bring your angel capital to their rescue.'

'Understood. I'm already familiar with Marseille, since they mirror what I came across both in Portland and Wilmington. With my reputation, experience and US dollars, we can make that happen. Regarding Zeebrugge, let me dig into that a little deeper.'

'Now, Ben, do you know a man by the name of James Macrae?'

'Yes, I know of him. I don't know him personally, but

he now heads up Macrae Shipping. In fact, I believe they have just merged with another company forming a large logistics company, Macrae-Claybourne Logistics. They own the terminals in Valencia, Genoa, Piraeus, Istanbul, and Yanbu. I also think Claybourne owns a significant chunk of the Immingham terminal in the UK.'

'That is correct. When you have taken over Marseille terminal, you will cut your dock and pilotage rates, increase turnaround efficiency, and suck all their business away from them. I believe you can weaken their Genoa and Valencia terminals with this strategy. After that we can swoop in and take them over. Eventually I want you to buy up all of their ports so keep an eye on what they are doing.'

'Sounds like I am going to be busy,' Armstrong replied, raising his eyebrows.

'Yes, you will be. You stand to make a great deal of money if all goes well. Now, one further matter. I need access to all your financial accounts on an ongoing basis. Remember, Ben, you are working directly for me now so you will focus on only my objectives. Your other work will cease. One last thing, my overall objective is for you to break Macrae-Claybourne Logistics.'

14

Chapter 14

'Mason, can you wheel the bikes out of the garage while I sweep out the floor.'

'Daaad! Do I have to?'

'Yes, you do! We all have to do our share to help out.'

Mason sulked. 'It's not fair. Why aren't the girls helping?'

'Don't worry, your mom has plenty for them to do.'

'Okaaay.'

'This will be a good job done. I've been wanting to do this for weeks now. You and I can go on a bike ride later.'

'James, phone for you! It's the police,' Sarah shouted through the kitchen window.

James picked up the receiver of the home phone. 'Hello?'

'Mr Macrae?'

'Yes, this is James Macrae.'

'Hello, Mr Macrae. This is Detective Inspector Hudson of the West Midlands Police. I'm sorry but I've got some bad news.'

'Oh? I thought all the bad news was over for a lifetime last year.'

'I wish that was true but, unfortunately, it's not. Hugh Stanfield and Dan Nash escaped from Brixton Prison this morning.'

'What!' he exclaimed. 'I don't believe it. How is that possible?' James put his hand to his forehead and fell silent trying to contemplate what it might mean for him and his family.

Hudson continued. 'We don't have the details yet, but I wanted to give you a heads-up just in case they try to contact you, your family or your business. We've already alerted the local police and they are stepping up security for you.'

'Is that possible? I know the police have limited resources.'

'Let me put it this way, Mr Macrae. We think there's a possibility they might want to get even with you. Stanfield and Nash are hardened criminals, and it might be an opportunity for us to get to them first.'

'I see.'

'This has already escalated to a worldwide manhunt. All airports, private and commercial, as well as ports, have full security surveillance measures in place.'

'Thanks, inspector. I'll notify all our terminals to keep a look out for these bastards. Since our troubles last year, security at every workplace both here and at home has been strengthened considerably.'

'Good! Listen, we'll keep you posted. As soon as we get any further developments, I'll let you know. I'll also send you my contact information.'

James turned to Sarah and filled her in. She paled immediately.

'Oh god, James. You'd better let Richard and Mary know straightaway. Does this mean we have to live the rest of our lives in fear?'

'No. It does not. We've already stepped up our security and a worldwide manhunt for these criminals is underway. Surely they can't get far.' James hugged her tightly.

Next, he went to his study and opened his locked gun cupboard. He checked his stash, cursing quietly that he hadn't thrown Stanfield to his death when he had the chance. He wasn't sure if those two would come after him, but he knew he would not make the same mistake twice.

******

James grabbed his raincoat off the passenger seat of his Range Rover and dashed across the paved area to the front of office reception. It was 7:30am. He had already had his early run in the rain before showering and getting ready. With the new day he felt invigorated and raring to go, feeling more confident that the security forces would be able to find Stanfield and Nash sooner, rather than later.

James put his head round Chris's office door. Chris had just got there as well. 'Sorry to spoil your Sunday yesterday, but you needed to know straightaway.'

'Yes, thanks. I got a call shortly afterwards from DI Hudson. They will be keeping a look out across all our operations and houses.'

'Let's hope they get an early result!'

James went to his own office and booted his computer up to view his daily KPIs – key performance indexes. These were measures of the company's performance. They were like a set of flight instruments. You could see the general direction the company was going in and you could see how close to the ground you were. In other words, whether the company was heading for trouble. Today's results were looking very positive; all indices were pointing upwards.

Chris put his head round the door and James looked up.

Chris frowned and came up in front of James's desk.

'Obviously yesterday's news of the escape wasn't good, but have you seen the latest edition of *Mercantile News*?'

'No, I haven't got round to looking at it yet. Why?'

Chris turned round the copy of the magazine in his hand and slid it across the desk for James to see. The frontpage headlines hit James square in the face.

Shanghai Port Authority 1 Macrae–Claybourne Logistics 0

By: Greg Driver Mercantile News – Special Correspondent

After several years in development, Shanghai Port Authority opened its doors to the world this week and what a shock it was! Now the busiest port in the world, in terms of cargo tonnage, it proudly displayed its enlarged deep seaport and river port.

The port covers an area of over 3000 square kilometres and is now the flagship terminal for the world's fastest-growing economy. The scale of the port is like nothing else on the planet, handling over 30 million twenty-foot containers and 400 million tonnes of cargo last year. The totally automated container-handling systems have revolutionised the industry and will put all their competition to shame.

This compares starkly to the relatively poor performance and disappointing launch of Macrae-Claybourne Logistics last month with their touted increases in efficiency at their ports in Istanbul, Piraeus, Genoa, Valencia, Yanbu and Immingham. To make matters worse, Macrae-Claybourne Logistics claimed at their launch that they had developed 'Tomorrow's Technology Today', a logistics software program, when it is now apparent that it was in fact 'Yesterday's Technology Today'. The Shanghai Port Authority had already developed this unique logistics software system and was using it well before Macrae-Claybourne Logistics copied it.

Things don't seem to be going well for the newly launched British logistics company. After a series of accidents and mis-management last year, they appear to be slipping badly, especially now, since Mercantile News has received several reports of customer dissatisfaction about the company. We have tried to contact the company several times for comment, but they have not returned our calls.'

Placed within the article were two graphics showing screen shots of the software system.

James put both his hands up and started to rub his eyelids.

'It never bloody rains, but it always pours! Holy fuck! I can't believe this!'

He looked up at Chris shaking his head. Chris turned round and closed the door to the office. Next, he came and sat down, facing James.

'My reaction entirely!' Chris exclaimed.

James's voice became more subdued as he went into con-trolled combat mode.

'I can't believe this is the same journalist that wrote that glowing article on us last month. This just doesn't make sense.'

'I agree, James. I get the feeling we are being set up. None of this is true.'

'Absolutely! This magazine is going to have a lot to answer

for. To say that we copied software that you and I both know we developed in-house is a blatant lie. This means we have a leak inside our own company if they do, in fact, have the same software. This alone will result in legal action from us. I believe we will also have a legitimate defamation claim.'

Chris was also marshalling his thoughts and continued, 'Certainly, but there's more to hit back on. To use the words "touted increases in efficiency" is libellous as well since we have the stats to prove our increases in efficiency. Not only that, to my knowledge, no one has called either you or me to comment on this report. That goes for our managers as well. Every one of our staff would have informed us if that had been the case.'

James smoothed his hair back. 'You are right. Regarding customer complaints too, both you and I see every one of these and sign off on them after action has been taken to resolve any issues. Again, since we merged, we have not received any. On the contrary, our customer satisfaction index is climbing. Let's get Janet in and see what she thinks.'

There was a knock on the door and James responded, 'Come in.'

'Good morning, Janet. Have you seen this article?'

Janet read through it quietly. She placed the magazine down in front of her and immediately said, 'These graphics are a complete rip-off. This is a copy of our software. To me it looks like they have manipulated the data; more specifically, changed customer names, dates and ports.'

James pushed up the sleeves of his shirt and started to scribble on his pad. 'Okay, so let's firstly investigate where the leak came from. With only a permissions-based hierarchy, access to each individual database is restricted. Only Janet has access to the complete system code.'

Janet responded. 'Our mutual hacker friend, Shad, by the way, has not been able to break the encryption to access this logistics software, so we know we still have the untouched virgin software. Looking at these graphics, I think that's all they have. I'm wondering if our "leaker" has only been able to get these screen shots out so far. If that's the case, we are still leading the world with this technology.'

James and Chris looked at each other and smiled for the first time.

Janet sat back and folded her arms. 'I'm confident they haven't got hold of our software. Each of our software developers only worked on certain sections of code. We then used ODBC, open database connectivity, to access the different database management systems and link them together.' The three of them huddled closer to the desk.

James continued. 'We need a plan of action. Let's get our company lawyers to launch a lawsuit against the publisher, the editor and the journalist based on each defamation contained in the article.'

'I agree,' Chris replied. 'Having said that, I hate legal action. I much prefer face-to-face resolutions. Personally, I'd like us both to confront the journalist and editor face to face, but we cannot do that if we go legal. With this blatant attack on our company, though, we have no choice but to go legal.'

James put his hands together and made a pyramid shape. He rested his chin on his fingertips. 'I feel that's the right thing to do, although in my gut I too would like to drive there right now and confront them physically as well. Common sense, though, tells me not to do that.'

Janet stepped in. 'Why don't we go legal right away, as you

suggest, but let's carefully analyse how we can stop these people messing with us once and for all.'

Janet paused while James and Chris remained silent and then continued with her train of thought.

'Lee Yuen is a brilliant programmer, which is why Lisa hired him. He's originally from Hong Kong so may have links to China. I know he speaks Cantonese and there are many similarities with Mandarin, but it doesn't mean he could be the leaker. Lisa is also highly experienced, and I respect her. Tell us more about her, Chris.'

'Well, I hired her three years ago when I decided our management systems were falling behind and could not handle our expanded business volume. She came to us through a head-hunter; she qualified at the University of Warwick in computer science. Before she came here, she was head of IT for UK Media and Telecoms in London, but, after her marriage failed, she wanted to return to her home city of Birmingham. This is where her parents live. To tell you the truth, I can't believe either one of them would do this to us.'

'I agree, Chris,' said Janet. 'They have both been excellent at their jobs and appear to be totally above board.'

James stood up and started to walk around behind his desk. 'I had a similar situation last year with Hal Spencer, the CFO. He was not easily identifiable as a traitor, so I did two things. First, I hired a private investigator to check him out and, secondly, I asked Janet to let me have access to all his communications. It was only then that I was able to catch him.' He stopped, shook his head. 'Christ! I can't believe we're in this situation again!'

Janet sighed. 'Why don't we do the same again? I can get Shad to help us. Once we've identified who it is then, maybe, we can manipulate them to turn the tables on our enemy. What do you think?'

James and Chris both raised their eyebrows, looked at each other and then back at Janet.

'Agreed,' they said in unison.

15

Chapter 15

Ben Armstrong was nervous. It was the first time he was doing Pair-Tree Capital business in public for his new, undisclosed employer; the Chinese government.

He checked over the correspondence from the EU Government one more time concerning the ownership of the Zeebrugge terminal. He'd already forwarded copies for General Shen to keep him updated. Buttoning up his dress shirt, he tightened his new silk tie and threw his light suit jacket over his arm. He grabbed a cab for the three-kilometre ride from his exclusive five-star hotel suite overlooking La Grande Place, Brussels to the Department of Mobility and Transport of the European Commission. Their office was located in the government building on Rue Jean-Andre de Mot. He arrived promptly for his ten o'clock appointment.

His meeting was with the director-general after arranging the necessary paperwork and wire transfers to take over ownership of the Port of Zeebrugge. The fairly new government building stood in stark contrast to the three-storey seventeenth-century houses surrounding it. Armstrong cleared security in the reception area and took the elevator to the tenth floor. He was met by the director-general's secretary. She showed him directly into her boss's rather plain grey office.

The tall Dutchman stood up and came to greet him from behind his desk. 'Good morning, Mr Armstrong. Welcome to Brussels and the European Union.'

'Thank you, sir. It is an honour for me to be here.'

'Would you care for coffee?'

'Thank you. That would be kind.' Armstrong smiled and continued, 'I'm pleased that we were able to complete the ownership so swiftly. I have to confess that I thought it might take longer.'

The director-general smiled at his guest.

'Well, that would be a perfectly normal thought. We government people do tend to take a long time to make our minds up. In this case, however, before you even enquired about it, the Commission had already made the decision to sell the port and wanted to act swiftly. Zeebrugge has always been an underdog port compared to its neighbours, but it has the potential to be a lot busier. Moreover, with the current labour situation, we needed to get our workers back on the job. Remember we are politicians, not business managers. We would not know how to operate such an organisation. To be honest, you have solved a headache for us, after the European Commission took away ownership from the Euro-Asian Shipping company.

'Thank you, Mr Van den Berg. Just out of curiosity, were there any other interested parties in taking the port over?'

'There were but, out of confidentiality, I can't tell you who they were. I can tell you though that you were the only bid that had the necessary resources to invest to bring all the port facilities, equipment, road, and rail links up to date. That, coupled with having a branch office based in London, together with your experience and commitment, clinched the deal.'

'Good. I'm glad we were able to help each other out. While we have this opportunity, I have some interest in a few other ports which I believe could be of further benefit to the European Union. After my Portland and Wilmington acquisitions, I have become an experienced port operator and want to expand my business portfolio for this vocation.'

The director-general placed his coffee cup back on his desk. 'What do you have in mind, Mr Armstrong?'

Armstrong leaned forward in his seat. 'Well, firstly, I'm interested in Marseille. I say this because I believe they have fallen behind during the last twenty years or so. The size of ships has increased substantially, which means larger berths and more efficient handling equipment are needed to handle the larger cargo capacities.'

Van den Berg pursed his lips and nodded his head. 'You are very astute, Mr Armstrong. This is, indeed, the case. What do you have in mind?'

Armstrong tilted his head back to gather his next words. 'Well, from what I have seen, the port needs to modernise its links with France's waterway network, Medlink, to the terminals in Lyon. Several roll-on/roll-off terminals would need to be designed and constructed to accomplish this goal. I also believe that more berthing stations and transit areas for twenty-and-forty-foot containers would need to be provided. This is not to mention a complete modernisation of the necessary rail links to handle the increase in capacity. All of this would require a substantial injection of capital. As the sole owner of my merger and acquisitions company that specialises in this area, I would welcome an introduction from yourself for me to meet with the current owners of the port simply to discuss these ideas.'

'Very interesting,' replied the director-general. 'Your observations would appear to be in line with our mobility and transport mission. I can tell you, this would be of interest to the EU for a couple of reasons. Firstly, we need to step up our handling facilities for all our trading partners outside the EU and secondly, by modernising Medlink, it would reduce the amount of goods transported by road with a resultant reduction of greenhouse gas emissions.'

'So, does this mean you would support an approach to the Marseille Port Authority?'

'Absolutely. Of course, I know the president of the Port Authority there well. Let me speak to him to see if they would be open to your ideas.'

'That would be good, Mr Van den Berg. With some sort of partnership arrangement, we could certainly find the necessary capital to finance such a venture.'

The director-general stood up from behind his desk and started to rub his chin. Armstrong stood up also, thinking the meeting had come to an end. To his surprise, Van den Berg looked at him and said, 'No, don't get up. I'm thinking on my feet.' Armstrong sat down again and remained silent.

After several moments, Van den Berg spoke. 'As a Dutchman and the former transport minister for the Netherlands, I have first-hand knowledge of the port of Rotterdam. For centuries it's been a busy port. Today of course it handles a huge amount of volume for the petro-chemical industry and general cargo, but what it lacks right now is a deep-sea facility to handle ultra-large vessels for containers. There are plans to construct such a terminal. Would a venture of this magnitude be of interest to you, Mr Armstrong?'

Armstrong was completely taken aback. He was delighted that the Zeebrugge deal had been sealed so quickly and easily, but he had not expected such cooperation for his inquiries for the port of Marseille. Now, out of the blue, a massive opportunity was opening up to him in the heart of Europe. Rotterdam was almost like the hub of a spoked wheel. The port would provide a huge leap forward for his business and his Chinese owners. He tried hard to contain his enthusiasm and retained his negotiating non-committal face.

'Well, I suppose I could be interested. A new port of this nature would require a huge investment. Perhaps I could see some preliminary plans to see what the whole project would entail? Are there preliminary estimates for the investment required to complete such a venture?'

Van den Berg nodded. 'I can tell you that Rotterdam will shortly be issuing a tender proposal. You could be added to the list of invitees. They would then provide you with the scope of proposed development, basic plans and preliminary estimates of expenditure.'

'That would be much appreciated, Mr Van den Berg.'

'Excellent! Well, Mr Armstrong, it has been a very productive meeting. I look forward to speaking with you again soon.'

'Thank you to you too. It seems we could be on the same wavelength for some time to come.'

Armstrong left the government offices and started to walk back in the direction of La Grande Place. He found a small café and sat outside on a patio under a red sun umbrella and ordered a caffé latte. He could not believe how quickly the acquisitions of European ports were opening up to him. All this through the top man in the EU Transport Division! He'd expected he might have to bribe someone like this, but this morning seemed to be happening without the use of any levers. Somehow, he still had to find a way to take over the Macrae-Claybourne terminals.

16

Chapter 16

With a face as black as a gathering storm, Li Ming burst into General Shen's rather sparse west wing office unannounced. General Shen looked up and closed the file he was reading.

'Mr Ming, to what do I owe this honour? I didn't think our liaison meeting was until next week.'

'It's not. We have a problem. Stanfield and Nash have escaped from prison. There's a massive manhunt on for them. We need to decide how to handle this?'

Cool as ever, Shen looked at Ming directly for a few moments, putting his index finger to his lips.

'Interesting. Our Mr Stanfield is a very resourceful individual. Let me think about this.'

Shen thought he saw a moment of panic in Ming's expression, probably because he feared that it might reflect badly on him by the chairman. Whatever he saw, it was gone in a flash and Ming's stony demeanour dropped back into place.

Shen continued. 'Well, it's likely Stanfield does not have deep pockets, since Euro-Asian Freight is no more, and he's lost his access to his Swiss bank accounts. That tells me he can't hide for ever. Also, being in custody for nearly a year means that the British and Europeans probably think that our planned expansion of using his company to crush Macrae Shipping has come to an end. What they don't know is our plan to use Ben Armstrong and Pair-Tree Capital to continue that strategy.'

'So, are you saying that Stanfield and Nash are not a threat to us?'

Shen looked up at the ceiling, rubbed his chin and then back to Ming.

'I'm saying that they are less of a threat now than before. Certainly, they will never be able to return to the shipping business. That would be out of reach.' He thought some more. *My god, this guy Ming is slippery. He already knows this. He's playing the simple secretary just to find out how I would react.*

Ming nodded. 'Stanfield and Nash are probably more worried about us catching up with them and finishing them off. What if I sent word to our agents to find these two before the authorities do and use them to finish off James Macrae once and for all? If we take the head off the Macrae organisation then they would be lost and vulnerable to our advances.'

Shen thought some more. 'Can you make that happen?'

'Yes. I can.' Ming smiled back. 'Walk with me in the compound. It's so beautiful at this time of year.'

Shen was suspicious. *What's the little ferret up to now?* He suspected he didn't want to talk further in any of the offices since they were bugged.

As they walked through the compound gardens, the fragrance from the trees and bushes engulfed them. The myriad of colours of the blossom trees appeared like an explosive grand finale of a gala fireworks display. Plumes of red, white and pink burst forth in front of them. Shen waited for Ming to start the conversation.

'Ah, this is my favourite time of year. Everything is so new and fresh.' He remained quiet for a few further moments. 'So, General, what's the latest with our plan? I see we have already deposited substantial funds with Pair-Tree Capital?' Shen thought quickly. *So now its 'our' plan, not 'your' plan.*

Shen stopped and looked at Ming. 'I will be brief, but will give you a full written report at our meeting next week. To summarise, we have already completed the purchase for the Zeebrugge terminal. Ben Armstrong is couriering all the original ownership papers to myself. He will keep copies in the London and Boston office. We will shortly be tendering bids for a limited share of the Marseille and Rotterdam terminals. We are not sure who else is submitting bids but, of course, we will have to outbid them. Ben Armstrong seems to think he has a good relationship with the director-general of the EU Transport Section in Brussels.'

'That sounds excellent,' Ming said as he sniffed in the scent of the flowers.

Shen continued. 'In terms of our cyber warfare plan we are preparing to receive a full copy of the Macrae-Claybourne Logistics software from Zichan, our asset within the company. Once we receive that, we will utilise it for ourselves across all our Chinese seaports. This will save us at least two years of software development. In return we will ensure that their original software is corrupted. This should prove catastrophic for Macrae-Claybourne and will further weaken them, ready for Pair-Tree Capital to step in. Zichan is proving to be a very effective undercover contact. Zichan was able to obtain screen shots of their software that we used for the Shanghai press conference.'

'Good. Our plans seem to be well on track. Corrupting their own software will be an added bonus. I look forward to the chaos that we will create!'

'Yes, it's a good plan. At the press conference, we were able to make it look as though the system was already up and running. One correspondent in particular asked some searching questions as to the origin of the software, but we were able to convince him that we had, in fact, designed, developed, and deployed it ourselves. This particular journalist has been compromised and has already written a damning article for the front cover of his magazine condemning Macrae. The disinformation strategy is already in high gear.'

Shen stopped and looked out towards the lake. 'Regarding compromising the international press, we have made a good start. We were able to compromise seven other journalists that attended the Shanghai launch. Of course, everything that they publish from now on will project favourable images of China's trade with the rest of the world and, in turn, subtly hurt their own country's interests. The UK journalist, Greg Driver, will publish a second article next week giving examples of Macrae-Claybourne customer dissatisfaction.'

'Excellent work, General. What else do you have up your sleeve?'

'Oh, there's more where that came from. If Macrae thinks we've gone away, then he's delusional.

17

Chapter 17

'I can't believe it's Friday night again. Where the hell do the weeks go?'

James leaned back against the kitchen counter and slipped off his necktie.

Sarah grabbed a cold beer from the fridge and thrust it in his hand. 'You better believe it; they seem to fly.' She kissed him on the lips. He put his other arm around her and hugged her.

'You look tired.'

'You could say that. It's been a crazy day. I had to finish architectural plans that were needed for the restoration of Warwick Castle, so rushing between there and then picking the kids up from school has been hectic.'

'How was your day?'

'It's been a busy week at work, but "good" busy. The company is firing on all cylinders.'

'Well, that's good! Any news from the police yet?'

'No. It all seems to have gone quiet. Apparently there have been no sightings of Stanfield or Nash over here, although the press have reported sightings in many faraway places.'

Sarah checked the oven. 'Listen, dinner's nearly ready if you want to go and round the children up. I was going to serve it up outside on the patio, but it looks like we're just about to get a shower.'

The five of them sat around the kitchen table having lasagne and salad when suddenly, completely out of the blue, Olivia asked, 'Mommy, where did I come from?'

Sarah giggled and said, 'Mommy's tummy and so did Mason and Mia.'

'Yes, I know that but how did I get in there?' Olly asked with a very serious and inquisitive look on her face.

Sarah looked at James for a moment and then replied quite seriously. 'Well, you came from a seed.'

Olly sat there for a moment thinking about it and then turned her big blue eyes back at her mom. 'Was there a picture of my face on the packet?'

They all roared with laughter, including Olly. Sarah looked at James and said, 'You know I should write these things down and publish them one day!'

James, still laughing, replied, 'Yeah we should! Remember Mason was about that age when he suddenly said once to me,

'Thank you for coming to see me when I was born!'

They all burst out laughing again. Mia was laughing so much she grabbed her side, tears streaming down her cheeks.

Once the children were finally in bed, James and Sarah went outside and sat on the patio in the swing seat looking out over the flower beds and lawn to the corn field behind their garden. The short shower had passed, and the warm summer air had quickly dried the ground. The sweet smell of the earth and the effects of the wine felt particularly soothing. As they sat in the fading light under a darkening red sky, James took a sip from his wine glass and sighed, 'Ohhh, I needed that.' Sarah could see him starting to unwind.

'So how did it go today? Did you talk to your lawyers about launching a libel suit against *Mercantile News*?' Sarah asked.

'Yes, we did. Martin Farley believes we have a good case for defamation and so does our law firm. They will draw up all the necessary documentation, file them with the court and then serve them on *Mercantile News*. Personally, it's hard to see how they can wriggle out of this, particularly when it comes to them saying that we copied Shanghai's logistics software. We have also launched a press campaign of our own demonstrating all the benefits we can offer our customers. We are taking the high road.'

'That's a good plan. Is Chris all okay with this?'

'Yes, he's one hundred percent in agreement. The longer we work together, I think the stronger we grow together.'

'I'm so pleased. Listen, on another note, my mom rang today to say that her friend is going to sell her house on the coast and downsize. Evidently it is happening faster than I thought. Her friend asked if we could go up this weekend and look at it before they put it on the market?'

'Ouch! That was quick. Look, I've got a meeting at work tomorrow morning, but it should only take an hour or so. Perhaps we could go to Wales after that and leave the children with your parents in Caernarfon?' He took another sip of wine. 'Are you sure we are doing the right thing?'

'We both love to escape to the Welsh mountains when we can, and my house is just too small now for the five of us. There aren't many properties that come up for sale there and I know my mom's friend's house. I'll wait for you to see it, but I think it would be ideal.'

'I know you're right, it's just that...'

'James, I know what you are thinking, but we can't put our lives on hold forever after what happened a year ago. Look, we've stepped up security on this place, we can do the same at this other house, if we decide to buy it. As long as you are in business, we are always going to have enemies.'

'But that's just it. These enemies don't play by the normal commercial rules. It's the underhand hybrid warfare that troubles me. You never know what they will do next.'

'That's true but, let's face it, we are all super careful these days, including the children. Not only that, but you've also been forewarned after last year and now we have some of our own tricks up our sleeve. Right?'

'Yes, you're right. I'm glad I taught you how to defend yourself if you ever needed to use the pistol. At least all the authorities know who we are so we're never too far off their radar. The survival of our shipping terminals is in the national interest. So, okay. Let's go up to north Wales tomorrow after my meeting. We'll drop the kids off at your mom and dad's and go and see this property. Tell you what, let's have a date night tomorrow. Dinner at the Vaynol Arms and then the cottage.'

'It's a deal. I'll go and make the arrangements.'

After dropping the children off at Sarah's parents the next day, James and Sarah drove south-west in his Range Rover along the winding coast road. It was mid-afternoon, and the sun was still high in the sky. White fluffy clouds peppered the blue sky, scurrying in from the Irish Sea. The air smelled salty and fresh. Sarah read out the instructions to James that she had been given by her mother's friend, Megan. She had explained to Sarah that their house position could not be located by GPS.

Around ten miles from Caernarfon, the narrow coast road started to change as the terrain rapidly started to gain altitude. Green grass-coloured hills with rocky outcrops exposed to the prevailing westerly winds, stood proudly defying what millions of years of weather had thrown at them. After a succession of turns down narrow lanes, they encountered a wooden five-bar gate across the road. It had a large 'Private' sign and a cattle grid straddled the width of the entrance. Sarah hopped out of the Range Rover, opened the gate, and waited for James to drive through, then closed it. Hopping back in the SUV, she said,

'Wow, this is just as I remember it. Of course, you can't see the house from here. It's about another mile away, overlooking the sea from a vantage point above the cliffs.'

They sat there for a few minutes, closing their eyes in the sunshine. The sun shone in the west, reflecting off the deep-blue sea stretched out beyond the cliffs.

James whistled.

'This is exactly what we love about Wales. It teems with beauty everywhere you look. Great thing too; we're not too far away from your parents and Snowdonia National Park.'

'And Llanberis is only twenty miles away. Come on, let's see if you like the house.'

They pulled up on a light-coloured gravel courtyard in front of the house surrounded by red and pink rhododendron bushes. Fragrance from honeysuckle bushes added to the welcoming feel. The house itself had been converted from an old woollen mill where local farmers would bring their fleeces to be spun into yarn and woven into blankets. The structure had thick Welsh stone walls, a sloping slate roof and had been modified to take large modern framed dormer windows with shutters. The mill's original water wheel was still intact and was fed by a fast-flowing stream. The front door opened, and Megan and her husband came out to greet them. Sarah hugged Drew and Megan straight away and introduced James.

Drew was rather elderly and moved slowly. He smiled warmly. 'It's good to meet you both. Thank you for coming so promptly. We didn't realise you were house-hunting until Sarah's mother called. We hope you like the house as much as we have, but, to be honest, it's been a labour of love. Given our age now, it's time to move on.'

As they went through the sturdy wide front door, they were greeted with a reception hall with a high vaulted ceiling with sky lights. Stone walls and stout timbers gave the house a homely feeling from the moment you entered. Being converted from a mill, the house possessed a unique character that begged to be lived in. Entering from the hallway was a large open-plan kitchen, adjoined by a good-sized, cosy family room with its own huge ingle-nook fireplace. The picture windows from these adjoining rooms all faced west out towards the cliffs and sea beyond. It was breath-taking. Sarah came closer to James and squeezed his hand. He squeezed it right back.

Outside, there was an expansive flagstone terrace, plus a gazebo on a slightly raised deck. A perfect happy hour spot. The patio area nestled between the well-maintained gardens with mature trees and shrubs surrounding the house. They viewed the rest of the house, which included four bedrooms, two bathrooms, a master bedroom with ensuite and an office. To the side of the house was a detached stone double garage with a workshop and a studio upstairs. Drew took James aside.

'This is my secret hideaway. I can spend hours in here making furniture and whatever else. When we built this, since I spend so much time in here, I had a tunnel constructed to link with the house. As you know, we get very strong gales that come through here, especially in winter. The woodstove keeps this place beautifully warm. James blew out a short whistle. 'You're right, this is every man's dream, although I might have to fight Sarah for it. This would be perfect for her architect studio.'

James and Sarah sat with Drew and Megan for some time on the back patio drinking tea and coffee discussing the property and its price. They agreed to buy the house; Drew and Megan were happy and so were James and Sarah. It was perfect for all of them.

As they drove back to Sarah's house in Llanberis, James and Sarah could not have felt happier. Don Henley's 'The Boys of Summer' came on the radio. Sarah turned it up as loud as she could. Their lives were settling down again and they were embarking on a new and exciting chapter in their lives.

18

Chapter 18

Oh god! I feel like I'm slipping into a dark and cold place that I can't get out of.

Greg Driver sat at his desk trying hard to suppress the ever-increasing yawning spasms that had overcome him. He felt his eyelids begin to close and shook his head to snap himself out of it.

The light outside the office was starting to fail as a weather depression moved in from the east. Even inside, the air felt heavy and damp. It was turning into that kind of day when the cold penetrated whatever clothing you were wearing and went straight into your bones.

Since returning from China, he was in a deep chasm of depression. He felt distant from his new wife which he put down to his feelings of guilt. He could not stop thinking about the sex with Meili. She haunted him relentlessly. One minute he was obsessed with her, then, in a flash, he was angry at her. Trouble was, and he knew it, underneath everything, he was angry at himself for being such a fool. He wondered what would happen at Macrae-Claybourne Logistics when they read the article. Every time the phone went, he cringed, thinking he would be balled out by them. He knew they didn't deserve this kind of treatment. They were good people, but he was in a corner. All he could do was wait it out and hope the situation smoothed out in time.

He shivered as his phone rang.

'Greg. Would you come to my office straight away!'

Greg entered his boss's office. There were four other people in there, besides his boss sitting around the conference table. Two of the men were the brothers who owned the magazine. He didn't know the other two. Phil West didn't engage in any pleasantries.

'Sit down, Greg. You have some explaining to do.'

'I don't understand, Phil. What's going on?' Greg answered.

Harry and Henry, the two owners, leaned closer towards Greg.

'I'll tell you what's going on, Driver. We've been hit with a multi-million-euro lawsuit by Macrae-Claybourne Logistics. Unless you and your boss can justify and fully defend this article that was published in this month's edition, this company is finished.'

They thrust the twelve-page legal document into Greg's hand. He looked at it, scarcely registering what the words meant. He put his head in his hands.

Harry, the elder brother, spoke.

'Mr Driver, these two gentlemen are our legal counsel. You will answer every question they have for you in detail. You will not go home until we are completely satisfied with your answers. It's going to be a long night. Phil, you are just as much in the hot seat, so you better have everything crystal clear. Do you both understand?'

Phil looked terrible; utterly drained. Greg started to shake.

The first lawyer, an owl-like elderly man with a hook nose and round metal-rimmed spectacles took off his tired pin-stripe jacket and produced a tape recorder, while the second younger man sat down next to him with a pad and multiple pens.

Owl Face scowled at Greg. 'So, tell us, Mr Driver, how much of your article is true?'

Greg leaned back from the table, swallowing hard.

'Well, you need to know that I ran the article past my editor first. He was the one that signed off on it.'

Owl Face looked at the brothers and then back to Greg.

'That we know. It's standard procedure, but that was not the question. I repeat, how much of this article is true and, more to the point, verifiable?'

Greg sat up straighter. 'Could I have a glass of water, please.'

'I'm waiting for an answer, Mr Driver.'

'Everything in the article is true.'

'Okay. That's a start. Consider this, though. Companies don't launch multi-million-euro lawsuits and seek damages unless they truly believe they have been defamed. They are accusing us of libel. I don't need to tell you that anything that is written down and falls into the libel category will be taken very seriously by a court, since the damage to the injured party can last for a very long time.'

'I repeat, everything in the article is true.' Greg reached for the glass of water that had been handed to him; it took two shaking hands to lift it to his mouth.

'Alright. Let's start at the top. Last month you wrote a glowing and complimentary piece about Macrae-Claybourne after, I gather, a very successful launch of their new partnership. I understand that Macrae-Claybourne is now the largest logistics company in the UK and contributes substantial amounts of money to our balance of payments. This is not a fly-by-night company by any stretch of the imagination. So, here's the question. How can you give someone accolades one month and then rip them to pieces the following month?'

Greg exhaled loudly. 'We spent two days in Shanghai port. It was on such a vast scale that none of the other journalists, nor me for that matter, had ever seen before. That's a fact. Not only that, but their fully automated container-handling equipment is a first anywhere. I know Macrae-Claybourne has automation, but not to that scale.'

Owl Face looked at his partner, who was scribbling down notes. He continued, 'But why did you write such an incendiary headline? That's a square punch in the face for any company.'

Greg looked at his boss for support, but his boss averted his eyes and looked down at the table.

'Well, I thought I needed what we call 'a grabber statement' seeing how this was going to be on the front page.'

'Well, you certainly achieved that! The trouble is, if anything, and I mean anything, even one word could be construed as libellous, then we could be in trouble. If you care to look further at the lawsuit document, they have listed twelve separate defamatory statements that they consider damages their reputation. We need to go through each one in detail, word by word. If you can't back up your accusations, then we will be held accountable.'

Greg looked at everyone peering at him. He'd never felt so cold and alone in his life before. His brain was in a complete turmoil. *Should I come clean and tell them the truth or just stack up more lies and hope that this all goes away?*

19

Chapter 19

Lee Yuen hopped off the number X22 bus on the Bristol Road in Deritend, Birmingham, and walked down Wrentham Street to visit his mother. Redbrick terraced houses, with small bay windows and front doors opening straight onto the pavement lined each side of the street. There were no trees or grass verges, just bricks and mortar. Several children idly kicked a ball about in the road. A child's bike lay abandoned on its side on the pavement. It was Sunday and he bought with him a bunch of flowers. Sundays were sacred. They would have a lunch together, sometimes play cards and then would often take a walk in Highgate Park before enjoying a big Sunday dinner together.

As the front door opened, Lee had a big smile on his face.

'Hi, Mom! How are you?'

Jinni scowled, turned around and left him standing on the front doorstep. Lee followed her into the kitchen. 'I've bought you flowers.'

Jinni still scowled. She took them, unwrapped them and stuffed them into a vase on the kitchen table.

'Mom, what's wrong? Are you feeling poorly? You don't seem to be right.'

Jinni turned on him and stamped her foot. 'I'm so upset with you I can hardly speak. You make me so angry!'

Lee stood in the small and cramped kitchen completely shocked. Spreading out his hands either side of him, he stammered,

'What, what have I done? I don't understand. You were okay on Thursday when I phoned you so what's happened in between?'

'You don't know! You don't know!' She started to cry and tried desperately to get her words out in between sobbing and shaking.

'After all I've done for you, and you repay me with such dishonour!'

Lee tried to move forward and give her a hug, but she pushed him away.

'Mom! I still don't know what I've done.'

Jinni took out a handkerchief, tried to dry her eyes and blow her nose. Her face was very red.

'I've worked my fingers to the bone bringing you up and tried to teach you honesty all your life. But now you've lied to me and I'm so disappointed in you. How could you do this to me?'

'Mom, I'm sorry, I still don't understand. What did I do?'

'I've found out by accident how much you paid for your new fancy apartment and there is no way you could afford that without doing something underhand.'

Lee stood there, mouth wide open, completely lost for words. Finally, he asked, 'where did all this come from?'

'I'll tell you where. My boss mentioned yesterday that

he hadn't seen you with me for a while and asked me how you were? Proudly, I told him you had just bought your new apartment overlooking Winterbourne Gardens in Edgbaston. You know what he told me?'

'No. I don't.'

'He told me he looked at those new apartments with his wife because they were thinking of moving out of their own flat above the restaurant. They want to move to the west end of the city, but one hundred and fifty thousand pounds was just too expensive for them!'

'What! What! And you think I've done something dishonest?'

'You must have done to pay that sort of money!'

'I didn't do anything underhand. I paid the down payment myself and have a mortgage based on my income. I haven't lied!'

'You haven't lied? You have and you know it, so don't tell me otherwise! You forget I've been brought up the hard way. I'm streetwise, but I'm honest; most of all honest to myself!'

'Mom, I know, and I respect you for that! But tell me how I have lied?'

'Son, you are not being honest with yourself. That's why I'm ashamed of you. You told me how much you earn, and I know you could not have afforded that place on your level of income. You are no better than the rest of those people in Hong Kong who worship nothing but money and possessions. God knows, I could have made a fortune selling my body there, but I took the hard alternative of staying honest to myself and others by just working hard. I did it all for you, to give you a better start in life than I had!' She burst out crying and collapsed onto a kitchen chair.

Lee stood there in silence, stuck for words. Fighting back tears himself, he looked at the ceiling and then down at the floor. Taking in a deep breath, he sat down on the opposite chair and broke into tears himself. Stuttering his words out, he said, 'Mom, I love you! I know what you did for me, and I'll be grateful for ever.'

Jinni sat there, still sobbing, but gave him a dismissive wave of her hand.

'So, tell me what you have done!'

'Mom, I didn't do anything dishonest, but I didn't tell you something at the time either.'

'Tell me what?'

'At the university, when I met Lisa Taylor, my boss at Macrae-Claybourne Logistics, I was also approached by the Chinese Trade Commission. They are paying me a monthly retainer as a computer consultant. Each month I fill out a report describing the latest trends and developments in the hardware and software business. There was nothing dishonest in that.'

'Oh, Lee.' Jinni sighed and looked back at him. 'You've got so much to learn. Don't you know what they are doing?'

'No, I don't!' he replied angrily. 'I'm well qualified and if someone wants to pay me for my expertise then I'm going to take it.'

'So, what else have they asked you for?'

Lee didn't answer. He looked down again.

'You didn't answer me.'

Slowly Lee responded. 'This week they asked me to send them a complete copy of the logistics software that my employer has developed.'

'That's what I thought; you are being sucked in. Lee, you

are being paid to spy! Don't you see that, or is money the be all and end all for you?'

'Oh god!' He groaned and shook his head. 'I didn't see it like that at the beginning.'

Jinni didn't let up.

'So why didn't you tell me you were being paid by the Chinese Trade Commission at the same time you were working for Macrae-Claybourne? I thought you and I didn't have any secrets between us. You know what value I place on honesty. So, tell me why?'

Lee was quiet, expecting Jinni to say something more, but she did not break the silence. Finally, after looking at the floor again, he looked up.

'You're right. I should have known better. I suppose I've been suppressing my unease for a while. I think I've been stupid and mesmerised by money. Yes, you're right. I should have told you at the time. I'm ashamed now I didn't. I should also have seen that the Chinese Trade Commission would want more than just open market updates. Mom, I want to be successful and make a name for myself. I suppose I thought this might be a way to do it. I'm sorry.'

Jinni looked back at him sternly.

'Lee, the only way to make a name for yourself in this life is by honesty and integrity. Money and power just give you what I call "sunshine" friends. When there's no money the so-called friends are gone. Listen to me, have you given the Chinese anything you shouldn't?'

Again, she penetrated him with her stare.

'No, Mom. I haven't. I swear to you.'

'Alright. Now, don't ever lie to me again by not telling me the truth. That's as good as a lie! I didn't scrape a living, educate you and take you halfway around the world for you to end up in prison. You have let me down and shamed me!'

With her shoulders slumped, she stood up, straightened her body out and held her head high.

'Now, terminate your agreement with the Chinese Trade Commission immediately!'

Lee sobbed and looked solemnly up at his mother.

'Okay. I will do that. I'm so sorry I was not honest with you. It won't happen again. You are my everything.'

20

Chapter 20

Why are you keeping Nash around now you've escaped from the joint? I can get rid of him if you want.'

Keeping his voice low, Thornton had made sure he was alone with Stanfield at the other end of his large transport warehouse away from the apartment. They stood behind a Volvo three-axle twenty-four foot box van.

Stanfield replied, equally quietly, 'I know you can, but I need him to help us leave England once and for all. He's a good ally to have for any dirty work. Besides that, he can help generate some quick cash to help us do that.'

'Okay, Hugh. Whatever you say. Just let me know when it's time.'

'Just play along for now and be nice!'

****

Thornton popped his head up from behind the camera. 'Holy smoke, Hugh, you look like a cross between Boris Johnson

117

and Buddy Holly!' He stood back and took a second take of Hugh Stanfield.

'Who the hell is Boris Johnson?' asked Nash.

'Oh, he's a journalist for the *Daily Telegraph*,' replied Thornton. 'He always looks like he's just scrambled out of a nearby hedge. His hair looks like a busted mattress!'

The previously dapper Stanfield now had a Boris hairstyle and black thick-rimmed glasses. The smart suit, shirts and silk ties were gone. It would be hard to recognise Stanfield as he was now. He also sported a well-defined five o'clock shadow, and appeared taller, after utilising lifts in his shoes.

Conversely, Nash – who had tidied up his appearance prior to his arrest – looked like an out-of-work musician. His hair had grown, covering his ears, and he now sported an overgrown, full beard. He wore a pair of perfectly round spectacles, John Lennon style. The glasses helped disguise the distinctive shape of a nose that had been broken several times. It was also hoped these new appearances would help fool the face-recognition software that had previously been used to identify Nash and assist in his arrest.

Thornton set the camera up and took several passport regulation shots of each of them.

'Okay. I'll take these down to our mutual friend and get your new identity passports, driving licences and papers all organised. Should take a couple of weeks. I'll take the cash out of your Andorra account.'

'Go ahead, Charlie. Can't wait to see what the outside world looks like,' Stanfield replied. He knew he could trust Charlie, at least for the time being. So far so good.

It had been over a month since Stanfield and Nash had escaped. They had remained completely out of sight in the transport warehouse on the Blackwell Trading Estate while the biggest manhunt in the country went on since the Yorkshire Ripper murders carried out in the 1980s.

'Put the news on, Dan. Let's see where we've been spotted today!'

Nash laughed. 'We should start a betting pool. What a great way to generate income!'

'Shhhh. Look, there's our old photos again!' They listened carefully to the report and then both erupted into laughter.

'I used to think John Cleese was funny, but the news is now the best comedy show ever. Captain Kirk couldn't have done better by delivering sightings of us in Brazil, Argentina and Australia all on the same day!'

Charlie was back within the hour. The three of them sat round the wooden kitchen table in the apartment.

'Right, let's put all the ideas we've had on the table for getting out of England.' Stanfield spoke like he was still the owner of Euro-Asian Freight, addressing his staff. Thornton and Nash grinned at each other.

'First, we need to generate some more cash. My savings are getting lower, and we can't stay here for ever. We all agree we can't get back into the maritime shipping business. It would take too much capital, too long to set up and we are too well known. Secondly, we have to stay clear of the Chinese. Of course they will know everything by now as we are world celebrities. It's probable they want us killed for all that we know. I'm sure people like General Shen and Ming would consider us dangerous since we are a party to their global expansion plans.'

Thornton nodded.

'To tell you the truth, Hugh, I wouldn't mind expanding

my transport business. I only started this when Jack Carter and I got into the bigger league of burglaries and we needed larger trucks to move all the goods. The Brinks Mat warehouse job at Heathrow airport twelve years ago necessitated that. The seventy-six cases of bullion needed to be whisked away very quickly. Jack and I used some of our share of the loot to buy this warehouse, as well as more trucks and trailers. We operated a legitimate transport business, laundered money, and used the equipment to transport our stolen goods when necessary. Now Jack's gone, I'm running this business on my own.'

Nash sat quietly listening, his eyes widening. These were huge revelations. He knew Stanfield was into arms smuggling and running his legitimate shipping business, but he had no idea his old mates were into crime so deep. The Brinks Mat robbery had been front-page news globally and had stunned the world. What a fucking unit!

Stanfield mulled over what Thornton had said.

'I have an idea. The little bit of capital I have left in Andorra could be used to expand the business, but what I have in mind is something very different. What if we got into human smuggling? It would be a cash only business and there is a huge demand. I'm sure with our combined knowledge of the shipping business and your knowledge of transport, we could make a fortune. It would set us up for a very comfortable retirement somewhere nice and out of the way!'

Thornton moved both sides of his mouth down in thought. He remained silent.

Nash shifted in his seat and replied.

'Travelling around the world these last few years in the various ships I worked on, I spent a lot of time hanging around the low dives around the ports. I know that China is a major source of men, women and children who are enticed to Europe on the promise of legitimate jobs. These people are then forced into slave labour or the sex trade. I've heard they pay up to fifteen thousand pounds to get to the UK.'

Stanfield calculated that ten people in one container would yield a gross income of one hundred and fifty thousand pounds. Thornton wasn't far behind him.

'Holy shit!' Thornton exclaimed. 'Now that's a good day's work. I'm beginning to like this idea. Hugh, you're fluent in Mandarin. You could organise the Chinese end and handle the passengers.'

'Yes, I could do that from here.' He thought some more, scratching his head. 'You know, there's a growing number of Chinese millionaires, and billionaires, for that matter. These people can never be sure if they will be allowed to keep their earnings or have to forfeit them to the Communist party. We might be able to tap into a growing market. These people will want to escape before they lose everything. I'm thinking we could fly them from China to tourist hot spots in Western Europe such as Paris, Brussels, and Amsterdam as though they were completing a multi-city sightseeing package holiday. Then, instead of them returning home, we pick them up and transport them across the channel by truck. It's way too far to bring them in containers all the way from China. Too dangerous. After all, we want them to get here in one piece. There have been too many deaths of people stuck in containers.'

Thornton thought some more. 'You know, I don't like the idea of bringing people over in standard twenty and forty-foot containers for several reasons. One, most smugglers use this method, and the authorities know it worldwide. X-ray machines, heat sensor and carbon dioxide machines are starting to be introduced to scan containers. I know that because I frequently go back and forth from Dover to Calais using the truck ferries. Secondly, containers are too inclined to be stuck in transfer terminals which increases the danger to the humans. I need money, but I don't want to have a load of deaths on my hands.'

Nash and Stanfield both looked at each other and shrugged. They had already committed that crime.

Stanfield got up from the table and walked around the kitchen deep in thought. He turned to the others.

'For us to be successful and charge more money for upscale customers from China, we need to do things differently. We would need equipment that is more sophisticated.' Stanfield the shipping entrepreneur was getting into gear. He continued. 'Dan, you are an engineer. Could you devise a container that could be ventilated and prevent X-rays from penetrating the interior?'

Nash nodded and turned to Thornton.

'Can you get me a pad and pencil? I've got an idea.'

21

Chapter 21

'Good morning, Mr Macrae. DI Stella Hudson.'

'Good morning, Inspector Hudson. Any news of Stanfield and Nash?'

'Not as yet, Mr Macrae. Listen, I wanted to call you personally to make sure you don't let your guard down. I know the press thinks they've already left the country, but we don't believe so. We are letting the press carry on with these stories, hoping Stanfield and Nash will get more confident to emerge from their hideout.'

'What makes you think they are still here?'

'This may sound strange, but we have to thank the IRA for many of our security upgrades. We don't publicise these, but within minutes of the Brixton escape the country's borders were locked tight. They still are.'

'You sound pretty sure of this.'

'We are. We're systematically going through every known contact that Stanfield has had in the past. We're also checking every known contact of your wife's kidnapper, Jack Carter, and anyone else who could be linked to the Bulldog and Beaver pub. Stanfield and Nash must have had outside help for them to disappear so quickly outside the prison walls.'

'Okay. Got it. We'll make sure we don't let down our guard. Thank you.'

James carried his freshly poured coffee and placed it on Chris's desk. Whereas James had pictures of their cargo ships in his office, Chris had large photographs of their trucks all in their various working situations on two of his office walls. The other two sides to his office were floor-to-ceiling windows overlooking the transport yard.

'Morning, Chris, howya doing?'

'Bloody good and you?'

'Not sure. On the one hand I'm very happy but I'm also wary. Just had a call from Stella Hudson, one of the team tracking Stanfield and Nash. She still wants us to be vigilant. The police think they are still in the country.'

'Interesting... Well, one thing's for sure, James. Because we are in the international shipping and transportation business with bonded warehouses, our security is tight. No harm in putting out another reminder, though!'

'No. Let's do that. As for being happy, I just got the last quarter's figures, and we are up substantially.'

'Yes, I just saw them too. Well done! Our economies of scale are already showing some early signs of success.'

James took a sip of his coffee.

'I've asked Martin Farley to join us this morning. We've just received invitations to bid on two tenders. One is for the port of Marseille and the other is for Rotterdam. The request for proposals, RFPs, both want injections of capital to upgrade their port facilities in return for a share of ownership.'

'Are we ready for this so soon after our merger?'

'I believe we are. We know the business and even if we lose the bids, we'll learn more about their future plans and how they might affect our existing terminals.'

'Ummm. Good thinking. Let's see what Martin has to say. He can advise us on any legal pitfalls.'

The three men sat for the next hour poring over the documents.

Martin was wary.

'On the face of it, both of these proposals are very similar. They both call for substantial injections of capital in return for a percentage share of the business. Obviously we will need to assess each of the ports assets, value them and then work out how much we invest into the existing business and work the ownership calculations from there.'

James replied, 'I'm okay with that. Chris and I can easily visit their facilities and have discussions with the present owners. We both speak French so it will be helpful. Martin, you are completely fluent in the language so that will help us tremendously.'

Chris tapped his pencil on the pad in front of him.

'I agree. James and I can easily assess the current value of each business, but I don't like the clause in here that they want to include 'goodwill'. In my book, goodwill is like a handful of nothing. How can you put a value on that?'

Martin agreed.

James looked up at the ceiling and then pondered, 'You are both right, of course. There's also something I don't like in either of these RFPs and that's the flexibility to negotiate the stage payments of the investment from the new potential owners after the bid has been submitted. To me, that gives them the right to move the goal posts if they feel they need to set one bidder up against another. Then it just becomes a bidding war, and the sellers can jack up the bids once they have them all in front of them.'

'Mmmm.' Chris frowned. 'Yes, that's certainly possible. I wonder how many bids they will receive. One thing's for sure, Euro-Asian Freight won't be bidding, so that should keep the Chinese at bay! I suggest we go in with a fixed bid, fixed stage payments that fit the various stages of expansion and stick to it and we exclude "goodwill".'

James nodded, in full agreement.

'Agreed. Martin?'

'Agreed.'

'Chris?' Chris's secretary put her head around the door.

'This letter has just been dropped off by courier. I believe it's from the law firm that *Mercantile News* engaged to defend the libel suit. It has 'private and confidential' on it, so I didn't want to open it.' She passed it to Chris. He checked the envelope and passed it to Martin. 'Martin, you're the lawyer, you better see what they say.'

Martin slid a letter opener through the top of the envelope. He remained silent, finishing one page, then reading the second in more detail. He went back to page one and read the letter again. Finally, he looked up. 'Can you believe the balls of some of these lawyers!'

Martin shook his head and continued, '*Mercantile News* denies any wrongdoing and rejects any claims of defamation. They are prepared, however, to make an out of court settlement as a matter of goodwill! More goodwill. That sum would be ten thousand Euros in return for a signed confidentiality clause!'

'James, I know what my reaction is, how about you?' asked

Chris.

James thumped his fist into his other hand. 'Tell them we will see them in court. They cannot be allowed to get away with this. We are being made to look like a bunch of liars.'

Martin nodded. 'Okay, but I have to warn you, a defamation case has to go through certain legal protocols before it can reach the courts. It could take years! The downside of this, of course, is the damage to our reputation while this carries on.'

22

Chapter 22

'Bloody hell, mate. This could be expensive!' Stanfield blurted out.

'Of course it'll be expensive! What did you think it was going to cost?' Nash threw his hands up in the air. 'You said you wanted to create a market for Chinese millionaires to illegally enter the UK. If you want to evade the law, this is what it's going take to do it and you are going to have to charge the price accordingly.'

Nash leaned back in his chair and folded his arms. He had spent a painstakingly amount of time drafting out a detailed design for a container to smuggle the human cargo.

Stanfield looked at Thornton.

'How much do you think this will cost, Charlie? Between the three of us, we don't have that much left.'

'Okay, settle down, guys. This is what I have in mind.' Nash pointed to the design on the writing pad.

'My plan is to have a professionally built tank container designed to carry hazardous materials in bulk. We can use a cylindrical stainless-steel tank, enclosed in a standard twenty-foot ISO container frame. I estimate the size of the tank could be twenty-five thousand litres. That will give us enough volume for carrying up to, say, ten adults. These tanks are rigid and leak resistant and are strong enough to prevent tearing or bursting under normal handling conditions. They would also carry the necessary hazard warnings, the Dept of Transport shipping name and identification number.'

Stanfield and Thornton remained silent, carefully studying Nash's design.

'We all agree that smuggling humans in standard containers is too dangerous. Suffocation, leaking body fluids and lack of sound insulation are all problems. So, we need to overcome these obstacles. With my design, I can guarantee we can resolve these difficulties.' Nash stood up from the table, pacing up and down the room.

'Our biggest challenge is to deter Customs and Immigration from inspecting our specialised container too closely. Believe me, no inspector is going to want to open our container because of what we say we are carrying. Medical waste, such as contaminated blood and the by-products of radium used for treatment, is enough to put anybody off.'

Stanfield looked at Nash, tilting his head and squinting his eyes, but remained silent.

Nash continued. 'These containers are designed for multi-modal transport and can be used for transporting, processing and pumping of both radioactive and medical waste. They can be monitored by on-board programmable logic control systems that control both the inlet and outlet valves located above and below the tank.'

Stanfield put up his hand.

'I'm not an engineer, but are you saying you can control the air input and internal temperature of this tank?'

'Yes. I am. So, we've eliminated the danger of suffocation. Not only that but the air pumps will help dilute the carbon dioxide gas emitted by the people inside. We can therefore avoid detection with the CO2 monitors. We can also collect any body fluids safely. These tanks incorporate double-shell designs and are tested for leak detection. The double skin will also mean our occupants won't be heard outside, should they move around or talk.'

Thornton nodded. 'Dan, I know just the manufacturer. There's one located somewhere in northern England that manufactures standard and customised tanks for the waste industry. We could order a standard stainless-steel tank designed to carry liquid medical waste. They manufacture to what's called ADR standards, which conform to UN standards, for carrying dangerous goods internationally.'

Stanfield finally spoke. 'But we can't afford to buy a tank container like this.'

Thornton held out both hands and lowered them slowly. 'Hugh, easy. If we lease it through my business, we will only have monthly payments instead of buying it outright. If we work the tank hard, make some quick cash, we can just disappear and leave it behind.'

'Okay. Once we've got our tank container, I can modify the internal structure of the tank here in this warehouse. If we order it with two baffles – partitions that prevent liquids from surging from one end to the other under braking and acceleration – then we can use a concealed area between them for transporting our human cargo.'

Nash looked back at them both, seeming to enjoy keeping them in suspense.

'We can handle the temperature sensors issue easily. Radium waste emits a higher temperature than its surroundings because of the radiation it releases. So when we go through this check, with the body heat of our humans, there is nothing abnormal. Now to beat the X-rays. Part of my modification will be to line the inside of the concealed section with lead sheets. No way anyone can see what we are carrying then!'

Thornton gave a wide smile. 'Bloody hell, Dan! This is brilliant. But we can't be seen to be buying that amount of lead. It'll look suspicious. Not only that, but it's also sodding expensive. We'll have to nick it!'

'Damn right we'll have to nick it,' Stanfield retorted.

'Let me take care of that,' said Thornton. 'We can use one of my trucks to carry it. I believe there's a big sheet lead supplier somewhere near Nottingham. I'll get some of the boys together. We can't risk you two doing it.'

'No, Charlie, Dan can go with you. He knows what he wants and can help with the break-in. He looks very different now and has a completely new identity. We must get out of here sooner or later. Might as well start now!'

'I'm okay with that.' Nash nodded in agreement. 'I'm going to need stainless-steel welding equipment, plus some metal working tools. I'll get a full list together of what I will require.'

Stanfield flipped over the page on Nash's sketchpad. He wrote down a list of points. Looking up, he spoke thoughtfully, 'We will need to find genuine pick-up points of medical waste on the continent, pretend we go there and then pretend we visit the reprocessing facilities here in the UK. The driver's logbook will have to show this every time we pick up our human cargo and drop them off. We are going to make a fucking fortune!'

Stanfield sat quietly for a few more moments, tapping his pencil on the tabletop.

'You know, once we've got the ball rolling and we've got some money stashed away, the last thing I want to do before I leave this country is get even with that bastard Macrae. And you are going to help me.'

23

Chapter 23

Ben Armstrong looked down from his Lear private jet as it banked to starboard on its final approach to Marseille airport. The sun's early morning rays suddenly lit up the cabin interior. His mood brightened. Work, that he had thrown himself into after his marriage breakup, was becoming more and more rewarding. With so much on the go, his brain was fully occupied. His selfish wife and his two spoiled children figured less and less in his mind as time went by.

The flight path took them directly over the Marseille Fos harbour complex, forty kilometres south-east from runway two. The port was well laid out, clearly having an advantage over other ports; being linked by river, rail and road.

The current owners needed to expand the quay for larger container vessels. They also needed to expand the cargo transit area as well as completely update all the handling equipment, including the railheads. It would be a capital-intensive project. Armstrong knew he had a blank cheque book, but he still needed to go through the necessary steps to complete the RFP. He grinned to himself knowing that he could easily buy into the complex after Otto Van den Berg, the Director-General Transport Division EU Commission, had called the current owners to give them a heads-up that Pair-Tree Capital would be bidding on the RFP. While he had not said it directly, it was apparent that the director-general wanted to create some more competition for Macrae-Claybourne Logistics, otherwise they would have the largest market share with all their ports in southern Europe, especially if they bought into Marseille. Little did Van den Berg know that he was opening the door to the Chinese!

Armstrong had also recognised that the author of the RFP terms and conditions had intended those negotiations on stage payments could still be held with the various bidders, even after the sealed bid date had closed.

After a somewhat choppy approach and bumpy landing, Armstrong picked up his reserved Volvo SUV from the Hertz rental office and drove himself to the Marine terminal. As he entered the chairman's office of the Port Authority, a smartly dressed and distinguished grey-haired gentleman strode to meet him.

'Welcome, Mr Armstrong. It's a pleasure to meet you.'

Armstrong extended his hand.

'Monsieur Laffite. Thank you for taking the time to meet me and showing me your port facilities. I'm looking forward to hearing of your intended plans for expansion. This is truly the business I love. In fact, it's my passion!'

Laffite spread his arms out in appreciation.

'Excellent! I hear such good things about you and your previous track record in the industry.'

'Well, that's always good to hear. Perhaps you could

show me your existing facilities first and then we can look afterwards at your financial estimates of their total value?'

'That is precisely what I had in mind. Let me show you around the liquid bulk, solid bulk and Ro-Ro terminals first. Following that, I will show you our existing container facilities. Of course, this is going to be the main focus of our expansion. Sadly, we have fallen behind other terminals due to the ever-increasing size of the vessels and soaring volume of container business.'

As they toured the facilities, Armstrong took photos and detailed notes. He also paced out certain areas of the terminal and noted measurements. It was clear that Monsieur Laffite was very proud of his terminal.

'Mr Armstrong. Before we return to the office and study the financials, I suggest we go to lunch. I can recommend L'Epuisette. It is a magnificent restaurant set on a rocky promontory with beautiful panoramic views of the coastline. The food is exquisite!'

'I like the sound of that. It sounds perfect. So, why don't we take the financials with us and that way we don't have to rush back?'

Armstrong would normally have skipped lunch anywhere else in the world, but he knew lunch was sacred to the French. Also, he wanted to get close to Mr Laffite. It might be possible to sweeten the deal with perhaps, some personal inducements, since he knew Laffite would still have to win over his board of directors for his choice of the winning bid.

'Splendid idea, Mr Armstrong. You like French culture?'

'I absolutely do. If we are able to reach an agreement, I intend to buy a house here. Your outlook on life and living is the best!' Laffite nodded in appreciation.

'Excellent! Let me order a taxi and we'll get straight off.'

They sat at the end window of the restaurant facing the sea. The view was glorious; the sun shone down brightly on the brilliant-blue, shimmering sea. A small harbour to the side provided a backdrop of bobbing fishing boats, while a string of rocky islands stood out to sea. The ambiance could not have been better.

Laffite put on his half-moon reading glasses.

'The wines here are particularly good. All the Bordeaux reds listed are excellent.'

'I'm ready to have what you decide. What do you recommend for lunch?'

Clearly delighted by the question, Monsieur Laffite replied enthusiastically, 'Well, we could start with fois gras pâté and then go with the lobster thermidor. You will see why they are listed in the Michelin guide.'

Ben Armstrong looked around the dining room as it started to fill up.

'Well, I must say this is a real pleasure for me. Rarely do we get to do business in such a relaxed atmosphere. I would love to work with you going forward.'

The waiter brought a bottle of Château Ausone Saint-Emilion Bordeaux and uncorked it at the table leaving the wine to breathe, while another waiter brought an 'on the house' teaser of devilled eggs with crab.

'Let's not discuss the RFP right now, Mr Armstrong. We can do that later. Tell me how you turned around your Portland and Wilmington terminals?'

While Armstrong relayed details of his former successes, they savoured the wine. After having finished the devilled eggs, they sat for some time before the fois gras was served.

Unlike most restaurants outside France where courses of food were served quickly, this was the opposite. Quiet and leisurely was the order of things. They were on their second bottle of wine by the time they ate their lobster thermidor.

Armstrong patted his mouth with his white linen serviette.

'Monsieur Laffite, I have to say this is the finest food I have ever tasted. Your recommendations were perfect. Thank you!'

'We are not done yet! With our coffee and cognac, we will have Mocha Pots de Crème. Most satisfying.'

As the waiter served coffee and two glasses of Remy Martin XO, Monsieur Laffite bent down and produced the set of financials from his briefcase. His face was starting to redden as he raised his brandy sniffer.

'There you go. À votre santé!' They clinked glasses, sniffed, and sipped the cognac.

Armstrong felt a warm glow flow down inside him. He sat back in his chair and stretched out his legs, feeling extremely comfortable. But was he trying to soften up Laffite or was Laffite trying to soften him up? Whatever it was, he would play along with it. Armstrong studied the figures. It was clear that the value of the assets of the port had been inflated. That he had expected, but it was heavily padded everywhere. He raised a question. 'I see you have put a value on 'goodwill'. I'm not able to assess that, of course.'

'I understand, but over the years we have built up a long list of established customers and our relationships with them go deep. There is a distinct value on that if you had to replace them from scratch. You have to trust us on that one.'

Armstrong replied immediately. 'Of course, you are right.' He knew full well that was a stretch, but he would let it pass. Laffite ordered a couple more cognacs and a top-up of coffee, which arrived with some squares of dark chocolate. By now the restaurant was nearly empty.

They chatted some more over the financials, each of them feeling the effects of the alcohol.

'Well, Mr Laffite, everything looks perfectly in order. I shall now put together my estimate as to what will be required to make up the necessary upgrades to the port and complete the RFP once I get back to my office in London.'

'Excellent, Mr Armstrong, but please call me Andre from now on.'

'In that case, please call me Ben. By the way, Andre, you mentioned over lunch that you intended to visit the United States with your family later on this year?'

'Yes, that is my plan. I will visit with my wife and our son with his wife and two children aged twelve and ten. It's a special wedding anniversary, but I won't tell you the number!' He laughed loudly.

'Tell you what. I have a house in the Hamptons. Why don't I lend it to you for the duration of your visit? It has extensive grounds and a private beach. Your grandchildren would love it!'

'My word! That is very generous of you! Thank you!' He thought some more. 'I'd appreciate it if we kept this just between us.'

24

Chapter 24

The three-axle heavy-duty Volvo truck with its large twenty-four-foot box van body drove slowly by the Electricity Board transport and equipment yard on the outskirts of Nottingham. Charlie Thornton and Dan Nash carefully checked out each piece of equipment parked inside the yard. It was late on a Saturday afternoon.

Thornton had brought his close friend Jaspal Gupta and one of his other trusted gang members, Prakash Kumar, to assist with the theft of lead and anything else that was of high value from a warehouse not far from this yard. They would need specialised equipment to access the warehouse. They had all been part of the gang that carried out the Brinks Mat Heathrow Airport robbery twelve years before. Gupta and Kumar drove an unmarked DAF medium-duty box van truck behind them.

They had already checked out the Metal Distribution company's yard and warehouse. The yard was surrounded by an outer wire and inner electrified fence, hence the need to use specialist Electricity Board equipment to break and enter the warehouse. Two reinforced high-tensile steel gates with strong locks were the only entry point into the premises. A security guard was installed in the office building. He could control the electric fence and gate locks from his office.

'There you go, Dan. That's the one we want.' Charlie nodded his head slightly to the right as he kept both hands on the steering wheel. He had picked out a truck with a large, extendable three-stage hydraulic bucket lift and boom installed behind the cab.

'We also need to check out the toolboxes on the side to make sure they have the insulated heavy-duty wire cutters and thick rubber gloves that we will need.'

'Okay, Charlie. Keep going and then we can pull into the nearby motorway services and wait until dark.'

Half an hour later, the two vehicles pulled into the Moto Trowell southbound service area and parked separately. They met up in the cafeteria, grabbing hamburgers and coffee. It might be a long night. At 9:00 p.m. it was dark enough to provide cover and they returned to the Electricity Board vehicle storage yard.

'I'm going to park the truck near to the fence at the rear of the premises, Dan. That should give you and Gupta enough cover to cut the interlocking wire fence. Kumar will park his DAF away from us and scan the police VHF frequency bands. Get your latex gloves on.'

Their cell phones vibrated.

'Okay, clear to go ahead. Repeat clear,' Kumar whispered.

Nash looked at Gupta.

'Ready?'

'Let's go!'

Nash and Gupta crouched down, cut a hole and crawled through the wire fence. Using bolt-cutters they broke the locks on the toolboxes of the bucket lift truck and checked the contents. Inside were two insulated heavy-duty cable cutters complete with sets of thick rubber safety gloves. They closed the toolboxes. Nash stood with his back to the vehicle, checking his cell phone. As everything was still quiet, he gave the signal to Gupta. Gupta smashed the driver's window and accessed the cab. Lying on his back, he quickly pulled away the plastic cover underneath the steering column, shorted the ignition and started the diesel truck. A large black exhaust cloud belched out of the exhaust pipe but quickly dissipated. Nash, in the meantime, had cut the locks on the entrance gate. As he opened the gates, Gupta drove the utility truck straight out of the yard and waited for Nash.

Nash closed the gates and hopped into the passenger seat of bucket lift truck as it pulled up. They drove straight to the metal warehouse ten miles away. Gupta followed Thornton's Volvo truck while Kumar brought up the rear in the DAF truck.

The police bands remained fairly quiet, except for central dispatch who called in several squad cars for a disturbance at the Fox and Goose pub in Nottingham city centre. The three trucks passed in convoy by the metal warehouse. Being a Saturday night in an industrial area, there was no traffic. From previous intelligence they had gathered before this trip, they knew they had to get over both fences to get at the security guard and access the central control and alarm system.

Gupta, driving the bucket lift truck, pulled up alongside the outer fence on a blind spot from the warehouse office. Nash hopped out of the passenger seat and climbed into the bucket hoist behind the cab. As Gupta engaged the power take-off from the engine and extended the truck outriggers for stability, Nash, using his hand-held control, raised and extended the hydraulic boom high into the air. As gently as he could, he extended the secondary boom horizontally across the two fences. The metal boom swayed up and down like a pendulum, inches above the electric fence. He held his breath and swallowed hard. One touch and he and Gupta would be toast. He froze for a moment, not wanting to move.

Slowly, Nash regained his composure. He lowered the third stage gently onto the ground inside the warehouse yard. The metal boom was perilously close to the electric fence.

He climbed out of the bucket, pulled on the thick rubber gloves, and grabbed the heavy-duty insulated wire-cutters and hid behind a stack of metal bars waiting to see if all was clear. The cell phone remained quiet.

Gupta took control of the bucket lift from the cab and carefully stowed the booms and outriggers back into position on the deck of the truck. He drove the truck around the corner to an adjacent street and parked it with the driver's side close to a brick wall of a warehouse to hide the smashed window.

The cell phones buzzed again. It was Kumar.

'Take cover. Quick! Police coming!'

Gupta scrambled across to the passenger side. He got out, closed the door, and left his truck, diving through a gap in between two dark buildings. He pressed himself hard against the wall in the shadows.

Nash was about to cut the electric fence cable but swiftly retraced his steps to stay out of sight behind the metal bars. He lay flat on the dusty ground, mind racing, wondering if his freedom would quickly come to an end.

Thornton drove his truck towards the entrance to the industrial estate and turned out onto the main road.

Jaspal ducked out of sight in the DAF cab. He had parked on

a forecourt without its lights on, close to the entrance of the industrial park. From his position on the floor of the cab he heard the police car pass by. A search light passed over his truck and through the windows. His heart was thumping hard. Uncomfortable as he was, he knew he couldn't move out of his pretzel position. Once they had passed his vehicle, he dared to stick his head up and stretch his cramped legs. Using his mirrors, he saw the squad car moving slowly further into the estate. It was evident that there were two policemen in the car. The passenger was working the search light mounted on the A pillar of the vehicle.

The police car went deeper into the industrial estate and then stopped outside the metal warehouse. The searchlight penetrated the outer yard systematically, while the driver got out of the vehicle and tried the front gate.

Nash did not dare move. He kept his head still and tried to control his breathing to remain perfectly still. He swallowed hard several times, trying to contain a dry cough. The irritation got worse. As the search light approached the rack of metal bars, he tried hard to suppress the cough, but, finally, he had to let it out.

25

Chapter 25

'So, what did you make of our meetings with Monsieur Laffite and the other Port Authority staff, Chris?'

The Macrae-Claybourne company jet had just taken off from Marseille airport, climbing steeply into the sky. As the pilot changed the angle of their ascent and commenced his turn to the north, James unbuckled his seat belt.

Chris frowned. He also unbuckled his seat belt, adjusted his seating position, and stretched his legs out.

'You know, it's hard for me to say. I'm normally pretty good at reading body language but the French always confuse me. They speak with so many facial expressions and multiple hand gestures and everything seems so emotional. If I had to say anything, I would say that their financial estimates of their worth are wildly overstated and while they want us to bid, Laffite didn't seem too enthusiastic about a partnership with us.'

James nodded quietly and thought for a few moments. 'Interesting. That's exactly how I feel. We would need to plough in huge capital to fund the expansion and upgrades without a realistic percentage of the partnership. It almost seems that they want us to bid so they can push up the other offers of investment and lower the ownership share. I overheard him say to one of his own colleagues that he was anxious to see what the American will commit to in their RFP. I think there are probably going to be three or four bids in total.'

Chris yawned, holding his hand in front of his mouth.

'If it were me, I would invest more in their warehouse expansion with more cross-dock facilities than they seem to think they need. That would give them more flexible opportunities to split incoming bulk cargo from the sea into smaller quantities to distribute these separate loads inland either by barge, rail, or road once they reach the port. Same goes for exporting in combining the same type of cargo into one bulk quantity. Somehow, our ideas and theirs didn't seem to mesh. They were on a different wavelength to us.'

'Why don't we complete our RFP exactly the way we see it and cut out all the padding on their own financial worth. Even if we don't get chosen, we still have got them surrounded with our Valencia and Genoa terminals. Goods travelling across borders within the EU have no hold-ups so we can easily compete with them when they have completed their upgrades.'

'Hundred percent, mate. We have a good business already. We don't need to practice anymore.'

James got up. 'Do you want a sandwich from the galley?'

'Sure, I'll have chicken, and I need a coffee too. Thanks.'

The plane levelled out at 39,000 feet; the company Cessna Citation often flew higher than commercial aircraft. Thin whisps of cirrus cloud drifted below in a veil of cream and white.

Chris finished his coffee. 'You know, James, I'm still in a quandary about who leaked those screen shots of our software system to the Chinese and why the *Mercantile* journalist did a U-turn on us. I know we questioned everybody individually and, of course, everyone denied any knowledge of it. Even their body language didn't reveal anything. It's a mystery.'

'Janet seems to think it could be anyone of three people. Lisa Taylor, Lee Yuen and another person in IT who maintains the PCs and servers.'

'You mentioned before we left for Marseille that Janet had checked our network security and that a copy of several screen shots and one separate database were downloaded onto a recordable CD-ROM on Lee Yuen's computer. I know he's originally from Hong Kong but, if anything, you wouldn't expect him to be sympathetic to the Chinese. As far as I know, the people of Hong Kong would prefer to stay with Britain. And anyway, why would he use his own computer if he wanted to do it secretly?'

'Good point, Chris. Whoever it is, we'll catch them once they attempt to copy any of the other databases. We need to keep them thinking that it was just a journalist that shot photographs of our screens when we invited them to our open day. Nothing like giving them a false sense of security.'

****

Nash's body convulsed again. He pressed himself harder to the ground and slowly moved his gloved hand across his mouth to suppress the cough. A small cloud of dust surrounded his head. He cursed the waterboarding he had endured over one year ago at the hands of the Chinese. His lungs had never recovered.

The search light suddenly jerked towards the rack of metal bars and meticulously swept from side to side around him. Nash kept his head down, not daring to even peep at the light.

The other police officer shouted from the front gate. 'It's okay, Matt, Fred's just signalled back from the gatehouse that all's okay. Let's go and get some tea!'

'Wait a minute, Mac. Something's not right here! I thought I heard a cough.'

'Don't be a prat, Matt. Who the hell would be in there? If there was somebody, they'd smell like fried bacon by now. Come on, let's get that cup of rosy.'

The search light did one final sweep of the yard and then the police car finally left the industrial estate. Nash felt breathless and weak. He managed to get up on his knees and tried to clear his throat as quietly as he could.

Jaspal quietly spoke into his cell phone: 'All clear. Green light everyone!'

Nash looked out from his hiding place and spotted the electric cable that he needed to cut. He ran, crouched down, back to the fence, and severed the electric cable easily with the powerful jaws of the wire-cutters. He dropped the cutters and rubber gloves out of sight behind the metal bars, pulled out his Glock from his jacket and raced as fast as he could alongside the warehouse to the office entrance.

As expected, the security guard emerged from his office door. The guard put his hand to his forehead to shield his eyes from the glare of the security lights and peered into the warehouse yard ahead of him to see why the power to the fence had cut out. He was too late to react to the pistol clubbing him over his head. Only slightly stunned, he lashed out at Nash. Nash ducked and clubbed him again heavily on the side of his head. The guard dropped to the floor unconscious, blood seeping from his ear. Nash put the boot in just to make sure he didn't wake up. He took the walkie-talkie and phone from the guard and dragged him back inside the office.

Quickly locating the controls for the two sets of gates and disarming the alarm system, he opened the gates. Next, he opened the large warehouse doors. Thornton had returned in the Volvo truck and immediately entered the yard and backed his truck inside the warehouse. Kumar arrived with the DAF and also reversed in beside the Volvo. Gupta came through the gates on foot.

Nash closed the main gates and the warehouse doors. To the outside world everything looked in perfect order. Kumar remained near the office door and continued to scan the police network.

Nash took charge inside the warehouse. 'Okay, so far so good. Let's be quick. Get the roller shutters up on the trucks and prepare the cargo straps. I'm going to look for lead.'

He spotted an electric forklift and started it up. Circling around the stacks of sheet metal and bars, he returned with sheets of lead loaded on a wooden pallet. Thornton guided the load into the back of the Volvo, while Nash pushed the load as far forward as he could using a set of extended forks.

'Have you got enough lead there, Dan?' asked Thornton.

'No. I still need more as well as sheets of stainless steel.'

'Okay. I've also spotted some brass and aluminium. Let's get that as well. It's easy cash down the East End.'

'Will do.'

Meanwhile, Gupta had found another forklift and was

loading the DAF with sheets of copper, brass and silver ingots. After more than an hour, they had filled the trucks estimating they were not overweight. The last thing they needed would be to be caught with an overloaded truck on one of the Ministry weighbridges on their return to London. They lashed down their cargoes, then made sure there were no fingerprints, or any other clues left behind. Kumar finished clearing all the security camera footage.

Nash went into the office and checked on the security guard. He lay in a pool of his own blood, mouth and eyes wide open.

Kumar looked at Nash. 'Don't worry, Dan, he's dead. He's not gonna grass on us.'

Nash shrugged.

Kumar smiled back. 'Just part of the job. All clear outside.'

Thornton leaned down from the cab. 'Get in, Dan. Gupta, get the lights, the warehouse doors, and the gates. Talk on the other side.'

Nash hopped into the Volvo and they drove out of the warehouse and yard. They waited outside while Kumar drove his truck into the street behind them. Gupta turned out the interior warehouse lights and closed the doors. Next, he flicked the switch to close the front gates and sprinted across to them to get outside before they closed. He jumped into the DAF cab and both trucks sped off into the night, taking separate ways back to London.

'Well, Dan, we've got everything we need to get our escape and retirement funds started. I'm tired of looking over my shoulder. You, me and Stanny boy deserve an easier life! Women, cars and alcohol – here we come!'

Dan smiled to himself. He wasn't sure who would survive out of the three of them. Self-preservation and greed were a potent combination.

26

Chapter 26

'**M**r Macrae, Mr Claybourne and Mr Farley. Before we meet the legal representatives of *Mercantile News* with the mediator, you are all going to need a lot of patience both today and over the coming months, if not years.'

James looked at the lawyer Martin Farley said was their best choice for suing *Mercantile News* for defamation. The lawyer, Geoffrey Ravenhurst, was a smartly dressed man in his fifties and was a specialist in media and communication claims.

James huffed. 'That's not what I wanted to hear.'

Ravenhurst nodded his head in acknowledgement.

'I understand, Mr Macrae, however the courts will treat the standards set out in Pre-Action Protocol as the usual, reasonable approach for parties to a media and communications claim. The courts will expect parties to have complied with this protocol in good time before proceedings are issued. Should a claim proceed to litigation, the extent to which this protocol has been followed by the parties will assist the court in dealing with liability for costs and making other orders.'

Martin looked at James and Chris. 'He's right. The two parties must attempt to settle the issues without issuing proceedings. We have to do this in writing, so we can be seen to understand each other's position and have attempted to settle these issues by this method.'

'But we've done that already. We issued our Letter of Claim with supporting documentation for the defamation,' James replied.

'Yes, you have,' Ravenhurst agreed. '*Mercantile News*, however, has rejected the claim and both parties, you and they, have exchanged key documentation to that effect.'

'So, this is what we are doing today. Taking it to the next step?' asked Chris.

Martin looked at Chris and James. 'Yes, we are. We now have to decide if we want to proceed with a form of alternative dispute resolution, or ADR as it is called, without going to court.'

Ravenhurst chipped in. 'Although ADR is not compulsory, the court will expect the parties to have considered ADR. A party's refusal to engage with ADR might be considered unreasonable by the court and could lead to the court ordering that party to pay additional costs.'

James nodded. 'So, if I understand this, this is a form of facilitated negotiation using an independent, neutral third party.'

'Yes, it is. If this ADR does not work out, you can then proceed to court action. So, are you ready to proceed with this right now? It's all been arranged, but you can still say no.'

****

Light poured in from the tall waist-to-ceiling windows either side of the ADR meeting room. Heavy wood panelling surrounded the walls underneath the windows as well as the ornately corniced mouldings and roof.

'Good morning to you all. My name is Allan Jennings and I am to act as your facilitator to help you both try to reach a satisfactory resolution before your defamation case reaches court. You should know that I am completely neutral in this matter and that I am a lawyer specialising in this area of the law. I have thoroughly studied all of your submitted documentation. Now I want to hear what you consider your position to be in this matter.'

James Macrae pushed his finger in between his neck and shirt collar, moving his neck from side to side. On the other side of the room, the two brothers who owned *Mercantile News* sat, stony-faced and still.

Jennings continued. 'Right, Mr Ravenhurst, as the representative for Macrae-Claybourne Logistics, please proceed.'

Ravenhurst stood up. 'Mr Jennings. In every case of defamation, there are three rules of precedent that must be met: One, the defendant must have communicated a false statement of fact and not mere opinion; two, the statement must have identified or referred to the plaintiff and, thirdly, the statement must have been published.'

'In the case of point one, *Mercantile News* clearly issued false statements regarding the authenticity of our software, as well as negative statements of our company performance and increases in our efficiency.'

Jennings nodded and scribbled some notes down. 'I see. Carry on.'

'As for rule number two and three, these points are also

beyond doubt. *Mercantile News* clearly identified Macrae-Claybourne Logistics, the plaintiff and the article in question was indeed published in their magazine. It was written by Mr Greg Driver, their special correspondent.'

Jennings pondered for a few seconds, tapping his pen on the pad.

'Okay, let me hear from the *Mercantile News* legal representatives.'

The owl-like elderly man with the hook nose and round metal-rimmed spectacles stood up. 'Mr Jennings, sir. My name is Barclay Blake. As for rule number one, it seems to me this is what this whole case rests upon. Clearly this is a complicated case. As with all cases of this nature, the burden of proof is for my clients, the defendants, to prove that their statements are true.'

Everyone remained silent.

As if he was talking to himself, Owl Face continued. 'The plaintiffs, Macrae-Claybourne, have taken exception to the words, "touted increases in efficiency". In my considered opinion, this is not libellous since their business did falter after the series of accidents and misfortunes that they encountered recently as per these submitted reports from *Mercantile News*.'

Ravenhurst jumped up from his seat.

'Objection, sir!'

Jennings immediately exclaimed. 'Please sit down, Mr Ravenhurst. We are not in a court of law.'

Owl Face continued.

'And furthermore, it is clear to me that a number of customer complaints were actually made against the company. I have had each of these complaints verified.'

Ravenhurst interceded: 'I'm sorry, Mr Jennings, but these complaints are old and were raised at the same time as a number of sabotage acts were carried out against the company over one year ago. I may add that the sabotage acts against my client were proven in a court of law. My clients dealt with each of these complaints and down-turn in business at that particular time. Since these unlawful acts of sabotage have ceased, my clients have enjoyed increased customer satisfaction, efficiency and profitability, therefore *Mercantile News* have, indeed, committed libel.'

Jennings made more notes. 'Carry on, Mr Blake.'

'This brings me to what I believe is the whole crux of this case. The accusation of libel clearly rests on the statement in the *Mercantile News* article that, and I quote: "To make matters worse, Macrae-Claybourne Logistics claimed at their launch that they had developed 'Tomorrow's Technology Today', a logistics software program, when it is now apparent that it was in fact 'Yesterday's Technology Today.' The Shanghai Port Authority had already developed this unique logistics software system and was using it well before Macrae-Claybourne Logistics copied it."'

Owl Face let the last sentence hang in the air. He took off his reading glasses and placed them carefully on the table in front of him. He looked from side to side around the group assembled around him and then continued, 'Sir, I do not profess to be an expert on computer software and that is why we consulted with a number of computer software experts. After lengthy consultations and submissions, we discovered that the Shanghai Port Authority version of the software program is indeed their own. The programming language they used is completely different to the programming language used by Macrae-Claybourne Logistics.'

He put on his reading glasses again and checked his notes carefully, running his bony finger across the typed sentences on the sheet of paper in front of him.

'The programming language used was Perl in the case of the Shanghai Port Authority and C in the case of the plaintiff. They are clearly not the same.'

Jennings made further notes. 'Mr Ravenhurst. What is your considered opinion?'

'Mr Jennings, this does not prove anything since C language can easily be translated into Perl. The Shanghai version that Mr Blake and his subject matter experts have seen is only one database and not the complete system that Macrae-Claybourne Logistics uses. We insist that the defendants are guilty of libel, and we seek damages for their actions.'

'Are there any further points?' Jennings paused. 'No? So, I will take everything into consideration and get back to you with a proposed resolution within a month.'

James and Chris looked directly across the room at the owners of *Mercantile News*. Both brothers averted their eyes.

****

The drive back to Birmingham started off in silence. Chris drove, James deliberated. Martin had stayed back in London for another meeting with Ravenhurst.

'Penny for your thoughts, James?'

'Hmm. I'm thinking we should continue to publicly take the high road in all our dealings and statements, but I want to do more. Firstly, I want to grab that little fucker, Greg Driver, by the throat and find out why he lied about us.'

'Amen to that!' Chris nodded vehemently.

James smacked the dashboard. 'I'm getting very tired of all this bureaucracy. It takes so much time, meanwhile the public still sees the published lies that Mercantile News continues to peddle. You and I have worked so hard to build a strong business that is honest and customer focussed. Now our customers just think we are charlatans. I'm sick of trying to play by the goddamn rules. They just don't fucking work! I think it's time to contact Scott Farmer, the private detective I used last year against my old CFO, Hal Spencer.'

'Yes, you're right. Let's do it.'

27

Chapter 27

The old mill stood back against the gorse covered hills, surrounded by the resplendent red and pink rhododendron bushes on the one side and the open coastline of rugged cliffs on the other.

Sarah stood outside their new home, her face lit up from ear to ear as James pulled into the gravel courtyard. While James had remained at work in Birmingham, she had spent the last two weeks with the children there on their summer holidays. The converted mill they had recently purchased looked more homely than ever. Bright-red geraniums poured over the tops of window boxes and the surrounding trees and shrubs were all in full bloom.

James beamed back and jumped out of his Range Rover.

'Jimbo! Oh, it's so good to see you! We've missed you these past weeks.' Sarah put both her arms around his neck and gave him a full, warming kiss on the lips.

James held his wife tightly to him, not wanting to let her go. He whispered in her ear, 'I love you, Sarah Macrae!'

'I love you too, James Macrae!' she exclaimed. 'How was

your drive up?'

'No problem at all. It took me just under three hours. Just about the same time as it took to get to the old house.'

He stood back and admired their new home. 'The house looks like ours already. You've been busy!'

'Well, I have to confess, my mum and dad helped out a lot. The contractors are just about finished now, but I can update you on all that later.'

'Thank god for summer holidays! I'm so looking forward to mine. It will give me a chance to unwind and help us fully settle in. So, where are our three little monkeys?'

'Oh, they're out back. Mason has discovered a secret path down the side of the cliffs and onto the small beach below. It's a very secluded and safe cove. No one can access it. I'd forgotten all about the path and it hadn't been used by Megan and Drew for several years. It was quite overgrown.'

James looked alarmed, raising his eyebrows.

'Is it safe?'

'It is! You can't see the path either from the top or the bottom, as it winds between the outcrops of rock and thick bushes that cling to the sides of the cliff. There's no way I would allow them on it if it wasn't. You know me!'

'Okay, let's go find them.'

Sarah led James over the patio, by hand, across the lawn and then through some thick gorse bushes and there, sure enough, was a winding single file path down the cliffs. They descended the track and came out behind a large rock on the sandy beach. Mason and the girls were playing tag. As soon as they saw James, they rushed towards him.

'Daddy! Daddy!'

James hugged and kissed each one of them. 'I've missed

you all so much! So, how do you like the new house?'

All of them shouted at the same time. 'We love it!'

Mason continued, 'It's so much fun. We have our secret path, although the girls aren't allowed on it unless I'm with them. We've also been helping Mum, together with Grandpa and Grandma, to move in.' James smiled. Whenever he wasn't with them, they all tried to act so grown up and responsible, rallying around Sarah. The episode last year had brought them even closer together.

James closed his eyes, relishing having all his family around him. The sea air smelled fresh and stimulating, the sun warmed his face and the soothing sound of the waves all blended in with the chatter and laughter of his family. It left an indelibly printed image in his memory.

James opened his eyes. 'Okay, last one up to the house is a rotten egg!'

The children squealed and sped away to the path. James linked hands with Sarah and followed them up to the house.

'Dad, you're the rotten egg!'

'Oh no! Not again! Now, come on show me your bedrooms and then we can play monster.'

They ate on the patio outside and when the children were clearing the table and washing up and wiping, James and Sarah had a moment to themselves.

'So, all the contractors have finished?'

'Yes, they're nearly done. The alarm system has been fitted, including cameras to the house, garage and workshop.

James nodded. 'This puts my mind at rest. Oh, by the way, I almost forgot, my parents asked when they could visit us. They would love to see the house.'

'That would be great. We could invite them up, say, on your

last weekend before you go back. How are they?'

'They're good. I had dinner with them this week. Dad's taken up golf again and mum is still doing her volunteer work at the hospital. They seem to be settling down well in their retirement. They both seem very happy and relaxed.'

'That's really good news. I wasn't sure Richard would be able to adjust so easily.'

'Well, if it wasn't for his heart attack, I don't believe he would have done either.'

Sarah smiled. 'Let's be thankful it all turned out well in the end.'

For the next few days, James helped put up pictures and unpacked boxes of their belongings, trying to find the right place for everything. There was no need to do any renovations or change the decor; it suited them perfectly. The house had been left in excellent order.

'James, can you get that? I think it's your phone. It was on the kitchen table, last time I saw it.

James looked up from his project of setting up a swing set for the children in the garden. He got to the kitchen just as it stopped ringing. He picked it up and saw Chris had called him. Knowing that they never bothered each other on holiday unless it was important, he called him back straightaway.

'Hey, Chris, what's up, mate?'

'James, sorry to disturb you on your holiday, but we have a problem. One of our container vessels lost over one hundred and fifty containers overboard in the Indian Ocean. It hasn't got out to the press yet, but it won't be long before it does. I've spoken to the captain, and he is at a loss why the containers should have been displaced. He said the sea wasn't particularly rough, neither was the pitch and roll of the vessel.

Certainly not enough to set off a parametric roll causing the stacks to lean too far over and break the lashing systems.'

'Oh shit! This is a disaster. I better get back straight away. Any other news?'

'Yes, we got the results of the Marseille and Rotterdam bids. We lost both of them by a huge margin. I'll show you when you get back, although they have not yet officially awarded the contracts.'

'Bloody hell, Chris. I thought we were in for a period of plain sailing. We've just had a great financial quarter and now this. I'll get back to the office early tomorrow morning. By the way, did we hear anything back about the arbitration proceedings?'

'Nothing yet, but that little shit, Greg Driver, has published yet another negative article about us. For some reason he's got an axe to grind with our company.'

'Okay, I'll check with our private detective if he's dug up anything yet once we've got this latest crisis under control.'

James got off the phone and broke the news to Sarah that he would be returning to work earlier than he had anticipated. He felt his mood slowly slipping back into the river of darkness he had experienced last year. His life was becoming a seesaw of light and dark.

28

Chapter 28

Ming looked up from his desk, 'So, General, do you have good news for me to report this month to the president?'

Shen smiled back and sat down in front of the secretary's ever-clear desk. Absolutely nothing to read upside down.

'Yes, Mr Ming, I do. Since our last meeting, we have made good progress with our strategic plan.'

He leaned down by the side of his chair and produced a manila folder from his briefcase.

Ming received it with an expectant air of approval. He opened the cover to reveal the first page detailing the Executive Summary. He adjusted his glasses and quietly scanned the bullet points, moving his head slowly from side to side.

'My congratulations on your progress so far. So, tell me how you think we are doing.'

Shen looked at his own copy of the report and referred to the bullet points one by one.

'We believe we are making good progress with our bids for part ownership of both the Marseille and Rotterdam port authorities. In each case we have bid the highest investment dollars for upgrading the port facilities. At the same time, we are the lowest bidder in our request for a percentage of the partnership.'

Ming interrupted.

'Just so I understand this correctly, the other bidders clearly wanted to invest less dollars than us, but wanted a higher percentage of ownership in each of the two terminals?'

'Yes, Mr Ming. That is correct. It means we should be the clear favourites for the final choice of partner. Once we have part ownership, our foot is in the door.'

'Excellent, General. When do you expect to hear the official results?'

'We don't have a specific date yet. Ben Armstrong has been in touch with the EU Transport Director-General to try to find out if he has heard anything. He has not, but while he agrees that Pair-Tree Capital are in a strong position, it does not guarantee us success.'

'Okay. Keep me posted and let me know immediately you hear something.'

'I will. Remember, once we have the results, I will need immediate access to the funds for our down payment, as well as each stage payment. I did copy you on each of the bid documents so you have the exact figures that we will need.'

'You did indeed, General. The president will sign off on them once we have received official notification. By the way, I was going through the accounts of Pair-Tree Capital for the last two months and I noticed that office expenses, as well as advertising and promotion entries, seemed rather high. I will need an explanation.'

Shen stared straight back at Ming. His face remained

impassive.

'Of course. All expenses must be accounted for correctly. I will have the costs and invoices sent over to your office. Every invoice is jointly signed off by both Ben Armstrong and myself. Of course, we also need a slush fund; to bribe certain individuals. Again, these transactions will be recorded properly, purely for our own internal purposes.'

Ming jotted a note down on his pad. Shen tried to read it.

'Good. Let's proceed with your report, General.'

Shen went back to his copy of the report on his lap.

'Next, our disinformation campaign is working well. There have been a number of international reports reflecting badly on the Macrae-Claybourne company published by the compromised journalists that attended the Shanghai launch. Each published article is in the appendix to this report. In addition, there have also been many positive media reports on China's friendly cooperation with a number of countries where we are investing in their infrastructure to help build our new silk road. These reports are also included in the appendices.'

'Good! Now, what happened with the lawsuit brought against *Mercantile News*?'

'The libel suit that Macrae-Claybourne Logistics launched against *Mercantile News* has not reached the court system yet. There are a number of protocols in English law that have to be followed before a defamation claim can get to court. A case like this could take years.

'This is excellent, General. I assume this leaves both the magazine and reporter to carry on with their negative reports?'

'Yes, it does. Greg Driver has already published another article focussed on poor customer reviews of the Macrae organisation, compared to the greater efficiency of the Chinese ports. He then surmises that if this is the case, then it will not be long before the Zeebrugge terminal starts to out-perform all other European terminals since it is being set up the same way as Shanghai in terms of the harbour redesign!'

Shen paused and grinned.

Ming, for once, chuckled in response while shaking his head.

Ming then referred back to his copy of the report.

'Now, what is the status of Zichan? Has our contact delivered the software yet?'

'Yes, so far we have received one database. Macrae-Claybourne are using multiple databases to run their entire operations, so we will have to get each one separately. This will take some time, but at least we can start to use the software piece by piece.'

Ming tapped his fingers rapidly on the desk and scowled.

'General Shen, start to put pressure on Zichan. We need that software yesterday! We are under pressure to get our terminals operating at the same level of efficiency as Macrae-Claybourne. In reality, I have it on good authority that they are outperforming us. This must stop!' His voice was raised by the time he finished the sentence.

Shen sat calmly with an air of confidence.

'It will be done, but I will not jeopardise our contact within their organisation by hasty and reckless actions. This person is too important for us to put at risk. You must remember, Mr Ming, I informed you that, once we had the complete software system, we would infect their own software to cause maximum chaos and destruction in the Macrae-Claybourne organisation. This will be a huge weapon to use and enable us to step in and eventually take over their operations. You must be patient on this one!'

Shen sat back in his chair and coldly stared straight into Ming's eyes. The only sound to be heard was the slow spin of the large ceiling fan mounted above them. Ming looked at the floor.

Shen cleared his throat and went back to his executive summary.

'As for our other strategy of pushing countries into debt and grabbing strategic footholds of critical commercial and military waterways, I'm happy to report that we have now completely taken over the port of Hambantota in Sri Lanka after they failed to repay their debt. We also have 15,000 acres of adjoining land. This gives us a base that we can use for military purposes only a few hundred miles from our rival, India.' He remained silent.

'General Shen. You have excelled yourself! The president will be very pleased. Now, is there anything else?'

'There is, Mr Ming. What is the status of your enquiries about Stanfield and Nash? The sooner you can locate them with your network, the better. I want to use them to get rid of James Macrae once and for all.'

'No news yet, I'm afraid. I have all our agents on full alert. Stanfield and Nash have gone to ground, but we will find them. We always do.'

Shen left Ming's office. The meeting had gone well. He smiled to himself, having already squirrelled away over two hundred thousand dollars in his offshore accounts. All the dollars had been neatly paid out through Pair-Tree Capital to bogus suppliers that Shen had created. His insurance policy was getting stronger, should he ever need to pull the ripcord. Once the Marseille and Rotterdam transactions were completed, he would have an even firmer financial cushion to fall back on, if he needed it.

Chapter 29

At 8:00 a.m., Lee Yuen made his way to the corner office.

'Hello, Rachel, do you think I could speak to Mr Claybourne?' he sheepishly asked Chris's secretary.

'Oh hi, Lee. I should think it will be okay. You know him, his door is always open. Just let me check.' She hopped up from behind her desk and walked into the corner office

'Come on in, Lee!' Chris shouted from inside the office. Rachel came back out smiling.

Lee entered the office. As he started to speak, his face reddened.

'Mr Claybourne. I need to speak to you, but could we close the door?'

'Sure. Come on in and sit down.' Lee closed the door and sat opposite his boss, leaning forward on the chair and somewhat short of breath.

'You looked troubled, Lee, what's bothering you?' Chris sat back in his chair, wanting to put Lee at ease.

'I'm not sure where to begin. We all know about the

Mercantile News article that mentioned that we had copied the Chinese software.'

'Yes, that was most unfortunate.'

Lee clasped his hands tightly together on his lap. 'I'm sorry to have to tell you this, but I think it's the right thing to do.'

Chris looked back at Lee, slightly tilting his head with a puzzled look on his face.

'As you know, my background is IT security. I recently installed spyware on my computer.' Lee waited for a few moments for his words to sink in, then he continued.

'Someone used my machine to download screen shots several weeks ago and, later, my machine was used to copy the individual logistics database that I am responsible for. It was copied onto a CDR recordable compact disc. The network password was used; not my password. The thing is, there are only three people that have access to the network password for my machine that I know of. Janet Rushton, Lisa Taylor and the other is Paul Adams, who maintains the PCs and servers.'

Chris took a few moments. 'So, what you are saying, Lee, is that Janet, Lisa or Paul could be a traitor to this company?'

'Yes, sir. I am.' He let out a huge sigh.

'Thank you for telling me this. Leave it with me.'

Lee got up to leave. 'I'm so sorry, sir. I would never do anything to harm this company. You gave me my first break. Thank you for listening to me.'

Chris sat quietly for a few minutes frowning and stroking his chin continually, when James walked in.

'James, I'm glad you are back. Sorry to drag you off your holiday but we have a mounting list of problems. We need to get down to it straight away.'

'Okay, Chris. Give me the bad news and let's get on it!'

'First things first. I need to bring Janet in.'

Chris, James and Janet all sat around the conference table. The office door was closed. Chris updated them on his conversation with Lee.

Janet was the first to speak. 'It would seem that if Lee is telling us the truth, then either Lisa or Paul could be trying to throw suspicion on Lee. But there again, Lee could be the one downloading the software and trying to throw suspicion on the other two. Can I use your computer, Chris?'

'Go ahead, Janet.' Janet got up and sat behind Chris's desk, furiously clattering away on the keyboard.

'While Janet's doing that, I'll give you the story on the container loss at sea.'

James remained solemnly quiet. He already felt his heart starting to race.

'I got a call early yesterday from Captain Hill on our container ship, *Inverclyde*. He estimates we lost more than one hundred and fifty containers overboard. He's making his way to Yanbu for inspection and repairs. I've already dispatched Jason Ferreira, our safety manager to investigate what happened. As I mentioned yesterday, the ship was not in heavy seas. There were no injuries to the crew.'

James took in a large deep breath. 'At least that's something! Was Captain Hill able to give you any idea at all how it happened?'

Chris shook his head.

'No. He simply said that nothing makes any sense. He was on the bridge at the time and as the ship gently rolled to starboard, a central stack of containers above the deck folded over like a pack of dominoes, taking the other stacks around them over the side. The bottom layer of containers remained on deck, safely secured with the lashing rods and turnbuckles.'

James sat forward in his seat. 'I don't understand it either. Our stevedores are trained in load securement and ensuring container twist locks are engaged.'

Chris continued. 'Strangely enough, we also lost two twenty-foot containers off one of our trucks the day before when they simply rolled off the trailer on the M6 slip road exit in Walsall. I've had them brought back to our yard. The body shop guys are taking a look at them now. Something doesn't seem right to me.'

'Okay, once *Inverclyde* gets back to Yanbu, we'll get them to take inventory and we'll notify the customers and insurance accordingly. We have a good safety record.' He then added, 'At least, up to now.'

Chris frowned some more. 'More bad news, I'm afraid. *Mercantile News* has continued to print negative press about us. The story of our rollover on the M6 yesterday is already online, together with photographs showing huge traffic jams on the motorway and surrounding roads. This news story, coupled with those published articles of customer complaints of our poor service, feels like an organised attack on us. Greg Driver has also been calling our customers, looking for anything negative he can find to dredge up against us.'

'I would have thought that his editor would have been keeping a tight rein on him,' James remarked.

'Yes, you'd think so, but these are verifiable stories – unlike the software allegations.'

'I guess that's true.'

Chris continued. 'Trouble is that these negative reports are already having an effect on our business. Sales are falling. Our drivers are getting twitchy. The media are also making a big deal on the pending lawsuit. It's appalling that a lawsuit of this nature should be in the public eye for so long before it even reaches the courts.'

'Just when I thought we had turned the corner. Right, what else do I need to know?'

He turned to face Janet, still tapping away on the keyboard.

'How are you getting on, Janet?'

'Firstly, I've checked with Shad. He confirms that our firewalls are secure and have not been breached. So, any leaks of our software have come from within our own company. Lee's machine was definitely used to copy one database onto a CD.'

'Janet, can we tell what time of day it was copied and then we can check who was here at the time?' James asked.

'We can, but whoever did it could have manipulated the time on Lee's machine to make it look like he was actually here and then restored the time clock back to the true time. It will be inconclusive.'

Chris's cheeks flushed bright red as he suddenly blurted out raucously, 'I want to drag all three of them in here right now, interrogate them and shake the bloody truth out of them!'

James got up from his chair and clenched his teeth.

'No Chris!'

Chris crossed his arms. 'Why not? I'm tired of always being the nice guy! We need to jolt this place up out of all this complacency – right now!'

'Chris, I know how you feel, but consider this: Let's allow Lee, Lisa and Paul to stay where they are, working as normal and pretend we don't know anything. Sooner or later, they will try to get the rest of the databases. Once we know who it is, we can let them have a corrupted database that is infected with malware and see where it ends up.

Chris remained silent pondering James's suggestion. Slowly he uncrossed his arms and then he smiled.

'Newton's third law of motion redefined by none other than James Macrae. Yes, that's far more subtle, let's do it and strike one for revenge.'

James looked directly at Janet. 'Would you be willing to infect a copy of our software? Get Shad on side.'

'Of course. This is our product and our technological advantage over our competition. Let's teach whoever is on the receiving end a lesson! I'll contact Shad.'

'Good. Thanks, Janet.'

After the meeting, James and Chris walked down to the body shop, careful to walk within the yellow-painted pedestrian lines. The yard was busy with tractors and trailers arriving and departing. Compressed air sanders and the sound of hammers on metal competed with the radio blasting from the back of the body shop. Hot, glowing Arc welding sparks flew up in the air as a welder repaired the frame of a skeletal container trailer. The body shop foreman saw them coming and signalled to a panel beater to turn down the radio.

Chris spoke first.

'Hi, Sam, any update on why those two containers rolled off in Walsall yesterday?'

Sam rubbed his hands on his coveralls.

'Good morning. I was going to contact the manufacturer and send them photos of the corner castings on the container where the twist locks insert. Seems to me, the holes are too big to engage the lock. The driver claims he locked the twist locks when he picked up each container. He's one of our longest-serving drivers and has won several of our safety awards in the past. It's not like him to make a mistake. To me, this is a design and manufacturing error.'

Chris frowned. They both inspected the castings. James looked at Sam.

'Sam, these containers have our serial numbers on them alright, but the manufacture of these two containers looks different than our regular supplier. You see here.' James pointed to the bottom corners.

'They are missing the reinforcing gussets that we insist are welded onto our containers.'

Sam looked carefully at the corners. 'I did notice that, but presumed we had mixed container designs since we merged the companies.'

James looked at Sam. 'Sam, what do I keep telling everyone?'

'Don't presume.'

'If you are unsure of anything, ask!'

'Sorry, James. I should have done.'

'Okay, don't let it happen again.'

James pulled Chris to one side.

'Chris, are you thinking what I'm thinking?'

'Yes I am. Sam's correct. Instead of having the regular ISO large oval hole, the opening is circular in each of these corner castings. When you're securing a container to a flat bed or another container, it would be difficult to spot. And then, when you're twisting to lock and engage it, it would twist normally, except the lock is not engaged with the corner casting.'

James clenched his fists. 'This is not a manufacturing error, it's bloody sabotage! These are not our containers, but someone has painted them and inserted our serial numbers on them.' He called Sam over to them.

'Sam, if you had to guess who manufactured these two containers, who would it be?'

'I would say they are Chinese.'

30

Chapter 30

Nash flipped his safety visor up and turned off his brazing torch. The molten stainless steel cooled and formed a perfectly proportioned flowing joint along the seam of the inner tank wall. He wiped his hands on his leather apron and exited the trailer through the lower access hatch towards the bulkhead. He rubbed the back of his arm across his sweaty forehead and removed the visor. He nodded to Stanfield, who passed him a cold beer.

'That's the second done.'

'Good work. You can't see any of the modifications that you've made from the exterior. Let me look inside.'

'Wait a few minutes for the fumes to clear. I've had the air-circulation pumps working while I was welding so it won't take long.'

'They on now?'

Dan nodded, intent on taking gulps of his beer.

'You can't hear anything! No one would know we are circulating air through the inner tank. It's perfect.'

'Give me a minute and let me get washed up.' As Dan

removed his apron and changed out of his welding boots, Stanfield circled the exterior of each tank in the warehouse. The polished ISO twenty-foot stainless-steel tanks were completely identical from the outside to the ones they had received from the manufacturer one month before. The tanks were housed in a standard steel cage conforming to all required ADR Standards to carry dangerous goods internationally.

While Nash had worked tirelessly, fitting out the interiors for their human cargo, Stanfield had set up multiple bank accounts in fictitious company names to receive payments from customers who wanted to enter the United Kingdom illegally. He used a trusted contact in China to act as a liaison between the customers who would become illegal immigrants. Each person would pay the equivalent sum of fifteen thousand Euros. Stanfield's target market would be wealthy Chinese who wanted to disappear with their families and set up new lives in the United Kingdom. The price would cover their journey to Europe and then their passage across the Channel inside the tankers.

'Okay, let me show you the outside first.' He pointed to the temperature gauges corresponding to each tank compartment within the trailer.

'These show the exact interior temperature measurements of medical waste that we will be carrying. We will not trigger any heat sensors at border control since each trailer will be the correct temperature for our cargo.'

He paused for a few seconds. 'Charlie is sorting official signage identifying the types of waste we will be carrying. We will also have the correct paperwork. Each compartment will have a shipper's sealed tag put in place at the time of pickup. Equally, any X-ray machines will not be able to see humans inside since they will be shielded by the lead lining that I have installed in the concealed compartment.'

Stanfield's eyes widened.

'Bloody good. Love it! Now, let's see inside.'

Dan led Stanfield to the lower access hatch and pointed to the round hatch as it swung downward.

'This access point is a standard fitting. It is opened when the tank is cleaned between shipments; each empty tank is purged with steam.'

Inside, they walked – crouched down – on the polished stainless-steel cylindrical floor through a sealed compartment door.

'This partition forms one of the baffles in the tank to prevent medical waste liquids from surging inside the rest of the tank.'

Inside was a compact, lead-lined oblong room. It was lit up using the twenty-four-volt electrical system.

'The room will be well ventilated at all times to prevent suffocation. The occupants will also have a supply of drinking water.'

There was a small hole in the corner.

'Any grey water will be caught in a sealed tank below the floor.'

Stanfield ran his eyes over the dimensions of the inner room. Deep in thought, his brow furrowed as he clasped his hands together.

'You know what, Dan, we could squeeze more than ten people in here,' he said with a greedy look in his eyes.

Nash held both his palms out in front of him.

'Steady on! It will be packed already. Anymore and you would overcrowd this space! Remember, they will need to sit on the floor for most of the time, especially if there are any delays. Claustrophobia could lead people to panic. Anyway, I thought we were trying to get maximum money from upmarket customers? Too many people in here and the air supply could also become a problem.'

Stanfield frowned.

'Yeah, I suppose you are right.' He remained quiet for several moments and then looked up.

'So, what's above us, Dan?'

'Well, we have the real tank compartment that will actually carry liquid medical waste. The tank extends downwards front and back on either side of this section. Our occupants are completely sealed off from the waste tank. If any customs officials do inspect the hatches and dip the tanks on the topside, they will see real medical waste.'

'Excellent! So, I have everything set up at the China end. We have at least forty customers already. Charlie Thornton has also sourced several customers in both Belgium and France to dispose of their liquid medical waste. We will have scheduled pickups in Brussels and Paris and then dispose of the waste through a legitimate waste management company with the EU-approved incinerators in Greenwich, not far from here. That way we can drop off our fare-paying customers at secure points somewhere between Dover and London.'

As they exited the trailer, the sensor went off on the yard gate. Billy Blowtorch checked and then opened the gate for Charlie Thornton to bring in a truck and flatbed trailer. With the warehouse doors now open, he drove the rig completely inside.

The shutter on a camera clicked.

31

Chapter 31

James stormed back to the office with Chris after the visit to the body shop to inspect the faulty containers.

'Those bloody bastards are at it again! They never fucking stop! I'm sick of these attacks on me and my family and now I've dragged you into it.'

'James, James, calm down. Yes, now I'm involved so let's sit down and analyse the situation.'

'How can I calm down? It's all becoming clear to me now. Think about it!'

Chris remained quiet.

'First the Shanghai Port Authority tries to steal our software, then there's a slew of negative press against us – from a journalist that was invited over there – and now we have these rogue containers loose in our fleet equipment. God knows how many there are or where they are for that matter!'

'Yes, you're right, but you have to calm down and then we can make a plan to fight back.'

James's face was still the colour of beetroot. 'Well it's no use relying on the authorities, is it? The fucking court system is letting our libel case fester in public like a malignant cancer, then there's the police. They don't seem to have made any progress with Stanfield and Nash. The goddam politicians say we've got your back, but it's all bullshit! Now more sabotage.'

Chris moved closer to James and put his hand on his arm, lowering his voice. 'Agreed, so let's sit down and make a plan. First we have to defend ourselves and then we have to retaliate, go on the attack. You did that last year, alone. Now it's different; I'm involved and I'll help.'

James sat down, twisting the wedding ring on his finger. 'Sorry, Chris. What started last year hasn't gone away. I thought the storm was over, but it seems we are in the eye of the storm. Our dear hybrid friends, the Chinese, must be behind this. They have to be! Them and their bloody silk road; trying to be all sweet and friendly with everyone while secretly developing their hidden agenda of world domination.'

'That's how I see it as well. They still want our ports. So, come on, let's see if we can turn this around. I'll go and get us coffee.'

When Chris returned, James was already jotting on a pad.

'Got some ideas, I see.'

'Yes. First these containers. Don't let's waste time with the manufacturer or the police. Instead, let's circulate photos to all staff of the rogue containers with the sabotaged corner castings and without reinforcing gussets. We'll get them to identify them and put them to one side. I'm thinking that when *Inverclyde* arrives at Yanbu for inspection, she may still have some of these containers on board. It would certainly explain the spill overboard of the hundred and fifty or so containers. In fact, I bet these containers were picked up in a Chinese port.'

'We'll check it out.'

'So next we repaint and change the serial numbers on these rogue containers and insert them back into the Chinese system. Just like last year, we have to fight fire with fire. It's no good trying to play by the rules anymore. These guys need to be taught a lesson. The gloves are off! What goes around, comes around.'

Chris smiled. 'Or, in this case, what comes aboard, goes overboard.'

'Exactly! Next, we apply pressure on that journalist Driver to find out why he's done what he's done. I'll get our private detective to step up the squeeze on him. And then we'll press on to catch whoever is leaking our software to the Chinese.'

Chris thought some more. 'What worries me is what else is up their sleeve?'

****

Scott Farmer peered through the café window at the old warehouse in the East End that had been converted into office space. He was dragging out his second cup of coffee, trying to quench the taste of the stale ham sandwich he'd just eaten. James Macrae had asked him to step up enquiries into a journalist by the name of Greg Driver. Farmer's interpretation of the message had been to give his quarry a good shake-down and find out why he was crucifying Macrae-Claybourne.

As dusk was falling, around 8:00 p.m., Farmer saw Greg Driver leave his office building. He left his coffee and hurried to catch him up. It wasn't difficult. Driver slouched along to what Farmer presumed would be Aldgate tube station. He already knew he lived in Romford, Essex. He'd been there and found his empty flat. According to the neighbours, his wife had left him.

Farmer buttoned up his old navy coat and pulled down his baseball cap further on his head as a chill wind blew across the expanse of water in Shadwell Basin. Driver seemed to be in a trance and continued to traipse along, not noticing he was being followed. Seemingly on impulse, he entered the old White Hart pub.

Farmer followed him in a few moments later. He was already sitting at the bar drinking a pint of beer. Farmer stayed at the other end of the bar, ordered a brown and mild, a packet of pork scratchings and took a seat at the rear of the pub watching Driver through a haze of cigarette smoke. The pub was noisy with excited chatter and clinking glasses, but Driver just sat alone, shoulders slumped, not talking to anyone. As he drained his first pint, he still didn't speak, but the barman brought him another one in any case. Farmer decided to check out the men's toilets. Being an older pub, they were outside, across a cobblestoned yard. There was a dark space between the toilet block and a high wall. Farmer went back inside the pub and saw Driver was still there, slightly swaying on his bar stool.

By the time Farmer had finished nursing his pint, Driver had already downed three pints and had ordered a double scotch. He slid a handful of notes across the old wooden bar, had one more belter of scotch and then slid off his stool and headed out to the toilets, somewhat unsteady on his feet.

Farmer followed him outside. It was now dark. He waited for Driver to come back out of the toilet and then grabbed him from behind and dragged him into the dark space at the rear of the toilet block. Driver's legs sagged as his body slumped in

Farmer's grip. Farmer pinned Driver against the wall, holding tightly onto his collar and pinning his right arm up higher above him. Driver's head moved from side to side, trying to comprehend what had just happened.

He slobbered, 'What the...what the...you can take what you want, mate, I don't care. I don't care about anything anymore.'

Farmer knew Driver was pissed as a rat, so tried to lead him on.

'Yeah, I can take your money, but you sound like you couldn't give a shit. Why not?'

Driver looked up. His eyes were wide and unfocussed.

'I'll fucking tell you why. I've already lost everything. My wife has left me and my job isn't worth shit. I don't even know who I am any more.'

'So why's your life not your own, my friend?' Farmer asked in a soothing tone.

Driver used his free arm again to wipe his nose and eyes on his sleeve.

'Cause it's not, that's why. That's my life, mister. I've got nothing. My life is finished.'

'I don't understand. Things can't be that bad, can they?'

'I'm not even a writer anymore. Everything I do is done by someone else and they put my name on it. *My* fucking name! And I had nothing to do with it!'

'So who's forcing you to do this? Can't you just say no?'

Driver tried to look up again, and stammered almost incoherently, 'Those bastards in Shanghai and my beautiful Meili. She was paid to seduce me and they're blackmailing all of us writers...my Meili, my Meili...' His eyes rolled and he passed out.

Farmer released his hold on Driver, letting him crumple slowly to the floor. He pulled out Driver's wallet and checked the contents. He found a photo of a beautiful woman inside. He removed it and placed the wallet back inside Driver's jacket. Farmer listened for anyone that might be in the toilet. It was quiet, so he quickly dragged Driver back into the toilets and left him on the floor. He stuck his head out of the toilet, checking the courtyard was empty, then walked back through the pub and left. He had what he wanted.

****

The ops room at the Metropolitan Police Headquarters was busy with chatter from all the officers on the team both answering and making telephone calls. Every wall was decked out with large white boards containing names, photographs, arrows and dates.

'Hudson, any progress on finding contacts of Stanfield and Carter?'

DI Stella Hudson looked up at DCI Thomas. 'Sir, I've got a few mugshots for Mr Macrae to look at. I've also analysed the old video footage from street cameras that were close to the Beaver and Bulldog. There are certainly some people of interest that we need to follow up.'

'Okay, what else?'

'My team have been going through the national company register for any companies that Stanfield, Nash or Jack Carter might have been involved with. This might give us a better idea of any friends or acquaintances from the past who could have conceivably assisted Stanfield and Nash in their escape. This list is being analysed as we speak.'

'What about any mercenaries that would be happy to paid for aiding the escape?'

'We've checked out all our snitches but have not turned anything up so far. The street is quiet.'

'Keep the pressure on, Hudson.'

'Yes, sir.'

'Lastly, the information phone line that was set up for information, has that turned up anything yet?'

'The reward offered, of course, is bringing up the usual cranks. Trouble is, it takes a lot of resources to follow up everything. I have to visit Birmingham tomorrow, so I'll check in with James Macrae and show him the mugshots.'

'Good luck!'

****

With sweat pouring off him James bent over, panting hard, as he got back to his Worcestershire home after his morning run. He wiped his forehead with his forearm as the salty taste of the sweat ran across his mouth. He checked his watch for his time and then stretched out his hamstrings one at a time. As he opened the back door, the house had a forlorn and empty feel to it. It wasn't the same when Sarah and the children weren't there. They were still staying at the new house in Wales for the holidays.

Hopefully he could still join them for the few remaining days of his holiday. He picked up a glass, poured himself some cold water, and sat at the kitchen table.

He checked his cell phone, listened to a voicemail from Scott Farmer, and then rang him back to get updated on the private detective's enquiries.

'Thank you, Scott. Good job getting that information out of Greg Driver. This starts to put more pieces into our jigsaw puzzle conundrum. We couldn't understand why he did such a U-turn on us, but now the endless string of negative press starts to make more sense. Can I ask how you got this information?

'You can, but I'm not sure it would stand up in a court of law as being admissible evidence. There's no doubt his wife has left him, and I also found a photograph of a woman who is not his wife in his wallet. In addition, I managed to get in front of Driver's editor, posing as a newspaper journalist investigating the pending lawsuit between you and them. Obviously he couldn't say much, but they are convinced Driver's published stories are reliable. I believed him, so Driver must not have told them he is being coerced.'

'Ummm. Doesn't look as though we can use this in our case, but I have an idea. Let me have your written report and the photograph as soon as you can.'

'Will do. Thank you, Mr Macrae. Let me know if I can do anything else.'

James finished his water and then filled his glass again.

Ummm. Should I or shouldn't I? Oh bollocks, I might as well.

He called Jeremy Hirons's cell phone number. Jeremy worked for MI6 and had been a key ally in helping James last year in exposing Hugh Stanfield's illegal activities and also identifying Hal Spencer, his old CFO as the traitor in his own company. Not only that, but Jeremy wasn't afraid to bend the rules a bit either. Like James, he privately shared his disdain of politicians.

'Jeremy, James Macrae. Can you talk?'

'Give me five minutes and I'll call you back on a secure line...

'

'Okay, we're good. How have you been, James?'

'Well, that's the reason why I'm calling. It seems that our old friends are at it again. My partner and I believe that our ports are under threat once more from the Chinese.'

'Why? What's happened?'

'You've probably seen that we are suing a trade magazine alleging that we have copied software from the Shanghai Port Authority, plus a series of other defamatory articles from a journalist who works for them by the name of Greg Driver.'

'Yes I have.'

'Well, it's just the opposite. Someone in our organisation has leaked some of the software to the Chinese. We've also come to know that Driver is being blackmailed by the Chinese to write these articles. Apparently a number of foreign journalists were compromised at a recent open house event in Shanghai. I think you guys call it the honey trap.'

'Yes, we do. It's the oldest trick in the book and it still works. I won't ask you how you found this out. Let me talk to Jack Fox, MI6 Director. He is still wary of Chinese expansion, so maybe we can assist you. I've no doubt, if we can, it might help your case. Remember, our dear friends in Downing Street still say they have the Hong Kong handover as a lever to keep the Chinese at bay.'

'Yes, I know, but what they say and what they do are two different things.'

'I know. Anyway, let me talk to my boss and maybe we'll pay a visit to Mr Driver and his magazine. After all, it's in the national interest.'

'One last question, Jeremy. Have you heard anything regarding Stanfield and Nash?'

'No. I don't have any news on that front. Seems they've gone to ground for the time being. There is still an extensive search, but no positive sightings yet. No one is letting up.'

'Bloody hell. How can they just vanish like that?'

'Well, I can tell you this, we'll get them in the end. Remember, it took us four years to find Charles Wilson – the great train robber – but we finally got him.'

'I hope it doesn't take that long again. Retribution is on the cards. Both ways.'

James showered and drove to work. He selected a song from a CD he had recorded of his favourite songs. Bob Dylan ignited his sound system with a song called 'Pressing On'. It was nothing like anything Dylan had ever written before, or even sang, but it suited James's melancholy mood. The combination of blues, soul and gospel, welded together by the unique swampy sounds of the Muscle Shoals recording studio, gave him inspiration.

He would be pressing on.

32

Chapter 32

Ben Armstrong could feel his own heartbeat as he sat in the Marseille Port Authority boardroom waiting for his first board meeting to start. He looked around the room with quick glances at nothing in particular. He was now an official fifteen percent owner.

The décor of the room looked tired and old, as if from a bygone age. Heavy brocade curtains restricted the view through the expansive windows to the harbour terminal and pictures of former directors adorned the faded beige-patterned wallpaper. The whole room smelled musty and damp.

Andre Laffite stood up at the head of the boardroom table and addressed the five directors.

'So welcome, Mr Armstrong, to Marseille Port Authority! We are so happy to have Pair-Tree Capital as one of our new partners. It will enable us to carry out the necessary upgrades to our terminal that we so desperately need.'

'Thank you, Monsieur Laffite. It is an honour for me to join your board.'

Armstrong looked around the table at each director in turn. With his best smile, he continued, 'I look forward to getting to know each of you as we progress with our expansion plans. It is certainly a well-trodden path that we have been on before at Pair-Tree Capital.'

He paused slightly as he saw one of the other directors give a slight sneer.

'My colleagues and I were so happy that you accepted our bid and detailed upgrade plans without any modification. With Monsieur Laffite's guidance we are hiring local contractors to start the work immediately. Furthermore—'

There was a loud bang from across the table. The sneerer slapped the table hard with the palm of his hand and stared straight into the chairman's face.

'This is the first I've heard of this! What's going on, Laffite?'

Laffite spread out his hands, turned down his mouth on either side, and shook his head. He replied quietly, 'Monsieur Bourassa, you know as well as everybody around this table that we were going ahead with the RFP and we agreed, as a board, that Pair-Tree Capital was the best partner for us.'

'Well, I didn't agree then and I don't agree now. You certainly didn't tell me we were starting construction already! We need to consider these plans more carefully before we forge blindly ahead.' Bourassa sat back with his arms firmly crossed.

'If I remember correctly, Monsieur Bourassa, you were the only director that voted against the motion. Since you only own fifteen percent of this company, you were outvoted. You have to accept that.'

Bourassa's face reddened. 'I don't have to accept starting construction immediately and I certainly object to some brash American barging into this company and throwing their weight around. Typical American behaviour!'

He turned his glare directly across the table to Armstrong. 'When will you people with your big mouths ever learn that you are not superior to the rest of the world?'

Laffite prepared himself to reply, but Armstrong held up his hand to stop him. Armstrong lowered his voice, 'Monsieur Bourassa, I'm so sorry you feel that way, but my company has done everything on the specific instructions of this board. I also understand that there were three other bidders to this RFP, so how have we barged in here? I simply don't understand.'

'Well, I'll tell you. I don't like you or your company! You are asset strippers and don't care a hoot about anyone except to swell your own wallets and sit on your fat arses.'

Monsieur Laffite stood up and shouted, 'Monsieur Bourassa. That's enough! How dare you treat our newest member with such contempt. You are not worthy to be on this board, behaving in such a manner. Apologise right now or I must ask you to leave this meeting.'

'I will do no such thing! In fact, I'll do better than that! I'm selling my shares immediately. This company is going down the toilet. You have my resignation, and I will sell my shares to whom I like.'

Laffite sat down again and, in a soft voice, replied, 'I'm sorry, Monsieur Bourassa, but that is not possible. For any director to sell their shares, they must first be offered to the other members of this board. Our rules then say that each director must approve of the sale to one or several of the other members, before these shares can be offered on the open market.'

Bourassa shook and clenched his fists. 'I will not apologise!'

He scribbled on his pad furiously and handed his resignation to the chairman.

Laffite said firmly, 'Let the minutes state that I have received, and accepted, Monsieur Bourassa's resignation. His fifteen percent share will now be offered to the remaining members of this board. Goodbye, Monsieur Bourassa, and thank you for your past services to this company. I will have all the official paperwork sent to you.'

Bourassa gathered his papers, scowled at everyone, and left the room, slamming the door behind him.

'I'm so sorry, Monsieur Armstrong, that you had to witness that. To be honest with you, the rest of the board members and myself thought something like this might happen. Unfortunately, he has fought us all the way down the line. Bourassa wants to keep everything, as we say, laissez-faire.'

Armstrong puffed out his cheeks and blew out a long breath.

Laffite continued, 'So, gentlemen, we need to ask if any member of this board would like to purchase the fifteen percent shares now available?'

Each board member looked around the oblong table. No hands were raised. The value of the shares had increased considerably in value with Pair-Tree Capital injecting so much more capital into the business.

Armstrong looked up, 'Well, if no one objects, I would like to offer to purchase the shares.'

Laffite waited a few moments. 'The motion before this board is that Pair-Tree Capital buys the fifteen percent available from Monsieur Bourassa. If accepted, this would mean Pair-Tree Capital owns thirty percent of the Marseille Port Authority. Monsieur Armstrong would remain on the board, but because he would have the majority share of the company, myself owning twenty-five percent, and the rest of the members owning fifteen percent each, then the position of chairman will become vacant and be filled by the majority shareholder. Is the resolution clear to each board member?'

A reply in unison came back. 'Yes.'

'All those in favour, please raise your right hand.'

All hands were raised. Laffite continued, 'Motion carried.'

Armstrong glowed. 'Thank you, everyone, for your faith in me. I pledge that I will do everything in my power to make the Marseille Port Authority a world leader in port facilities and performance.'

33

Chapter 33

General Shen presented his Lei Wen passport, identifying him as the Managing Director of Shanghai HVAC Controls, as he passed through Customs and Immigration at Heathrow airport.

'How long will you be staying, Mr Wen?'

'One week. I have business meetings here in London.'

While the immigration officer thumbed through Wen's passport, the security camera behind him took a photo of Shen. It was not able to identify Lei Wen as General Shen. With his passport stamped, General Shen cleared Customs and took a cab to the luxury Connaught Hotel. The taxi made its way through the elegant five story buildings to the corner of Carlos Place and Mount Street in the heart of Mayfair. He checked in and then immediately left for his meeting with Ben Armstrong at the new Pair-Tree Capital office in the Gherkin, located in the financial district.

'Good afternoon, Ben. How are you?'

'Good! It's a pleasure to see you, Lei! Welcome to our new London office.'

'Looks good. This was an unexpected visit, but I have other business here in London, so I thought I would combine everything together.'

'Sure, why not. It's the perfect time for us to meet. I have good news and more good news.'

'Oh?'

'Yes, I just got back from Marseille. Let my assistant get us both coffee and I'll tell you all about it.'

They sat at a glass table in Armstrong's office, looking south-east towards Tower Bridge.

'So, tell me this good news!'

'As you know, we won the tender for the Marseille project by offering to only take a fifteen percent share in the company. The port authority had vastly overstated their value which must have been apparent to every bidder, including us. I also learned that Macrae-Claybourne Logistics put in a bid but wanted a thirty percent share of the business. Frankly, their estimate of the net worth of the Port Authority was bang on. Bottom line, we are in the door!'

'Good job, Ben. That was our prime objective. Did they make any suggested changes to our plans for modifying and upgrading the terminal?'

'No they didn't. Not a single one.'

'Splendid. The plans for the expansion of the deep-water terminal, cargo transit area, handling equipment and rail heads must be complied with. No alterations may be made to the specifications that we supplied you with from Beijing.'

'Yes, that was fully understood from our last discussion.'

'Good! Now what's the other good news?'

'You are never going to believe this, but I have another requisition for more funding for Marseille.' Armstrong almost burst out laughing. 'Another fifteen percent ownership just fell into our laps. I have to say that it was unexpected, but I dived straight in!'

Shen's eyes widened and his face lit up. 'That's the last thing I expected to hear at this stage of the game!'

'But that's not all. I am now the fully elected chairman of the board, being the majority shareholder. Now, Monsieur Laffite, the ex-chairman, owns twenty-five percent and I believe I can persuade him to sell me his share soon. He is near retirement age and clearly can be manipulated. He accepted a free family vacation from me this summer in my house in the Hamptons. He loves the high life!'

'Well done, Ben. You have done well, but how did you acquire the other fifteen percent?'

'One of the other shareholders was clearly against Pair-Tree Capital. He claimed we were asset strippers and would ruin the business and put people out of work!'

Shen laughed out loud. It was one of those rare moments when he let go.

'God, if they only knew the truth!'

****

The black cab waited at the traffic lights on New Cavendish Street to turn right onto Portland Place. Attractive five and six-storey Edwardian buildings lined the wide street, punctuated with mature deciduous trees planted in the central divider.

General Shen paid the cab driver outside the Chinese Embassy. He entered the six-story building through the white stone portico on Portland Place opposite the tall bronze statue of General Sikorski of Poland.

He sat down with the London branch head of security, Peng Zheng, at a conference table in a soundproof room.

The security chief passed a photo to Shen that had obviously been shot from a distance, the image being somewhat grainy. Shen remained quiet for a minute or so, scrutinising the print very carefully. Finally, he looked up.

'It's a possibility it's Stanfield, but a bit of a stretch. The hair, the height and the five o'clock shadow could be disguises. I'm not sure. What makes you think it could be him?'

'Frankly, it's a long shot, but we have been combing through old company records to try to find any businesses that Jack Carter was involved with. Unfortunately, we could not find any until we started to search through the numbered companies. You remember Carter was a former partner of Stanfield before James Macrae killed him. We figured Carter may be involved with other people and Stanfield might know who these people were and used them to help with his escape. We finally found a numbered company that is a transport business owned by a man named Charles Thornton. He was apparently in business with Jack Carter some years ago, so we waited and watched his business. Finally, we got this photograph. We carried out further surveillance, but drew a blank. It seems it is a legitimate business. Charles Thornton has regular employees, one of whom resembles the photo you just saw. It seems he has a family and lives in Stepney. It certainly is not Stanfield. I was instructed from Beijing to do nothing further until you arrived in London.'

'Yes, that is correct. No doubt Stanfield and Nash had help from outside. As head of our security here in the UK, what is your opinion of Stanfield and Nash. Are they still a threat to China?'

'No, I don't believe so. The British and American authorities would have interrogated them thoroughly by now. All their former activities would easily have been exposed by the very evidence that sent them both to prison. There would be nothing further for them to give to the Brits, Europe or the US.'

'Yes, that is my point of view as well. By now, Stanfield must be short of money so that would prevent him from entering shipping business again. Also, China's economic and political relations with the rest of the world have certainly not been affected by the conviction of these men. We still have the usual cordial relations with everyone, even though we follow overseas attachés.'

Shen paused for a few moments. 'I'm thinking Stanfield and Nash could still be useful to us, even if we don't manage to find them.'

The security chief smiled. 'Are you thinking of finishing off James Macrae and making it look like Stanfield and Nash did it for revenge?'

'Exactly. Stanfield and Nash would still have the will and a grudge against this man. My thinking is they would have gone to ground after their escape to plan their next moves, which would include finding money from somewhere to extend their freedom. That said, however, they must be scared we will kill them to shut them up for good. If it was me, I would think that way. Nevertheless, we should still exert every effort to find them.'

The security chief nodded, patting his fingers on the table.

'Yes, we will continue to search for them and, yes, we could certainly frame them to make it look like they finally kill Macrae off.'

Shen frowned and thought some more. He got up and started to roam around the room. Shaking his forefinger in the air, he murmured, 'The trouble is...' He paused again.

'The situation's different now. Macrae Shipping has now been split into two companies. The property assets of the terminals are owned by Macrae Holdings, while operations are now owned by Macrae-Claybourne Logistics or MCLO as they are branded. James Macrae's father, Richard, and his wife Mary own the majority of shares in Macrae Holdings.'

'What if he and his wife met with a fatal accident?'

The security chief tilted his head to one side and thought about it.

'Logically, the shares of Macrae Holdings would fall to James Macrae.'

Shen opened his hands and leaned forward across the table.

'That would be my guess too. So, let's work on a plan to kill Richard and Mary Macrae first. This would be the only path for getting hold of the actual property that the Macrae-Claybourne operations work from. That's an essential step for China.'

Zheng nodded. 'Yes, and I have a specially trained team that we use for undercover operations. I can put them at your disposal. Mr Ming has made it clear that I am to give you any resources that you might need.'

Shen started to rock backward and forward on his feet and continued, 'Excellent! Then we could kill James Macrae and make it look as though Stanfield and Nash are behind it. From past encounters with these two in China, we can even plant their DNA at the scene! China would be clear of all suspicion.'

'This is a workable plan, General.'

Shen continued to pace around in front of the conference

table.

'After the Macraes are dead, we will take over all strategically located terminals through our mergers and acquisitions company, Pair-Tree Capital. The financial incentives that we will offer to do this will be too generous to refuse.'

'This is doable.'

'Yes, once we've got Istanbul, we can control access to and from the Black Sea. That means we have a grip on the Russians. With the other terminals we can take control of all of southern Europe and North Africa. Our silk road will be unstoppable.'

34

Chapter 34

The stereo blasted out the words of the Dylan song just as James pulled into work. They suggested that nothing could hold him down.

He had played the song 'Pressing On' just one more time. While he certainly wasn't a religious man, his mood had lifted exponentially. He smiled, grabbed his briefcase, and went to his office.

'Hi, Rachel, you're in early.'

'Yes, I had to drop my husband off early for work as his car is in for a service. When will you go back to Wales? You're supposed to be on holiday, you know!'

'Yeah, I know. I've got a meeting with one of the detectives working on the Brixton prison escape first thing and then one with Janet. After that I'm going to finish the last few days of my holiday back in Wales.'

'Oh, I'm glad you will get a chance to get back with your family. That's good. Just a sec!' She lifted her phone. 'Oh! Your visitor is here already, in Reception.'

'Great. She can come straight up.'

****

'Good morning, Mr Macrae.'

DI Hudson entered James's office. She looked fit, alert and oozed a 'down to business' demeanour. For her, the devil was in the details. She was a relentless pursuer of the truth.

'Good morning, Inspector Hudson. We finally meet. How can I help?'

'Well firstly, I want you to know that we have a full team working 24/7 to find Stanfield and Nash. We believe they had outside help for their escape, so we're looking for links to likely suspects. I have some photographs I'd like you to look at. We know that you visited the Anglo-Asian Freight offices and also spent some time at the Beaver and Bulldog last year and wanted to know if you've seen any of these people before?'

She spread a number of photos on his desk.

James studied each of them carefully. His mind filtered through the images in his memory, but, finally, he looked up.

'No. I'm sorry, I can't say I recognise any of these faces.'

'What about anything unusual since Stanfield and Nash escaped? Have you or your family noticed anyone hanging around or anything like that?'

James shook his head. 'No, none of us have. My family is habitually vigilant after the events last year. Regarding the company, we stepped up our alert level across every branch and terminal once we heard of the escape. Again, there has been no suspicious activity.' He did not say anything about the faulty containers, firstly because he believed the police would not be able to prove anything and secondly, he wanted to plant the sabotaged containers back in Chinese hands.

Hudson continued. 'What about all the negative press

you've been getting. Could that be linked to Stanfield and Nash, do you think?'

'That's a good question. As it happens, I've spoken with MI6 about this already. We believe these stories are originating in China. I would suggest you speak to them. There's quite a history there. I can give you the name of the agent. Of course, we have taken legal action and launched a defamation lawsuit against *Mercantile News*.'

'Yes, I saw that. But do you think that these reports have anything to do with Stanfield and Nash directly?'

'I would think not. My guess would be that they would be too focussed on more direct action rather than a disinformation campaign such as this.'

'Thank you, Mr Macrae. Just one more thing. We are also focussing on any companies that Stanfield, Nash and Carter were involved in. Are you aware of any at all?'

James thought for a moment. 'Apart from Anglo-Asian Freight and the Beaver and Bulldog, I'm not aware of any other.'

Hudson stood up. 'Okay, thank you, Mr Macrae. If you do think of anything, anything at all, please let us know.'

James watched her leave from the office window above. Her shoulders were slightly slumped, not quite as straight as when she entered his office. James murmured to himself, *'no point in talking to her about the leaked software or sabotaged containers. Too much bureaucracy and political bullshit to deal with. We can move faster than either the police or the government.'*

He turned around and spoke aloud to himself,

'No. This time I'm going to do it my way!'

****

Janet Rushton sat alone in her car, parked away from work. Her clothes were ruffled, and her shoulder length blonde hair was not as tidy as it normally was. She picked up her burner phone and punched in a number from memory.

'Shad. Can you talk?'

Shad was a man of few words. They had known each other from their early teens; computers being the common interest between them. With their close friendship, their trust in each other was implicit. He was a brilliant self-employed computer programmer and worked from his home in West London for a number of different clients.

'Yes, I can. It's a safe line.'

'So, what's your plan?'

'I've studied your software and will write the malware program also in C. I will develop a polymorphic virus called Chameleon, except that it will be modified and enhanced to a degree that has never been used before. In turn, this virus will work in conjunction with a network virus that will travel through all network connections and replicate itself through shared resources.'

'That's good. Can we be sure it will not be detected by any anti-virus software?'

'Don't worry. This virus relies on mutation engines to alter its decryption routines every time it infects a machine. This way, traditional security solutions may not easily catch it because they do not use a static, unchanging code. The use of complex mutation engines that generate billions of decryption routines make them even more difficult to detect.'

'So, what happens then?'

'Once the virus has been triggered, destructive payloads are launched throughout all program files. It then becomes a multipartite virus that infects computer systems multiple times and at different times. Bottom line, when combined with other malicious routines, polymorphic viruses pose even greater risk to its victims.'

'Brilliant. Can we be sure that it will spread fast, cause complete destruction and cannot be traced back to us?'

'Come on, Janet! You know me!'

'Sorry. I should know that! Listen, I've got a meeting to go to but I'll work from home for the next few days so we can work on this together.'

****

'Hi, Janet, let's chat. Chris is in Immingham today.' Janet came into James's office and closed the door.

James stood up to his full height of six foot two. They sat around his conference table.

Janet lowered her voice. 'Okay, James. The wheels are in motion. I will work with Shad to bury multiple viruses into a copy of our entire logistics system. It'll be better if I work from home on this.'

'I agree. How long will it take?'

'I'm thinking a couple of weeks. We have to make sure our hybrid virus can be buried so deep that it can't be spotted. And then it has to be perfect. We will only have one chance to get this right.'

'Yes, we do. God knows what would happen if we were ever found out!'

'I spoke with Shad this morning and I have utmost faith in him. Don't forget I'll be with him every step of the way. The viruses will be designed to trigger chaos at key decision points and then splinter afterwards, leading to a multitude of actions downstream that would affect each stage of the logistics programs at every step in every port. It will be impossible to reverse the chain of chaos that it will create. Like a soft-nosed bullet, once it hits the main target, it will splinter into a million pieces that cannot be retrieved or reversed.'

James closed his eyes and just shook his head.

'Wow, Janet.'

'In short, James, we are creating a logistics software bomb of seismic proportions.'

****

James grabbed a set of the latest financials and stuffed them in his briefcase. He was just about to leave the office and return to Wales when Lisa Taylor stuck her head around his door. Lisa had lost weight over the past year. Her pear shaped body was not so pronounced as it had been. James wondered if she had lost the weight deliberately after her divorce or was it due to increased stress?

'Can I see you for a minute, James?'

'Sure, come on in. What's up?'

'Well, it's to do with the software that Shanghai claims to have. I believe I know who the traitor is. It pains me to say it because it was me who hired him. I've found out that screens shots a copy of one of the databases that we use has been copied from Lee's machine onto a recordable CD. I think he must be giving the Chinese this information.'

'Have you spoken to Janet about this?'

'No, I haven't. She's just gone home. That's why I came to you.'

'Thank you. I appreciate you telling me. Could Lee copy all the separate databases that go to make up the whole system?'

'No. He doesn't have access to every database. Each separate database is restricted, and permissions based. Janet controls the administration of the entire system. I know she keeps all usernames and passwords off-site.'

'Okay, I will contact Janet, but, in the meantime, Lisa, what do you think we should do?'

'I think you need to speak to Lee Yuen.'

'I agree. Is there anything further we should do?'

'Yes there is. As Janet is working on a special project at home, let me have access to all the databases so I can ensure they are secure. Janet needs to have a back-up in case anything ever happened to her. Then I can take over immediately if ever we have a problem.'

'Good idea. Let me contact Janet at home and I'll get back to you. I'm also going to get hold of Lee Yuen.'

After Lisa had left the office, James called Chris and Janet on their cell phones on a three-way call.

'Just had an interesting conversation with Lisa. She came to me to say that Lee is the one leaking the screen shots and a database to the Chinese. She apparently discovered the software had been copied on his machine. She said she would have told you, Janet but, of course, she knows you are out of the office.'

Janet replied, 'I thought this might happen sooner or later. As we said before, this doesn't mean Lee is the traitor. It still could be Lisa, Lee or Paul Adams.'

'I agree,' said James. 'I think I need to reach out again to our PI, Scott Farmer to investigate all three. We will need to work fast while you work with Shad. If we can find out who the leaker is, we can use them to deliver our malware present and ram it straight down the throat of our hybrid enemy.'

******

James finally left to resume his holiday in Wales at lunchtime. As the gently undulating fields of Shropshire subsided away into the hills and mountains of the Welsh countryside, James drove with his window down taking in deep breathes of the fresh air. The sky was hazy and the weather warm as he pulled up in front of his house in the late afternoon. As he opened his door and stepped onto the gravel courtyard in front of the house, he spotted his father's new maroon BMW 5 series E39 parked in the garage.

Sarah came out with her apron on, patting the flour off it.

'You made it!'

She hugged him and they kissed as though they hadn't seen each other for years.

'Yes, thank goodness I can get some time with you all. How is everybody?'

'We're all well and it's great having Richard and Mary stay with us. They're all down on the beach right now while I prepare dinner.'

James opened the back door of his Range Rover and produced a bunch of flowers. He grabbed his suitcase at the same time.

'Oh, James. Thank you!' She hugged him again.

As they walked through the front door, more of their belongings had been unpacked from boxes.

'You've been busy, I see.'

'Yes, Richard and Mary have lent a hand. It's given me a bit of extra time to do some jobs while they play with the children. All in all, I think we've got this place pretty well how we want it. Tell you what, why don't you go and join them on the beach and then we can have dinner afterwards?'

James got changed into his shorts and T shirt and went down the cliff path towards the beach. He stood for a few moments, savouring the view of his parents down below playing tag with the children in the sand. It was so good to see his mum and dad enjoying their retirement with their grandchildren, especially after his father's heart trouble.

He kicked off his sandals and felt the warm dry granules of sand filter between his toes. The sound of the waves added to his sense of contentment. He hugged everyone and joined in the game.

'Just in time, James!' his mother called out. 'I don't think we've got any more energy left!'

As they climbed the cliff path back to the house, Olivia asked, 'Nana, why do you use a stick?'

'Well, that's my hiking stick. It helps me when I walk over rough ground.'

Olivia thought for a moment. 'Are you like an old granny?'

Mary and Richard laughed. There was nothing like children to keep you young.

They all sat round the dining room table enjoying the shepherd's pie Sarah had made.

'Are we having apple pie and ice cream afterwards, Mum?' asked Mia.

'Oh yes. It's gramps's favourite,' Sarah replied.

'Mine too,' said Mia, smiling and looking up into Richard's eyes.

Richard winked back at Mia and then looked at everyone.

'Got to say, James and Sarah, this house is gorgeous. The views are spectacular, especially the sunsets over the sea. Doesn't matter what season it is, it will be a wonderful family home. It's certainly great for the children.'

Sarah smiled. 'It was meant to be. We'd only just decided we needed a bigger place when my mom and dad's friends wanted to downsize. If this place had ever hit the open market, it would have been gone in a flash.'

Mary lifted up her wine glass. 'Well, it's about time we had a run of good luck in the family. These past couple of years have been challenging, to say the least! Here's to all our health and happiness!'

35

Chapter 35

Charlie Thornton descended the steep four-lane highway towards the docks at Dover. He applied the engine brake to retard the momentum from the weight of the empty tank trailer pushing his Scania tractor unit forward. He would complete a test run to Brussels, pick up a load of liquid containing low-level radioactive medical waste and return to London with a full load ready for waste treatment.

Thornton braked to negotiate the roundabout at the bottom of the hill. He followed the road signs for Reservations. Next, he pulled up on the weighbridge and printed the gross vehicle weight of his truck and trailer and then followed the sign for Check-In P&O Ferries.

Pulling up in front of the kiosk, the lady behind the window immediately said, 'I know you. You normally come through here with a fridge-van trailer. How come you are now pulling a special ISO tank container?'

'Yes, I know. We've just got a new contract for taking back medical waste to the UK for reprocessing.'

'Okay, let's get you checked in. I will need to see your passport, HGV licence and reservation. Are you empty now?

'Yes, I am. Here are the papers and receipt for the tank purge and here is my Dangerous Goods Certification. I have all the necessary paperwork in this folder.'

The lady went through the paperwork meticulously. Thornton remained in his cab with the engine turned off. This was regular procedure. He had done it hundreds of times before, but this was his first time hauling dangerous goods.

'There you go, love. Everything is in order. Here's your barcode ticket for Lane 198.'

'Thank you. Much appreciated. See you again soon.'

Thornton followed the well-laid-out truck lanes and pulled his truck into lane ready to embark on the ferry. He entered the ferry, driving down the large ramp, and parked his truck inside the cavernous hold amongst all the other trucks.

At Calais, he set the cruise control at the designated speed limit of 90kph. He wandered into his thoughts. As a hardened criminal he had committed every crime known, or so he thought, and now he was into the crime of human smuggling, a completely new venture. Once there was enough money in the kitty, he was going to call it a day. It seemed inconceivable that he had avoided any kind of criminal charges, but he had done it. After all these years, he was ready to call it quits. It was tough to keep looking over your shoulder all the time. His friendship with Jack Carter and Stanfield went back years; to their upbringing in Bethnal Green when they stole coats and belongings from cloakrooms and sold them in the East End market. They had remained loyal to each other and had watched each other's backs on the mean streets of London. As for Dan Nash, he didn't care for him; nor did he trust him.

Had Stanfield not held him back, Nash would have been at the bottom of the river Thames by now. He was not worth one-third of the takings.

Thornton followed the E40 and R20 highways and covered the journey in just over two and a half hours. This was the quickest route, rather than take the ferry from Dover to Zeebrugge. He had always heard that Brussels was a beautiful city, but his approach on the six-lane divided highway with banks of grass and trees gave him no sense of what the city was really like. He followed the detailed instructions he had been given by the new customer. Closer to the hospital, he drove carefully on much narrower roads, lined by a mixture of old and new apartments, offices and shops.

Arriving at the cancer hospital complex of the Jules Bordet Institute in Brussels, he pulled inside an older building containing bays for all the waste trucks. This hospital was the central gathering point for all the medical waste from the surrounding regional hospitals. He had to enter loading bay 1. A diminutive man with greying hair and alert eyes greeted him. The man wore a white coat, gloves and hard hat. He checked his clip board as Thornton descended from his cab.

'Good afternoon, Mr...?'

'Thornton, Charlie Thornton.' They shook hands.

'So, Mr Thornton, I'm Pierre Bourellier. I trust you had no trouble finding us?'

'No. Thank you. Your instructions were perfect.'

'That's good, because it is a little tight to bring trucks in of this size so close to the city. There are plans for a brand-new hospital to be built to the west of the city, in the Anderlecht district, but that's probably years away.'

'This is no problem for us. That's why we are using twenty-foot containers instead of forty.'

'Good. So, I am the hospital waste supervisor and have been certified by the EU as a Dangerous Goods Certified Professional and can seal the load with an EU customs seal. Let's go into my office so we can check the paperwork.'

Thornton followed the man into the office and took a seat in front of his desk. He believed this part would flush out any weaknesses that they had in their future plans. His file contained his own dangerous goods handling certification, driver licence, passport and trailer manufacturer's ADR certification for carrying the classification of waste, UN 3291. He also had with him all the necessary signage that would be placed on the truck showing exactly what he was carrying.

'Wait here, please. I will return when I have inspected your equipment.'

'Yes, Monsieur Bourellier.'

Thornton waited in the office looking agonisingly through the window to the loading bay. He stood up from his chair and fiddled with his ignition keys in his pocket, constantly swapping his weight from one foot to the other. Bourellier checked the trailer VIN number and manufacturer's plates. Next, he climbed onto the top of the tank container and visually inspected inside each top hatch. Following that he checked each waste valve underneath the tank and then he went inside through the purging hatch.

'Well, Mr Thornton, everything is in perfect order. I must say that the tank manufacturer knows their business. Those baffles in the tank are extremely robust.'

Thornton let out an inner sigh of relief. He tried to hold his breathe back instead of letting out a huge gasp.

'Yes, we chose the best equipment we could for this contract.'

'Your rates are very competitive. The business is complicated and costly, especially conforming to EU regulation.'

'Excellent, we are an established transportation company, and we pride ourselves on our professionalism. By the way, we have another identical trailer built at the same time as this one. As well as me, we will use one of our most senior and qualified drivers to pick up your waste. The next time I come, which I believe is next week, he will be with me when we ramp up the disposal of your waste.'

'Good. I have to say, this is the first time in a long time any company has come in with the correct paperwork right off the bat. We had to terminate the previous company contract because of poor paperwork, and I will not jeopardise my credentials and that of the hospital organisation by letting people be sloppy. It's either right or wrong in my book.'

'Excellent. We have the same culture in our company.'

'Good, that's settled. Now let's get you loaded up and on your way.'

Returning to the port of Calais, Thornton drove through the X-ray scanner, heat and carbon dioxide sensors without incident. Customs checked the seal on the trailer, paperwork and signage. He checked in at the P&O office once more and boarded. By midday the following day, he had offloaded the waste, purged the tank clean and returned to the depot.

Once inside the warehouse with the doors closed, Stanfield and Nash sat down with Thornton.

'So how did it go, Charlie?' asked Stanfield.

'No problems at all, although the next time we go, I want Dan to drive the second truck, but we will keep it empty just to be on the safe side. The hospital supervisor is very thorough, and he will certainly want to inspect the second trailer. I will have people in my tank, but Dan can't have any for his first run.'

'That's settled, then. We'll be careful. This venture is too profitable to jeopardise right from the start.'

****

'Have you terminated your relationship with the Chinese, Lee?'

'Yes I have, Mom. They were very angry.'

'Of course they were angry! They wanted to use you as a spy.'

Lee Yuen looked down, walking slowly along the pleasantly winding paths between the plots of neatly cut grass and shrubbery beds in High Park, Birmingham, together with his mother, Jinni.

Chestnuts, ashes, laburnums, limes and other trees had been planted to make it look like a well-tended garden. It was a Sunday afternoon, and they were enjoying the early autumn weather. Leaves on the tops of the trees were starting to change to attractive russet reds and golds. The slight chill in the air gave a hint to the approaching season.

Jinni continued. 'Remember, you should have done this without my insistence. One of the reasons we left Hong Kong, before it is handed back to China, was fear of the future. Not that we know anything bad will happen, but when the chance came for us to emigrate, I took it. I needed to give you a better start in life than I had.'

'Well, I'm not going to screw it up again. This has been a big lesson for me.'

'Just live within your means, Lee. You will find yourself much happier in life.'

36

Chapter 36

'I hope I'm doing the right thing. What we're about to do scares the hell out of me!'

'Listen, Huan, we've gone over this a thousand times. How much more proof do you need! They're seizing the assets of successful entrepreneurs like you every day. Look at your friends who got rich and powerful and now they've lost everything. Some of them are even behind bars. That could be us! Who knows, our business might have been taken over already.'

Huan sighed. 'Yes, you're right. Let's wake the children up and get on with it. At least with the money we've transferred, we can start a new life in England.'

Huan Zhou hugged his wife Li Mei tightly and whispered, 'I'm scared.'

She whispered back, 'Me too, but we have to do this for our children's sake.'

They gathered up their two children, Kai, a bright ten-year-old girl and their son, Liang, six. Kai had long black hair and had a very pretty face. Liang had shorter black hair and looked more studious with his round glasses.

'Shhhh. We're going on an adventure, we all have to be very quiet.'

They gently closed the door of their Brussels hotel room. With two small rucksacks, Huang and Li Mei led their two children along the corridor, both holding their soft toys.

They had left China a week before on an organised ten-day sightseeing tour of Europe. Huan Zhou owned an electronics company that had grown and prospered significantly under Deng Xiaoping's economic initiatives. He had become increasingly paranoid as the Chinese Communist Party had been carrying out extra audits and inspections of his company recently. After discussing everything with his wife, they decided they could not wait to see what would happen to them and made the decision to start a new life by escaping to England.

At 5:00 a.m. they left their room and slipped through a side door of the Bedford hotel, close to the centre of Brussels. The early morning light was just beginning to break across the rooftops of the historic city centre. There was a slight chill in the air.

An unmarked white minibus stood across the street from them. Zhou approached the driver and simply said, 'Tourist bus 11?'

The driver nodded his head in response. He opened the sliding side door to admit them. Once inside, he checked each passport but did not engage in conversation. Satisfied, he drove silently though the quiet streets and made his way to a warehouse in the South Charleroi Industrial Park. Thornton had rented a smaller warehouse adjacent to the main industrial estate. It would enable them to bring in each shipment of clients unseen, load them into the trailers safely and then depart to pick up the medical waste. He had chosen this location as there were heavy trucks and trailers going back and forth twenty-four hours a day. Also, if they needed to pull the pin and escape quickly, there were excellent road, rail and inland waterways connected to the ports of Rotterdam, Antwerp and Le Havre. As a seasoned criminal he always had an escape plan. It had served him well over the years, having never been arrested.

Huan and his family shivered as they left the minibus.

Liang looked up tilting his head and furrowing his brow. 'Daddy, where are we going?'

Huan stopped and crouched down in front of Kai and Liang. 'It's a game of hide and seek, so we must be very quiet. Some other people will play the game with us. Okay?'

Kai and Liang nodded.

Once safely inside the warehouse, Zhou and his family were joined by two other well-dressed Chinese couples and two men. They had very little baggage with them. Inside the warehouse, the ten were marshalled together in a small room without windows. A Chinese man entered and held up his hand to gain attention from the group. He spoke in Mandarin: 'Welcome, everyone. Please listen carefully to what I say. Following these instructions will help ensure your success of entering the United Kingdom. You must remain quiet at all times. Our means of transporting our clients is secret and varies all the time. We will not tell you how you are being transferred. Are there any questions so far?'

Huan Zhou raised his hand. 'How long will the journey take?'

'It is possible it could take up to twenty-four hours.'

There was an audible gasp from the group.

The speaker raised both hands and then lowered them slowly.

'Please, do not worry! There will be sufficient water and dried food for you. From time to time, the light inside will go out and the fan will stop, but there is no reason to panic. You will have plenty of fresh air. Please ensure you visit the bathroom here before the next stage of the transfer.' He paused and then continued, 'For those of you who may suffer from anxiety, we have sedatives to help calm you. In a few moments you will be blindfolded and must remain here. One last thing. I will take your cell phones. Let me have them now.'

Huan and Li Mei blindfolded their children, whispering, 'This is going to be fun!'

The group, blindfolded, heard the doors of the warehouse opening and the sound of a truck entering. They were led hand-in-hand and carefully loaded through the hatch at the bottom of the tank. Once inside the secret compartment, they crouched down and took off their blindfolds. Inside the confined space, the group exchanged nervous glances at each other. A few tried to smile. The door to the lead room was closed, locked and sealed behind the baffle wall.

'Where are we, Daddy?'

Huan whispered quietly, 'It's a secret room so we all have to be quiet and patient.'

'Will there be a prize at the end of the game?' Liang asked.

'Oh yes, you and Kai will have a big surprise.'

Outside the tank, Charlie Thornton stepped down from his truck cab and handed the man a handful of cash.

'How did it go?'

'So far, no problems. They only saw me and the minibus

driver. The disguises are good.'

'Good! Next time we will load two trailers. This is a test run. All being well, we will be back in three days. That's when the next group arrives. Okay, lock up and make sure the minibus stays here inside the warehouse.'

As Thornton left the warehouse, Nash started up his truck, parked close by, and followed Thornton's tanker. They carefully followed a network of roads to the Jules Bordet Institute located in Brussels to load the medical waste into each trailer.

Once at the hospital, Nash followed him slowly into the waste bays at the rear of the hospital. He applied the air brakes, stepped down from his cab and stood by his vehicle.

Monsieur Borrellier emerged from his office.

'Good morning, Mr Thornton. I just need to check the VIN number of your trailer. As long as it is the same one as before, we can get you loaded straight away. For the second tanker, I will need to do a full inspection like the last time.'

'Of course! Go ahead.' As he said that, Bourellier looked over at Nash.

'I also need to see your driver's papers as well.' He looked at Nash, squinted his eyes and thought for a second.

'This is the driver you spoke of the last time?'

'Yes, that's him. Been with us for over fifteen years. He doesn't say much. He's a man of few words!'

'Oh? There's something vaguely familiar about him.'

Thornton quickly changed the subject. 'His trailer is exactly the same spec as mine, same manufacturer.'

'Good, let's get the inspection done and get you on your way.'

Bourellier carried out the inspection on Nash's trailer.

'Excellent!'

As both trailers were filled up with the contaminated medical waste, Nash remained at a distance from Thornton and Bourellier.

Inside the secret compartment, the overhead light went out and the air flow stopped. There was a cry of surprise. Huang and Li Mei held both children tightly to them. In the blackness, the faint sound of running liquid was heard. It felt like they were prisoners at the bottom of a well and would be drowned, slowly gasping for air with no way of escape. Muffled cries accelerated a sense of panic.

Someone made a 'shhhhing' sound, and all went quiet again.

****

Bourellier produced an EU customs seal for each tank trailer and attached the heavy-duty steel bolt coated with a yellow weather-resistant anti-corrosive plastic though the holes in the opening hatch catches. He clicked the bolt into the sealed barrel, forming a one-time lock and tamper-proof seal. Next, he took the identification numbers of the seals and inserted it onto each Bill of Lading.

He handed the completed paperwork back to Thornton. 'See you in three days.'

Thornton opened the door of his cab to get in. His eyes widened as he saw the switch in the downward position that worked the fans and lights in the trailer. He must have hit it with his knee when he got out. He quickly flicked the switch up again, hoping no damage had been done.

****

As Thornton and Nash left the hospital bays, Nash's rear wheel fenders clipped a concrete stanchion. Bourellier looked up, hearing the loud screeching noise. Something was bothering him. It took him a few minutes to work out what it was; Thornton had said that the driver was very experienced.

37

Chapter 37

‘Mrs Macrae?’

‘Yes, this is Mary Macrae.’

‘Good morning, Mrs Macrae. This is Denise from Central LPG Gas. We need to make an appointment for a safety inspection. According to our records you have a five-year-old 500-gallon propane tank which needs to be recertified before we can refill it. The inspector will also need to enter your house to inspect the gas lines from the outside tank and regulator to your gas burners inside your basement. He has to do what is called a "drop test". The whole visit should be done in less than an hour. When would it be convenient for him to come?’

‘Well, we’re home this week. I guess any day would do.’

‘Okay. How about Thursday at 3:00 p.m.?’

‘That would be fine.’

‘Good. The inspector’s name is Don Griffiths. We’ll see you then.’

‘Thank you, goodbye.’

****

The Central LPG Gas company service van pulled up on the driveway in front of the Macraes' bungalow. The driver, dressed in a Central Gas uniform, approached the house and knocked on the front door.

'Mr Macrae? I'm Don Griffiths. I'm here to inspect your propane tank, regulator and lines.'

'Ah, yes. My wife told me you were coming today. I think the tank is still about one quarter full. Can I see your credentials?'

'Of course! Here's my company and Gas Council certification.'

Richard Macrae checked the photograph of the inspector and the certification. 'I hope you don't mind me checking, but you have to be so careful these days.'

'Not at all, Mr Macrae. More people should do that. I'll start outside with the tank.'

'Go ahead. When you've finished, just knock on the door and I'll show you where the pipes enter the basement to the furnace.'

The inspector took out his tool bag and went to the propane tank, situated about twenty feet away from the side of the house. He inspected the exterior and all the seam welds together with the input valve. Next, he traced the pipe from the regulator to the side of the house.

The inspector knocked on the door. As Richard opened it, the inspector said, 'All is good outside.' He followed Richard inside the house.

In the basement, the inspector turned off the main inlet gas valve and then attached a pressure gauge to the pipe. Richard stood beside him. Next, he turned the main gas valve on again.

The gauge needle moved sharply up around the dial.

'Good. That's normal. Okay, now I have to go and shut off the valve on the outside tank and then wait for fifteen minutes. I'll be back after that. It's always a good time for me to do my paperwork while I wait in the van.'

'Okay. Give me a shout when you need to come back in.'

After just over fifteen minutes, the inspector came back to the door.

'Great, thanks, Mr Macrae. Okay, let's check to see if there's been any pressure drop.'

He checked the gauge.

'Nope. We're good.'

He disconnected the pressure gauge and reconnected the inlet pipe to the furnace. Keeping his body between the burners and Richard, he gently loosened the valve to one of the burners.

'Great. I just have to turn on the outside cylinder valve and we're done. Can you sign this for me please?'

Richard checked the work order after the inspector had inserted the readings from the drop test, signed and dated it.

'Thank you, Mr Macrae. I just have to attach a Gas Utilisation Regulation Pressure Test tag to the furnace, and we're done. You're good for another five years. I'm off now for the day. I've got tickets for the Aston Villa game tonight against Birmingham City. I'm a Villa supporter, but, to be honest, I don't know which team is worse these days!'

'Ah yes, the famous local derby. It's sad, isn't it? There aren't enough swear words to describe either of them nowadays. Take care.'

****

Later that night, Richard got up from his chair in front of the TV. He looked tired and pale.

'I'm getting a bit of a headache, I think I'll go to bed.'

Mary replied, 'Yes, I think I'll do the same.'

They lay in the dark for some time. Then Richard started to snore, keeping Mary awake. She thought she could smell gas. She lay there for a few more moments, then decided to go and check. She leaned over to flick the bedside light on. There was a massive flash and explosion. An erupting ball of fire came up through the floor beneath them. She was blinded by the flash as two outside walls of the bungalow were completely blown out. The ball of fire leaped high into the air.

Neither Mary nor Richard saw that.

38

Chapter 38

Dan Nash cursed himself for clipping the concrete stanchion after leaving the loading bay. He was supposed to be an experienced HGV driver and it didn't look good. He saw Bourellier in his side-view mirror look up when the screeching crunch occurred. He sensed Bourellier felt that something wasn't right about him. It was as though he had partially recognised him.

After a nearly three-hour drive, he followed Thornton onto the English Channel P&O ferry at Calais. Nash braked and followed Thornton slowly through the x-ray, heat sensors and CO_2 channel checks at Calais. The harbour terminal was busy with end-to-end trucks coming and going. He smiled as they passed through the checks, alarms remaining silent.

They both stopped for paperwork checks; having the correct hazmat signage meant no alarm bells were raised.

As they parked inside the huge, cavernous vehicle bay of the ferry, Thornton came up to Dan and whispered, 'We may have a mess on our hands.'

'Why?'

'When I got out of the truck at the hospital I must have turned off the air and light to the trailer.'

'So what? We've got their money.'

'We'll just have to find a quiet spot and dump 'em.'

'Yep. Better luck next time.'

****

Huan Zhou breathed deeply, trying to relax after the harrowing experience of near suffocation and the feeling of terror in the darkness. He tried to sip water and, as he did so, noticed the others taking in deep breaths. He checked his watch yet again. How could time go by so slowly? By now they had been inside the compartment for over five hours. Acute cramp spasms reverberated up his right leg. Would it be worth it? He started to breathe rapidly again. Eventually, the gradual rocking motion enabled him to doze off. When he opened his eyes, he saw his wife, children and others doing the same.

Huan noticed the rocking motion of the trailer stop. Everyone inside tried to move their limbs as best as they could. Still, no one spoke. After about two hours, Huan felt a sudden movement of the trailer. He smelled diesel fumes. Did this mean they had crossed the channel and were leaving the ferry? He had an idea it might be and gave his family a renewed squeeze. Kai and Liang smiled weakly back at him. Liang continually stroked her hair to one side, while Kia's eyes darted from side to side.

Surely they must be there by now? Huan felt his earlier optimism starting to vanish. The endless journey was starting to get to him. Li Mei took his hand. Huan closed his eyes and slid back into his crouching position once more. He put his head in his arms and sobbed without sound. e started H

****

Thornton and Nash entered the vast medical waste management centre in Greenwich just before midnight. Damp mist from the river Thames crawled over the whole complex. Yellow sodium lights scattered around the buildings, pipework, tanks and chimney stacks gave it an eery, almost science fiction appearance. Steam from exhaust valves periodically spurted out into the dark sky above.

As one of the few EU-approved facilities in Europe, they operated around the clock. A secure and fenced-off town within a city.

Thornton and Nash stood back from their vehicles as waste disposal officers connected the waste pumps to the tankers.

Huan jerked and came to from his semi-conscious state. He heard the gurgling of the liquid again and immediately perked up. Something must be happening soon. Would they ever be able to get out of their tomb?

The night foreman approached Nash. 'There you go. Here's your waste paperwork and receipts. See you next time.'

'Thanks, guv.'

Thornton signalled to Dan to follow him again.

Once they had emptied their tanks, they drove east to the rear of Beckton Sewage Treatment Works. It was a secluded, dark service road close to the University of East London and London City Airport.

Thornton and Nash jumped down for their cabs. Pale residual lighting from the sewage works would give them enough light to open the tank hatches.

Thornton rubbed his neck. 'This could be gruesome Dan. I'm not sure if we are going to have to dump ten bodies here?'

Nash shrugged his shoulders. 'So what? If we do, we do. Let's get on with it!'

Huan Zhou heard the panel to their compartment slide open. Huan helped Kai and Liang to their feet. They inched their way out to the hatch at the bottom of the tanker and managed to unfold themselves and stand shakily on the ground.

It was cool and dark. They stood clutching each other shivering intently.

Huan looked up to the sky and spoke quietly, almost to himself. 'We've done it. We're here.'

Li Mei bent down to hug Kai and Liang and cried.

Thornton was relieved. At least there would not be a mess to clean up. He spoke quietly to the ten illegal immigrants.

'Wait here, you will be picked up and dropped off in London.'

******

As Thornton and Nash drove their rigs back to the transport yard, Billy Blowtorch was there to open the gates. The outer gate and warehouse doors were then immediately closed. Inside the warehouse, Thornton and Nash dropped down from their cabs and stretched their bodies. Stanfield was waiting to meet them.

'That was a bloody close one, Hugh! I nearly killed them!'

Stanfield hissed: 'Shut up, you two! Listen carefully. Billy and I spotted two surveillance vehicles earlier. This place is being watched and we could be raided anytime. It's too late for us to get out of here now. Our best chance is for us to hide in here and hope for the best! Dan, you and I need to get inside one of the trailers and hide now. We have one of the other drivers, Harry, in bed in the apartment up stairs. Charlie, you need to lock us both inside the trailer and then get in the other bed quick. Billy, sleep in the front office. Go!'

At 4:00 a.m. a battering ram was used crash through the yard gates and the warehouse door. Heavily armed police officers with bullet-proof vests entered the warehouse and swarmed in. Billy looked up from his camp-bed and raised his hands. Officers ran up to the apartment.

'What the fuck!'

Thornton sat up in bed and stared at the man in front of him.

'Get up you, two! Now!'

Thornton and Harry did as they were told. With guns on them, they raised their hands as they stood.

'DCI Thomas and this is DI Hudson, Metropolitan Police. Where's Stanfield and Nash?'

Thornton squinted and looked confused. So did Harry. Spreading out his hands either side of him, Thornton pretended to shake off sleep.

'What the fuck is this all about?'

'You know very well!'

'I'm sorry, but I don't.'

' I wanted every inch searched.'

Turning back to Thornton, he continued, 'Now, you can either answer all my questions now or come back to the station. What's it to be?'

'I've got nothing to hide.'

Thornton and Harry sat down at the kitchen table. Thomas remained standing while Hudson took a chair opposite and produced a notebook. Meanwhile a fingerprint team spread out and got to work.

'Before we start, I hope you have a search warrant before you rip my place apart!'

'Of course!'

'Then let me see it!'

Hudson pulled out a sheet of paper from her pocket.

'Why?'

'Let's start at the beginning, shall we? You used to know Jack Carter?'

'Many years ago.'

'So, what's the story?'

Thornton shrugged. 'What's all this about?'

'Just answer the question. You knew Jack Carter, didn't you?'

'Years ago, he and I set up this business as partners, but it was basically a one-man show.'

Thomas remained silent. There was a long pause until Thomas spread out his hands as if to say, 'What does that mean?'

Thornton continued. 'It was me doing all the work. Not him. We fell out not long after and I bought him out. We hadn't seen each other since then. He went off and did his own thing with his pub. I heard he'd been killed.'

'But you know Stanfield and Nash?'

'No.'

'Of course you do. If you knew Carter, you would know Stanfield.'

'I don't! Do I need a lawyer?'

Thomas ignored the question and leaned over the table towards Thornton. 'Don't lie to me!'

'Listen, I read the papers like everyone else. Of course I

know who they are. Other than that, no, I don't know them. Why would you think I know them and why would you think they were here?'

Thomas gave Thornton a hard, intimidating look.

'I'll ask the questions, not you!'

'If you worked with Jack Carter then you must have known of his friendship with Stanfield?'

'Actually, no, I didn't at the time. I've only learned about his relationship with Stanfield through the newspaper reports of the trial last year. After Carter and I split up, we never had anything to do with each other.'

'Why did you split with him in the first place?'

'I told you. I did all the work to get this place off the ground and he did nothing. He wanted his share but wasn't prepared to work for it. To be honest with you, he was a lying, dishonest lazy son-of-a-bitch. I would have been a fool to carry on like that.'

'But you started this numbered company with him over twenty years ago, so you must have run into him and Stanfield during that time.'

'Once more. I did not!' Thornton looked over at the female inspector, 'Is your boss hard of hearing?'

Stella Hudson continued to write notes.

Thornton continued. 'Inspector Thomas, I've never been in trouble before, so why now?'

'You are on record as being a director of this company, originally with Carter.'

'That's a fact, so why tear my place apart?'

Thomas didn't answer Thornton's question. A police officer came up to him and shook his head. 'There's no one here, guv. Only the geezer in the front office.'

Thomas got up from the table and went to the outside staircase. He looked down to the vehicles parked below. Turning back to Thornton, he said, 'What's in those tankers? We need to take a look inside them.'

'I wouldn't do that if I were you, Inspector!'

'Oh, really? Why not? Scared we might find Stanfield and Nash, eh?'

'No, those tanks, while empty, will contain a residue of hazardous medical and radioactive waste. You see the signage on the outside. Your men could easily become infected from contaminated blood and anything else that was in there if you access those tanks.'

'But you said earlier you had emptied your loads in Greenwich last night.'

'I did and while the waste management company rinses the tanks out afterwards, they still contain some of the waste residue. Before we can even access the tanks and reload, they have to be purged by law.'

'What's involved with that?'

'We have to take them to a certified purging station who issue certificates so we can access the tanks and reload again. Those are the hazmat regulations.'

'Okay. How do they purge the tanks?'

Thornton tried to remain calm. He knew exactly where this was going. Thomas knew it and he knew it.

'They are purged with steam.'

'So, why haven't you done that?'

'Simple. Our on-duty driving hours are up and the station does not open until 6:00 a.m.'

'Get dressed, you two. These tanks need to be purged. Where's the purging station?'

As Thornton went to get dressed, the inspector grabbed him by the arm.

'Now, Thornton, do you want to tell me where your friends are before we poach them? It will be easier on you if you tell us the truth now.'

Thornton swallowed hard.

'Nothing to tell.'

39

Chapter 39

Sarah opened her eyes. One of the exterior sensors had triggered the alarm, together with the outside lights. She picked up her phone. 12:06 a.m.

'James! James! Someone's at the door.'

'Uh, what?' James groaned, trying to come out of a deep sleep as he lay curled up against Sarah in bed.

'Someone's banging on the door!'

James sat up. 'I'll go check the cameras.'

He went over to the side table and checked them. He was surprised to see a police officer and another man at the door. He put on his dressing gown and went downstairs. As he opened the door, the man in plain clothes spoke.

'Mr Macrae, I'm sorry to disturb you. I'm Inspector Garrigan. There's been a terrible accident.'

'What's happened?'

'Can we come in? I think you may need to sit down.'

Sarah came down the stairs, wrapping her dressing gown around herself. She pulled out a chair from the kitchen table. James also sat down, his legs suddenly weak.

Inspector Garrigan took a deep breath.

'Mr Macrae, I'm sorry to tell you that there has been an explosion at your parents' house. I'm afraid there's no other way to put this to you, but both your parents were killed in the blast.'

James's eyes widened and stared straight ahead. He couldn't think of anything to say. Sarah put her hand to her mouth and burst into tears. They looked blankly at each other and then held themselves tightly together.

Finally, James looked up. 'Tell me what happened, Inspector.'

Garrigan cleared his throat. 'We got the call an hour or so ago from a neighbour. By the time the emergency services got there, there was nothing left.'

'I need to go there.'

'That might not be such a good idea, Mr Macrae.'

'Inspector, they're my parents. I need to go there.'

James dressed and was driven to his parents' rural home close to the village of Pershore. Sarah stayed back with the children.

As he got closer to the house, the narrow lanes with their high hedgerows trapped a combination of mist off the fields and smoke. The air became acrid. When the police car finally turned into the drive, the house was surrounded by fire engines, ambulances and police vehicles. A river of water ran down the drive and across the road. The original structure was unrecognisable. Two of the outside walls were completely blown out. The other two were barely standing with visible cracks in the brickwork. Blackened roof trusses, still smouldering, tilted slantwise at a precarious angle. Shards of glass, smashed bricks, wood and roof tiles were spread all over the garden. Furniture had been reduced to firewood. Firemen were dousing the last of the flames. The flashing blue and red lights from the emergency vehicles strobed through the lingering smoke haze and steam.

The remains of his parents' bodies had already been photographed and transported from the house. The police had also ascertained that there were no other bodies in the house. James stepped over the maze of hose pipes and stood there in shock, eyes wide open. The blast must have been tremendous, given the radius of debris. He stood next to Inspector Garrigan. 'Can I see my mother and father?'

'James. Yes, we will need you to identify the bodies.'

He sighed and put his hand on James's shoulder. 'It's not pretty. They must have taken the full force of the blast from beneath them.'

James closed and opened his eyes. He shook his head. He felt dizzy.

'Our preliminary investigations suggest it was a gas leak. The fire marshall together with my team will be conducting an investigation.'

Police were scouring the grounds in a straight formation, shining powerful flashlights on the ground. A team of forensic detectives were already surveying the remains of the house.

James sat back in the police car, wrapped in a blanket. Anxious neighbours were all gathered behind a police barrier. An avalanche of despair hit him. Was there to be no end to the grief and sorrow that he had endured over the last two years? *Mother. Father. How can they be gone? When does this end? How much more can I take?*

Garrigan came back over to James.

'Tell me about your father's security system.'

'He has the same system as me. External and internal cameras, motion sensors and pressure pads around the property and double locks.'

'How long does the camera system keep the film?'

'One week.' James's mind was stepping up a gear. 'The recorder is located in a fireproof steel box in my dad's study.' He looked over at the remains of the house.

'The corner room where the two remaining walls are.'

'Back in a second.' Garrigan marched straight over to the house and talked to the fire chief who promptly disappeared into the ruined house. Ten minutes later, he emerged with the steel box.

Garrigan looked at James and said, 'Let's hope the recording hasn't been compromised. Now, let's get you home to your family, Mr Macrae. There's nothing you can do here while we carry out our inquiries. I'll call you in the morning.'

James was driven back to his own house in silence. He sat in the back seat slumped over with his head in his hands. Once inside, he called his Chris, his partner.

'Chris, it's James.' He swallowed several times trying to contain his tears.

'James? Is everything alright?'

James stammered back. 'No, it's not alright. My parents are dead. They were killed in a gas explosion tonight.'

There was silence on the other end of the line and then finally Chis answered.

'Oh my god, James! Did I hear you correctly?'

'Yes, they're gone.'

'I'm coming over.'

'No, Chris, not now. I want to be alone with Sarah and the children for now.'

'Alright, if you're sure? Listen, I'll take care of things at work for a while. Just let me know if you need anything else. Jenny can also come over in the morning.'

'Thanks, Chris. I'll call you.'

'James, I'm so sorry. We're all here for you.'

There was another silence.

Finally, Chris asked, 'Do you think this is related to last year?'

James answered slowly. 'Honestly, I don't know.'

'Okay, but in any case, I'll put out an alert to all our personnel. I'll also give my parents a heads-up. I'll call you back tomorrow.'

****

'I've got it. That's it!'

Pierre Bourellier sat at his customary patio table at the Bistro Porte de Hal in the Marolles district of Brussels. It was a clear, crisp morning and he was only a short walk away from his work at the Jules Bordet hospital. He was enjoying croissant, butter and jam with his early morning coffee. By the time he had finished his second cup, he had it! That was it!

Something had bothered him ever since the last shipment of medical waste had been picked up. He now knew the second driver he had seen two days ago. He resembled one of the men that had been circulated by Interpol. Photos were routinely distributed to personnel in the transport industry. The beard and glasses had not been enough to disguise the man, certainly not anyone as astute as himself. He was a stickler for detail. He made a mental note to call the authorities when he got to work. He paid his bill, dabbed his mouth with his serviette and got up from the table. e resembled the H

He walked east along Waterloo Boulevard to the hospital where the cobblestone pavement narrowed. He started to cross the one-way Rue Breughel when a Citröen C15 work van unexpectedly shot out on his left-hand side from behind a parked car, accelerating hard.

He stood frozen for a second, then tried to step out of the way. His world became upside down as he felt himself flying over the top of the van high into the air, then all became black.

The Citröen immediately turned right onto Waterloo Boulevard and was gone.

40

Chapter 40

'We're moving.' Nash tried to stand up in the sealed compartment, lost his balance, then fell backwards onto Stanfield.

Stanfield clawed at the door, trying to prise it open. He used both hands and feet, but could not budge it. 'Help me, for god's sake!'

'There's no way it's going to move. I designed it so it would be locked from the outside.'

'It's no use. Charlie's sealed us in and locked the door. The baffle wall will also be locked into position. There's no way out.'

Stanfield wiped sweat out of his eyes, heart thumping. 'Oh god, what's going on? We don't even know if the police have raided the warehouse?'

Nash settled down on the floor and wrapped his arms around his knees.

'Well, we can thank our lucky stars that the air pumps are working, and we can breathe. Hell, there's no water left from the last run! I guess Charlie doesn't think it's safe to let us out yet.'

'Bloody hell, you're calmer than me!'

'You're just feeling claustrophobic. It's normal. I know it's cramped, just relax. We must be patient. Believe me, I know. I work in confined spaces all the time for my job. You just have to settle down, breathe slowly and count to three. Try closing your eyes and imagine you are in a place that you feel safe.'

'Oh, fuck! I was beginning to panic there for a minute. Not sure though if this is better than prison or not. Thanks.'

After a while, the movement of the trailer stopped. All was still for about half an hour, then the trailer moved again. Shortly after, loud metallic sounds reverberated through the tank. They continued to sit in silence and then stared at directly at each other, eyes and mouth wide open. A loud gushing sound started as the temperature inside the compartment started to rise alarmingly. They both quickly stood up.

Stanfield screamed. 'Oh god. They must be purging the tank. We're going to be scalded.' He clawed desperately at the door again.

Nash tried to reassure his boss. 'Listen! Lead is more heat resistant than other metals except stainless steel. Hang on in there! Once the steam phase is finished, they'll flush the tank with detergent and give it a final rinse. The first phase must end soon. From then on, the temperature will begin to fall.'

Sweat poured off Stanfield. He felt his pulse rocket and the raging thirst was unbearable. He tried to lift his hand to his forehead, but he could hardly lift it. Black specks floated at the corners of his eyes and dizziness started to overtake him. The last thing he was aware of was Nash whimpering.

****

Outside the purging bay, Inspectors Thomas and Hudson stood side by side, watching Thornton and Harry, the other driver. Both suspects remained impassive, although Harry occasionally shifted weight from one foot to the other. He'd been involved with Thornton on a few jobs in the past, but nothing like this.

Harry felt sure Stanfield and Nash would be scalded to death and didn't know if he should intervene or not. He waited, grinding his teeth. *Should I stop it now or follow the boss's lead?* Thornton remained motionless and quiet.

******

Whack.

'Stand up! Stand up, goddamnit!'

Stanfield came round to Nash pulling him up by his collar, yanking him off the floor.

His hands throbbed. Stanfield looked down at his palms. They were badly scalded from when he had collapsed and put his hands on the compartment floor.

'I bet the police wanted to access the tank to find us. They must have suspected we were in the warehouse for whatever reason. If I was Thornton, I would have told them they couldn't access the tank because of the lingering carcinogens and other dangerous shit that was being carried previously. That's why the tanks are being purged now. We'd better keep quiet. Next thing they will be entering the tank.'

Stanfield felt his legs give way again.

****

James hit the switch on the kettle. It was almost 4:00 a.m. He sat at the kitchen table with his head in his hands while he waited for the kettle to boil. Sarah came down from the bedroom, pulling her dressing gown on. She kissed James on the head and put her hand on his shoulder.

He shook convulsively, the sobs getting deeper and deeper. Sarah held him.

Finally, he pulled away.

Sarah took a tissue from the box on the side and wiped his eyes.

She sat opposite him and held both his hands in hers.

He looked up at her. 'I'm in a deeper and darker place than I've ever been before. I don't know how I can bear this.'

****

Thomas signalled to a man in coveralls, hard hat and safety harness.

'Okay, open up both tanks!'

He looked back at Thornton.

'We're going to nail you and your fried buddies here and now! You can't tell me that you didn't know Stanfield after being in business with Jack Carter. You must have all been buddies at one time.'

The special ops inspector attached a rope to his safety harness and lowered himself down into the front compartment of the tank, into the dark cavern below. With little light from the top hatch, he flicked on his flashlight. It penetrated the black void with a powerful, thin beam. He felt a strange uneasiness. As a special ops police officer, this experience felt different. He felt a shudder go through him and an inexplicable fear, even though the temperature in the tank was still warm. He ran his flashlight over all the weld seams in the vessel. All of them had been professionally welded. He tapped on all the sides of the compartment and got the same sound each time. He came out several minutes later.

'Nothing in here, Inspector. I'll try the rear compartment.'

After a few more minutes he emerged again.

'Nothing in this compartment either!'

'Okay, check the second trailer. The bastards must be in there!'

The inspector lowered himself carefully down through the top hatch of the second tank. The feeling of trepidation returned. He repeated his search procedure, tapping on the internal tank baffle.

Inside the hidden compartment, Nash barely heard the taps as he lay on the floor. Stanfield remained unconscious, barely breathing.

The inspector looked again at the tank baffle, but there was nothing out of the ordinary. Finally, he popped his head out of the tank.

'There's nothing in here either, guv. These tanks are both empty.'

Inspector Thomas looked at Stella Hudson with a grim look on his face.

'Christ, I thought we had them!'

Hudson replied. 'So did I. Thornton's lying. I know he is. If he knew Carter enough to be in business with him, he must have known Stanfield. That's why I was also convinced they were inside the tanks.'

Thornton heard Hudson. He snarled: 'You two have a bloody cheek accusing me of hiding two criminals and ripping my place apart.' He sneered at Hudson. 'I run a respectable business and have never been in trouble with the law. You'll be hearing from me further!'

Thomas shrugged and walked out with a grim look on his face. As soon as he was gone, Thornton and Harry drove back to the warehouse as quickly as they could. Billy had already organised help to repair the yard doors. They drove the rigs straight into the warehouse, closed and locked the doors. Thornton scrambled up inside the tank as fast as he could and released the baffle to expose the lead-lined room. His mind was racing, expecting the worst.

Inside, Stanfield and Nash were curled up, motionless.

41

Chapter 41

'Well done, Ben! You pulled the Rotterdam deal off!'

'Thank you, Lei. I have to confess, even though we knew we were the highest bidder, it's taken a long time to officially hear that we were finally awarded the bid.'

Shen smiled down the secure phone line. 'This is excellent news. Again, did they try to change any of the specifications for the upgrades that we set out from Beijing?'

'They did, but I refused to budge. I know the specifications for the new berths and depth of water are critical for you. It seems as though the bids came down to two. Macrae-Claybourne and ourselves. They preferred the Macrae-suggested specifications, but money won in the end.'

'Okay, I need you to send the requisitions for funds to me so we can get underway immediately. Secondly, step up your efforts to finish construction at both Zeebrugge and Marseille. We need to get them up and running to give Macrae-Claybourne a run for their money.'

****

The early autumn air felt heavy and damp. It was a dull, dark, and oppressive kind of day. A few leaves were starting to turn yellow in the subdued light, James noticed as he stood outside in the garden. He had not slept after returning from what was his parents' home. Nor had Sarah.

'What should we do about telling the children?'

'We'll tell them when they wake. I'll let the school know what's happening.'

Mason put his head round the door. 'What's that, Mum?'

Sarah stood up. 'Hang on, let me get the girls.'

They all sat around the kitchen table.

James put out his hands on the table.

'Hold my hands, all of you.'

'Last night, there was a terrible accident. I'm afraid that Nana and Gramps won't be with us anymore.'

Silence. 'What does that mean, Dad?'

James swallowed hard. 'I'm afraid it means that Nana and Gramps both died in the accident.'

For a moment there was just a look of astonishment and then Olivia started to cry, then Mia, and then everyone else.

Finally, James spoke. 'I want to tell you a story. Sometimes, when I was younger away on business overseas, I talked to Nana and Gramps in my mind, if there was a question I had. Strangely enough, even though I couldn't see them, they still gave me an answer. He paused. 'It means you will always be able to talk to them, even if they are not here.'

'I'm going to miss them,' murmured Mia.

'I know. They will always be with us in our hearts and memories.'

****

James exited his driveway and drove south-west on the M5 from just outside Bromsgrove. Inspector Garrigan had called him to ask if he could come into the central police station in Worcester.

'Good morning, Mr Macrae. Again, I'm so sorry about your loss.'

'Thank you. I don't feel as though anything is real anymore.'

He passed James a coffee. 'Let's go into my office.'

'I'm afraid the security cam footage was too badly damaged; we were unable to see anything at all. The fire investigators are still on site.'

'Oh. I hoped the video might help us The box was supposed to be fireproof.'

'Yes, I know, but not to the extent of an explosion like that.' He stood back. 'Now the hard part. If you are up to it, I need you to identify the bodies. The morgue is located in the hospital next door.'

As the sheets on the individual trolleys were turned back, James took a step back as he looked at the damaged heads of his mother and father. Someone had obviously tried to tidy them up as best as they could, but there was no mistaking it was Richard and Mary Macrae. At least, not to their son.

James wiped tears from his eyes, kissed their foreheads, each in turn, then left the room.

****

Thornton dragged Stanfield's body to the edge of the access hatch. He then lowered him gently, feet first, down onto the ground. Harry, standing below, held Stanfield up and then lowered him onto the warehouse floor. Next, they did the same with Nash. Thornton crouched down next to Stanfield and felt his pulse. It was very weak, and his breathing was shallow. His body was still very hot. Harry had done the same with Nash, although his breathing was slightly stronger than Stanfield's.

'Let's get them both into the apartment. Billy, get some Gatorade from the shop! We have to get plenty of fluids down them. We can't get a doctor. Even if we could it might be too late. We'll just have to do the best we can. They're either gonna make it or not.'

Thornton and Harry manoeuvred them up the stairs and into the apartment and bed. Holding up their heads, Thornton and Harry tried to get water into their mouths.

Nash was first to cough and splutter out the water, but at least he was gaining consciousness. Stanfield did not respond. They kept trying. Eventually, he was able to swallow a few drops. They persisted until he regained consciousness. Billy returned with the Gatorade and once that was ingested, both Stanfield and Nash started to show more positive signs of recovery.

Thornton sat back. 'Holy shit, guys. That was close.'

Nash was the first to speak, albeit very weakly.

'Where are we?'

'Well, you're not in hell yet, if that's what you mean! We've got you back in the warehouse. Crazy as it sounds, this is probably the safest place right now.'

'What about Hugh?'

'He's getting there, slowly.'

'Tell me what happened.'

'We got raided. They ripped this place apart and then wanted to get inside the tankers. I tried to put them off – telling them it was because of the residue of hazardous waste – but they persisted. From then on, I had to go through with purging the tanks or you, me, and everyone else would be close neighbours in Belmarsh for the rest of our lives. Let's hope there's no lasting damage.'

****

James drove home from Worcester police station. Instead of taking the motorway, he drove slowly through the country roads, driving back to his parents' house. He felt he needed proof of what had happened.

The air still smelled acrid. Nothing was left of the house; only one wall still standing. In the cold light of day, the radius of splintered wood, tiles and brick debris was far greater than James had realised.

'Can I help you?'

'Who are you?'

'I'm the fire investigation officer. Who are you?'

'James Macrae. This was my parents' house. I was here with the police last night.'

'Oh, I'm sorry for your loss, Mr Macrae.'

'Thank you. What do you think caused the explosion?'

'I still have to write up my official report, but I've just let Inspector Garrigan know that this was definitely an accident. There's no sign of foul play. It was caused by a slow build-up of what we call fugitive gas in the basement, to the point that any small spark in the house could have set it off.'

James got out of his car. As he walked across the ground,

his feet crunched on the debris. He felt utterly desperate.

James left and drove back to his own home on auto pilot. On reaching home, he sat in his car outside the house for a while, watching Sarah and the children through the windows of the family room. He knew he needed to get a grip on himself and be there for them.

James spent the rest of the day at home with his family. They talked and played games, trying to lighten the mood as much as they could.

'Sleep well, Mason. Good night.'

They tucked him up like a bug in a rug, went downstairs and sat down in the family room.

'I need a scotch. Do you want one, Sarah?'

'Yes, I think I do.'

James sat in silence, taking sips of his drink.

'What are you thinking, James?'

James rubbed his hand back and forth across his brow.

'I don't know, really. It's just a feeling of uneasiness I've got.'

'What do you mean?'

'The death of my parents; while they say it's an accident, it somehow doesn't feel right. It's hard to explain, but now the reality of the situation is beginning to sink in, I'm starting to have so many "what if's" creep into my head.'

'You don't think it was an accident?'

'Honestly, I don't know what to think, but what if it wasn't? What could be gained from this?'

Sarah remained silent, deep in thought.

James continued to air what was starting to churn away in his head. 'After last year's attacks on our family, I can't help thinking this may be an extension of that. To date this year, we have had attempts to steal our software, a series of defamations and an infiltration of sabotaged containers. What if this is an escalation to try to take over business yet again?'

'So why would anyone target Richard and Mary?'

'Perhaps they see this as an opportunity to gain access to our terminals?'

'I see what you are getting at, but the investigation of the explosion doesn't point to that.'

'I know it doesn't. But something feels off.'

'Tell you what. Why don't you ring Inspector Garrigan tomorrow and ask him to look again? Surely he would have to listen after all that has happened to us.'

42

Chapter 42

'What the fucking hell have you done, Shen?'

Ming stood up abruptly. His office chair fell backwards, crashing on the floor. His lips were tight and drawn.

The whole Zhongnanhai compound in Beijing felt uncomfortable to be in. People looked down at the floor avoiding directly looking at others when passing in the corridors. Workers were keeping their heads down and staying close to their desks after hearing frequent outbursts of shouting from behind closed doors.

Shen sat coolly in front of Ming's desk, staring up at him.

'I don't know what you mean.'

'Of course you do! Don't play a smart alec with me. The president will have us both for toast because of what you did to the Macraes.'

'I saw the news like everyone else, but I can assure you I had nothing to do with it. Have you asked your London head of security the same question?'

'Of course I have, you fool! Like you, he says he had nothing to do with it either.'

'Then there you have it! As far as I understand it, it was a gas leak. They do happen. As for the president, he was very clear on his message that he did not want any killing on China's hands in order to reach our strategic goals. We dealt with that before with Stanfield. My plan was to do everything by purely commercial means. I have delivered you Marseille, Zeebrugge and now Rotterdam. If this unfortunate incident with the Macraes leads to us getting a foothold in their terminals, then you should be pleased. I'm sure the president will praise you for that.'

'You better be straight with me, Shen, or I'll have you in Quincheng prison before you know it.'

'Settle down, Mr Ming. Do you think I'm stupid? I've done everything by the book just as President Jiang Zemin commanded.'

Ming picked up his chair and sat down, adjusting his clothes.

'Alright. So, tell me what else have you been up to?'

Shen smiled and continued. 'I had several hundred containers manufactured with a defective design of their twist lock castings.'

Ming looked at Shen, questioningly. 'Twist locks? I don't understand what those are.'

'On each twenty-foot or forty-foot container, there are provisions for locks on each of the outer corners. When engaged, twist locks hold the container to either the truck bed, rail bed or another container. When containers are stacked on top of each other, they are locked together. So, for example, if we have a stack of, say, seven or eight containers above deck on a ship, if one of the containers lower down does not have its twist locks properly engaged, when the ship rolls, the container stack will simply fall off into the sea.

'Our containers have miraculously found their way into the Macrae fleet. This means their company will be losing a lot of their customers and, of course, our compromised journalists will be able to inform their readers. Mr Driver will then report the increasing number of accidents that will, unfortunately, soon be occurring. It's only a matter of time before these containers part ways with the ships and trucks that carry them, if they haven't done so already!'

****

'Inspector Garrigan, I wanted to call you because I don't believe the explosion at my parents' house was an accident.'

'Oh, why would you say that?'

'Given the history of the attacks on my family and business, we knew that our foreign terminals were under threat. I believe they still are. Removing my parents would put my enemies one step closer to their objective.'

'I see. However, we have absolutely no evidence to say that the explosion was intentional.'

'So why now? Why so soon after last year? Surely you can see a pattern developing here?'

'I repeat, Mr Macrae, I have absolutely no evidence to support opening a murder inquiry, which you seem to think this is.'

'I do.'

'Look, I had a forensic team comb the scene all night and yesterday morning. In addition, the fire investigation officer, a thirty-year veteran, has confirmed it was a fugitive gas leak. I have read his report. It is meticulous in its findings. I'm happy for you to see the full report, if it will help put your mind at rest.'

'Yes, you can send it to me, but I still believe that my parents were targeted.'

'I'm sorry, Mr Macrae, the case is closed.'

James replaced the receiver. He felt himself getting hotter.

'What did he say?' Sarah asked.

'The case is closed and he will not reopen it. He has no evidence to suggest it was intentional.'

James gritted his teeth and started gently thumping his fist on the kitchen table. 'I'm gonna call Jeremy Hirons again. If anyone will listen, it'll be him.'

Finally, after several hours, they were able to connect.

'Jeremy, I need your help. You've no doubt heard the news.'

'I have and I'm very sorry. You have my condolences.'

'Thank you. The more I think about this, the more I believe my parent's death was not an accident.'

'Okay, tell me what you're thinking.'

'There's too much coincidence. If I was a betting man, I would say our European terminals must still remain a strategic target for our enemies. My parents' death removes one more obstacle for the Chinese to take us over. Add this event with the recent attacks on our company; the attempts to steal our software and discredit us in the press means that our hybrid enemy has not gone away!'

'James, I can assure you, the Chinese are completely under control. There is no way in hell they would do anything like murder your parents!'

'Why not, for god's sake?'

'It's simple. We are less than two years away before Hong Kong reverts back to China. They will absolutely not jeopardise that!'

'Jeremy! You have to listen to me. I'm sure they've done it.'

'I'm sorry, James. With all the information I'm party to, no, they would not have done it.'

James started to pace around the kitchen table.

'Well, what about Stanfield and Nash? They could have done it!'

'James, please settle down. I know we're still looking for those two, but there have been absolutely no sightings of them. Look, while we've been talking, I've pulled up the police report on your parents' accident and there is categorically no evidence to support your view.'

'So, are you saying you won't do anything?'

'I'm sorry, I can't.'

'Okay. How about Greg Driver of *Mercantile News*? What's happening with him?' Surely that would be a reason for you investigate further.'

'It might, but I don't have good news for you on that front.'

'Oh?'

'When we hauled him in, he denied that he was being blackmailed by the Chinese. He said he printed the negative articles about Macrae-Claybourne Logistics because they were true. We also visited *Mercantile News* ourselves and questioned both his boss and the owners. They, in turn, denied any wrongdoing. Greg Driver has since gone missing. He hasn't turned up for work in the last few days.'

James dropped his hand to his side and slumped his shoulders.

'That's not surprising.'

James put the phone down and frowned. 'Looks like we're on our own.'

'So, what do you want to do now?' asked Sarah

James shook his head. 'I'm so angry inside, but I know that's not going to help matters. I need to think things through some more.'

'Well, you told me that you have your private investigator working on who leaked your company information to the Chinese, so why don't you get him to take a look at the gas explosion while the evidence is still fresh?'

James sat up.

'Good idea! It's clear the police and MI6 won't do anything further.'

He walked backwards and forwards.

"This is crazy! These threats are staring us straight in the face! Why can't they see them?'

****

'What kind of fear or promise of a new life would possess people to take such drastic action, Charlie, especially if there's a high risk of dying?'

'Fucked if I know, Harry. All I see is money in those tanks.'

They stood back from their rigs parked inside the south Charleroi warehouse on the outskirts of Brussels, watching another group of illegal immigrants clamber up into the tank trailers.

'Gotta say it's a bit different to robbery, at least the kind we're used to.'

'Who cares. It's a great way to make money quick. If there's any casualties, we just dump 'em and move on.'

The bottom access hatch was secured.

'Okay, we're loaded. Let's go!'

The two tractor trailers emerged from the industrial area and made their way towards the Jules Bordet hospital.

Thornton picked up his CB mic. 'Everything okay, Harry?'

'I'm okay, boss. I'm still behind you. I'll come up closer to you now we're getting closer to the hospital.'

Harry hung up his mic and accelerated his Scania truck to close the gap with Thornton's tanker. He reflected on how much longer he could push his luck. Since the Brinks Mat robbery twelve years before, he and Thornton had managed to remain below the radar. The raid by Thomas and Hudson had shaken him; however, Stanfield wanted to cram in some more runs. He figured he would carry on for now and take Nash's place for the time being. He'd make some good money standing in for Nash. It certainly felt strange watching a scared bunch of humans climb up into the tanker wondering if they would ever come out alive. If he was stopped, he would deny any knowledge of this. After all, he was just a driver, wasn't he?

Thornton slowly drove his tanker trailer into the loading bay of the Jules Bordet Institute and applied the air brakes. Harry followed with the second tank. Thornton jumped down from his Scania cab and was met by an older man in coveralls with a clipboard. He had a photograph of Thornton attached to the top of a form.

'Monsieur Thornton, I presume?'

'Yes, sir. I am. Monsieur Bourellier is not here today?'

'I'm afraid not. He was killed by a van in a hit and run accident three days ago.'

Thornton looked surprised. He took off his company cap and rubbed his head.

'Oh my goodness! That's terrible news. I'm so sorry.'

Inwardly, he smiled. It was clear Bourellier had recognised Nash the last time when they picked up the medical waste. Something had to be done and quickly. Had he been left alive, their cash cow would have gone up in smoke before it got really started! Their network of international contacts was as efficient as ever.

'I'll be taking care of dispatch until they can find another qualified replacement. I've checked all your previous paper-work, and all is in order. M. Bourellier was very efficient. I'll just check your trucks, VIN number of the tanks, together with your drivers' credentials. I see you've got the correct hazmat signs displayed. 'Okay, let's get you loaded up.'

He signed the EU certification and sealed the load. Nothing could be heard on the outside of the tanks that would suggest twenty people were couped up inside the two trailers.

'Okay, Harry, follow me back to Calais. When we get to the x-ray and CO_2 checks, don't forget to flick the switch off for the air ventilation fan just while we go through the CO_2 check. Don't stop or look around; just drive through slowly and keep looking ahead as you would normally.'

They took their reserved places on the P&O ferry. The ferry was running on time, and they made it back to the Greenwich medical incinerator plant again around midnight. They repeated the cycle of emptying their tanks and driving east to the rear of Beckton sewage treatment works to drop off the Chinese illegal immigrants.

They pulled into the warehouse around 2:30 a.m. Harry smiled when Thornton thrust a handful of bank notes into his hand. 'I could get used to this, Charlie! I know it's risky, but the money's good!'

'It sure is.'

Harry was a good stand-in and Thornton trusted him. Now might be the best time to get rid of Nash once and for all.

****

'Scott, I need you to do some more detective work for me, but before we get to that, have you made any progress into who leaked the one database to the Chinese?'

'I have, Mr Macrae. I've narrowed your three suspects down to two. I've eliminated Paul Adams from any possibility of leaking your software.'

'Are you saying it's Lee Yuen or Lisa Taylor?'

'I am. Yuen has purchased a very expensive apartment in Edgbaston, way beyond his means. As for Taylor, she appears to be a loner. From what I can see, she doesn't have much of a social life, but what's interesting is she's just dropped a healthy deposit on a new house being built in Sutton Coldfield. I can tell you it's quite a posh development. On checking her divorce settlement, it's doubtful it would have covered the amount she put down. It's obvious she wants to move from her parents' house. I think I'm pretty close to having an answer for you. I just need to carry out another enquiry.'

'Good! The sooner you can solve this, the better. Now, you've no doubt seen the press about the explosion at my parents' house?'

'I have. I was very sorry to see that.'

'I don't believe it was an accident. I believe it was murder.'

'I see. Why would you think that?'

James got up from the chair in front of Farmer's desk and started to walk back and forth wrapping his arms around himself.

'I don't have any proof, but it fits into a pattern of sabotage and murder against my company and family. Maybe my mind isn't straight and I'm in a dark place right now, but with all the funeral arrangements and dealing with winding up my parent's affairs, I've become pre-occupied with conspiracy theories. Let me remind you of all of the events that took place last year, some of which you were involved in yourself, and bring you up to date with what's happened this year.'

Farmer stood up and used his whiteboard and marker to list out the chronological bullet points that James relayed. When James had finished, he stood back and studied each point

'Ummm. I agree with you, Mr Macrae. There's a clear pattern here alright.'

James looked Scott Farmer straight in the eye, swallowed hard and then spoke: 'Last year's events taught me much about hybrid warfare. Hybrid methods of warfare, such as propaganda, deception, sabotage, and other non-military tactics are being used to destabilise my company. The Chinese want my international terminals for the expansion of their silk road. They needed to kill my parents to free up title to the property on which these terminals stand on. They know title will pass to me. Therefore, they will continue to undermine my business. Of course it's conceivable they might try to kill me and my family.'

Farmer nodded his head.

'Yes, it's the sort of thing you read about in the news, but most people never really take any serious notice of it because it doesn't affect them directly. But I can clearly see now why you think this.'

'Frankly, Scott, you're the only one who agrees with me. The police have just taken the fire inspector's report on face value and MI6 is following the stupid politicians' naïve belief that China won't do anything to jeopardise the return of Hong Kong in two years' time.'

'Got it! You know Napoleon once called China 'a sleeping lion'. I'm beginning to think the lion is now fully awake and on the prowl. Let me get to work.'

43

Chapter 43

'Hugh, let me do it. Let me get rid of him now. Harry is doing a great job driving the second truck. What's more, I trust him and he's a better driver than Nash. There's no point in keeping him alive. He's too much of a risk and why split any of the money with him?'

'No! Just hang on a bit. We've now got some serious cash in the bank and my injuries have healed. We're close to escaping from here, but, before we leave the UK, I need him to help me kill Macrae and his family.'

Thornton shook his head. 'Why the hell can't you leave that one alone! There's no point!'

'Not for you there isn't, but I need to get even with that bastard! He's robbed me of my business and my life. Besides, if I left him alone, I would look weak in the underworld. You know as well as I do, if I do that, I'm vulnerable to anyone who wants a reward. Fear of reprisals from me, if I do this, will help us steer clear of trouble in the future.'

'I think you're wrong. Just leave it, let me get rid of him and let's get the hell out of this country!'

Stanfield gritted his teeth and wagged his figure at Thornton. 'No! Not now. And that's final!'

****

It began with a few gentle spots of rain. A few of the mourners let out their umbrellas and huddled closely together, but by the time the vicar was winding up his dedication and Richard and Mary Macrae were being lowered side-by-side into their graves, the rain had become more intense, pummelling the tops of the canopies. The chill wind and pungent smell of the earth added to the sheer and shocking spectacle of the end of James's parents. His tears mixed with the rain and fell into his parents' grave.

****

Sarah kicked off her shoes and slumped in the chair. The last of the funeral guests had just left the house and Sarah's parents had taken the children with them for a short holiday at their home in Caernarfon.

'Phew! Thank god that's over!'

James took off his suit jacket, slackened his tie and undid the top button of his shirt. He closed his eyes and lay back on sofa. He let out a long sigh.

'I feel completely empty and lost.'

'I know.'

They sat in silence for a while each in their own space. Finally Sarah came over and lay next to James, placing her head on his chest.

'So where do we go from here, James? I want to help.'

'I've been thinking about that. We are the only people, apart from Chris and Scott Farmer, who think this was not an accident. If I go back to work, can you work with Scott and try to get to the bottom of everything? He's a good detective, but he only has limited resources. My gut feel is that we have to move fast and try and pre-empt any further attacks on us.'

****

James looked up just as he booted his computer up.

Janet stood in his office doorway. 'Oh, hi, Janet. Thanks for coming to the funeral. Sarah and I appreciated everyone's support.'

'I'm so sorry for your loss.'

James nodded in appreciation.

'Chris is taking few days off. He's been wonderful at taking care of everything since I've been gone. Let me close the door and we can catch up.'

'How is our malware project coming along?'

'Shad and I have spent over two weeks working on it. He has custom-built a series of layered viruses that will work in conjunction with a network virus. The tricky part was finding a way for the virus to lie dormant while any anti-virus software is in operation. He's still beta testing everything, but when it hits a network, it will spread corruption in every file like wildfire. There's no reversal once it has access to a computer or a network.'

'So does it just shut everything down automatically?'

'No, it doesn't. Because it is customised on our own logistics system, whoever uses the malware can enter their own information into the various data fields. For example, ship names; dates of arrival and departure; details of different cargoes; customers; container sizes and harbour berth sizes.'

'I assume the system looks normal to them when they do this. And then what happens?'

'It does, but once they start to use the system, it will mix and match all the information to the point it will create chaos.'

'Excellent. We just need to identify who our leaker is, so they can personally deliver our surprise package!'

As Janet left, Martin Farley put his head around the office door.

'James. Good to see you back!'

'Thanks, Martin. I gather you've been busy while I've been off.'

'I have. You know of course that we lost the Marseille bid to Pair-Tree Capital and that we were not the best bidder on the Rotterdam tender either.'

'I did, although the Rotterdam tender wasn't officially awarded before I left.'

'That's right. Before it was finally awarded, we were asked to justify our specifications for the port expansion facilities, which Chris did. It would appear our proposed enhancements for the rail heads, deep-water port and container-handling equipment were the best of any of the proposals. So we went back and forth, but Chris refused to increase our bid.'

'Yes, our bid was definitely firm.'

'Anyway, Pair-Tree Capital were awarded the tender despite their different port upgrades. Their valuations and required ownership percentage absolutely didn't make sense. It was the same in Marseille. They overvalued the existing facilities and asked for a lower percentage of ownership.'

'Ummmm. What does that suggest to you, Martin?'

'I'm smelling a rat.'

'Me too. Pair-Tree Capital has paid way over the odds for Zeebrugge, Marseille and now Rotterdam. For a supposed asset stripper like Ben Armstrong, it doesn't make any sense. I'm thinking we have another Euro-Asian Freight on our hands.'

'So it would seem. The Chinese must be up to their old tricks again.'

James picked up his phone.

'Chad, got a few minutes? I'm just in my office with Martin.'

Chad Greening, Director of Sales, came in and sat down next to Martin.

'So, what do sales look like right now?'

'Honestly, it's flattened out after a great boost in sales following the merger. While our systems are working perfectly, we are seeing a downtrend. It seems the outstanding legal action with *Mercantile News* and all the negative press has undermined confidence in our company. I'm also noticing that Zeebrugge is slashing their rates. Seems our competitors see a weakness and are piling on the competitive pressure.'

'Ummm. I suspected something like this might happen. Martin has told me that Pair-Tree Capital has now finalised their deal with Rotterdam. While we don't necessarily compete head to head with these two ports in northern Europe, I'm thinking that Pair-Tree may cut their rates next in Marseilles. That, in turn, has the potential to affect our terminals in Genoa and possibly Valencia.'

'Yes, it's certainly a possibility. Let me keep a close eye on their rates and if we need to adjust our rates, I'll let you know.'

'Thanks, Chad. Just make sure you and your team stay close

to our customers with personal visits and assure them that we value their business. Personal relationships are everything in our business.'

****

Scott Farmer wore a smart suit, light coat, trilby hat and carried a leather briefcase. He did not look out of place in the new luxury apartment block overlooking the exotic Winterbourne gardens in Edgbaston. He knew Lee Yuen was at work. James Macrae had given him the green light. It was late in the afternoon. He found Yuen's apartment on the sixth floor and walked confidently to the door. With his back to the corridor, he slid a special tool between the door jam and the lock. The door opened, he entered and closed it behind him.

He scouted out the apartment and found a filing cabinet in one of the rooms that was being used as an office. Before he entered the room, he looked to see if there were any cameras. There was one clipped to the top of a computer screen. He checked to see if it was off. It was, but he still placed his light raincoat over the camera and screen.

He opened the bottom drawer of the filing cabinet and worked his way upwards. The top drawer gave him what he was looking for. He took out the bank statements and meticulously went through them. Bingo! Every month a numbered company had deposited the same sum of money into Yuen's account. This was in addition to the bi-weekly salary deposit from Macrae-Claybourne Logistics. The numbered company deposits coincided with his start date at Macrae-Claybourne, but the deposits had stopped over two months ago. Farmer photographed the statements, put everything back as he had found it and gathered up his coat.

He was just about to leave the room when he heard a key in the lock.

****

'University of Birmingham. How may I direct your call?'

'Good morning. Can you put me through to the Employer Relations team, please?'

'One moment please.'

'Employer Relations, Ed Cousins speaking.'

'Ah, Mr Cousins. This is Lisa Taylor from Macrae-Claybourne Logistics. I wanted to know when the date of the next open house is being held for potential employers and the new graduates?'

'Hello, Ms Taylor. We have one next month on Friday 23rd. I know you've attended before and hired some of our best graduates.'

'We have and, I may say, we have been extremely happy with them. Your standards of education are exceptional. We would like to attend again this year.'

'Excellent, I will add you to the list.'

'Thank you. Oh, by the way, do you have a list of the other employers attending.'

'It's not up on the website yet, but I can tell you that it's pretty much the same as the last two years. Those that have attended in the past are listed on our website.'

'Excellent. Thank you so much, Mr Cousins.'

Sarah Macrae put down the phone and pulled up the university website. She printed out the list of past employer attendees. Amongst all the companies listed was one that struck her: The Chinese Trade Commission.

****

Scott Farmer stood behind the office door in Lee Yuen's apartment, clutching his briefcase. He would use it as a weapon if he had to. He heard the person enter and close the front door.

A female voice shouted, 'Hello, Lee. I'm back!'

Next, he heard a bunch of keys land on top of a kitchen counter and a bag drop on the floor. He inched his way silently into the hallway and peered into the kitchen. A woman with long black hair had her back to him and was unpacking a shopping bag and loading the contents into the fridge.

Silently, without any sudden movements, he opened the front door and closed it quietly. The lock sprang back and made noise. Without waiting to see what happened, he walked to the fire escape stairwell and left the building.

He had what he wanted.

****

James placed the Thai takeaway on the kitchen countertop. He unpacked them and put the different dishes of food on plates in the oven to warm up. He'd picked it up on the way home as Sarah had been working with Scott Farmer for several days. She'd left him a message to say she would be late home and Scott would join them.

Sarah came through the door from the garage. Scott Farmer followed her. Before she even took off her coat, she grabbed

James by the arm.

'James, James, we've got some news! We have to update you!'

'Good news, I hope! It's been another tough day.'

They all sat down around the kitchen table.

'I found out this afternoon that your parents had a visit from the gas company the afternoon before the explosion!'

'What!'

'Scott asked me to make enquiries around your parents' house to see if they had seen anything unusual. I called on all the nearby neighbours. They all said that the police had asked them the same questions, but nobody had seen anything. As I was leaving the area, I saw a man walking his dog. Apparently, he lives over a mile away from your parents' house and walks that way most days. Anyway, he remembers seeing a Central LPG Gas van there the afternoon before the explosion. You take it from there, Scott.'

'When Sarah told me that, I phoned the gas company to ask if they had made a service call there. They said that they had not. I persisted in my questioning and eventually I was able to speak to the service yard foreman. He told me that one of their service vans had gone missing for a few hours from the central yard that day. He found it a few hours afterwards back in the same yard. Since nothing had been taken and no damage was done, he didn't report it and never thought anymore about it.'

James thought for a moment. 'Sounds like an impersonation by someone to try gain entry to the propane tank and lines.'

Scott nodded. 'It definitely looks like it. I've also been following the Stanfield and Nash developments. Sarah had asked me if I thought they might be behind it. While it's a remote possibility, with my contacts in the local police, they have definitely not been seen around here. My sense is this was an organised crime. Someone must have made an appointment. I don't believe your father would have allowed anyone in 'cold' to his house and obviously the van had to be organised as well.'

'So what do you suggest next, Scott?'

'I think we should report our findings back to Inspector Garrigan. If I were him, I would have his men check all the security camera videos along the high street in Pershore. That van must have passed that way on its way from the Central LPG Gas company to your parent's house. Maybe we get lucky and match the plate to the missing service van. If we are even luckier, we may get a mug shot of the driver.'

'Good. Let's do it.'

Sarah nodded. 'You should also contact Stella Hudson. She should know this too.'

James agreed. 'You're right. We will. So, any further news on our own saboteur?'

Scott looked at Sarah. She smiled nervously. Next he looked at James. 'Yes. You're not going to like this, but Sarah and I are sure we have the right person.'

'Go on. Let me have it!'

'It's Lisa Taylor.'

'Christ almighty.'

'Here's where it gets worse. The two of them were being paid by a numbered company that I have traced back to Chinese ownership. They were recruited two years ago at the Birmingham University open house. Both were paid monthly fees, but Yuen's stopped over two months ago before your database was copied. Lisa Taylor is still being paid. It would also explain how she was able to put down such a hefty deposit on her new house.'

James clenched his jaw.

'I bloody knew it! The Chinese are still after our terminals. They've murdered my parents and tried to sabotage my company again! When will it end?'

44

Chapter 44

'**C**hris! We need to meet. Can you come to the office today? It's urgent!'

James floored the accelerator of his Range Rover, throwing a shower of gravel high into the air behind him as he pulled out of his driveway. He punished the engine, going into the red on the rev counter on every gear change. His knuckles were white as he flung the steering wheel around all the corners. As he pulled into work and slammed the driver's door hard, the smell and smoke of the brake pads and discs filled the air.

Chris closed the office door and sat opposite James. He remained stone-faced and silent.

James launched straight into what he wanted to say and spat his words out venomously. 'We can't afford to wait for the next action by the Chinese. Instead, we have to go on the offensive and provoke our enemy to make a move that we've already anticipated. At the same time, we need to punish them – hard!'

Chris put up his hand. 'Slow down, James, bring me up to

speed will you!'

James put both hands in the air. 'Oh sorry, Chris, I didn't mean to launch into you, but I'm so fucking angry.'

'I get that. Tell me what's happened since I've been away and then we can work out what we need to do. Okay?'

'Here goes. First, we now know my parents were murdered. It was not an accident and was probably carried out in an organised way by the Chinese. We are trying to get the police to reopen the case.'

Chris remained quiet.

'Second, the Chinese recruited Lee Yuen and Lisa Taylor nearly two years ago. Yuen is no longer working for them, but Taylor is. She's the one who leaked the database to the Chinese.'

'Oh shit!'

'Third, I'm bloody sure Pair-Tree Capital is working for the Chinese. To pay out what they did and take less ownership shares for Marseille and Rotterdam terminals does not fit in with the characteristics of an asset-stripping company. Also, they paid way over the odds for Zeebrugge.'

'Agreed.'

'Couple this to the Chinese containers that have found their way into our fleet and the lies that have been fed through a blackmailed journalist, my conclusions are irrefutable. So, as well as punishing them with our virus, let's provoke them to come after us.'

'Sorry to interrupt you, but what do you mean by that?'

'Let me give you an example. I'm now in my enemy's shoes. They want our shipping terminals for their silk road objective and possibly for naval and military purposes at some future point. They've removed one obstacle, my parents, thinking the shares of Macrae Holdings will pass to me. Logical?'

Chris nodded slowly. 'Yes, that makes sense.'

'So let's think what their next step might be? They would then have to murder me, Sarah, and my children. But it wouldn't stop there either. They would have to come for you and your family.'

Chris's eyes widened.

'To answer your question, I'm proposing we provoke our enemy into showing us who they really are. If we play with them and maybe suggest to them that we might sell our business, that will slow them down in terms of coming after us personally.'

James put his fore finger in the air and continued. 'I'm thinking that Pair-Tree Capital is now secretly owned by the Chinese. As Anglo-Asian Freight has been dissolved, this must be the replacement. So, my plan, if you agree, is to set up a meeting with the owner of Pair-Tree Capital. His name is Ben Armstrong. Why don't we get him here on our own turf and tell him we are thinking of selling our joint business. Let's see if he brings up Macrae Holdings and Claybourne Holdings as well. If he bites, he'll make the trip here. We could ask him an outrageous price and see what happens next.'

Chris sat quietly. James also remained silent. Finally Chris said, 'How about if we push this a little further. If he accepts our outrageous price for all the terminals and the whole of our operations business, including Macrae and Claybourne Holdings, then we'll know categorically it's the Chinese. They'll probably congratulate themselves on killing your parents and bringing us to the table.'

James smiled for the first time.

Chris continued. 'What if we then tell him we've had a

change of heart and we've decided not to sell after all. That would drive Pair-Tree Capital and the Chinese wild! The next step for them would be to definitely come after us.'

James grinned. 'Now you're thinking like a hybrid enemy, Chris, except this time we'll be ready for them!"

****

DI Stella Hudson, on loan to the Met squad from the West Midlands force, sat at her desk on the fourth floor of the Metropolitan Police headquarters located on the corner of Broadway and Victoria Street in London. She took off her glasses and rubbed her tired eyes. A dull pain was beginning to form across the bridge of her nose. She'd seen something come across her desk in the last few days, but she was having difficulty joining the dots together; linking this event with her current assignment of locating and capturing Stanfield and Nash. It was past 7:00 p.m. and the autumn shadows from the nearby buildings were getting longer.

DCI Thomas, her boss and partner, got up from his nearby desk and stretched himself to his full height.

'Wanna take a break, Hudson?'

Stella looked up. 'Yeah. Good idea. Going back to Detectives 101 is bloody tiring. Most people think our jobs are glamorous and exciting, they have no idea of the drudgery that comes with it. Sooner or later, we've got to come across some further clues to track those slippery bastards down.'

'Come on, mate, let's get a pie and a pint at the Feathers around the corner. It'll do us both good.'

They grabbed a small table inside the snug oak-panelled bar and got stuck into two chicken and mushroom pies and a couple of beers. Thomas took a long swig of his pint and let out a long 'ahhhhhh'. He wiped the back of his hand across his mouth, while Stella sat silently contemplating.

'Go on, spit it out, Hudson!'

'What, the beer or what I'm thinking?'

Stella looked at her boss in earnest. 'There's a link some-where to our guys that's sitting there so close I can almost touch it. It just hasn't hit me yet.'

'Give me a hint.'

'Remember when we went to that transport yard thinking we'd found a lead on Stanfield and Nash. Those tankers had been carrying medical waste and I seem to remember them saying that they had just returned from Brussels and dropped off their loads in Greenwich.'

'Yes, they did.'

'Right, but in the last little while I've seen a report or something from Interpol that is staring me in the face. But what's the something?'

Thomas put down his cutlery. 'Oh shit, I know what it is. Let's finish up and get back quick. It's that hit and run death report of that hazmat shipper and receiver at that hospital in Brussels. That's the link you're looking for!'

'Come on. Let's go!'

45

Chapter 45

Ben Armstrong drove his black Mercedes S 500 AMG into the Macrae-Claybourne visitor's car park at their head office in Aston, Birmingham. The late afternoon was unseasonably warm being in the mid-twenties Celsius. A cloud of dust blew up in front of the car from the electric thermo-fan as it continued to rotate. He gathered his suit jacket off a hanger in the back seat, stuffed his white shirt tighter into the top of his trousers and put on his jacket. He strode purposely with his briefcase into the reception area.

James and Chris looked down from the boardroom window. James looked directly at Chris.

'Well, this is it! We've made the move, now let's see if we can provoke the lion and bring him out into the open.'

'That we have, James. Good guy, bad guy routine, right?'

'Right.'

James's secretary came in. 'I have Mr Armstrong of Pair-Tree Capital here to see you both.'

'Thanks, Rachel. Please show him in.'

Outside in the car park, a workshop technician walked by

Armstrong's car carrying a tyre gauge. He spun it up in the air, tried to catch it with one hand but missed it. It fell to the floor. He bent down to pick it up on the blind side of the office and attached a magnetic transponder to the underside of the Mercedes.

Armstrong was hardly through the office door when he boomed,

'Good afternoon, gentlemen. It's a pleasure to meet you both.'

James and Chris stood up from the boardroom table. James spoke first, smiling warmly at Armstrong.

'It's a pleasure to meet you too. We've both heard a lot about you and your successful track record with your American terminals and now your expansion into Europe.'

Chris stood back and was more reserved. Rachel brought in coffee and water.

They all sat down at the boardroom table, Chris and James on one side and Armstrong on the other.

Armstrong took off his jacket. 'I must say, James, I was taken completely by surprise by your phone call last week. To be honest, you are the last company I would have expected to have heard from.'

Chris retained a stony demeanour. 'And why would that be, Mr Armstrong?'

'Well, you have not long merged your companies and with two well-established businesses, I would imagine your balance sheet is very strong.'

'Thank you, Mr Armstrong.'

'No, please call me Ben.'

James spoke next.

'Okay, Ben. Yes, we do have a very good business but certain events that happened recently have given us cause to reflect on the finality of life. Neither of us have ever had time to smell the roses. That was the reason for my contact with you and why we are sitting here today.'

'James, I did hear of your parents' untimely death. You have my sincere condolences. Your parents certainly never had a chance to enjoy their golden years.'

James looked down at the table. 'Thank you.' He paused. 'Suddenly you begin to realise that life is finite. As for us, we don't really see our own children grow up. We are always preoccupied with work and less time for the family. I mean, look at me. I've been married for fourteen years, and I've only been home for seven of those years. The rest of the time was spent working at all of our European and Middle Eastern terminals.'

Armstrong looked over at Chris. 'How about you, Chris. Do you feel the same?'

Chris frowned. 'I understand James's point of view, although I don't think I'm ready to walk away from the business just yet. I think you have to know in your own mind when it's time to retire. Honestly, this is James's idea.'

Chris adjusted himself in his seat and leaned forward. Staring directly at Armstrong he continued, 'The only way you can convince me to sell is money. Our families and us two have worked our asses off for what the company is today. To budge me, you would have to make the offer so attractive that I could not refuse. Do I make myself clear?'

James shifted uneasily and winced. Armstrong caught the moment. James then said, 'Of course, the price must be realistic. As a private company we have a wealth of plant, equipment and retained earnings.'

'Chris and James. Let me assure you that Pair-Tree Capital appreciates free enterprise and know how to value it, so everyone is happy. To make mutual agreements, both buyer and seller have to feel they are more than satisfied with the eventual deal. Negotiations in good faith can be the only way to go.'

Armstrong bent down and picked up his briefcase. He extracted a folder and shuffled some papers.

'I see that Macrae-Claybourne Logistics only owns the operations of each branch of the company, but the land is owned by Macrae Holdings LLC and Claybourne Holdings LLC respectively. Operations lease the fixed assets from both holding companies.'

Chris answered first. 'Let me be clear, Mr Armstrong, we are both possibly open to the idea of selling Macrae-Claybourne operations, provided the price is strong enough to convince us both. Claybourne Holdings LLC is off limits. They own all our terminals in the UK. As for James, the sale of Macrae Holdings is up to him.'

Armstrong remained quiet. Looking uncomfortable, James swallowed hard.

'I'm with Chris on the possible sale of the operations company, but now I'm the sole owner of Macrae Holdings I'm open to selling all our European terminals but, and it is a big but, you would have to pay an astronomical price to buy me out on that branch of the company. My family swore they would never sell that business, but with the tragic accident of my parents, I think it is time to rethink my life. I need to learn to relax.'

Armstrong thought for a few moments.

'So, just to summarise what I think I've heard this afternoon.

Both of you would consider selling Macrae-Claybourne Logistics, the operations side of the business; James, you would consider selling Macrae Holdings LLC and, Chris, you do not want to sell Claybourne Holdings?'

Chris laid his hands flat on the table. He leaned forward again.

'That is correct, Mr Armstrong. We do not want to waste our time unless you are serious and pay a price that more than satisfies us. By the way, at the risk of being rude, would your company have the resources to buy us out completely?'

Armstrong raised his eyebrows.

Chris continued, 'I'll be honest, we are an entirely different beast than either Marseille, Zeebrugge or Rotterdam and we're not looking at selling just a piece of our company for part ownership like the others. James wants to get out completely and I get that. But if he goes, I go.'

'Yes, Chris. I understand your point. We are all realistic businessmen. As for the resources, you let me worry about that. I'm wealthy in my own right, my company is very strong financially and I have the backing of Wall Street. Us Americans, we like to make money – same as you. If I didn't see potential, I would not be here.'

James grinned. 'Okay, now we've got that out of the way. We have a confidentiality agreement and non-disclosure agreement for you to sign. Once we've done that, we can enter into due diligence.'

'Excellent, James and Chris. I appreciate this opportunity. Thank you.'

'So, would you like to join us for an early dinner at the Bartons Arms? It's just across the way from the office. You can leave your car here and we can walk over.'

'I'd like that. I only flew in from New York yesterday and popped into our London office this morning, so dinner would be most welcome. Let me use the washroom first.'

Armstrong left the boardroom and went off down the corridor. Chris leaned over to James and whispered, 'That was a smart move telling Armstrong you were the sole owner of Macrae Holdings. With Sarah and the children also being shareholders, you've now taken yourself and them off the target list for the time being, if our friend is truly in bed with the Chinese.'

****

Thomas and Hudson rushed back to the Met from the pub. Thomas pulled up both reports they were interested in.

'Yes, you're right, Hudson. That guy Thornton, the one who did all the talking when we raided the transport yard, did say they had returned from Brussels with hazardous medical waste.'

He flicked over a couple of more pages.

'When we checked out his story, they had actually picked up the waste from a hospital called the Jules Bordet Institute.'

Stella had the other file in her hand. 'Bingo! The guy who was killed by the hit and run driver was a Pierre Bourellier, the waste supervisor at the same hospital. Coincidence?'

'I don't think so.'

'Neither do I! Let's dig a bit deeper into the link. We could be onto something.'

46

Chapter 46

James, Chris and Ben Armstrong left the office and crossed the road to the Bartons Arms.

'My word! This is a pretty unique pub,' exclaimed Armstrong as he entered the heavy mahogany-panelled Victorian pub, complete with stained-glass windows.

'It's downright gorgeous!'

Chris answered. 'Yes, it's over one hundred years old. A great local to have next to our business! Beer's not bad either.'

They sat in the restaurant, Armstrong looking around to take in all the detail of the room.

'What's good on tap here?'

'They have a new craft beer here called Oakham Green Devil IPA. It's quite a hoppy beer, but I like it.'

He didn't tell him it was slightly on the strong side.

The chat over dinner was very informal. Armstrong told them of his inheritance from his grandfather and how he built his venture capital business. James and Chris talked of how they had both been brought up in the business. It was an easy conversation.

Armstrong sat back in his chair. 'James, if we are to reach an agreement, how would you spend your time?'

Chris sat silently at the table, watching Armstrong closely. He concluded that Armstrong was a good card-player too. While he had spoken freely, he hadn't given much away. Time to loosen him up.

James replied. 'That's easy. More time with my family. We love to walk, and I love to climb.'

'Interesting. And, Chris, what would you do with your time?'

'Before I answer, let's have another pint.' Chris signalled to the waiter, who promptly returned with three more pints. By now they had sunk three pints and shared a couple of bottles of Châteauneuf-du-Pape.

'Well, to answer your question, I love rebuilding old cars.'

'Fascinating, what cars do you have?'

'I have a 1969 Porsche 908 Spyder, a 1950 Ferrari 250GT and a Citröen Deux Chevaux.'

They all laughed. Chris continued, 'Honestly! I love driving around in that old Citröen.'

The waiter brought coffee. The chatter around them in the restaurant got louder and louder as more people and alcohol fused together. Armstrong leaned back and loosened his shirt collar and necktie.

'Would you like your usual with the coffee, Mr Macrae?'

'Why not. Do you like Aquavit Ben?'

'Can't say I've ever tried it? What is it?'

'It's a Swedish spirit with a very distinctive taste. I got introduced to it when I tried to buy into the Gothenburg harbour terminal. Loved it ever since!'

'Well, if we're going to do business together, why not. I

guess I can leave my car at your office and take a cab back from here. I'm staying at the Grand Hotel.'

James smiled.

'No worries. Let's see if we can make a deal together. For me it would be a new life.'

Chris's demeanour changed. 'Hey, James, don't let's get too pally-pally, we're not going to sell unless the price is right!'

The waiter handed out the three shots of Aquavit. Armstrong sipped his.

'Wow, that's rocket fuel. What a taste!'

James laughed.

'That's not the way to drink it. It has to be knocked straight back. Skål!'

James and Chris knocked their drinks straight back. Armstrong followed suit. What he didn't know was that James and Chris had already arranged with the waiter that they would be drinking shots of water. Aquavit was a clear alcohol. They downed several more shots.

Chris smiled. 'Okay, Ben, I'm curious to know how you can raise the finance to buy all of our operations, as well as Macrae Holdings. Do you honestly think it's possible to do such a huge acquisition?'

Armstrong remained poker-faced.

'You let me worry about that. Yes, it will be the biggest acquisition that I've ever done but with my partners I'm sure we can arrange the necessary funding.'

Chris frowned.

'You know we're talking billions and not millions of dollars, right?'

'Yes, I know. I promise you my partners have the capital if it makes sense to them.'

'So, who are your partners?'

'Oh, apart from my own capital, I have a group of companies and individuals that can put up the money. You don't have to worry about that!'

James looked at Chris.

'Chris, that's not our business. All we have to do is receive Ben's offer and say yes or no.'

'Yes, you're right, James. I'm always the sceptical one,' said Chris.

He turned again to Armstrong and, half smiling, continued, 'You know there are others interested in buying us out as well?'

Ben smiled. After a cool start to the meeting earlier in the afternoon, he felt he was starting to build a good relationship with both of them.

'That, I'm not surprised to hear. Of course there are.'

Chris looked contented, but then added, 'Remember, Ben. You only get one bite of the cherry. Your offer has to be your final one. Do we understand each other?'

'Absolutely, I will not disappoint you.'

Good! Do you want to go to a club afterwards?'

'Sure, why not? Let me get the bill for dinner, though. This has been very enjoyable.'

They left the Bartons Arms just after 10:00 p.m. and walked a short distance to The Elbow Room. As they reached the top of the stairs to access the club, a wall of smoke, chatter and loud music hit them head-on. It was a small, intimate club with a dance floor filled with couples surrounded by others drinking and talking in booths. Behind the central bar was another quieter room filled with couches and small tables. The three of them slouched down into the comfortable seats. They idly continued to chat when they were joined by three very attractive ladies.

'You guys look like a lot of fun! Can we join you?'

The one girl looked at Chris and winked at him on the blind side of Armstrong.

'Sure, go ahead,' said Chris.

After a couple of bottles of champagne and some dances, Chris and James got up to leave. 'Sorry, everybody, but we have to get home. Ben, are you coming with us?'

Ben sat looking up at both of them with an extremely satisfied grin on his face. One of the girls moved her hand up and down his thigh.

'I think I'll stay a bit longer and then cab it back to the hotel.'

'Okay, Ben. Neither of us will be at the office tomorrow, but you can pick up your car whenever.' They shook hands.

Ben exhaled loudly. 'I'll get back to you once I receive your asking price and I've evaluated it properly.'

'Take care, Ben, and don't get into too much trouble,' said James, laughing.

Ben went back to the Grand Hotel with his escort after leaving the club sometime after James and Chris had left.

He made it to his room with her but passed out on the bed. She undressed, stripped him off and then opened the door to his room. The other two girls came in, stripped off and took compromising photographs of the scene. Afterwards, they left him tucked up in bed.

Downstairs, they left the hotel by the side door on Church Street and hopped into the back seat of a BMW 740i waiting across the street. James and Chris turned around from the front seats and grinned.

'Did you get it all?'

'We sure did. It was easy. You guys sure softened him up in

more ways than one!'

They all laughed.

'Here's the camera. It's all on there.'

James handed over an envelope full of cash.

'Thanks, girls. It's much appreciated!'

After the girls had left the car, Chris turned to James.

'Well, we've done it now. We've broken the ice.'

James rubbed his hands together.

'Yes! Let's see if we've woken the lion up and he takes the bait.'

****

The Cathay Pacific Boeing 777 throttled back the two large GE90 turbo fan engines and lowered the two sets of wing flaps in preparation for the final approach to Boston Logan International airport. It had flown non-stop from Hong Kong.

General Shen looked down from his window seat through the wispy cream clouds at the bright-blue rolling sea and white caps in Massachusetts Bay. He yawned, trying to clear the slight pressure in his ears. He had decided he needed a personal meeting with Ben Armstrong after receiving Armstrong's latest message. Customs and Immigration was cleared using his Lei Wen, Managing Director, Shanghai HVAC Controls identity. That was the alias he always used with Armstrong.

Shen checked into his luxury suite at the Liberty Hotel, located at Beacon Hill and overlooking downtown Boston. His stay would be short but busy. His meeting with Armstrong at the Pair-Tree Capital head office on Federal Street was to be in two hours. Time for a shower and some personal business.

He sat at the ornate rosewood office desk in his suite and logged onto the internet using his own laptop. He was invisible to the outside world with his secure VPN connection. Next, he logged into his secret offshore bank accounts. Now that the Marseille and Rotterdam ownership contracts had been completed, he noted he now had over three million us dollars in his private slush fund. He was satisfied.

He changed the VPN server location to Hong Kong and for the next hour and a half, he set up a fictitious company that provided freight tonnage statistics to Pair-Tree Capital. Shen listed the name of only one director and owner, except it wasn't himself. It was the name of Li Ming. He transferred two hundred and fifty thousand dollars into the new company account via an intermediary account and then promptly closed the intermediary account. He smiled to himself. Not only had he set himself up to be financially secure, in addition he also had a fall-back plan if everything was to go wildly wrong with the scheme he had set up to terminate the Macrae's once and for all.

Armstrong's downtown office was large and sumptuous. It was heavily carpeted. There were pictures of his grandfather and a number of harbour terminals adorning the walls.

'Lei! It's great to see you again. Welcome to Boston. I wasn't expecting you to come so quickly!' Armstrong looked tired as he sat down at the conference table with his visitor.

'Me too, but after I received your call – given the seriousness of the developments – we could only discuss this face to face.'

'Agreed. Frankly, I can't believe how quickly this has all transpired. I guess you heard that James Macrae's parents died in a dreadful gas explosion?'

'Yes, I saw the news. While it was a terrible accident, it

seems it has opened a path for us to acquire the Macrae-Claybourne terminals.'

'It sure has. After I received a call from James Macrae indicating that they were thinking of getting out of the business, I went immediately to see him and his partner at their Birmingham headquarters. I have to say it was a difficult meeting to start with. Claybourne is a guy that doesn't want to sell. He will have to be bought off. It's Macrae leading the charge for the sale.'

'How so?'

'Well, it's clear to me that James Macrae has re-thought what he wants out of life. He's lost his parents and realised that life doesn't go on for ever. It seems he wants to spend more time with his family.'

'So where are we at now?'

Armstrong smiled.

'I believe I have built a good relationship with both of them. Got to say, it was hard work, but I think I won them over in the end. They, at least Chris Claybourne, had difficulty understanding how I could raise such a huge amount of money to buy them out.'

'I don't blame him. That's only natural given the size and scope of their business. I would query that as well. What did you tell him?'

'I told him, apart from Pair-Tree Capital, I had several companies and private investors that were all looking for good returns on their money. I also told him I have the backing of Wall Street.'

'Good. That's all they need to know. Once the money is transferred, what do they care?'

'Exactly! Last night I received a large courier package containing their estimated value of each individual business. That is, the operations of each of their four European terminals as well as their value on the partnership with the Saudi Company that owns Yanbu. In addition, they included the asking price for Macrae Holdings.'

'This is a truly remarkable development. I wasn't expecting Yanbu to be included, let alone Macrae Holdings.' Shen looked deadly serious.

'Do they say how they estimated their selling prices?'

'Absolutely. Apparently, they had just completed a company audit. It seems their bankers wanted up-to-date valuations of all their assets. Not only were their last set of financials included, but Deloitte carried out their complete audit. Can't argue with that. Of course, I had to sign a non-disclosure and confidentiality agreement.'

Shen nodded.

Armstrong slid a large file across the desk to Shen. Expressionless and taking his time, Shen looked through each executive summary of the reports for each individual company in the group.

'Have you authenticated these accounts and audit reports?'

'I have. My staff and myself worked all through the night. With the time difference between ourselves and Europe, we were able to contact the relevant parties. It's all above board. There's more though.'

'Oh?'

'Yes, Macrae and Claybourne left me in no doubt from our meeting that we would have to pay over the odds to buy them out. They've thrown in an obscene valuation on top of the figures you see in that file. They're couching it under "goodwill". Claybourne also hinted during our meeting that there were other interested parties as well.'

'Umm. I guess that's to be expected. You said Macrae wants to sell but Claybourne doesn't?'

'Yes. It was made very clear to me.'

'Ben, given what we paid for our shares in Zeebrugge, Marseille and Rotterdam, are the Macrae valuations in line with them?'

'Bottom line? Our partners' assets were all inflated with "goodwill", so I would say yes.'

Shen drew in a large breath and sat back in his chair, contemplating everything that he had read and heard.

'Frankly, nothing is much of a surprise to me. They know the strategic value of their business. It's a real jewel. Let me have this file and you retain copies. I will have to get back to you regarding what we pay for their assets. This is a significant amount of money.'

Shen remained sitting back in his chair. Inside, he knew he would get instant approval from his bosses. It was a no-brainer, except he would have to get formal approval from the president. This was way out of his authority. Maybe he could gain some rungs up the ladder for himself.

Chapter 47

'I'm scared, Huan!'

'Listen, Chyou, it will be alright. If we can do it, you can too.'

Huan Zhou felt a cold shiver run down his spine as he remembered the claustrophobic horror of being crammed into a small hidden compartment with his wife, his two children and others for over fifteen hours, as they entered England illegally.

'Look, big sister, we've been here for over two months now and we've managed to start a new life. By this time tomorrow we should all be together again. I have a job for your husband already. Just try to relax and tell Shoi-Ming that it's a game of hide and seek.'

'I'm still not sure, Huan.'

'Where are you now?'

'We were picked up from the hotel this morning in Brussels and now we're in some sort of warehouse waiting with another group of other people.'

'Okay, you're on the last leg. Listen, you've come this far, just see it through. These guys know what they're doing.'

Thornton and Harry entered the warehouse and stood back while the passengers were loaded into the two tanks.

Thornton patted Harry on the shoulder.

'Well, that's it, mate. Another load of cash! Come on, let's get to the hospital.'

****

'DCI Thomas, I've just heard from Border Services that Thornton passed through the docks at Calais, coming off the P&O ferry from Dover. That was over one hour ago. The two tankers are travelling together.'

'Okay, Hudson, I've already got the Belgian police armed squad on standby. Let's see if we can rattle Thornton's cage and see what happens. There has to be some kind of a link between him, the death of the hazmat shipper at the Jules Bordet Institute and maybe Stanfield and Nash.'

DCI Thomas hoped to hell there was. It had been weeks of no results and he was under serious pressure from his superiors.

****

Thornton and Harry negotiated the twists and turns of the narrow streets of Brussels in convoy.

'Everything okay, Harry?'

'Yep. All good. This heavy rain and low cloud doesn't give us much visibility, though.'

Oblivious to the pouring rain outside the two tanks, the fourteen adults and six children remained quiet. The sedatives were working. Huan's sister, Chyou, bit her lip constantly to the point it started to bleed. She clutched her son close to her, while her husband held her hand. She tried closing her eyes, but couldn't help peeping at the others in the tank every so often to see what was happening.

'Okay, Harry, I'm just turning right onto Rue Héger-Bordet. I'm scheduled for Bay 1, you are Bay 2.'

'Got it, boss.'

As the overhead doors opened up, Thornton and Harry inched their way into the loading bays, the dripping tractor trailers drenching the concrete floor with water. Their cab windows misted up with the temperature change. A loud hiss from the air brakes being applied echoed against the bare concrete walls and support pillars. It seemed unusually quiet.

Thornton sat in his cab for a few moments, listening and staring around him. The hair on the back of his neck started to rise and he could feel goosebumps on his skin. He left his engine running. Before he could alert Harry, Harry had already jumped down from his cab, looking for the waste supervisor.

'Hands up! You! Get out of the cab. Now!'

Thornton looked down through his cab door window. He found himself facing the barrel of a gun. Harry was already surrounded by two heavily armed officers. Thornton quickly grabbed his mobile and immediately sent a message. The message consisted of one letter: E. He rammed the truck into first gear and released the air brakes. As the veins in his neck started to throb, the cab reared up and shot forward from the drive-through bay. He braced himself hard behind the steering wheel. There was a loud bang as he rammed a police car that was blocking the way. He managed to push it aside. He made a sharp turn at the road but to no avail; two other police cars blocked the way. He was trapped. He put his hands down and slumped his head forward onto the steering wheel.

Harry's reactions were equally swift. He took advantage of the crash distraction and managed to dart to the side of the bay. Panting hard, he slowly inched himself into a dark corner and located an exit door. He felt for the bar, opened it and fled blindly into a side street. He felt his feet slipping on the wet cobble stones as he tried to gain traction. He could hear police officers close behind him. As he brushed his wet hair from across his face, he found himself on another narrow cobblestone street. He ran as fast as he could back towards Waterloo Boulevard. He could hear the footsteps and yelling behind him for him to stop getting louder. He tried to increase his speed, but his steel-cap safety shoes were not the most flexible. With his heart pumping faster and faster, he turned right, crashing into several pedestrians and knocking them flying. Strewn shopping bags across the pavement did not slow his pursuers. Glancing behind him, he could see the long line of traffic coming to a halt as the police squad spread out across the street behind him. He took advantage of a break in the traffic and ran towards a castle on the other side of the road. As he sprinted towards it, a security guard – on seeing the police squad chase their man – stepped out from the Porte de Hal museum located in the old gatehouse of the former fortified city walls. He tried to grab Harry, but Harry side-stepped him, jumped over a low chain-link fence and proceeded to run through an adjoining park, dodging amongst the trees. The squad were catching up with him, so he abruptly changed direction and ran across a large flower bed, making for an exit from the park into another adjoining street. Gasping for breath, his boots sank into the soft, wet earth. The mud stuck in heavy layers to the bottom of his soles. As he looked up to spot the exit to the park, his path was blocked by more heavily armed police. He was surrounded. He sank panting to the ground, a beaten man.

Thornton slowly raised his head from the steering wheel. He gaped through all his cab windows and saw armed police officers surrounding his truck. He closed his eyes, let out a long sigh and got down from the cab. With pistols facing him, he felt his wrists grabbed from behind and the handcuffs roughly being closed on his skin.

******

Inside the tank, Chyou felt the rocking motion of the trailer stop. She clung to her son and held her husband's hand tightly. There was eery silence. Still no one spoke inside the tank. Could they be at the docks already? She didn't know. She closed her eyes and tried to slow her breathing down.

****

The last of the compromised containers that had been designed with the defective twist lock castings and planted in the Macrae-Claybourne fleet had been repainted and renumbered by the Macrae-Claybourne personnel. The containers were infiltrated back into the Chinese carrier system. An intermediate carrier had been used to transport them through a third party broker back into the system.

Several days later, the Chinese, fully laden mega container vessel *MV Jinsha II* slowly manoeuvred out of the port of Felixstowe on the east coast of England and headed south, making its way through the North Sea towards the entrance of the English Channel. It was a calm evening, and the sea was placid.

Within hours, a powerful weather front quickly blew up from the east. The wind started to whistle and howl amongst the hundreds of stacked containers above deck. The shrill noise became piercing to the ear drums. Huge waves began to form very quickly in the shallow sea and white foam streamers started to break off from the white caps in the roaring gale. Low, heavy clouds swarmed towards the ship as the visibility dropped dramatically. Intermittent sheet lighting illuminated the thick grey and black clouds from behind while deafening thunder bolts roared overhead.

The ship's giant port side profile against the wind and waves provoked a violent rolling motion. The captain clung to the brass handrail on the bridge. 'Hard to starboard!'

The vessel was slow to respond due to its sheer size. The captain continued to strain his eyes through the rain and salt spray being hurled against the bridge windows.

'Bloody hell, boys, this is a bad one! Hang on!'

As the vessel rolled to starboard, stacks of containers became loose. With their defective twist lock castings, there was nothing to hold them together. Hundreds of containers were violently thrust overboard, crashing into the raging surf below. Some sank immediately, some bounced and bobbed like corks in the confused sea.

'What do you think, Captain?' said the first officer.

'Honestly, I'm not sure we going to make it. Take a look amidships, it looks like the deck is starting to sag. It can only be a matter of time before the hull cracks. Put out a Mayday call and prepare to abandon ship!'

Within minutes the entire crew had gathered on deck. A number of life rafts were jettisoned off the ship and a cargo net was attached to the coaming and slung over the side. The captain was the last person to join the rest of his crew in the fully enclosed lifeboat.

'Okay. Let's go!'

The crew braced themselves for impact with the water as the large orange watertight lifeboat slid down the chute at the stern of the ship.

With the challenging sea conditions, the surf became even more treacherous with floating containers that threatened to crush the lifeboat.

As the lone ship continued to roll, the centre of gravity of the ship moved to starboard, accentuated by the momentum of the shifted cargo. She leaned heavily into the water, inviting the dark, furious sea to sweep into her gaping open holds. The double hull design of the ship was no match for the weight of the thousands of tonnes of water that poured in through the open deck. A massive creaking and tearing moan consumed the vessel. The hull shuddered as its steel structure was viciously ripped in half. The bow section stood momentarily erect against the ink black sky, while the stern, housing the bridge, pivoted high up above the water.

As the fully covered lifeboat was thrown about in the surf, the crew remained stiff and silent in their seats. The captain looked over at his first officer.

'By god. That was a close one!'

He peered through the lifeboat window. Within minutes, each half of the ship disappeared below the frothing turmoil of angry sea beneath it.

Then there was nothing left to see, except the debris of

containers being tossed about like plastic bath toys. It was as though the ship had never existed.

48

Chapter 48

Janet stepped into Lisa Taylor's office. It was already late afternoon. The watery sun was getting lower in the sky, casting long, pale shadows across the room. She let out a huge yawn.

'Oh! I'm so sorry, Lisa!'

Lisa let out a chuckle.

'Oh, don't worry. I feel the same too.'

'It's been a long day. Can't believe the summer's already over. Feels like I missed out this year with that spell I had working at home and no real holiday. I think I'm going to need a winter break this year, somewhere warm. How about you?'

'Oh no such luck for me, I'm afraid, Janet. I've bought a new house in Sutton Coldfield and I'm moving out of my parents' place. Can't wait, to be honest. It'll be the first house I've ever owned on my own. Living with my parents after the divorce was my only option. At least now I can afford somewhere where I can please myself. I'll have a lot of expenses getting the house to how I want it, so there will be a lot to do.'

'Congratulations!'

'Thanks!'

Lisa got up from her computer terminal.

'I wanted to ask you what happened when you questioned Lee Yuen about the leaked software?'

'Well, that's partly why I'm here.'

Janet took out a 3. 5-inch computer disc from a file she was holding. 'Here are the access codes for each of the databases that comprise our whole proprietary logistics system. I can't think why I never gave them to you before.'

'Oh, that's great! Thank you. At least you've got a back-up should we ever need it.'

'You'll also find the password for the firewall if you ever need to access the system remotely. Working from home caused me to rethink how we can work smarter if we are not able to get into the office.'

'Wow! That's terrific. Thank you.'

'Regarding Lee, I've got him on a really tight rein right now. Confidentially, I can tell you this. I've got a recruitment agency looking for a replacement for him as we speak. Once they've found the right candidate, I will let him go. If I could do it now, I would, but we need someone who can replace his particular skill set. He's a unique database programmer.'

'Yes, he is. How long do you think it will take to find a replacement?'

'The agency thinks that by the end of next week, they will have two individuals to choose from.'

'A week, eh?'

'That's what they say. Let's hope they can. I'll be glad when this is all behind us.'

'Yes, you're right. It's been very worrying for all of us.'

When Janet had gone, Lisa made copies of the databases, after entering the access codes she had received on the computer disc. She left the office just after 6:00 p.m. She drove her silver Volkswagen Golf GTI out of the employee car park and threaded her way towards the Walsall Road and made her way north.

She did not see the dark-coloured Toyota Camry following several vehicles behind her. She pulled into the Malt Shovel and parked her car at the rear of the pub. The dark-coloured Toyota pulled in and parked several spaces away from her. The driver pulled down both sun visors and slid low in the seat. Lisa remained seated in her car.

A black BMW M5 entered the car park not long after and circled the pub three times before pulling into the space beside her. Lisa hopped out of her car into the passenger side of the BMW. The driver of the Toyota found it hard to see through the tinted windows of the BMW but shot multiple photographs of the vehicle using a powerful telephoto lens.

****

Stanfield had just finished up arranging for more illegal immigrants to enter their pipeline when a text popped up. E. Within seconds, he had levered off the plastic cap at the foot of his tubular metal-framed bed and extracted a tightly rolled up piece of paper that contained the usernames and passwords of his secret bank accounts. He then grabbed his Oh shit! bag, inserted the sheet of paper in his pocket and ran downstairs from the apartment into the warehouse.

'Dan, come with me!'

'Get out now, Billy! Get out!'

Billy didn't need any further warning. He exited the office and hurried off down the street, leaving the yard gates wide open.

Stanfield and Nash ran out to Thornton's Ford Transit parked across the road. Stanfield's heart pumped harder and faster. He drove out of the industrial estate only to see an oncoming group of police cars and personnel carriers racing into the area. He kept his head down.

'Where are we going, Hugh?'

'North. I just got the emergency code from Charlie. It means the police are on to us. If all goes well, we'll meet up there and start our getaway from the UK.'

****

General Shen walked briskly along the winding path through the gardens of the Zhongnanhai Compound towards Li Ming's office. The weather was cooler, and a heavy mist hung over the lake, adding to the silence. While it was a national holiday in China, the government compound was working normally. He clutched his briefcase tightly, containing copies he had made of the Macrae-Claybourne financials.

As he walked into the conference room next to Ming's office, he was surprised to see five other men dressed in smart suits around the table. Ming introduced the Minister of Finance, together with his aides. As Shen took a seat, Ming placed a call from the central conference phone in front of him.

'We are ready for you now, sir.'

The men all sat in silence for a few minutes and then stood up abruptly as the president of the People's Republic of China entered the room.

President Jiang Zemin sat down at the head of the table. Adjusting his thick black-framed spectacles, he looked down at the paper Ming slid across to him. He then looked up and stared at every man present with his piercing eyes. Still silent, he picked up the paper with both hands and brought it closer to his eyes. He then placed it back on the table.

'This is a huge amount of money.'

Deep in thought, he rubbed his hand several times across his chin. Turning to his Minister of Finance, he asked, 'What is your opinion?'

'President Zemin. Yes, it is a large amount of money, sir. My department has analysed all the figures. Valuations of all the Macrae-Claybourne assets, both their operations companies and their real estate company reflect current market price levels. The audit carried out by Deloitte's is completely authentic. What is not realistic is the valuation placed on "goodwill". This figure is not based on anything tangible.'

Zemin frowned. 'I see. What's your opinion, Ming?'

'President Zemin. I agree with the minister.'

Zemin turned to Shen. 'General Shen. And what is your opinion?'

Shen sat up in his chair and placed both hands on the table.

'Sir, while the "goodwill" aspect is certainly ambitious, it is not unexpected. James Macrae and his partner know full well the true value of their locations. Macrae clearly wants to show something for his family's four generations' worth of efforts. Claybourne, his partner, on the other hand is reluctant to sell and the only way he will sell is to basically ask a ridiculously high price. The message is: "if anyone's willing to pay this much, they can have it". Having said that, he is keeping hold of Claybourne Holdings. This company owns property in Immingham, London, Birmingham, Manchester and Glasgow.'

Zemin nodded, acknowledging Shen's point of view and then turned to Ming. 'Ming, pass me the file with the audit reports.'

Ming slid the file across the table.

Zemin opened the file and studied each executive summary one by one. The room remained completely silent. Finally, he took off his glasses, rubbed his eyes and looked directly at Shen.

'So, tell me what you would do if you were in my shoes, General?'

Shen was taken aback by the question but tried not show it. He did catch sight, however, of Ming, clearly upset that he was the person that Zemin was looking to for advice.

General Shen focussed solely on the president and replied with an assured and confident voice.

'President Zemin, I believe we should move forward immediately with the purchase of both Macrae-Claybourne Logistics and Macrae Holdings. Of course, it is an exorbitant amount of money but within the context of our silk road policy, it should be viewed as a wise investment.'

'Um, so you say we should just go ahead and pay the asking price? You don't think we should counter the offer?'

'No, sir, I do not. We should take this deal off the market as soon as possible before anyone else gets a chance to close it.'

Shen paused momentarily. 'With respect, President Zemin, my four-step plan was to do exactly this. Step one was to set up a mergers and acquisitions company based offshore and buy up all the seaports that we consider desirable. This included the ports of Macrae Shipping. They are strategically positioned for us to use Turkey as the gateway into Europe and create footholds along the Mediterranean Sea and southern Europe. Not only that, but we would control the entry and exit to the Black Sea. We will always need to keep Russia in check. Should we need any of these ports for geopolitical purposes later, we have them in our pocket.'

President Zemin made a pyramid with his fingers. He closed his eyes and thought for a few more seconds. He opened them again and turned to his Minister of Finance. 'What do you think we should do?'

The minister cleared his throat. 'I think we should counter the offer. This amount of money is unacceptable. As Minister of Finance, it is my responsibility to safeguard our spending.'

His aides all nodded in agreement.

'And, Ming, what do you think we should do?'

Ming puffed himself up in his chair. Angered by Shen's prominence in the meeting, Ming now saw his chance to belittle Shen.

'I categorically agree with the minister. We should counter the offer. That is what any sensible person would do. With respect, Shen is a military man while we are all businessmen.'

The president nodded. 'One more question. I need to be assured that the death of Macrae's parents had nothing to do with us?'

Ming sat up again. 'No, sir! My head of security in London has made extensive inquiries and it is clear the police are treating this as a fatal accident.'

The president turned to Shen.

'General?'

'Sir. No, this is nothing to do with us.'

'Good. We will continue our silk road expansion by purely

commercial means. I do not want any blood on our hands. Our long-term strategic objective to dominate the world must be made without any acts of terrorism or murder. You must use all hybrid methods of warfare available to you. Understood?'

Shen nodded. 'Yes, sir. Perfectly.'

'Okay. Here's my decision on our offer to buy out the Macrae-Claybourne businesses. Halve the value of the "goodwill" portion and pay out the full price for the assessed value of the assets.'

He turned to the minister.

'Prepare our offer accordingly and give it to Shen to pass to Pair-Tree Capital. I want it done immediately!'

He got up and left the room.

Ming scowled at Shen as he left the room.

49

Chapter 49

'Hey, Chris, any news yet? Have we heard anything from Armstrong?'

'No, not yet. It's only been a couple of days since we couriered the financials to Boston!'

'I know. I know. I'm an impatient bastard. I just want to finish this up as soon as we can. I need to get back to a normal life.'

Chris stepped forward from his desk and put his hand on James's shoulder.

'James, just settle down and be patient. We have to wait. If we try contacting Armstrong, we will lose the upper hand. We're doing everything we can to force an end to this. Sit down for a minute. I do have some news. Just hang on while I close the door.'

James remained quiet.

'Look at this news article that just came in.'

Chinese mega container vessel sinks in the North Sea.

Early reports are coming in that the MV Jinsha II broke up and sank in gale force winds yesterday off the coast of Margate after a number of containers shifted and fell overboard. Her twenty-five crew members were able to abandon ship just minutes before she sank.

According to MV Jinsha II's captain: 'It was a miracle there were no injuries or loss of life and it proved the effectiveness of ongoing training, and competence of everyone on board.'

All vessels in the area should be aware that a large number of floating containers are also posing a hazard to shipping.'

Chris remained silent while James read the article.

'Bloody hell, Chris, I bet those sabotaged Chinese containers were on that ship. Thank god no one was hurt.'

'My feelings exactly. It's one thing to cause damage, it's another thing to lose innocent lives. My understanding is that the vessel pulled out of Felixstowe believing they could outrun the storm. Instead of being downwind of it in the Channel, they must have caught the full force of the gale broadside on. If she keeled over, there would have been nothing to stop the sea pouring into the hull. Probably broke its back and sank quickly after that.'

James sat silent for a while. 'Godamn it. They are the ones who started this! What a dirty, filthy business this is turning out to be.'

Chris changed the subject. 'So, what else has been happening?'

'Well, following our hybrid warfare model, we are on the offensive. Janet gave Lisa copies of the codes to access the bogus firewall, in addition to the username and passwords to access the infected logistics software. Lisa then made copies of these and left work.'

James continued, 'She was followed by Scott Farmer, the private detective we hired. Apparently, she drove to the Malt

Shovel pub in Great Barr and made a rendezvous with another person in a BMW. Our man took photos of the car, the driver and the plate. When Lisa got back into her own car, he then tried to follow the BMW after it left the car park. Seems it was travelling south on the M6 towards London when he lost sight of it.'

Chris propped his head up on his hands. 'Do you want to pass this information onto MI6?'

'No. I don't. There's going to be all manner of shit hitting the fan if this software goes to who we think it will go to. Logically, we have the potential to wreck not just Shanghai, but if we are right about Pair-Tree Capital being used as a front for the Chinese to take over various seaports, then we can maybe wreck Zeebrugge, Marseille and Rotterdam as well. Better to keep it at arms' length.'

'Fair enough. I'm like you, James. I can't wait to see the carnage this is going to create!'

'So, on the other front, you and I have set the trap for Pair-Tree Capital. There's no way any company would make an offer for us at the price we've demanded. If they come back to us quickly, then it must be the Chinese bankrolling the venture. When we turn down their offer it must provoke a strong reaction. That's when we have to be prepared for them to come for us.'

'That's for sure. We can also discredit Ben Armstrong with our compromising photos. The Chinese certainly wrecked the life of Greg Driver, the journalist. We can do the same to them.'

There was a knock on the door. Rachel, James's secretary, poked her head round the door.

'Excuse me interrupting, but this fax just came in. Thought

you might want to see it immediately.'

'Thanks, Rachel.'

James got up from his chair and took it from her. He read it and then passed it to Chris. James smiled for the first time that morning. Chris looked back at him with a wry grin.

****

Thornton and Harry, still handcuffed, were taken in two prison vans from the Jules Bordet Institute and transferred in an armed convoy back to England. Neither Thornton nor Harry said anything about the twenty Chinese nationals still hidden in the tanks that were left behind in Brussels. Ever optimistic, they felt they might get released on some technicality or other. There was nothing at all to pin on them. The police still didn't know about Stanfield and Nash. It was only suspicion. They certainly didn't know about the illegal immigrants and how could they know anything about M. Borrellier's fatal accident? Once on the street again, they could flee, without ever admitting culpability.

****

Inside the hidden compartment of the tanker, Chyou, her husband and their son, Shoi-Ming, sat amongst the others.

Chyou whispered to her husband. 'There's been no motion of the vehicle for a while. I wonder if we are on the ferry.'

'Could be. I can't wait to start our new life.'

Chyou gave him a weak smile back.

****

DI Stella Hudson wound her way through the bleak maze of security gates and corridors in Brixton Prison. As each barred gate was closed, the loud sound of metal on metal sent a hollow resounding clang bouncing back and forth off the bare concrete walls. The prison officer opened one of the solid cell doors. Hudson looked through another set of stout iron bars into the small, windowless cell.

'Ah, Mr Thornton. We meet again. Welcome back to England! You will be facing numerous charges including obstruction of justice and aiding and abetting known criminals.'

Thornton stared straight back at Hudson. 'Nice try, Inspector. I've done no such thing. How many times do I have to tell you muttonheads, I run a legitimate transport business? I even told you before that the Jules Bordet Hospital is one of our main contracts. They pay good money for the disposal of their waste. It's never been a secret. I need to be released right now, I've got schedules to keep! We can discuss the harassment and false arrest suit later on.'

'We'll see about that. Oh, I forgot to mention Monsieur Borrellier, the dispatcher at the Jules Bordet Hospital. That's another set of questions for you, but all in good time.'

Thornton laughed. 'You're wasting your time, inspector. You're on a fishing expedition! I'm getting my lawyer in here.'

'Excellent. You're really going to need him, especially as we have found the fingerprints of Stanfield and Nash all over your so-called transport business premises.'

Thornton tried to remain stone-faced, but started to feel his stomach fill with acid.

Hudson went down to the next level in the prison.

'Ah, Harry, the ever-faithful driver loyal to Charlie Thornton. If you cooperate with us, you may be able to avoid being transferred to Belmarsh at Her Majesty's pleasure.'

'How can I cooperate with you? I'm just a driver, an employee of Thornton.'

****

Stanfield accelerated the Ford Transit van onto the M40.

'Pass me Charlie's cap, Dan. You never know who may see us.'

'There you go. So, what's the plan, Hugh? I know you said we were close to pulling out of the UK, so you must have one.'

'We do. Charlie rents a large barn near Hereford. It's in a remote part of the country to the west of the city. He's had it for years, well before the Brinks Mat robbery. He's got plenty of gear in there that could be useful to us. If the plan falls into place, Charlie will join us there.'

'Okay, but that doesn't help us escape the country!'

'We've a few loose ends to tie up first. For a start, we're gonna get even with James Macrae and his family. I have a score to settle with him. Once we've got rid of him, the plan is to get to the fishing port of Fishguard on the Welsh coast and take a fishing boat to Rosslare in Southern Ireland. We can decide where we go from there.'

'Somewhere warm, I hope!'

'Definitely.'

Stanfield didn't think to mention that Nash would not be with them.

****

Two heavy-duty truck drivers from the Belgian police drove

the trucks and tank trailers left behind at the hospital, to a secure police compound on the outskirts of Brussels. They had not been filled with medical waste, but would be kept as evidence and inspected later by the UK authorities. The two tanker rigs were parked safely side by side and locked up. The fresh air fans continued to work, bringing oxygen to the hidden occupants. As the evening approached, the autumn temperature began to drop rapidly. The battery power for both trailers started to deplete as the truck engines were no longer operating to charge them.

No sound could be heard from inside the tankers.

****

The black BMW M5 that had picked up the computer discs from Lisa Taylor at the Malt Shovel pub pulled off from the M1 at the Newport Pagnell service area. The driver needed to make sure she had not been followed. She waited in her car, carefully watching other cars pull in after her. She started her engine, and slowly drove around to the blind side of the building, waited, and then did the same around the fuel station. She watched the exit slip road and when two heavy trucks were gathering speed to exit the area, she accelerated hard and cut in just before them. She left the motorway abruptly at the next exit, making her way to a business centre car park close to Bletchley Park. It was an ironic switching point. Bletchley Park was the place where the mathematician Alan Turing and his team deciphered the German Enigma machine used for sending secure messages during the Second World War. A maroon Ford Escort was parked amongst several other vehicles close to the office block. The driver exited the BMW, walked over to the Ford Escort, opened the driver's door, and drove off.

50

Chapter 50

James and Chris both read the fax that had just arrived.

'Offer coming by courier. Will call tomorrow. Ben Armstrong – Pair-Tree Capital, Boston MA.'

James ran his hand over his head. 'Bloody hell! I know I was being impatient but gotta say, that's quick!'

'Yeah, you're right. It is!'

James sat down again and clasped his hands in front of his face.

'You know what this means, don't you?'

He didn't wait for an answer.

'It conclusively proves, at least in my book, that the Chinese are financing Pair-Tree. Think about it! I'm sure both Pair-Tree, various independent investors and Wall Street could not have agreed to a deal so quickly. There would be too many variables to discuss among all the different parties. Right?'

'Exactly! It would take time to agree on a final offer and then there would be the question of percentage of shares amongst all the various parties. No, to turn this around so quickly, it must have been one party or, at the most, two. Let's face it, we gave them a ridiculous sale price.'

'Well, let's wait and see what they offer. Whatever it is, they are going to be really pissed when we turn them down. I wish I could be a fly on the wall when that happens.'

****

Inspector Thomas was back in the manhunt operations room at the Metropolitan police headquarters. He stared at the large white boards on the wall. Names, places, times and events were all linked together like an elaborate cobweb.

A forensic team had worked through the night at Thornton's transport yard. Positive fingerprints had been found for both Nash and Stanfield. They'd been living in the apartment at the warehouse after all. He'd been right the first time. He checked the forensics report in detail and then the photographs that had since been developed in the police lab. All the photos suggested normal living habits; food, clothes, reading material etc. There were bandages and burn cream was lying on a vanity unit in the bathroom. Thomas frowned repeatedly twizzling around the pen in his hand, his ever-inquiring mind filtering all possible permutations of where this would take him.

Thomas was still fiddling with his pen when DI Hudson came in.

'Morning, Hudson. Did you rattle the cages of Thornton and his driver?'

'Sure did. Thornton tried to hide it, but he was alarmed when I told him we'd found the fingerprints of Stanfield and Nash. Right now, Thornton and his driver are claiming complete innocence. We should let them stew for a while.'

'Agreed, Hudson.'

'So, apart from the prints were any other clues found at Thornton's yard?'

'There were. We found bandages and burn cream.'

Hudson took a large gulp of her coffee and then choked. She coughed loudly and managed to recover, wiping her mouth with a tissue.

'Sir! When we raided the warehouse, there was no sign of Stanfield and Nash. What if they were hiding in the tankers when they were purged with steam? That might account for burns?'

'We searched the tanks afterwards. There was nothing. There would have to be some kind of hiding place in there. It's plausible.'

They both sat in silence and then both stared at each other, their eyes wide open in horror. Thomas spoke first.

'Oh my god! Try this one on for size. There's only one reason for a concealed compartment. It's either contraband or maybe humans? Perhaps carrying medical waste was meant to keep customs inspectors at bay?'

'That's it, sir! We'd better get the Belgian police back there immediately to inspect those trailers in Brussels.'

'You go and I'll stay here. Chances are Stanfield and Nash are on the move, either there or here.'

****

The package from Pair-Tree Capital arrived by courier. James and Chris sat alone in James's office, just staring at it. They sat side by side, knowing they could only choose one path. There was an air of palpable solemnity. The noise from the busy transport terminal outside was dulled by heavy carpeting and triple-glazed windows.

James opened the package slowly, took out the enclosed folder and put it down if front of them. As he opened it, they both scanned the top page in silence. Waiting for each other to finish reading, they flicked over the other pages until they reached the final offer page. It was a huge sum of money, but less than they had demanded. They both looked up at the ceiling and let everything they had read sink in.

James let out a huge sigh. 'It's a massive amount of money, but less than we asked for.'

Chris grabbed the calculator from James's desk. He tapped at the keys, checked the sum with the figure on the sheet and then tapped again.

'I see what they've done. They've taken the full valuation of all the companies from the Deloitte audit and then halved the figure of our goodwill.'

'Hmmm.' James smiled.

'What they've done is given us both the chance to be bad guys! I'm gonna enjoy this. After two years of fighting these sneaky bastards, it's our turn to bring them out into the open and deliver a knockout punch.'

'Hundred percent! Let's wait for Armstrong to call and then we can both bite his head off. Can't imagine what will happen when he tells his bed partner that it's all gone to shit.'

The phone rang. James picked it up, thinking it was Armstrong on the line.

'James, it's Scott Farmer. Listen, got some news. Lisa Taylor just received a fifty thousand Euro deposit into her bank account today. From what I can deduce, it looks like it's a stage payment, suggesting there is more to come. It came through the same numbered company that has been paying her the monthly fee.'

****

Meili Shabani, the driver of the BMW M5 and Ford Escort arrived at Shanghai Pudong International Airport on a BA flight direct from Heathrow. She immediately took a cab to the Shanghai Port Authority, where she met with the president and the IT team leader.

'Did everything go according to plan, Meili?'

Meili replied. 'Yes, sir, it did. No problem whatsoever.'

'Excellent.'

The president turned to his IT manager. 'Take these computer discs, make sure they are virus free, then customise the software for our terminal here, as well as Zeebrugge, Marseille and Rotterdam. Once you've done that, infect the discs for them to be returned to Zichan, our contact at Macrae-Claybourne Logistics and have her re-install them.'

Meili spoke. 'Do you want me to pay the balance of her commission once that has been accomplished?'

'I will need to speak with General Shen first. He may decide to have her terminated.'

51

Chapter 51

Chyou slowly opened her eyes and looked around. The overhead light was becoming dimmer by the minute. Everyone had a grey tint to their skin and blueish lips and most could no longer stand, desperately conserving oxygen. One man tried to stand up, clambering desperately on top of the others, trying to suck air from the overhead air vent. The cries from the others had long been weak and slurred. She tried to speak to her son, Shoi-Ming, but all he could do was give her a weak smile back and then closed his eyes. Her husband was cold to her touch and did not respond. Another person by the name of Zhang was convulsing, foaming at his mouth. The light went out. Chyou let out one last whimper as her eyes closed.

****

It was lunchtime when the call came through to the Brussels police secure vehicle compound to check inside the tank trailers. Being understaffed, the call was not picked up straight away but went to voicemail. The compound supervisor and his assistant were sitting in the lunchroom munching away on sandwiches and discussing Anderlecht's chances of winning their soccer league. Three police cars pulled up at the gate with their full sirens and light bridges blazing.

The supervisor opened the gate. 'What the fuck's going on?'

'Don't just stand there, get the keys for those two trucks and trailers that were brought in here yesterday!'

The supervisor didn't need to be told twice. He ran to the office.

As the trucks were being started, two policemen climbed the steps to the top of the tanks, opened the compartment lids and shone flashlights down inside. 'Nothing here, sir!'

'And nothing here, sir!'

'Okay, let's try these hatches underneath both tanks.'

Each hatch was lowered, and the inspectors looked inside each compartment. Their flashlights revealed nothing. 'Alright, someone get us a couple of measuring tapes.'

For the next half an hour the compound supervisor and his assistant clambered inside both tanks, measuring the internal length of the compartments with the outer layer of the tank's double skin. They looked at each other when they compared notes.

'Santa Maria! There must be a hidden compartment in each tank! Let's get back in there and find out how to access them.'

The supervisor and the assistant went back inside the tanks. Eventually the assistant came back out as fast as he could. He doubled over and threw up all over himself and the ground. Two minutes later, the supervisor appeared. He was white-faced and retching.

'You better get a load of body bags. It looks like Auschwitz in there.'

****

'Hello, James. It's Ben Armstrong. How are you?'

'Hang on while I get hold of my partner.' He kept Armstrong waiting several minutes.

'Okay, we're both here now. You're on speakerphone.'

'Hello again, James, and hello, Chris. I take it you've had time to consider our offer?'

There was silence on the line. Finally, James spoke.

'You've fucked it up!'

'Pardon... Excuse me?'

'You fucked it up! You heard me!'

'I don't understand. How did I do that? I believe we've made you a perfectly good offer!'

Chris spoke this time. 'I thought I made it crystal clear that I didn't want to sell. It was James who was driving this, not me. I told you several times that I would only sell if the price was right. Those were our terms.'

'But I think this offer is more than fair.'

James jumped in. 'We also told you in plain language that you would only get one bite of the cherry. Keeping Chris happy was the key to me leaving and starting a new life.'

'I'm sorry, James, I don't remember that.'

James raised his voice. 'You had this in the palm of your hand, Armstrong. If you'd have given us our asking price straight off the bat, it would have kept Chris happy and stopped me from rethinking my position. In short, you've blown the only chance you had!'

'So, what if I can come back with a better offer?'

'Too late. I've now decided not to sell, irrespective of your offer. I can find other ways to smell the roses and spend more time with my family.'

'James and Chris, please let's not leave it like this. What if I tell you, here and now, I will match your price, one hundred percent?'

James shouted, 'You're not listening to me. You've upset my partner and now I've reconsidered my position. Honestly, if you had any integrity at all, how could you now offer the full price, just like that! I'm not going to sell and that's final!'

'James and Chris! At least give this new offer consideration. Let me call you tomorrow. That will give you time to reconsider.'

'Too late!'

Chris jumped in again. 'I think we're done here. Good day!'

Armstrong was left holding the phone in his hand. He was stunned. He honestly thought he had forged a strong enough relationship with both James and Chris to make a deal.

He put down the phone, took a deep breath and phoned Lei Wen, alias General Shen. He wondered what would happen next.

52

Chapter 52

The London head of security of the Chinese Embassy, Peng Zheng, took an early lunch. It was a warm, overcast autumn day. He strolled north along Harley Street in between the elegant, large Georgian-styled town houses with their black wrought-iron balconies and railings. He wondered how many doctors had practised here over the years behind the large, rectangular sash windows. He made his way across Marylebone Road into Regent's Park. It was something he did often. The peace and serenity of the vast park with its expanse of lush mature trees, neatly trimmed lawns and flourishing flower beds was the perfect place to think and unravel his often dark and sordid world. He found an isolated bench and sat down.

He had a big decision to make, one that could make or break him. Should he choose his present boss, Li Ming, the head of the MSS, the Ministry of State Security, as well as the private secretary of the President or General Shen?

He had been told by Ming recently to give Shen every support and assistance he could provide when Shen had visited London. From the moment he met Shen, it was apparent that he was a man on the move upwards. Not only was he affable, he was a clear thinker. He made things happen in a positive way. Conversely, Ming was too slippery to be trusted. He never felt secure under him. In a way, he had already made that choice when he arranged to take out Richard and Mary Macrae in collaboration with Shen. He had then denied to Ming that he had anything to do with it. Now it had come to his attention from an anonymous source that Ming was siphoning off money from China into a secret bank account of his own, located in Hong Kong. Having checked the story out, he considered it to be credible. He got up from the bench after a long break and returned to the embassy. He would alert the president's own agents and circumvent Ming on what he had discovered.

All he had to do now was wait and lay low.

****

The Shanghai IT manager loaded the Macrae-Claybourne logistics system onto his isolated computer. His advanced system virus checker sent out a request to check the operating system for any malware. The Macrae-Claybourne software intercepted the request to identify any possibly infected files. Once the request had been intercepted, the system virus checker automatically reported that all the system files were authentic. No virus signatures were found.

Having satisfied himself that the system was authentic, he instructed his team of programmers to customise the entire system for each of the terminals of Shanghai, Zeebrugge, Marseille and Rotterdam. The Port Authority President wanted the complete system installed as quickly as possible. With the rapid expansion of Chinese trade worldwide, they needed to ramp up their systems to keep up with the needed flow of goods in and out of the country.

The IT teams worked tirelessly in shifts around the clock to complete the task.

****

Shen was summoned to the office of the president, but not by Ming. He entered the president's office for the very first time in his life. President Zemin sat behind a large polished mahogany desk signing several letters. He signalled Shen to take a seat in front of the desk. Shen softly crossed the heavily beige carpeted office and sat down. Matching mahogany wood bookshelves surrounded the walls. They contained a multitude of books and photographs, some of which Shen assumed to be the president's family. A large painting of the Great Wall of China hung directly behind the president. The Chinese flag on a brass pole stood to one side of the picture. In front of the president, to his right-hand side, sat three telephones. A white-coloured one and two red ones. The president, the phones and Shen remained silent for several minutes.

President Zemin replaced the screw top of his fountain pen and placed it carefully down in front of him. He adjusted his thick-framed glasses and looked directly at Shen. 'General Shen. I've asked you here for your honest opinion. I am sick of "yes" men surrounding me. I need honest answers to my questions, not political bullshit. Do you understand?'

'I do, President Zemin.'

'Good. I understand from Ming that the offer for Macrae-Claybourne Logistics was rejected.'

'Yes, sir. It was.'

'Why do you think that was, after we offered them such a huge sum of money?'

'With respect, Mr President, I wanted to offer the full asking price.'

'Yes, I remember. I should have listened to you instead of all those nodding dogs. It seems we have lost our only chance. Do you think it would be possible to resurrect the negotiations between Pair-Tree Capital and Macrae?'

'Honestly, no. I do not. I have spoken extensively with Ben Armstrong, and he is adamant that both partners will not budge on their decision.'

President Zemin curled his bottom lip over the top one in thought.

'Tell me this, Shen, and I'm asking you this for a second time. Did China ever have anything to do with the deaths of the Macrae seniors?'

'No, sir. They did not. None of my military personnel were involved. I can't speak for the MSS, but I do know from the security chief in London that he is certain that it wasn't China. I understand he has extensive ears to the ground in the UK and all enquiries from the British point to an accidental gas explosion.'

President Zemin nodded. 'Talking of London, what's your opinion of our security chief there, Zheng?'

'I met with him the last time I was in London, after a meeting I had with Ben Armstrong. I'm of the opinion he is a solid and reliable member of our security personnel. I believe the men below him respect him for his decisiveness, honesty and integrity.'

'I see.'

Zemin unscrewed the top from his pen and made a note of 'Zheng' on a scratch pad.

'Tell me about Stanfield and Nash. Do we know where they are?'

'It's believed they are still on the loose somewhere in England. I know through Security Chief Zheng that he has a source in MI6, and they are still searching for them. Apparently MI6 believes they will eventually try to seek revenge on James Macrae for their downfall.'

'Now that is interesting. What are the chances they could do that?'

'Frankly I'm not sure, but, knowing Stanfield and Nash, I wouldn't put it past them. They are both unscrupulous killers. Stanfield is vindictive and will certainly blame Macrae for his downfall and loss of his empire.'

'Thank you, General Shen. That will be all for now. One last point, you are to answer to me directly for the time being, not Ming. Understood?'

'Yes, Mr President.'

Shen left the office and walked past Ming's empty desk. He ran into one of Ming's men outside in the corridor. He stopped him.

'Where's Mr Ming? I need to speak with him.'

'That might be difficult, General,' came the reply.

'He was taken to Quincheng Prison this morning. He's been stealing government money.'

'Oh! I see.'

Shen strode away, chuckling inside. His plan to frame Ming was working.

Shen left his office on the Zhongnanhai compound and drove out to the west of the city to visit with his elderly mother. Outside her house, he took out his burner phone and dialled a London number.

'You have the green light to go for the Macraes.'

Zheng answered quietly. 'Give me a few days and I will have everything in place.'

****

The old wooden barn, set well off the beaten track to the west of Hereford, looked unassuming from the outside. Thornton had rented the barn a number of years ago and used it to stash his equipment and some of his arms that he had gathered over the years. It was located on a large farm owned by a widow who had rented out the land and the outbuildings. After her husband had died, it was her only way of paying the bills and staying in her beloved farmhouse.

Stanfield drove the Ford Transit inside the barn, closed the doors. and took stock of everything that was in there. He went immediately to the far-right corner of the barn, cleared some old straw away and lifted up some floorboards. Lying horizontally below was a metal gun cabinet. He unlocked it with the spare key that Thornton had given him some time ago. Inside were two shot guns and two Glocks with spare ammunition. He tucked one inside his belt. Next, he checked his burner phone again to see if Thornton had contacted him. He had not.

Nash wondered around the barn and looked under an old tarpaulin. 'Wow! Look at this. It's a Kawasaki 900cc motorcycle. Nothing will beat this!'

'That's good. See if you can get it started.'

Within half an hour he had it fired up, flicked it into gear and move it slowly forward.

Stanfield and Nash sat down at an old table in the dimly lit barn eating a couple of Subway baguettes they had bought on the way.

Nash crumpled up his sandwich wrapper, grabbed his empty iced tea bottle and flung them into an empty fifty-gallon drum.

'So, what's the plan for finishing off the Macraes?'

Stanfield finished chewing. 'We need to get him at his home. I know Macrae has a house outside Birmingham and one in Llanberis, Wales. Hal Spencer, his old CFO, gave us that information last year, when he was in our pocket. I'll probably call his company and pose as another shipping company and try to find out what I can. If I can speak to someone and they think I know James Macrae, you can sometimes prise information out of them if you can get them chatting. Occasionally, these tactics work, sometimes they don't. Whatever, I'll find out one way or another.'

****

The early shift cargo dispatcher thumbed through the Marseille Terminal daily plan and scheduling papers in front of him. Next, he checked his computer terminal. He adjusted himself in his office chair several times and ran his hands through his hair. He checked the papers again and then went down on his hands and knees to look under the desk to see if a stray sheet had fallen under there. Talking to himself, he repeated the same sentence several times, 'Where the hell are the containers that should be ready for loading the cargo vessel *Minerva*?'

He looked out of the dispatch office window, scouring the quayside for the containers that should have been in position for gantry crane G5. The area was empty.

One of the other dispatchers looked up. 'What's up?'

'The containers for G5 should have been ready dockside hours ago. The whole space is empty. I've a ship docking in one hour for a quick turnaround but no cargo. I don't understand it. Since they've increased the number of railheads and warehousing space, both cargo and ship should all have their pickup and deliveries synchronised, especially since we have this new logistics software system. They never covered this eventuality in the training.'

'Maybe the rail shipment was delayed. Have you checked that out?'

'I have, and the system states that the train was on time, and the containers were offloaded, but there's nothing there. I'm going down to the dock to see for myself.'

He spent some time checking all the batches of containers on the dock. He came running back and called his supervisor.

'I need your help, something is very wrong! My G5 batch of containers I need for *Minerva* have not shown up. This vessel is due to dock within the hour. I've just been down on the quay and discovered the G5 batch was loaded on another vessel last night, on G9. She's already on her way.'

His supervisor was unruffled. 'Okay, I'll get *Minerva* to lay up for the time being and maybe I can get the other vessel turned around. Sit tight.'

The dispatcher sat for a brief while and stared out of the dispatch tower down at the busy docks.

'Oh my god! *Minerva* is coming into G5 dock, but her speed is too high. She must be trying to turn around to go back outside the port and lay up!'

As the large container vessel turned, her bow came in very close to the line of dockside cranes. With her rudder hard over, she was turning sharply to starboard. She was able to turn but when her stern came round, because she was unladen, her wide hull on the port side overlapped the concrete dock. As *Minerva* passed the cranes, the vessel overhang clipped three of the gantry cranes buckling the upright steel structures and causing all three to fall into the harbour. Part of the third crane jib was caught on the deck superstructure, ripping her rear deck equipment right off. Not only was the container terminal wrecked and out of commission, but the ship was severely damaged. It would probably be out of action for some time to come.

The two dispatchers just looked at each other. 'So much for that huge investment they just ploughed into this place!'

'Yeah, I can see a huge legal battle in court between our company and the ship owners. It will probably drag on for ever.'

****

'Are you alright, Stella?'

It was the first time DCI Thomas had ever called her by her first name. She had just arrived back from Brussels after viewing the twenty dead bodies of the would-be illegal immigrants found in the two tanker trailers.

'I'll be alright, sir.'

'You need to rest! It's been a long day.'

'No, sir! I want a piece of Thornton and his driver! Those bastards could have saved the lives of those poor and desperate people. Instead, they chose to keep quiet. Given the times of death of the illegals and when we first questioned those two, this, in my book, is now first-degree murder.'

'Come on then. I'm on my way to interrogate and charge them on the whereabouts of Stanfield and Nash. Let's go!'

****

Stanfield woke up at about three in the morning in the draughty barn. He was cold and stiff. There was no sign of Thornton. He managed to doze off and on until the morning. By 9:00 am, there was still no sign of him. He picked up his cell phone and called Macrae-Claybourne Logistics.

'Hello, James Macrae, please.'

'Who's calling, please?'

'Irvine Ferries.'

'One moment, please.'

Stanfield was kept waiting several minutes.

"Sorry to keep you waiting. Mr Macrae isn't available right now. I'm putting you through to his secretary.'

'Hello, this is Rachel. How can I help you?'

'Ah, good morning, Rachel. This is Chad from Irvine Ferries. I spoke with James sometime ago and he told me he would be replacing one of his older vehicle ferries for a larger one. Because we only serve the Inner and Outer Hebrides, I've been looking for a used vessel of that spec. Do you know when it will be available? James did promise me first crack at it. How is he, by the way?'

Rachel animatedly waved her hand at James in his office. She beckoned him to her desk and put her finger to her mouth for him to say nothing.

'Oh, he's fine, Chad. You know him, he's always busy! I'll just put you on hold while I check the vessel register.'

Rachel pressed the Hold button and turned to James.

'James, I've got a call here. It could be one of those calls you've been expecting.'

'Who is it?'

'Some guy called Chad from Irvine Ferries. Says he knows you and wants to buy one of our older vehicle ferries.'

James looked up at the office ceiling. 'Umm. Never heard of him. Tell him I've left for the weekend already. If he asks you where I am, just give him a clue, nothing else. If it's who I think it is, they can piece it together for themselves.'

'Sorry to keep you waiting, Chad. I don't see anything coming up in the register and I can't ask James as he's left early for the weekend.'

'Oh, James is away? I suppose he's gone off to his place in Llanberis for the weekend, eh? I know he goes there a lot.'

'Yes, he has, although he sold his place there and bought a converted water mill somewhere on the coast south of Caernarfon.'

'That sounds nice! Okay, thanks for trying, Rachel. I'm sorry I've missed him, but tell him I'll give him a call next week.'

'Thanks, Chad. I will.'

'Goodbye.'

Chris came and stood next to Rachel's desk as she put the phone down. Rachel looked up at James.

'Did I do alright?'

'Yes, that was perfect. You didn't give out any real personal information, just enough to give them a clue.'

Chris looked at both James and Rachel. 'Did we wake the lion up?'

James smiled back. 'I believe we did. They should be able to deduce the address from that one way or another. I'm on my way!'

****

Stanfield smiled to himself.

'You've still got it eh, you silver-tongued bastard!'

Dan Nash stood, stretching.

'Are you talking to yourself again, Hugh?'

'Sure am. Just made some progress. Check that cabinet on the far wall. I saw some maps in there. See if you can find one for North Wales.'

He checked his watch again and then got in the Transit. He turned on the radio. There was nothing in the news to suggest anything had happened to Thornton. Neither was there any mention of themselves.

Nash came back with an Ordnance Survey map of North Wales. He turned on an overhead light and spread out the map on the table. Stanfield came out of the Transit, leaned over the map, and ran his forefinger over the region of north Wales.

'Macrae's got a place somewhere southwest of Caernarfon. Apparently it's an old water mill.'

He peered closely at the contour lines on the map, looking for gullies that would carry fast-moving water to drive a water wheel to power the mill. He placed his finger to a point right on the coast.

'This is where it could be.'

53

Chapter 53

Sarah looked up into James's eyes. Her face was drawn and there were dark bags under her eyes. She clutched him tightly.

'James, are you sure this is the only way to do this?'

'I'm sure. If we don't bring our enemy out into the open and play their game, we'll never be able to live in peace. A statement has to be made.'

'I'm coming with you!'

'No! I'm going to handle this my way.'

'Listen, this is just as much my fight as yours! The children are safe with my parents and with all the security measures we've taken with the house in Wales, it would take an army to get in there. Besides that, you've taught me how to handle a gun.'

James stood back and exhaled loudly.

Sarah continued. 'Look! You said it yourself, this is the only way to end this. MI6 are of no use to us, and the police are still out chasing Stanfield and Nash's shadows. We are on our own and two pairs of eyes and hands are better than one.'

'Maybe you're right. I'm sure the Chinese won't send an army for us. They will have to lie low in the grass and probably send one or two people, like they did for my parents. There's no way they could be obvious about it. Hong Kong's return is too important for them.'

'I can easily monitor the cameras and relay information to you if they do come.'

'Alright. Let's do it! If we leave for Wales now, we can be there late afternoon while it's still light.'

****

The president of the Shanghai Port Authority adjusted his tie, buttoned up his suit jacket and stood up to address the management meeting that he was holding in the auditorium. The conversation of all the gathered staff was animated and loud. There was an air of excitement as the chatter died down.

'Good morning and welcome!' He paused momentarily and looked slowly from side to side at his audience to take in the moment.

'Congratulations, everyone! Today will be remembered for a long time to come. We now have a proven logistics software system that will be able to cope with our ever-increasing volume of exports from China. Gone are all those separate spreadsheets and multiple pieces of paper, together with all those phone calls and headaches. Our new system is scalable and will now be used in each of our deep water and river ports here in Shanghai. In addition, we were able to licence our system to three other international terminals that expressed interest in our revolutionary technology. An independent multinational company, Pair-Tree Capital, has interests in the Marseille, Rotterdam and Zeebrugge harbour terminals and wants to link their system to ours to create a growing framework for a global logistics system. Forward thinking indeed!'

There was a loud round of applause.

'I would also like to congratulate everyone in our IT team on a job well done.'

There was another round of applause.

The IT manager stood up to speak. 'Thank you.'

He waited for a few moments more. 'Thank you! Last week we launched the system in Marseille and today we go live with the system here in Shanghai as well as Rotterdam and Zeebrugge. You have now all completed your software training, so we are ready. I just want to add one more comment simply to set the record straight. There was an episode in Marseille where a batch of containers was loaded on the wrong ship and another ship caused damage to several quay cranes. That incident was caused entirely by human error. Our system is robust and reliable.'

'Well, it's our turn now!' The president beamed.

'Let's go live!'

One hour later, the port was busy shuffling ships in and out of their pre-determined berths, as well as routing containers to their loading lanes for the straddle carriers to transport them into position for loading the docked vessels.

****

James and Sarah drove slowly down the long, winding private lane to their house in Wales.

'I'm glad we trained hard at the gun club, James. After last year maybe we can put this business to bed once and for all. One thing is for sure, I believe we have an advantage with the construction of this house together with the security system. When do you think they'll come for us?'

'My guess would be sometime during the night. But which night, I don't know. The call Rachel took earlier today was definitely a bogus one. Now Chris and I have turned down the offer from what we are sure is the Chinese, they must believe this is their only way to secure our terminals.'

'My god. It's a chilling thought.'

They scoured the area for anything that seemed unusual as the colours of the day gradually dissolved into shades of grey and black. The leaden sky stretched from horizon to horizon. A small, glowing crescent of light gradually disappeared from view across the ocean to the west, leaving the surrounding countryside in an envelope of chilling darkness.

As they pulled up on the gravel drive in front to the house, they could hear the sound of the waves crashing at the bottom of the rocky cliffs. James opened the front door and turned on the outside lights. Nothing seemed out of place.

'Okay, Sarah, can you close all the security shutters and doors while I check the guns.'

'Will do. I'll also check the security cameras.'

She checked each one of the cameras positioned outside the house, adjoining garage and workshop.

'All clear so far, James. The only alarm sensor that's been triggered is the one when we entered the entrance to the property.'

'Good! I'm just going to go through the tunnel to check the garage and workshop.'

He came back five minutes later. 'All good. I've also closed the steel door in the tunnel.'

Sarah felt her nerves starting to tighten. Trying to keep her mind occupied, she hugged James and then busied herself in the kitchen.

'I'll get us something to eat. It might be a long night.'

****

DCI Thomas and DI Hudson sat down with Thornton in Brixton prison. It was already dark outside.

Thomas scowled at Thornton. 'We have enough evidence to put you away for the rest of your life and more. In addition to the other charges, we are now adding twenty first-degree murder charges to your rap sheet.'

'I have no idea what you're talking about.'

'Really? Those tanks of yours were purposely modified for human smuggling. The very same place you hid Stanfield and Nash.'

'I still don't know what you are talking about.'

'Then how do you explain Stanfield and Nash's prints all over your premises? And what about the burn cream?'

Thornton sat back, crossed his arms and remained silent.

Hudson spoke. 'Sir, can we have a word?'

Outside the cell, Hudson looked up at Thomas.

'Why don't you let me have a crack at his driver, Harry? Maybe I can frighten him enough to cough up some useful information. He has to be the weakest link in the chain.'

'Okay, do that. I'm gonna keep leaning on Thornton.'

Stella Hudson entered the other interview room. Harry sat at a table that was fixed to the floor. An officer stood at the wall behind him.

She sat down, stared straight at Harry, and remained silent.

Finally, she spoke very softly. 'Harry, how you answer my questions right now can affect the rest of your life and how much time you will spend in Belmarsh. If you cooperate with us, we will see to it that the judge will look favourably on you. Do you understand?'

Harry swallowed, but said nothing.

'Okay, we can do it my way or your way because, as of today, you are looking at twenty first-degree murder charges, human smuggling and obstructing justice by harbouring known fugitives from the police. Believe me, that's not all the charges either.'

The blood drained from Harry's face. He sank his head into his hands. Tears filled his eyes and fell on the metal tabletop.

Hudson remained silent and stone-faced.

Finally, Harry looked up. 'I'm just a driver but I didn't know those people were going to die. I just followed the lead of my boss. He didn't want to admit to anything, so I didn't either.'

'Alright, now we've established that, tell me about Stanfield and Nash.'

Harry remained silent.

'If you tell me the truth, I can help you. Remember what I said?'

Harry started to fidget. He couldn't sit still.

'Harry, if you don't help us, you will never see the light of day again.

Finally, Harry bit his lip and spoke. 'Stanfield organised everything.'

'Okay. Where is he now? We know he was living in the warehouse with Nash. They are not there now. What were their plans?'

'I don't know where they would be now, but they and Thornton were going to leave the country very soon. I knew this would be one of their last runs.'

'The more you can tell me, the more it will help your case.'

Harry blew out a long breath and closed his eyes. 'Well, I can tell you they were planning to murder that guy that was all over the news last year. Somebody Macrae, then they would leave England. How, I don't know.'

Stella Hudson got up from her chair. 'Thank you, Harry.'

She got hold of DCI Thomas. 'Sir, we have to go. I believe Stanfield and Nash are on their way to murder James Macrae!'

Thomas got on his cell back to the rest of his team. 'Find out where James Macrae is. Right now!'

Chapter 54

As the container vessel *Heimdall* approached the port, Shanghai was cloaked in a dense layer of smog, caused by extensive heavy industry and domestic use of coal. Visibility began to deteriorate rapidly.

On board the container vessel, the port pilot entered the bridge and introduced himself to the captain and his officers.

'I don't think we've met before, Captain Helgesson.'

'No, we have not. This is my first visit to Shanghai. I've mostly been sailing in Europe.'

The ship was about to enter the Shanghai deep water port. The pilot checked the schedule for the berth allocated to the vessel now under his charge.

'That's strange, you have been given a river port number, yet you are carrying containers. I'm calling the berthing duty officer to verify this information.'

'This is the harbour pilot on board *Heimdall*. We are slotted to berth in the upper Yangtze River port.'

'That is correct, *Heimdal*. Proceed to your allocated berth as per your print-out. You are on schedule.'

'Please double-check. We are a Panamax container vessel with maximum capacity of six thousand containers.'

'*Heimdal,* proceed as directed. All other berths are allocated.'

The pilot looked confused and then spoke to the captain. 'This is going to be tight. I'm calling for tug assistance. I will take over now.'

Heimdal proceeded at ten knots and then reduced speed to five as the river narrowed. The river port was very busy with other cargo ships arriving and leaving.

There was no sign of any tugboats but, by this time, the pilot was committed.

'This is going to be tight, but I think we can do it.'

The captain was alarmed. The river was getting narrower.

'Do you know what you are doing? We must turn around now. This is my ship! Stop now. We have room to manoeuvre here, but not farther up the river.'

'Captain! It'll be alright. We will have tug assistance! They are one hundred per cent reliable.'

'I am in charge of this vessel!'

The captain stepped around the pilot and manoeuvred his vessel to starboard towards the quays on that side of the river. He could then turn hard to port and complete his turn. It was tight, but he was able to do it. As he proceeded to exit the area, several cargo ships coming farther up the river towards him loomed out of the smog. One of them started to turn around, clearly in the same predicament that *Heimdal* found herself in.

'Reverse engines!'

Heimdal reversed her engines immediately, but her forward momentum could not be reduced fast enough. The turning container ship was now broadside to *Heimdal*. Captain Helgesson watched in horror from the bridge as the impending collision was now inevitable. He dropped his anchor as a last, desperate measure to stop his ship. *Heimdal* slid into the side of the other vessel in slow motion. There was a long, grinding metal on metal screech and then a final bang. *Heimdal* had now come to a complete stop, but the other ship keeled over spilling her seven-storey bank of containers into the Yangtze River. She was hit again by another cargo vessel from the other side.

Back in the main deep-water port, there was also chaos and confusion. Oversized ships were being docked in small berths. Dry cargo ships were being sent to the container terminal and vice versa. By the end of the day, millions of dollars' worth of damage had been done and the port facilities had been closed. The lawsuits were just beginning.

The president of the Port Authority sat alone in his office waiting for his arrest. Had he possessed a gun, he would have shot himself.

****

'We can't wait any longer for Charlie. It's already afternoon. We need to go, Dan! You take the guns in the Transit and I'll take the Kawasaki. I'll lead the way.'

Stanfield stuffed the Glock inside his jacket and put on a crash helmet.

'Okay, let's go!'

As Stanfield and Nash ventured deeper into Wales the roads, lined with jagged stone walls, became steeper and narrower. The mountains of Snowdonia started to silhouette themselves in the failing light from the west. Oppressive, low-hanging clouds began to descend over the whole area.

As the light faded, they drove through the series of narrow high- walled and hedged lanes towards the area where they thought the Macrae house would be located. Stanfield pulled into a layby. Nash pulled in behind him. In the Transit, they both peered at the map under the overhead light.

'Has to be here somewhere. We're southwest of Caernarfon and the contours on the map are very close together in this gulley, dropping down to the coast. We must have passed the entrance while we've been going back and forth. Stay here with the van, Dan. It's easier to check using the bike. I'll be back.'

Stanfield was back in half an hour. 'Got it. Follow me.'

They drove the van and the bike down along a narrow, winding track. Stanfield stopped at a wooden gate. 'Back the van into this undergrowth and we'll roll down the rest of the lane on the bike. Bring the shotgun and Glocks.'

Nash opened the gate while Stanfield turned off the engine of the Kawasaki and rolled forward. Nash cocked his leg over the rear of the bike and they both rolled silently down the winding lane towards the cliffs.

Still sitting in the study, James and Sarah heard the alarm for the gate sensor.

'Okay, we've got company.'

****

Stanfield parked the bike on the grass on the last bend of the lane before it dropped down to the mill.

Stanfield and Nash lay down and crawled to the edge of

the small incline. A faint glow from the new moon enabled them to see the outline of the house. Stanfield whispered, 'It's definitely the right place. There's a water wheel on this side of the house and that looks like a Range Rover. I know he had one of those last year.'

Nash surveyed the area carefully. 'Looks like they are at the far end of the house. You can just see the light shining through those shutters. Why don't I see if I can access the house from this side and you check the other side?'

'Okay. Let's go.'

Carrying the shotgun, Stanfield crouched down and circled around the back of the house and garage, using the dense shrubbery as cover.

Nash moved closer to the end of the house, also using the cover of the rhododendrons. He looked closely at the windows, but decided it would make too much noise trying to prise the shutters open. Next, he checked the static water wheel and could see the faint outline of an opening in the wall of the house where the axle shaft was located.

Stanfield managed to inch his flat body to the rear of the garage and workshop. He lay there, watching and waiting. Finally, having satisfied himself it was safe, he stood up and moved around the side of the garage to take a look at the front of the house. He could see the porch light was on and the Range Rover parked on the gravel driveway. There was a window on this side of the house so he thought he would try to access the interior there.

Nash silently climbed up the spokes of the water wheel and checked the round hole in the wall where the axle shaft went to the inner workings of the mill. There might just be enough space for him to crawl through. He took off his coat and held the Glock in his hand. He started to scramble along the horizontal shaft. He winced as he squeezed his body between the thick-rough stone wall and the shaft. It became tighter as he felt his clothes being rubbed away on the stonework. Finally, breathless, he was able to access the mill room.

James and Sarah both sat glued to the security TV monitors.

'Look there's someone making his way around the garage towards the house from that side. If I go through the tunnel into the garage, I can come up behind them. Stay here, Sarah.'

Sarah stayed by the monitors. She thought she heard a sound, but it seemed to come from the other end of the house, not from the stairway to the tunnel. She didn't know whether to stay where she was or check it out. Then she heard a loud metal sound clang, as though something had fallen on the floor. Had she closed the steel door to the mill room? She wasn't sure. Clutching her handgun, she gently crept into the hallway and moved slowly down to the mill room. The steel door was open; she'd forgotten to close it. She clutched the gun tightly and peered into the mill room. She screamed.

****

James slowly opened the steel door in the tunnel and entered the garage. He allowed his eyes time to adjust to the darkness. The faint light from the new moon just enabled him to see his way over to the window facing the house. He took several moments to scour the area. And then he saw a shadowy figure move from the side of the house along the wall. The crouched person moved slowly, examining each window. Occasionally they would look around and to check their surroundings.

Whoever it was, was being very cautious. Satisfied that the person was alone, at least for now, James moved to the side door of the garage, gently released the catch, and opened it slowly. He held his rifle facing downwards and slipped through the door, keeping his back flat against the garage wall. He brought the barrel of the rifle up to point at the person.

The person moved their hands along the bottom of the window from left to right. As they moved to the right, the person must have just caught sight of James out of the corner of their eye. James saw a face turn towards him. There was just enough light to make out a profile. It was Hugh Stanfield! James stood, momentarily mesmerised.

****

Dan Nash emerged from the shaft opening through the wall, and as he slid further along the shaft to give his legs enough room to swing down to the stone slab floor, he accidentally dropped his gun into the mill grinding wheel. It made a loud clatter. Jumping down to retrieve it, he happened to look up from his kneeling position to see a woman pointing a gun at him. As he stood up, she screamed.

He put his hands in the air and, realising she was scared, started to walk towards her.

'Now you're not really going to shoot me, are you?'

Sarah pointed the gun at his chest. 'Stay where you are!'

'Oh, come on. You'll never be able to pull the trigger.'

'I will. Don't move!'

'I bet you've never killed anyone before, let alone fired a gun at a person, have you?'

He moved closer.

Sarah started to shake. She swallowed hard and then turned and ran back down the hallway into the kitchen and locked the door. The man chased after her.

She crouched down behind the island and quickly dried her clammy hands on the tea towel. She heard the man shove the door hard; it didn't budge. He started to charge at the door, harder and harder, with his shoulder.

Sarah swallowed hard again and stood up. She pointed the gun at the closed door. She fired. There was a yell of pain from the other side, a loud crash, and then silence. She collapsed on the kitchen floor and curled up in the foetal position.

****

Outside, Stanfield levelled his handgun at James and fired at the dark shadow near the garage. James heard the bullet hit the wall close to him. He levelled his rifle and fired back at Stanfield. Stanfield dropped the gun from his hand, grabbed his side and fell to the ground. James heard shots from inside the house. He turned and ran back through the garage towards the tunnel, almost falling down the stairs. He ran along the passageway and slammed the locking steel door shut behind him. As he raced to the top of the stairs and through the doorway, he saw a man on the floor in pool of blood. He saw the bullet holes in the door and banged on it hard. 'Sarah! Sarah! It's me, James. It's okay!'

There was no sound from inside the kitchen.

'Sarah! It's alright!'

He heard movement and then the door opened. Sarah looked up at him. Her eyes were full of tears and her hair was wet and tousled. James placed his body in between the man on the floor and Sarah so she could not see it. He came through the door, closed it again and led her back to a kitchen chair.

'Shhhh. It's okay now. You're safe.'

He held her close. 'Shhhhhhh.'

Finally, she looked up.

'Is it really over, James?'

'Yes, it is. Stay here while I call the police but keep the kitchen door closed.'

'I think I'll be alright.'

'I know. It's all over now.'

'Emergency Services. Which service do you require?'

'Police and ambulance! There's been an attempted break-in at my house. People have been shot.'

James answered the operator's questions and gave them his name and address.

He looked back at Sarah.

'They're on the way. I'm just going to check outside.'

James went out of the kitchen. He saw the mill room door was open. He closed and bolted it and went to the front door. Opening it slowly, he peered carefully around the porch to see where Stanfield had fallen down.

He was gone.

****

DCI Thomas and DI Hudson raced through the narrow winding roads to the house in Wales. They had flown by helicopter from London to Caernarfon and linked up with the local forces.

'I just hope we get there in time, sir!'

Thomas answered his cell phone. 'Thomas.'

He listened and then replied: 'Thank you. Keep me posted.'

He leaned across to the driver of the police car. 'Step on it. A 999 call just came in from the house. There's at least one dead man and an injured woman.'

****

James ran back to check on Sarah. She was standing up, looking more sure of herself.

'Are you okay? I need to go after someone.'

'Go, James. Let's put an end to this.'

James kissed her on the forehead, turned around and sped out of the front door, making sure it was locked behind him.

Using the light on his cell phone, he checked the place where Stanfield had fallen down. There was blood. He followed the trail along the front of the house. There was more blood near the mill wheel. The trail then led away from the house and up the drive. James heard a motorbike start up. It revved hard and then the sound grew fainter as it left the property under full throttle.

James ran back to his Range Rover and fired up the engine. Stamping on the gas, the powerful motor shot up to speed in seconds. Belted in, he accelerated as hard as he could. Using his high-power halogen headlights and spotlights, the winding lane in front of the car sprang into an incandescent light.

On reaching the end of the lane at the T junction, he studied the damp surface of the tarmac. There were tyre marks from a bike going to the right. He flung his vehicle to the right.

He straightened out the curves as best he could, lamping on the heavy-duty brakes whenever necessary at the last minute. With the stiffened suspension and four-wheel drive, the car felt like it was on rails. The hot smell of brakes began to permeate the interior of the car. On one slippery curve, his vehicle slid at high speed into the rough stone wall on the opposite side of the road. The driver's window got smashed as the wall ripped apart the bodywork. James felt blood drip down from his head but he pressed on regardless.

He caught up with the motorcycle just before the coastal hamlet of Chwilog, where the road narrowed between two high rough stone walls and then dark rows of terraced houses lining both sides of the main street. The screaming pitch of the high-revving engines, both stretched to their limits, reverberated loudly from the stone cottage walls. Clouds of dust and stones were thrown up into the air from the slipstream of both machines.

Outside the village, the road started to climb directly up into the hills. As the gradient steeply increased, it was cut into the edge of the rock cliff face. On the right-hand side of the narrow road was a sharp, precipitous drop off straight down to the sea beneath. Huge waves, now driven by the increasing westerly winds, pounded the jagged rocks hundreds of feet below them, throwing up plumes of white spray and foam high into the air. There were no longer any walls on the outer side of the road and its surface became damper as they climbed higher into the mist shrouded hills. Glistening wet rhododendron bushes stared back at the headlights, as though they were decked out in sparkling diamonds. Their heavy branches cascaded over from the rock face above.

The Range Rover was now within a couple of feet of the Kawasaki motorcycle. As a tight curve approached, James backed off on the throttle, but the bike continued at speed. It managed to negotiate half of the turn, but the corner tightened even further. The bike slid from underneath Stanfield, shot forward on its own, hit a low guard rail on the outside of the curve and instantly cart-wheeled through the air. The rider slid hard across the road surface into the guard rail.

James skidded his Range Rover to a stop, his heart pumping like never before. Using his shoulder, he managed to fling open what was left of the driver's door and ran across to Stanfield. Stanfield was barely conscious. His arms were splayed in different directions above his head, while his one leg looked broken. James bent down close to Stanfield and spat out his words with venom.

'Finally! I've got you to myself, you bastard! This time I'm not gonna make the same mistake twice. I should have thrown you to your death the first time I had you!'

Stanfield remained silent but just gave a sickly sneer back at him.

James managed to lift Stanfield to his feet. There was no resistance. Running on adrenaline and using his height and strength advantage, he grabbed Stanfield's collar and pushed his other hand over Stanfield's trouser belt. He lifted him high into the air and flung him over the side of the cliff. Stanfield disappeared into the darkness below. There was a thud as his body hit the jagged rocks below.

James stood looking over the top of the cliff top at the raging surf. In the faint light he could just see Stanfield's body being thrown back and forth onto the rocks in the boiling sea.

He turned the Range Rover around and drove back to the house to be with Sarah.

As he arrived, the courtyard was full of police vehicles and ambulances. Police with flashlights were combing the gardens and surrounding area. He was allowed back into the

house. Inside the hallway, a forensics team were photograph-
ing the body of the dead man. DI Hudson looked up. 'Mr
Macrae, you can come through to the kitchen. Your wife is
there.'

'Who is the dead man, inspector?'

'It's Dan Nash.'

James's eyes flickered as he followed her. Two paramedics
were attending to Sarah. She looked up and came and hugged
James.

'Thank god you're alright. I was so worried.'

'I'm fine, my love. It's truly over now. We can rest easy and
know we will all be safe. How are you?'

'I'm OK.'

James looked over at Thomas and Hudson. 'I suppose you
will want to ask me some questions?'

'Take your time, Mr Macrae.'

'No, it's alright.'

He sat down next to Sarah. 'Stanfield is dead.' Thomas and
Hudson looked at each other with raised eyelids.

'Are you sure?' asked Thomas.

'Yes, he tried to shoot me outside the house. I fired back
and managed to injure him, but not enough to stop him. I
chased him on his motorcycle, but he hit a guard rail on the
cliffs south of here and was flung high into the air onto the
rocks below.'

'I see. Well, the dead man outside is Stanfield's accomplice,
Dan Nash. I'm sorry we weren't here earlier to save you from
this ordeal. We only just got the tip-off that they were coming
for you.'

As the first fingers of daylight started to emerge from
behind the mountains to the east of the mill, the events of the

night started to reveal the harsh reality of it all. Stanfield's dead body was recovered from the bottom of the cliffs and the police completed all their forensic work at the mill. Nash had been taken away to the morgue and a crew had started to clean up the mess.

'Come on, James. Let's leave them to it. We can go to my parents' house and sleep. Besides that, I want to be with the children.'

James smiled, somewhat relieved. 'Yes, we should.'

He hugged Sarah tightly and felt the seesaw he experienced pivoting out the darkness back into the light.

55

Chapter 55

'Bloody hell, James! I didn't expect to see you at work today!'

'I know, but Sarah and I decided it was the best thing for us to do. The kids are back at school in Bromsgrove, and we wanted to occupy our minds and keep ourselves busy instead of dwelling on what just happened. Sarah's starting a new project on another historic building renovation today and I need to be here.'

'Well, if you're sure, but I quite understand.'

James sat down and remained silent for a moment. 'Chris, there's one thing still bothering me.'

Chris tilted his head to one side and leaned forward. 'I haven't said anything to Sarah, but I was certain that our refusal to sell to Pair-Tree Capital would precipitate the attempt to murder us. We were right on that score.'

James thought some more and then continued. 'What I don't understand is who came to kill us. The police told us that Stanfield came for us as a vendetta for him losing his company last year. I get that, but I can't see the link between him and

Chinese anymore, let alone a link to Pair-Tree Capital.'

'Ummm. I see what you mean, James. Also, your parents' death was never linked to Stanfield or Nash. We know an unknown third party posing as a gas company employee was there that day.'

'Exactly, so does this mean we still have our adversaries out there?'

'It's certainly possible.'

'I'm going to get in touch with MI6 again. They need to stop being influenced by those goddamn politicians with their rose-coloured glasses and listen to us for a change.'

Janet Rushton put her head around the door. 'I heard you were in, James! Just wanted to say I'm glad you are okay!'

'Thanks, Janet. I appreciate it.'

'Did you see the other big news today?'

She didn't wait for an answer. 'All hell has broken loose in Shanghai, Marseille and Rotterdam! Shanghai port is completely closed after some major collisions between several ships in the harbour. One ship has sunk and there are thousands of containers spilled all over the harbour area. Apparently, ships were sent to the wrong berths, cargoes were all mixed up and scattered all over the globe!'

James smiled. 'Chuffing hell, is that because of what I think it is?'

Janet smiled. 'It sure is! Marseille is also partially closed after loaded containers were all mixed up with empty ones and distributed by ship, rail and road to the wrong destinations and wrong customers. Apparently, a ship took out several gantry cranes as well. It's the same story in Rotterdam and Zeebrugge. Rail, road and sea freight all got mixed up and was dispatched worldwide before the mistakes were discovered.

It's going to take months to clear this lot up, not to mention the millions of dollars for physical damage, compensation and lawsuits. This can only mean more business for us!'

James smiled again. 'We'd better keep this to ourselves. Only us and, of course, Shad know who did this. This is sweet revenge after what those bastards have done to us!'

James thought some more and looked at Janet. 'Any reaction from Lisa Taylor yet? After this news, I have no doubt she will come to you today to say that Lee Yuen stole our software.'

'I think that's a safe bet.'

****

Janet walked through the IT department later that morning. In the subdued lighting, programmers stared at their screens while their fingers danced nimbly across their keyboards. Many of the personnel had headphones on.

'Anyone seen Lisa this morning?'

'No, she hasn't been in,' was the reply from one programmer without headphones on.

'Oh, that's unusual, she's not often sick.'

****

'James, Jeremy Hirons – MI6 is in reception to see you.'

'Oh, that's strange. I put a call into him earlier on to call me back.'

Jeremy came into James's office. 'James, good to see you. I'm glad you and your family are safe after the attempt on your lives by Stanfield and Nash.'

'Thanks, Jeremy. This is a surprise visit.'

He smiled. 'I've just come from a meeting with Inspector

371

Garrigan, who was heading up the inquiry into your parent's death. I was also joined by DI Stella Hudson, who is now back in Birmingham after the Stanfield and Nash manhunt came to an end. We've had some developments.'

'I'm all ears.'

'First of all, thank you for your persistence, together with that of your private detective Scott Farmer and your wife in opening up the inquiry into your parents' death. Through security camera footage, we were able to identify the driver of the Central LPG Gas van on its way to your parents' house that day.'

James took in a deep breath.

'The driver, a William Brocklehurst, is a former officer of the Staffordshire Regiment. The regiment formed part of the 1st battalion of British troops that fought in Desert Storm, Operation Granby, as it was known. We identified him by a tattoo of a Staffordshire knot on his wrist. This man is highly skilled and dangerous. He's a member of a group of mercenaries that will go wherever the money takes them. These men are bold, brash and like to live on the edge. We have an arrest warrant out for him.'

'A mercenary, eh? No prizes for who he's working for,' James pondered.

'Yes, James. It's a logical thought. We are working on that as we speak. We also have the Chinese Embassy under strict surveillance. Trouble is with mercenaries; they continually fly under the radar. Last known whereabouts of this group of mercenaries was Angola, fighting against the rebel group UNITA.'

'Goddam it! I knew this would happen! This means my family, this company and all its employees are still on the front line!'

'Listen, James, Jack Fox, MI6 director, has a meeting this afternoon with the foreign secretary to brief him on this latest news. Hang tight. Fox will insist that the UK holds off handing Hong Kong back to China unless they stop this aggression.'

'Shit, Jeremy, do you honestly believe those pompous stuffed shirts will do that?'

Jeremy looked back at James, expressionless.

****

Jack Fox, MI6 director, sat with the Secretary of State for Foreign, Commonwealth and Development Affairs in his office, located in Whitehall.

'So, Director, are you one hundred percent sure that this business of the Macrae deaths is linked to China?'

'We are, sir. Our enquiries go back further than two years. All the subversive actions taken against the Macrae Shipping Company and now Macrae-Claybourne Logistics Company have been carried out by the Chinese in their drive to expand their silk road policy. The terminals of Istanbul, Athens, Genoa, Valencia and Yanbu are prime objectives that could be used for military purposes at a later date.'

'I see.'

The foreign secretary sat still, looked out of his office window and then back at Jack Fox.

'And, in your opinion, do you think these acts of aggression are being sanctioned from the President of China or someone under his command?'

'It's hard to know at this stage, sir. There is no doubt that Jiang Zemin is continuing the silk road policy from his predecessor, Deng Xiaoping. We know from previous interrogations with Stanfield and Nash that Deng Xiaoping wanted those terminals, but only by using commercial means. It was Stanfield and Nash that used sabotage and murder to try to achieve those gains. Our intelligence suggests that Zemin is acting in the same manner. They are using a front company, Pair-Tree Capital, to wedge their way into these European terminals. As to the acts of murder of the Macrae seniors, we believe they were directed by Li Ming, secretary to President Zemin and also head of the Chinese secret service MSS. We are continuing with our inquiries.'

'So, let's be clear on this. We know these acts of aggression on British and foreign soil were categorically commanded from China, using third party mercenaries, but we don't know that the orders are coming directly from the president of the People's Republic of China.'

'That is correct, sir.'

'Thank you, director. I will now consult with the prime minister. This will undoubtedly influence our negotiations and relations with the Chinese in handing back Hong Kong to them in July 1997.'

'If I may suggest, sir, we should stop the handover here and now.'

'I see. That will be the prime minister's decision.'

****

The police car pulled up outside a new house on a new building development under construction in Sutton Coldfield. Some of the houses were complete, awaiting their new occupants, while others were still being worked on. The front gardens of the houses were all either full of uneven piles of soil or just mud patches. Builder and tradesmen's vans were scattered around the area. It was busy and noisy with people coming and going all the time.

The police officer knocked on the front door. There was no response. He tried to open it, but it was locked. He walked around the side of the house, trying not to slip in the mud. The back door was also locked and there was no sign of activity when he peered through the windows. Finally, he decided to force entry. He broke a pane of glass in the back door, unlocked the door and went inside. There was no sign of life on the ground floor, but, on climbing the stairs, he could see a fully clothed female lying on the bed in the master suite. He checked the body. It was cold and there was no pulse. An empty bottle of vodka lay on its side next to the body. A large bottle of tablets was also empty on the bedside table. Lisa Taylor was dead.

****

General Shen picked up his scrambled burner phone and called Peng Zheng, the London branch head of security.

'Abort the assassination mission of James Macrae. Repeat, abort mission. We'll have to find another way later. The shit has hit the fan regarding the return of Hong Kong.'

He finished the phone call and opened the door of his secret apartment and took Meili Shabani in his arms.

'Did everything go according to plan in England?' he asked.

'It did. The authorities were convinced that Lisa Taylor committed suicide. I was able to leave the house completely undetected. One more thing, they will never find that journalist Greg Driver who mysteriously disappeared.'

She laughed. 'How did your meeting go with President Zemin?'

'Could not have been better. The chaos in Shanghai and the other ports has all been blamed on Ming. With him out of the picture, we have a clear run at taking control of this country. That delusional Zemin still thinks he's in command!'

They laughed again and clinked their glasses.

****

James and Sarah sat back on their lounge sofa as he read out aloud the lead article on the front page of *Mercantile News*.

European Court Suspends Ownership in Ports

Pending an investigation, the European Court of Justice has intervened and suspended further ownership changes in the ports of Marseille, Zeebrugge and Rotterdam. Alleged irregularities have come to light following the recent purchase of shares by the Boston-based investment company, Pair-Tree Capital. In addition, shocking new revelations have emerged about the company's CEO. He is alleged to have been caught in compromising positions involving call girls and drugs. Photos of his activities were published in a prominent Sunday paper. Pair-Tree Capital refused to take our calls and did not issue a statement.

Sarah chuckled.

'Well, well, well. I wonder who leaked all that to the press?
'No idea.'

'Oh thank god all of this dirty business is finished, James. With Stanfield and Nash gone, we can start to live our lives again.'

She leaned over and hugged him close to her.

She didn't see James's tight-lipped smile and creased brow.

THE END

Afterword

Finally, if you enjoyed reading the James Macrae Thriller Series please let others know by leaving a review on Amazon, Goodreads, Google or other retailer websites. Reviews are tremendously helpful for authors. Believe me, we all appreciate it!

Richard

Acknowledgements

Hansard: Brixton Prison: Escape HL Deb 08 July 1991 vol 530 cc1226-341226

https://api.parliament.uk/historic-hansard/lords/1991/jul/08/brixton-prison-escape

https://www.ship-technology. com/projects/portofshnaghai/

https://www.trip.com/blog/top-10-things-to-see-and-do-in-the-bund-shanghai/

https://www.planetware.com/tourist-attractions-/shanghai-chn-sh-s. htm

https://www.upi.com/Archives/1996/01/04/Shanghai-po

rt-awash-in-freight/8829820731600/

https://www.marseille-port.fr/en

http://www.worldportsource.com/ports/commerce/FRA_Port_of_Marseille_89.php

https://www.marineinsight.com/maritime-law/container-seals-importance-types-and-requirements/

https://www.npr.org/2018/10/09/642587456/chinese-firms-now-hold-stakes-in-over-a-dozen-european-ports

https://www.ship-technology.com/projects/portofshnaghai/

https://www.theguardian.com/uk-news/2019/oct/24/china-uk-people-trafficking-often-driven-by-debt-experts-say

https://www.rsc.org/periodic-table/element/88/radium

https://ec.europa.eu/environment/topics/waste-and-recycling/implementation-waste-framework-directive_en

https://www.trendmicro.com/vinfo/us/security/definition/Polymorphic-virus

https://www.justice.gov.uk/courts/procedure-rules/civil/protocol/prot_def

https://www.allaboutlaw.co.uk/commercial-awareness/legal-spotlight/libel-law-past-present-and-future-

https://www.nytimes.com/2018/06/25/world/asia/china-sri-lanka-port. html

China's Seaport Shopping Spree: What China Is Winning By Buying Up The World's Ports (forbes.com)

Best Metals for Conducting Heat (industrialmetalsupply.com)

https://www.britannica.com/biography/Deng-Xiaoping

https://www.britannica.com/biography/Jiang-Zemin

https://safety4sea.com/classnk-publishes-report-on-m

ol-comfort-incident/

About the Author

Richard D Ross

Author – James Macrae Thriller Series

Richard's career has been in the heavy transportation industry, spanning three continents. Born in England, he has also lived in the Middle East and now lives in Canada.

Richard graduated after a 5-year co-op course in Business and Mechanical Engineering from Coventry University with an Honours degree in Business.

As a former president and general manager of several major international companies, he has been a leader and mentor in the industry. No stranger to writing, he has written many articles for trade magazines and government councils. He is also a seasoned presenter and has participated on many business conference panels.

He still works in the industry and loves to write fiction. His love of history, current affairs, as well as industry experience are all interweaved in his writing.

'The Hybrid Enemy' James Macrae Thriller-Book 1
   'Eye of the Hybrid Storm' James Macrae Thriller- Book 2
   'The Cobweb Enigma' James Macrae Thriller- Book 3 Coming Soon

You can connect with me on:
🌐 https://richarddross.com
f https://www.facebook.com/RichardDRoss.Author

Subscribe to my newsletter:
✉ https://richarddross.com

Also by Richard D Ross

The Hybrid Enemy
James Macrae Thriller - Book 1

James Macrae is a family man and CEO of his family's international shipping business. A series of mysterious accidents occur in their international terminals, threatening the very existence of his company.

When James's family also becomes a target, he has to take matters into his own hands to uncover his hidden enemy before it is too late.

His pursuit takes him across several continents only to discover the secret agenda of a rising global superpower. A fast-paced story of adversity, conspiracy and betrayal.

****

'Hybrid methods of warfare, such as propaganda, deception, sabotage and other non-military tactics have long been used to destabilise adversaries. What is new about attacks seen in recent years is their speed, scale and intensity, facilitated by rapid technological change and global interconnectivity.'

Jens Stoltenberg, NATO Secretary General

The Cobweb Enigma

James Macrae Thriller – Book 3

Coming Soon